With our Blessing

JO SPAIN

Quercus

SHORTLISTED FOR THE RICHARD AND JUDY
SEARCH FOR A BESTSELLER COMPETITION

'Fiendishly clever . . . and a **big fat twist is lobbed
into the ending like a hand grenade**' *Irish Sunday
Independent*

'Brilliant! Fast paced, well researched and sensitive. **Jo
Spain is a sparkling new talent**' *Irish Examiner*

'An uncomfortable read that delves into [a] country's
dark secrets'*Irish Independent*

'**In a very strong year for Irish crime-fiction debuts,
Jo Spain's** *With Our Blessing* **is among the most
assured** . . . *With Our Blessing* picks at the scabs of
recent Irish history to reveal raw and gaping wounds'
Irish Times

'Spain's **vivid thriller explores the dark secrets of
Ireland's past** that are a real-life situation haunting
so many people within Irish society today'
Irish Country Living

'Takes the traditional "country house mystery" and
gives it an Irish twist. **Atmospheric and compelling**'
Sinéad Crowley, author of *Can Anybody Help Me?*

'Jo Spain's vivid thriller explores the dark secrets
from Ireland's past that continue to haunt Irish
society today' Martin Sixsmith, author of *Philomena*

Jo Spain has worked as a journalist and a party advisor on the economy in the Irish parliament. *With Our Blessing* was shortlisted for the Richard and Judy 'Search for a Bestseller' competition and became a top-ten bestseller in Ireland. Jo lives in Dublin with her husband and their four young children.

First published in Great Britain in 2015.
This paperback edition published in 2016 by

Quercus Publishing Ltd
Carmelite House
50 Victoria Embankment
London EC4Y 0DZ

An Hachette UK company

A CIP catalogue record for this book is available
from the British Library

PB ISBN 978 1 78429 317 8
EBOOK ISBN 978 1 78429 316 1

10 9 8 7 6

Typeset by Jouve (UK), Milton Keynes

Printed and bound in Great Britain by Clays Ltd, St Ives plc

For Martin, who made it possible

AUTHOR NOTE

While this book is fictional, Magdalene Laundries and mother and baby homes did exist, in my home country and elsewhere. *With Our Blessing* draws on the real-life accounts given by women who went through such institutions. However, the religious order mentioned in this book and the remote rural village named Kilcross in Limerick are inventions of my imagination and not intended to resemble any real-life people or places.

The following are just some of the books, programmes and websites I used for research during the writing of *With Our Blessing*:

Banished Babies: The Secret History of Ireland's Baby Export Business by Mike Milotte

The Light in the Window by June Goulding

The Lost Child of Philomena Lee: A Mother, Her Son, and a Fifty-Year Search by Martin Sixsmith

Sex in a Cold Climate directed by Steve Humphries for Testimony Films, Channel 4

Justice for Magdalenes (JFM Research) can be found at www. magdalenelaundries.com

www.adoptionrightsalliance.com/

1975

Her whole body shook as the adrenalin coursed through it. Sweat glistened on each unclothed patch of skin and relief from the pain washed over her like a wave. She knew, instinctively, that the physical ache would return between her legs and in the depths of her stomach but for now, in this instant, she was distracted by the little pink bundle and its continuous pitched wail.

'Let me hold my baby. Please. I think it's hungry.'

Her voice was plaintive, pleading.

The labour had been long and arduous. Fourteen hours of contractions with nothing to take the edge off and only harsh, scornful words from the woman meant to assist.

None of that mattered now. This baby had sprung from her womb, healthy and vital. She had created this miracle. It was the best thing she had ever done.

It didn't matter how the child had been conceived. The seed was nothing; it was the growing and nurturing that mattered. This small bundle of innocence, with tiny perfect hands and dainty poking feet, red mouth open like a hungry chick's and darting blue eyes – how could anybody blame it for anything?

'Please, please let me hold my baby.'

The mother tried to sit up, reaching out as the nun wrapped the newborn in a pristine white towel.

The movement in the bed alerted the sister.

She turned to look at the mother, lifting the baby so that all the young woman could see from her bedridden position was the back of its head. She could still hear the keening, though. The baby wanted the warmth of its mother's body, the sound of her heartbeat, the smell of her skin and her milk.

The nun raised a disdainful eyebrow.

'Do you really think I'm going to let you hold this precious gift from God? Do you really think Our Lord would allow you to keep this child? You, a whore?'

She spat the words.

With a curt nod to the sister by the bedside who had come to replace her, the nun turned and swept out of the room.

Sheer panic gripped the mother.

'Wait. My baby,' she choked, her heart racing. She tried to get up but, weak and dizzy, fell back.

There was a moment's silence.

Then she started to scream hysterically. The sound drowned out the wailing of the baby and the echo of sharp footsteps receding down the corridor.

It broke the heart of the nun left to tend to the woman.

She ceased trying to wipe the perspiration from the mother's brow.

'My baby!' the new mother implored, every ounce of colour drained from her face, her eyes wide with fear and disbelief. Then, overtaken by a primal reaction, she used every last ounce of her strength to raise her exhausted body and swing her legs to the floor. The sound that came from her throat was guttural.

She would get her baby back.

The young woman was possessed of a determination that was more powerful than anything she'd ever felt, but the nun beside her was physically stronger and hadn't been weakened by hours of labour.

She put her arms around the mother in both a comforting and restraining way, and they struggled.

'Don't. Please don't. You knew this would happen. There's nothing we can do.' The nun's voice broke on the last sentence.

The woman fought against her some more before collapsing back with a small cry. She looked at the nun, aghast.

'But it's my baby.' Her voice was now a haunted whisper, incredulous. She was in shock but she also knew, in her head if not her heart, that she was defeated. She *had* known this was going to happen.

Great shuddering sobs spilled from her throat and the nun held her tightly but gently, hot tears welling in her own eyes.

'I'm sorry,' she said to the mother, over and over. 'I'm

sorry this is happening to you. She will answer for her sins. I promise you.'

The desolate woman heard the nun through a fog of pain.

She collapsed back on the bed, turned over and stared at the white metal bars of the empty cot beside her.

'Was it a boy or a girl?' she whispered.

The nun told her.

The mother responded with a heartbroken sigh.

Hours ticked by, but the woman didn't move. Not when they washed her, nor when they wheeled the bare cot out and left her staring at the wall and the table of medical instruments.

She heard none of the compassionate words mumbled by the nun. She didn't taste or swallow the water that was held to her lips. The smell of the clinical disinfectant being mopped over the floor didn't reach her nose.

She lay there, feeling nothing, seeing nothing.

It was six hours before the madness came.

The return of the physical pain was nothing compared to the fury and the anguish that consumed her.

The light faded. The nun ordered to watch her fell asleep.

The woman in the bed wrapped her arms around herself. She began to rock. Then she began to whisper, over and over.

'I hate her. I hate her.'

The words filled the void. They were a comfort, a mantra to replace what had been taken from her. Her body lay empty under the coarse blanket. Her arms clasped herself, not her baby.

All she had now was grief and loathing.

2010

I am frightened. I keep thinking I can hear sounds. Doors banging. Footsteps.

The kitchen is a Christmas wonderland, with aromas of cinnamon and nutmeg. On the counter is a tray of storybook gingerbread men lined up to cool, delicate icing dotted down their fronts. Beside the tray is a red muslin basket of spiced buns, sugar frosted. It's early December and soon there'll be a Christmas tree in the corner, twinkling with lights and home-made ornaments from years past.

It's cold and the air smells of snow. I shiver and close the back door gently, shutting out the frost.

I cross the room, pausing at the kitchen door.

The wind has risen, shaking the window frame, and my hand trembles in concert with the old glass.

I steady myself. Close my eyes. Remember not to let fear get the better of me.

For years, I've been haunted by the feeling that someone is coming for me. I've a vivid imagination. Some might say I'm paranoid.

They haven't lived my life.

I open the door.

There's nothing in the well-lit entrance hall. Nobody up when they shouldn't be. No bogeyman ready to pounce.

Relief.

The kitchen door is heavy and crashes shut behind me as I cross the threshold, making a God-awful noise. I nearly leap out of my skin, my hand flying to my mouth.

It's a minute before I can breathe again. No one else seems to have heard; I've only scared myself.

I know it's important to let yourself be afraid. I learned the taste of fear early. It's a friend. Terror makes you alert.

I move across the hall, quietly, straining to hear if anyone else is active in the house.

There's a small walnut table just to the right of the door I'm approaching, a large vase of white lilies at its centre. Their smell is intoxicating, pungent, used for centuries to mask the stench of death.

The door leads to a corridor lined with stone alcoves. In each one sits a candle, lit earlier or later in the day depending on the season. The last person up, and it's always the same person, blows them out before the weary trip to bed.

The routine is the same. Step, step, step. Blow. A lick of the fingers and a hiss of the wick for good measure. All the way to the end. A lonely task.

I sense a movement to my left and whip my head round to see what it is, chest constricting.

It's nothing. The shadows of tree branches twisting in the wind, caught in the stained-glass window.

An involuntary laugh escapes my lips, breaking the tension. Not every sound is for me; not every shadow is the enemy. Even as I think it, I relax, the knots in my shoulders easing.

I'm at the door now. To my right is the light switch for the corridor. Buzzing fluorescent tubes overhead provide a guiding light back to the hall once the candles are extinguished.

I flick it. In the last few months the old-fashioned fuse box has been acting up, unexpectedly plunging the corridor into darkness. It's nerve-racking on a moonless night, but the trick is to leave a candle lit and use that to get back.

To the left of the door is an old coat rack, heaving with long winter garments. It's so wide and deep, an adult could hide in it and not be seen, head to toe.

As I stand by it, my imagination gets the better of me again. I wonder, is someone hiding there now?

I reach in tentatively and move my hands through the coats. I'm ready to snatch my arm out, petrified that someone will grab me by the wrist and pull me in, a cry dying on my lips before it has time to erupt.

There's nothing there.

I hear a noise. This time it's real and it's close. Footsteps are coming my way. I shudder as skeletal fingers crawl along my spine.

I dive into the coats, heart racing.

The door opens.

A woman steps into the hall. I can see her profile through the damp-smelling clothes.

My mouth is dry and I'm filled with dread.

It's actually happening.

Can she see me?

Her face is hard. Fearsome. Ever sneering. She's the one I'm afraid of.

For a second I think she has seen me. Every muscle in my body seizes with terror.

Then she turns away from me, places the last burning candle on the table. She raises her hand to the light switch to turn it off. She thinks the fuse has blown again and doesn't want the switch to be on when it's replaced.

Her hand freezes. The switch is off, but she knows she flicked it on before entering the corridor.

I step out of the coats, as silent as the grave. While she is standing there, puzzlement turning to unease, I raise the heavy torch I'm carrying.

Her body starts to quiver ever so slightly. She has sensed my presence but doesn't turn around. Maybe she thinks if she can't see me, I don't exist.

I do exist.

I bring the weapon down with just enough force. Not too hard, not too soft. I'm like Goldilocks and the three bears. My blow is just right.

It cracks against the back of her skull. Her right arm flails, her left twitches.

Too late, I see her trailing arm hit the vase on the table. It smashes against the wall with an explosion that sounds to me like thunder and a siren all going off at once.

Shards of glass explode in all directions as she collapses to the ground.

I've no time to react. No time to clean. I must move now.

I pocket the torch and hook my hands under her armpits.

There's barely a moment to savour what has just happened. All that watching and waiting. Over a year's planning.

Revenge.

I don't know if it's the Christmas spices in the air but it's true what they say.

Revenge is sweet. And I'm not done yet.

Day One

Friday, 10 December

CHAPTER 1

He was dreaming. He knew this, even though in his imaginings he was actually up and getting dressed, albeit in that sleepy, sluggish way of dreams. It was his day off and he was going to get the papers, breathing in the sharp winter air on the pleasant fifteen-minute walk to Castleknock village. No hurry. Maybe pick up some Danish pastries. He and Louise could light a fire in the old-fashioned grate in their bedroom and curl up under the duvet.

Louise. She was calling him now. 'Tom. Tom. TOM!'

He opened his eyes. Actually opened them this time.

His wife was leaning over him, her long brown hair tickling his cheek, amused brown eyes peering into his barely opened green ones.

'Calling Detective Inspector Tom Reynolds. Time to wake up, love. Do you fall asleep at night or slip into a coma?'

She wafted a mug under his nose. His slightly crooked nose, which she had decided early in their relationship was his most endearing feature, because it gave a manly unevenness to his handsome face.

He smelled coffee. Steaming and rich, strong wonderful coffee.

'For me?' he croaked, rubbing his eyes. He pulled himself up into a sitting position, running a hand through his thick, once black, now greying hair.

He reached for the caffeine. 'I was having the strangest dream, you know the type when you think you're awake, but you're still asleep ...'

'Tom.' Louise smiled and stroked his face, her fingers scratching his salt and pepper stubble. 'You're still half asleep. Ray is downstairs. You're needed.'

Tom grunted, sipping the coffee and grumpily batting her away as she ruffled his bed-head hair.

'What time is it?'

He wasn't a morning person at the best of times, but something told him this was earlier than even he was used to.

'It's just after six. I'd offer to make you both breakfast but Ray says it's urgent. There are some pastries downstairs you can take ...' She paused and patted his stomach. 'Though maybe some fruit might be better.'

Tom snorted at that, took another sip of coffee and felt it kick-start his synapses. Put the mug down and stretched.

'I'm an inspector in the National Bureau of Criminal Investigation. It's always urgent. God, why am I so tired?'

'Maybe because you stayed up until 1 a.m. so you could smoke a cigar after I'd gone to bed? Oh, I smelled it all right.'

She gave him a playful clip on the ear. He responded with a sheepish grin.

She hated him smoking, but he was nearly fifty and

couldn't kick the habit of a lifetime. He had a preference for intensely flavoured, if prohibitively expensive, Cuban cigars. Luckily, a few puffs were generally enough to keep him happy.

It was one of his only vices. His wife devoured crime novels populated by detectives who drank too much, suffered with depression, were addicted to painkillers – their list of afflictions endless, their lives unfailingly miserable. The fiction shelves had done a great job convincing the public that all police detectives were stereotypical flawed geniuses, battling secret demons. In reality, although the job took its toll, most of Tom's colleagues were normal men and women with all the usual human qualities and flaws, and most officers retired intact, not as quivering wrecks.

'I apologize. It's too cold to sit out back. I could get the flu.'

'I've no sympathy.' She shook her head. 'Not when you're worried about flu but not about lung cancer. Will I send Ray up? He's chomping at the bit down there.'

Tom nodded, braced himself for the cold air and threw his legs out from under the warm bedspread.

He had his trousers on and was buttoning up his shirt when Ray rapped on the door.

'It's okay, I'm decent,' Tom called.

Ray Lennon was fifteen years younger than Tom. His height, chiselled features, dark grey eyes and buzz cut all contributed to make him an attractive man. The intense, brooding appearance, however, belied a boyish sense of humour. That light-hearted aspect of his personality in turn masked an insightful intelligence, which explained his relatively swift rise through the ranks to become Tom's lead detective sergeant in the NBCI's esteemed murder unit.

Tom chose a navy tie and turned round. 'Cold got your tongue this morning?'

The teasing grin died when he saw his deputy's face.

Ray's features were grim, the colour faded from his cheeks. He looked shell-shocked.

'What is it?' Tom asked.

There had been a spate of gangland killings over the last few months, but the situation appeared to have calmed. Every guard in Dublin was praying the hiatus would last through December.

Ray swallowed, Adam's apple bobbing, still choosing his words.

Tom grabbed his suit jacket from the chair beside the en suite. 'Please don't tell me one of the scumbags has shot an innocent bystander.'

Ray shook his head. 'No. It's worse.'

'Not a child?' Tom's heart thumped as he said the words.

Again, a shake of the head.

'It's a woman, sir, an elderly woman. They found her body in the Phoenix Park.'

The inspector sat down on the edge of the chair, ostensibly to lace his shoes, but in truth because he felt he should be sitting for whatever was coming next. He couldn't imagine what could provoke such a reaction in an experienced detective outside of a child being harmed.

'Spit it out, Ray.'

'She's been crucified, Tom. An old woman has been crucified in the park.'

'What do you mean, crucified?'

Tom wondered for a moment if he was still dreaming. His house faced one of the outer walls of the Phoenix Park, a public green space that encompassed over 1,700 acres of Dublin city land.

'I haven't seen her. Michael and Laura were the first of our team at the scene. They just said she's nailed to a tree.'

Tom stared blankly at his deputy for a long moment before his senses kicked into action.

'Let's get down there. It's not in public view, is it?'

'No, it's off road.'

The two men hurried downstairs, meeting Louise in the hallway.

'It's cats and dogs out there, Tom. Take your raincoat . . .' She paused. 'What is it?'

Tom shook his head.

A look of well-worn understanding settled on his wife's face.

Tom took his heavy black coat from her outstretched hand.

'I might get a Christmas tree today,' she said, as he fastened his zip. The world he had to deal with outside might be brutish and chaotic, but she'd be damned if she'd let it infringe on their home life. 'And you said you'd order that mini skip for me for those boxes of junk in the attic.'

'I'll do it later.' His response was automatic.

'When you die, Tom Reynolds, I'm going to have "I'll do it later" inscribed on your tombstone.'

'As they say, love, if you ask me to do something, I'll do it. You don't need to nag me about it every six months.'

She raised one eyebrow in the 'I don't think you're funny' expression he knew so well.

'Anyway, isn't it a bit early for a Christmas tree? I won't be here to help you.'

'We're only a couple of weeks away. Maria can help.'

'Isn't she in college?'

Louise hesitated. It was barely noticeable, but long enough for her husband of over a quarter of a century to stop moving towards the front door.

She mentally kicked herself. Sometimes, it was necessary to delay the truth.

'It's nothing to worry about,' she said hurriedly. 'I'll fill you in another time. Go, do your job.'

Tom paused a moment longer, then leaned over to hug and kiss her goodbye.

Maria had been causing them more than a few headaches these last few months. She wasn't settling well in college and at nineteen years of age it had gone beyond the point of them telling her what to do. Tom was starting to wish, much and all as he loved her, that she would cut the apron strings and flat-share with a friend.

Louise closed her eyes and enjoyed the brief embrace, inhaling the smell of musk and toothpaste. He was on the brink of yet another case that would steal him from her, just when she needed him.

She sighed. Life with Tom was never boring, but it was often lonely.

CHAPTER 2

Traffic in the park was light in the still dark morning. In an hour, the roads would be backed up as people awoke to the heavy rain and decided to avoid unpredictable public transport and drive to work.

They were in Ray's car. Tom's mechanic saw more of the inspector's vehicle than he did these days. The old man had advised against an Alfa Romeo, but a pig-headed Tom had willingly sacrificed reliability for the car's magnificence when it was on top form.

These past two weeks, though, relying on either Ray or his oft-time garda driver Willie Callaghan had been painful. Both men observed the speed limit with what Tom considered undue reverence.

'You do realize fifty kilometres per hour in this park is for law-abiding citizens, not the police, don't you?' he griped, as they toddled down the Phoenix Park's main avenue.

A grim smile played on Ray's lips, but his eyes stayed focused on the road.

'I think you'll find, sir, the speed limit is for the benefit of the deer, who don't really care who's driving the car.'

The park was home to over 400 fallow deer, descended from an original herd introduced in the 1660s. Dublin residents knew to look out for them bounding across the main avenue at night, but many an unfortunate visiting driver had been known to swerve with fright into the roadside ditches upon seeing the magnificent animals canter out, eyes glinting in the headlights.

Tom and Ray had entered via the Castleknock gate and now took a right turn before the American ambassador's residence. Further on they took a narrow road to the left, freshly marked with police cones. A lone officer stood sentinel, hunched against the driving rain.

The uniformed guard peered through the car's windscreen from under his dripping cap as they slowed for him. Seeing who they were, he waved them through enthusiastically.

At the road's end they pulled in beside two other squad cars parked on the grass verge.

'Prepare to get drenched,' Tom warned, as he pulled his hood over his head and stepped on to the sodden grass. The smell of damp greenery assaulted his nostrils, followed by the uncomfortable sensation of wet seeping up his trouser legs. All the heat he'd absorbed in the car seemed to instantly leave his body.

Michael Geoghegan was waiting for them. He was wearing a heavy black Nike rain hoody, hands shoved in the pockets.

The inspector knew Michael was only back on the job a few days. He hadn't seen the young detective since

Michael's wife had miscarried three months previously. Anne had been almost halfway through her pregnancy and the baby's loss was a devastating blow to the couple. Michael had been granted compassionate leave, combined with overdue holiday time, so he could be with her.

Tom placed his hand on the other man's shoulder. 'Michael, good to see you. How are you? How's Anne?'

Michael shrugged and shuffled nervously. 'We're all right, sir; getting on with things.'

It was obvious the young detective didn't want to dwell on the tragedy.

'What have we got here, then?'

'We had a hard time finding her. The man who rang it in was incoherent and, to be honest, describing a wooded area — 'Michael cast his arm at the many trees in their vicinity '— well, one copse looks the same as the next around here.'

'Did you say corpse?' Ray looked astonished.

Tom rolled his eyes. 'Copse, you illiterate! It's a collection of trees. Carry on, Michael.'

'Right. Well, a patrol car was sent out first, but we were pulling an early morning shift and heard it on dispatch, so we got here minutes after the uniforms. Pathology and the Technical Bureau are sending teams. There were gunshots fired at a house in Clondalkin last night and an incident in town so they're stretched. I think McDonagh himself is coming. He gave me a big lecture about how busy he is, and put the phone down.'

Michael looked uncertain, as if he was wondering

whether he should have confirmed that the chief super-intendent in charge of the Garda Síochána Technical Bureau was indeed en route.

'He's on his way, Michael,' Tom reassured him. 'Have we secured the scene as much as we can for now?'

The Technical Bureau would assess the crime scene for forensics, but Tom's team would set up an outer cordon to protect against public or media intrusion.

'There's a guard at the entrance to the road you came up and another behind this set of trees, making sure no one can get in. The hollow where we found her is pretty much inaccessible, bar where you come off the main path. There are dense bushes and briars surrounding it.'

'We'll go as far as the hollow,' Tom said. 'We'd better not go in until the Bureau gives us the okay.'

They set off into the trees, taking torches from the car. Tom could see they were following a rough path, but he knew no woman would walk this route alone, day or night.

'Michael, the man who rang in – how exactly did he say he came across this woman? This doesn't look like the sort of place you'd be walking your dog.'

'He didn't. No name either.'

'Suspect number one, so,' Ray offered.

It took them five minutes to reach Laura Brennan. The youngest detective on the team was resting her back against a tree. Her copper curls hung forward, her face illuminated by the smartphone in her hand. Laura's fingers flew over the screen, issuing diktats via text. Unlike

Michael, who took casual dressing at work to a new level, the female detective always wore smart, well-fitted suits. She was young, so she dressed older to make a point. Right now she was wearing a sensible black parka over her tailored clothes to keep out the rain.

She looked up at their approach and hauled herself to a standing position.

'Morning, sir. The victim's in there.' She took a deep breath. 'It's pretty bad.'

'Nothing has been touched?'

'Nothing.'

Tom and Ray walked to the very edge of the dark hollow, careful to go no further for fear of contaminating the scene. Both men raised their torches. Their combined arcs of light illuminated patches of the clearing in the trees, casting a ghostly glow on the leaf-strewn soil.

At the same moment, both men trained their respective beams at the far side of the small circle.

Ray dropped his torch in shock. 'Christ,' he exclaimed, sinking to his knees and fumbling to retrieve it.

Tom was frozen to the spot, a slight tremor in his hand as he kept his light focused on the nightmarish sight in front of him.

The woman appeared to be standing, ready to meet them. Her head was positioned grotesquely to one side, resting on one outstretched arm. Her chest was exposed beneath torn, blood-saturated fabric. Thin strands of lank grey hair framed her wrinkled face. She was in her seventies or thereabouts. Nondescript clothing – a brown skirt and lace-collared blouse.

The elderly woman's facial features were frozen in a moment of terror, eyes wide with horror, mouth hanging open in permanent shock. Dried blood covered the bottom half of her face.

Her arms extended at an unnatural angle from her body, hands impaled on long nails hammered into the wide tree trunk. Her feet, barely raised off the ground, were joined and similarly affixed with a single nail.

As if the nails were not enough, a rope tightly cinched her waist to the tree.

None of it, though, shocked Tom as much as the words.

On the bare flesh of her chest, letters had been crudely carved.

The inspector had to squint to make out the words, barely discernible amid the congealed blood.

Satan's Whore

Tom instinctively took a step back. In that chilling moment, he was glad he hadn't eaten breakfast.

Behind him, Ray was polluting the outskirts of the crime scene, vomiting as he clutched a tree for support.

CHAPTER 3

'Good morning, Tom. What have we here, then?'

Emmet McDonagh, head of the Technical Bureau, walked briskly towards them. Two others followed, momentarily obscured by his girth.

'I thought I'd lend you my extensive expertise, as you're on my home patch. Where's the victim?'

Tom pointed into the hollow.

Emmet abruptly stopped and directed his torch nonchalantly into the dark space.

The accompanying technicians crashed into the back of him.

'Jesus Christ!' Emmet exclaimed.

'You did stop with no warning,' a woman's voice snapped, before its owner came round to stand beside him.

'I wasn't talking to you,' Emmet replied. 'Look.' He brandished his light at the hollow, creating a gruesome flickering effect on the victim.

The woman's eyes widened. 'Well. That's novel,' she declared.

Emmet shook his head and the mop of brown hair atop it, still distracted by the sight in front of him.

Tom reckoned he dyed his hair. Emmet had twelve years on the inspector and there wasn't so much as a grey strand in sight.

'Hell, Tom, a bit of notice would have been nice. I thought we were coming down for some gang shooting.'

'Michael didn't tell you?' Tom was surprised. Then he remembered Michael telling him Emmet had been his usual brusque self on the phone.

The other man shook his head. Without taking his eyes off the victim, he waved his hand at the two people beside him. 'Sorry, you know Ellie Byrne and Mark Dunne, don't you?'

Tom leaned forward to shake their hands. He'd seen both technicians on occasion, and he certainly remembered Ellie. The woman was beautiful. Long raven-black hair framed a love-heart face, her bone structure the envy of any model. Even exhausted from her heavy workload, with bags under her eyes, she was still breathtaking. He suspected Ray had a crush on her, along with most of the men on the force.

Both of them shook his hand distractedly, busy staring at the woman nailed to the tree.

'We need to secure this,' Emmet said. He shone his torch over the ground in front of them. 'Has anyone been in there?'

'None of our lot,' Tom said.

'Who left that?'

Emmet waved his torch at the rank-smelling puddle to the left of the entrance.

'We can account for that,' Tom replied, deflecting the question.

'Hm. I'll need some halogen lamps. It's at least another hour until proper daylight, and if it keeps raining it will stay dull.'

Tom spent most of the hour and a half that followed on the phone. The state pathologist was en route, along with Tom's boss, Detective Chief Superintendent Sean McGuinness.

When Emmet eventually allowed Tom into the hollow, he crossed straight to the victim, shaking his head in disbelief.

'What do you think, Emmet – mid to late seventies?'

His colleague walked over and joined him, nodding his head slowly.

They peered at her chest.

'She's been stabbed,' Tom said, aware he was stating what was probably obvious to Emmet. 'Repeatedly.'

He would take in everything he could before the pathology team arrived and took over. After that, they'd take the woman down from the tree. The inspector didn't plan on being in the hollow when they removed the nails from the victim's hands and feet.

A crucifix hung around the woman's neck. Tom pulled on a pair of latex gloves and very gently lifted it. The figure of Jesus hung on the cross. The hideous irony of the victim's crucifixion was inescapable.

He turned the cross over. There, on the back, were the initials MM.

They had been engraved. They didn't look like the mark of the manufacturer.

'MM,' he said to Emmet. 'That would be religious, rather than her initials, do you think?'

'Probably. It could be Mother Mary. Maybe a Roman numeral?'

Tom gently placed the crucifix back on the woman's neck.

'She's tall, but I'd hazard a guess she barely weighs seven stone,' Emmet observed. 'It would have been easy enough for her killer to tie her to this tree, once she'd been propped against it.'

'Even if she'd tried to fight?' Tom asked.

'She didn't fight. Not here,' Emmet replied. 'She wasn't killed here.'

'What do you mean?'

'I mean she was stabbed somewhere, bled out and was brought here afterwards. This body was arranged post-mortem. There would be far more blood if she'd been stabbed here. That's why I let you in so quickly.'

'Are you serious? Somebody brought her here and crucified a dead body?'

'Yes.'

Tom took a deep breath. He was relieved that the woman had not suffered the crucifixion while alive, but that begged a question.

'Why?'

Emmet shook his head. 'Mine is not to reason why, but to give you the clues regarding the how. It looks like someone wanted to make a statement.'

Tom wasn't listening. He was staring at the blood on the woman's chin. It looked as though she'd been punched in the mouth. But . . .

'God Almighty!'

Emmet jumped. 'What?'

Tom was staring into the woman's mouth, his eyes bulging.

'Her tongue. It's been cut out.'

CHAPTER 4

Tom gave the members of the pathology team a rundown as soon as they arrived. He left them to get on with their work and made his way back to the car with Ray.

The first of the press had arrived. The two officers ignored the reporters' scattergun questions as they got into the car, slamming the doors on the outside world. Headquarters would deal with media inquiries, and Tom didn't envy them the task.

'That Ellie is a looker, isn't she?' Ray said casually, retrieving a towel from the backseat.

'Why do you have a towel in your car?' Tom asked, distracted.

'Went for a beach run last night. I used it to dry off the sweat and rain so I wouldn't get cold on the drive home.'

'You make me sick.'

Tom rubbed at the condensation on the passenger window, then instantly regretted it. One of the rebuked reporters was staring bug-eyed at the car, and now he could be seen. The inspector sighed and turned towards Ray, his back to the window.

'Do you think she's single?'

This was their routine. When they walked away from a crime scene, they talked about anything and everything other than what they'd seen. It was a five-minute hiatus, their way of postponing the inevitable. It also meant Ray didn't have to discuss the incongruity of being a murder detective with an aversion to gore. Others might find it hilarious. Ray found it humiliating.

'I suspected you had a thing for her, but really?' Tom responded. 'Do you think the start of an investigation like this is the time to start courting? I don't know how you could have been eyeing her up, anyway – against that backdrop. It must say something about you psychologically.'

Ray glared at his superior officer. 'Courting? Oh, sorry, is this the eighteenth century calling?' He placed his hand to his ear, pretending it was a phone. 'It's for you. They want their turn of phrase back. I just wondered if she's single. You know, for the future.' Ray shook his head in exasperation.

No one would ever describe him as a Romeo. The demands of his job left little time to meet anyone, but he was in his mid-thirties now and single didn't feel as good as it used to, especially as invitations to old friends' weddings arrived with alarming frequency these days.

Within twenty minutes, the head of the NBCI, DCS Sean McGuinness, arrived. Tom watched as the chief's car sped towards the growing band of reporters, causing them to jump to either side of the oncoming vehicle.

As the big grey-haired man emerged, Tom could tell

from his gesticulations that he was blaming the pouring rain and sodden ground for the car's failure to slow down.

It took McGuinness a few seconds to spot Tom and Ray. He took long strides over to the car and banged forcefully on the roof before yanking open the driver's door. The young guard who had arrived with him caught up and tried to put an umbrella over his superior's head.

McGuinness flapped him away. 'Really? You think an umbrella will make much difference?' he roared, pointing to the open heavens.

The young officer scurried off, red-faced, but not so far as to be outside shouting distance.

'Staying nice and warm, are we, gentlemen?' the chief barked at them in his thick Kerry accent, as his dripping head poked into the car.

'Have we a mini-bar in here? Are ye having Irish coffees? No? Then get the hell out!' He roared this last part.

Ray put a hand over his mouth to stifle a laugh.

'Mind you don't get sick in there, youngster; news of your sterling performance has spread.'

Now Ray hung his head, mortified, not only by the other man's sarcasm but also because he had just realized Ellie Byrne would be bagging his regurgitated breakfast.

Tom took pity on his junior and decided to run interference.

Reluctantly, he got out of the warm car. 'Nice to see you too, sir.'

Tom was just less than six foot, but the chief soared over

him. He had height and width. His size and strength, even at sixty, abetted by his loud and dramatic personality, gave him an intimidating air. Tom knew it to be a front. Sean McGuinness was an old friend and, beneath the brashness, he was thoughtful, kind and good-hearted.

McGuinness's tone was discreet now, conscious of the watching reporters.

'I'm just wondering how a woman managed to get herself murdered in Garda Headquarters' back garden.'

His words implied that Tom's team should have been camped out in the park, ensuring no embarrassing murders were being committed.

The chief sucked air into his cheeks and then released it slowly. Running his hands through his shaggy grey hair, he wiped away the rain that threatened to blind him as it ran down his forehead.

'This is like manna from heaven for the press. Between the gang murders and budget cuts and internal politics . . . I don't know how we will cope.'

Tom nodded sympathetically. McGuinness would retire in a couple of years, and the path to his job lay open for Tom – yet he couldn't bear the thought of it. He couldn't stand the idea of having to stress about how to run a whole department on little or nothing and deal with growing crime levels, not to mention the media constantly editorializing on the police's failings.

'Did you hear?' McGuinness leaned towards him conspiratorially. 'On Tuesday a guard in Donegal had to get a home burglary victim to collect him from the station to investigate. Have you ever heard the likes? They only have one car in the station and it was out.' McGuinness shook his head. 'Anyway. That's not important now. This woman —' he gestured at the trees '— we won't let internal problems beat us on this one, eh, Tom?'

When they arrived at the hollow, two pathology assistants were examining the nails in the woman's hands, working out how to prise them from the tree with the hands still intact. McGuinness took in the scene and instantly spun round to escape it.

'Blessed Virgin, Mother of the Divine!' He made the sign of the cross, a reaction appropriate to a man of his generation, albeit inappropriate given the victim's circumstances.

Tom could hear Emmet yelling after them, 'This isn't a bloody tourist trail!'

'My God, Tom. What if a child had run down here and seen that?'

Ellie was walking towards them with plastic evidence bags destined for the lab.

'Anything?' Tom asked.

She shrugged. 'It's a public area. Any or none of this could be relevant. You do know what this place is known for, don't you?'

Tom looked at McGuinness, and they both shook their heads.

Ellie raised her eyebrows. 'It's a notorious rent boy run. This is where they bring their customers.'

'You're joking,' Tom choked. 'How do you know that?'

'I thought everyone knew that. But, you know, we are stationed just a mile or two up the road.'

The Technical Bureau was located in Garda Headquarters, which sat just inside the North Circular Road entrance to the park – its 'back garden'.

'So, there's no doubt she would have been found quickly,' Tom said.

Sean McGuinness shook his head. 'Barbaric. That's the only word for this. We're dealing with an animal. And speaking of . . . no one is to talk to that pack of rabid dogs at the cordon. We'll do a press conference later when we've established some facts.'

CHAPTER 5

By the time they arrived at the garda station in Blanchardstown village, an incident room had been designated. As head of the murder squad, Tom was generally based in Harcourt Street on Dublin's south side, but the place tended to be overrun with activity on any given day. When possible, he moved his team to the station closest to their most recent crime scene. Conveniently for him, Blanchardstown was near his home and a location to which he was accustomed.

He was gingerly sipping an insipid black liquid when Ray came in carrying two polystyrene cups from the Bistro, their favourite restaurant in the village.

'Oh. You've already got coffee.'

'That's stretching it.' Tom extended his hand gratefully for the fresh cup. In his book, instant coffee was an affront to humanity. If you weren't willing to grind good quality beans and preheat the milk, then you were as well getting your caffeine from a can of Coke.

'More instructions from the chief?' Ray indicated the phone in Tom's other hand.

'Yes. He wants this solved in time for the evening news.'

Before the hour was out the room was full. Those detectives who had visited the crime scene that morning were joined by four more team members and by the station's sergeant, Ian Kelly – affectionately nicknamed 'Hairy' by his friends, a tribute to his completely bald head.

Ian began arranging the photos sent over by the crime scene unit. The shots captured every gruesome detail of the woman's injuries. Even the seasoned detectives in the room found the images repellant.

'Okay, let's start,' Tom said. 'It's our job to discover this woman's story. Who is she? Who did this to her? Why?'

Tom paused. He was conscious that the men and women in the room were desperate for the Christmas break. It had been a long and punishing year.

'You are the most talented detectives in the force. You know this. That's why you're in the murder squad. We're going to have our work cut out for us here, but I couldn't ask for a better team.'

'There's no one else to ask for,' Ray snorted.

The others laughed.

The inspector smiled. 'It's true. This is going to take over our lives for the foreseeable, but at least McGuinness has moved our ongoing cases sideways. This is top priority.'

He looked at Michael as he said this, and thought of his young wife at home, mourning the loss of her baby. Should he be here at all?

Michael caught his superior's appraising look. He needed to be here so badly he couldn't put it into words.

This was awful, but it was someone else's awful. It wasn't his loss. It wasn't the pain that racked him every night as Anne lay on the far side of their bed, her stomach empty, aching for a baby that was no more.

His colleagues knew of their loss. They didn't know the couple had been trying for a baby for five years now and that this was the first time they'd progressed beyond the magic twelve-week mark. Eighteen weeks and it still ended up as a bloody tragedy.

Michael's face must have betrayed his desperation because Tom held his gaze only briefly before moving on.

'All right. What do we have?'

Ray stood up awkwardly. Being the centre of attention always made him nervous.

At that moment, the meeting-room door opened and a young guard came in wheeling a trolley of food.

'My apologies, Ray,' Tom said. 'I had lunch sent for. It will be a long day.'

The detective sergeant wanted to get his piece over with, but the rest of the team looked grateful. A couple had been glancing anxiously at the clock, wondering if their stomachs were going to start rumbling.

Even better, Tom had ordered the sandwiches and drinks from the Bistro.

Satisfied that everyone in the team had food to hand, and waiting until Ray had taken a particularly large bite of his sandwich, the inspector called the room to order.

His deputy almost choked. The rest of the team, with

no onus on them to speak, chewed happily and watched, amused, as Ray attempted to swallow the mouthful.

That would distract him from the nerves, Tom thought.

What an infuriating old git, Ray thought.

'Okay,' he eventually managed, taking a deep breath. 'The good news is the pathology office have bumped this above everything else and they're performing the autopsy today. From their preliminary examination, they've noted the victim's estimated age at mid to late seventies. They're already suggesting the six stab wounds she received may have come from a regular kitchen knife. They won't confirm that yet. The same weapon was likely used to cut out her tongue. She was alive for that, but they believe she was already dead when the words were gouged into her chest and she was crucified.'

The detectives who hadn't been at the scene that morning gasped at the tongue news and, to a man and woman, their eyes flew back to the photos on the wall, searching for visual proof of the heinous act. Those with less strong stomachs discreetly placed sandwiches back on paper plates.

Ray cleared his throat again. 'Approximate time of death is yesterday, Thursday morning, 11 a.m. They haven't found anything as of yet on her body to indicate DNA from her attacker. There are no broken fingernails, nothing to demonstrate she defended herself. More on that in a bit. The Tech Bureau has a lot of material from the scene to go through but they're not sure any of it will be relevant.'

Ray looked down at his notes. 'The pathologist says it looks like she was hit on the back of the head with a blunt object. There are no noticeable fibres in the head wound so he suspects some kind of metal implement, maybe aluminium.'

The room collectively winced, imagining the cracking sound the weapon would have made as it connected with the elderly woman's head.

'The perpetrator took a risk because a more forceful blow would have caused internal bleeding and could have killed her. Pathology found patterned ligature marks on her arms and legs, which indicate she was tied up at some point, maybe to a chair. So, if she regained consciousness that may explain the absence of defensive wounds on the body. They also found some lacerations to her right hand, caused by glass fragments.'

Ray wiped the sheen of perspiration from his brow. He could run ten kilometres and hardly break a sweat, but standing in front of a room of people to talk was a pressure like no other.

'They can't confirm exactly when she was brought to the park. The cold weather complicates their calculations. By the time we got to her, all night, obviously. Pathology suggests she was moved there on Thursday evening.

'Finally, as you know, pathologists don't theorize lightly, but our guy is willing to speculate that the first stab wound to the heart, perhaps in combination with the mutilation of the tongue, caused a myocardial infarction – a heart attack. That's probably what actually killed her, but he won't have confirmation until he does the full post-mortem.'

The room was silent.

Ray nodded at Tom, who stood up.

'Okay, folks. Here's our problem. We don't know who she is, why she was murdered, where she was murdered, or by whom. So, absolutely nothing, basically. This one is a standing start, I'm afraid.

'Our victim's identity is a priority. We'll do a press conference this afternoon and appeal for witnesses. The body was left in the Phoenix Park; there must be someone who saw something. And I want that anonymous caller—'

'Sir, what is the writing about?' Michael interjected.

'There's clearly a religious subtext, with the crucifixion,' Laura offered.

'Maybe there's some kind of satanic element?' Ian speculated. 'I can't recall anything like that happening before in Ireland, though. Don't the satanists use an upside-down crucifix?' Ian cocked his head slightly to the left as he looked at the picture of the dead woman, as though imagining her upside down.

Laura stared at him, appalled.

'Why was she left in the park?' asked one of the other detectives, Bridget. 'That wooded area is a bit off the beaten track but is still accessible. He could have brought her up to the Dublin Mountains and she might never have been found.'

'He wanted her found,' Tom answered. 'We've been told the area is a rent boy haunt, so it's out of the way but in use. Whoever hung her there must have worked fast, but the killer still risked being caught. What I'm wondering is why the tongue? What is the murderer telling us – that he's silenced her for ever? That she was a liar?'

'Does there have to be a reason for torture?' Michael asked. 'He could have cut her tongue out to stop her screaming.'

Tom shook his head, unable to rationalize the cruel act.

The inspector brought the meeting to an end by giving the team designated tasks. As the officers filed from the room, he turned to Ray.

'What time did it start raining yesterday?'

'About three. It was steady all day. I know, I was out running in it.'

Tom sighed. With rain, the park could have been deserted on Thursday evening, especially off road.

'Let's get a photofit ready in case nothing turns up in missing persons,' he said.

'I presume it will be us two telling the family?'

'Yes. If we can find any,' Tom grimaced.

What would be worse? he wondered.

To tell a family, or there to be no family?

CHAPTER 6

Tom looked at the number and address he'd written down. 'Are you sure? The anonymous caller rang from his landline?'

'Of course we're sure. Anyone could have tracked it down. We told your detective that.' The subtext being, don't waste our time with such elementary procedural queries.

'Thank you,' the inspector responded curtly, hoping the expert from the IT department hadn't been as rude to Laura.

He looked at the number again in disbelief. What kind of genius would make an anonymous call from their home phone?

Just as he was about to send a car out to pick up Gerard Poots – their now identified caller – Tom's phone rang, the screen displaying an internal number.

'Yes,' he answered.

'Sir, we have a man called Gerard Poots down at the front desk. Says he's the one who rang the park body in.'

Tom sat back in his chair. Curious. Of all the stations . . .

'Put him in an interview room and get detectives Brennan and Geoghegan in with him.'

He looked at the clock. It was 8 p.m. and he wanted to go home. He'd yet to solve a case on day one, outside of those where the perpetrator confessed up front. The press conference had been well attended and every media outlet they needed was now carrying the story. They'd kept back the gruesome details of the murder for now and just released information about the woman's appearance and where she was found.

Over the next twenty-four hours, that should translate into an identity. He hoped. Missing persons had turned up nothing.

He picked up the phone to ring Ray, just as the door opened.

Ray strolled in, brandishing his phone. 'You rang?'

'Now that's the kind of prompt response I like in a subordinate.'

Ray rolled his eyes. 'The caller is downstairs.'

'I know that, and I even know where he lives.'

'Really? And he hasn't even been interviewed yet. You're good.'

'I've sent Laura and Michael in to scope him out before we scare him with the big guns.' Tom flexed his biceps comically. He hadn't completely lost the muscle tone in his limbs from years of swimming and running, but he was sitting in a room with a man still in his prime, who happened to work out every day. He sighed and muttered:

' "An aged man is but a paltry thing, a tattered coat upon a stick." '

Ray drummed his fingers on the other side of the desk and raised an eyebrow.

'Forgot to take your meds?'

'It's William Butler Yeats, you philistine,' Tom retorted.

Twenty minutes later Laura and Michael arrived in Tom's office, shaking their heads.

'We left him down there giving a formal statement to Ian,' Michael reported. 'He's an emotional vomiter, told us all his problems as soon as we walked in. He's a married man, a solicitor, and he picked up the rent boy in the park around midnight. Not a pleasant character, but if he's the killer he'll be appearing in next year's Oscar nominations. Said he was in shock when he rang last night – frightened his wife would find out what he's been up to. Implied he was the one being taken advantage of.

'Anyway, they saw nothing and heard nothing, but at some point . . .' Michael coughed. 'At some point he said he felt like someone was watching them, which apparently isn't unusual among this fraternity, so he used his mobile to shine a light around the hollow. That's when the pair of them saw the victim. They fled the scene in a panic. He doesn't have a name for the lad, but Vice will track him. He's probably telling all his mates what happened. We're taking Poots' DNA now.'

'I think we should do him for using rent boys. I've seen those kids,' Ray said. 'Pitiful.'

'I know,' Tom said. 'But imagine what that would do for other potential witnesses. One member of the public comes forward to help and is done for soliciting. There'll be dog walkers out there trying to recall if they neglected to pick up their pets' poop, rather than what they might have witnessed.'

'Fine,' Ray said. 'Are we done for tonight?'

'Yes. Team meeting at 8 a.m. and let's see what we have then. I hope nobody had plans for the weekend.'

Tom managed to get out of the building without encountering anyone who might cause him further delay. One of the joys of working from a suburban station. Had Sean McGuinness caught him leaving at this hour he'd accuse him of taking a half-day.

He headed in the direction of the bus stop. The bus for town would leave him close enough to his house on Black-horse Avenue to walk the rest of the way. Someone could have driven him home, but he needed some alone time.

He sat, anonymous and freezing, waiting patiently for the elusive late evening bus, the *Pearl Fishers* duet blaring from his earphones.

The well-known piece of music was brutally interrupted by his ringtone.

It was Ian Kelly.

'I've just left,' he answered. 'What's happened?'

Ian hesitated before speaking. Tom sensed he was rattled.

'We've an ID. At least we think we do. I hope you're sitting down. You're not going to believe this.'

'Well? Who is she?'

Ian took a deep breath. 'She's a nun, Tom.'

The blood drained from the inspector's face.

'God,' he whispered.

'I don't think God had much to do with this,' Ian replied. 'There's another nun coming up from Limerick in the morning to ID her. But she said Reverend Mother Attracta – that's her name, by the way – has been missing since the day before yesterday and matches the press description.'

'Limerick? That's a bit of a stretch, isn't it – geography-wise?'

'A two-hour drive if you put your foot down, which I assume you would if you'd a body in the boot.'

'Well, if I'd a body in the boot I wouldn't want to risk being caught speeding, Ian. Hell, what are we saying?'

'Sorry.'

Tom turned over the news in his head. Could a missing nun from Limerick be their dead woman in Dublin?

'Tom? You know, I had this feeling she was a nun.'

Hindsight was a glorious thing.

'We discussed a religious dimension. Could it be someone hitting out at the Catholic Church?' Tom wondered aloud.

'There's been a lot of media coverage lately around the Church and abuse. I had a notion that was mainly directed at priests, though.'

'Mainly,' Tom replied. 'Why do I feel like a can of worms has just been opened?'

'Because it has. You'll be meeting Sister Concepta at Store Street station beside the morgue at 10 a.m. I'll ring Ray.'

Tom hung up as he saw his bus rounding the corner. Another one with the same number followed it.

There was truth in those old sayings.

The inspector walked briskly alongside the granite wall that circled the Phoenix Park. He had lived facing that wall for over twenty years. The park provided an amenity for all the city's residents, but particularly for the people who lived beside it. Now, a murdered woman had been hideously displayed there, a sinister addition to the handful of tales that scarred the park's history.

Tom was old enough to remember vividly the murder of Bridie Gargan. The young nurse had been sunbathing in broad daylight in the park in 1982 when unhinged society playboy Malcolm MacArthur bludgeoned her to death while attempting to steal her car.

Today's finding, though, was in a league of its own.

He slipped off his shoes in the hall, unknotted his tie and wondered why the house was so silent. Through the sitting-room door he caught a glimpse of an undecorated Christmas tree. He'd smelled it before he'd seen it.

Louise and Maria were huddled in conference at the kitchen table in the centre of the large kitchen/dining room. Their body language unnerved him. Maria was visibly upset.

Louise shot up in her seat when she saw him. His daughter just groaned and hid her head in her hands.

'Tom, you're home early.' His wife sounded guilty.

He glanced at the clock. Wondered if it was too late to turn round and go for a pint.

'Not particularly.' He nodded inquiringly at Maria.

Louise sank back into her chair, her beautiful face creased with worry. 'She was planning on telling you tonight, but with everything that's happened—'

'What is it?' Tom was suddenly alert.

When he needed to, he was very good at leaving his work at the door. His family took priority, no matter what he was dealing with in the job.

He pulled out a chair beside his daughter.

Maria's mop of auburn hair hung over her arms as she remained prone, head buried. Sitting there, in that position, she could have been ten years old again.

He placed his hand gently on her elbow.

'You need to tell him,' Louise said.

'I am mummified,' Maria mumbled.

'You're what—?' Tom asked.

'Tom, just listen to her,' Louise interjected.

'I am listening to her. She said she's mummified – whatever the hell that means.'

'Mortified, I said mortified!'

The voice came louder from under the hair.

Well, it was hard to hear anything the girl said when she mumbled it to the table, he thought.

'What's wrong?' he sighed, adding 'now' in his head.

She groaned again.

He took a deep breath and tried to be calm.

'I'm sorry you're upset, Maria. I just want to know what's wrong so I can help. I'm here for you. Are you in trouble? Is it college?'

Maria looked at her mother, and some sort of silent conversation was had between the two of them. It resulted in his daughter sitting up straight and collecting herself. The tears were wiped away and a loud sigh, complete with a sobbed hiccup, was emitted.

Then she hit him with it.

'I know this will come as a shock to you, Dad, but I'm not the first and I won't be the last. I'm pregnant . . .'

CHAPTER 7

At twenty-eight years of age, and to her eternal shame, Laura Brennan still lived with her family.

Up to a number of years ago they'd lived in Kerry. But as recession hit the country hard, jobs became thin on the ground in the Southwest. Although Laura was excelling professionally in the ranks of the guards, her parents had begun to worry about the prospects for the remaining four in their brood.

Laura could understand why. Most of her schoolmates had already emigrated, and she feared her younger brothers and sisters would follow.

Then her father's mother had passed away and left her only son her Dublin home. Her father, also a guard and nearing retirement age, found a desk job in Dublin shortly before Laura was offered her first detective post, based in the capital. The city, while reeling from the economic crisis, still had more to offer by way of jobs for her siblings, even if the move had been a wrench – especially for her mother, who was Kerry born and bred.

Laura wearily unwrapped her scarf and draped it on top of the many coats slung over the end of the banister.

Her brother Daithí, sixteen and one of the twin babies of the family, thundered down the stairs, carrying a bowl of grapes. He stopped on the last step, rocking on his heels.

'So, that old woman in the park – was it gory? What did they do to her? Was she butchered?'

Laura made a disgusted sound. 'Daithí, you really are a little freak.'

He popped a grape in his mouth and grinned as he chewed. 'Yuk! These have seeds in them. Really, why would you buy grapes with seeds in them? Mam is going Lady Gaga.'

Laura's other brother, Donncha, emerged from the sitting room, and she found herself trapped between the two of them.

'Somebody took the time to figure out how to cultivate grapes without seeds,' Donncha said, eyeing Daithí. 'If only they could figure out how to do that with morons. Stop them propagating.'

'I hope you don't mean me!' His younger brother was indignant.

Laura laughed.

Donncha was next in age to Laura. After some turbulent initial years, starting when she was four and their mother brought the little interloper home from the hospital, they had become the best of friends. They had to unite against the three that came after them.

'I'd love to have a bath and relax,' she groaned. 'Can't the children be put to bed?'

Donncha laughed. 'No such luck. Mam kept a plate warm for you, by the way – meat and two veg.'

'What else would it be? If she made a curry, I'd die from shock.' She gave her brother a conspiratorial grin before heading into the kitchen in search of dinner.

Her father was sitting in the corner in his pea-green recliner. When they'd moved, her mother had leapt at the opportunity to remove the offending piece of furniture from the sitting room, claiming lack of space. The colour green had never been her favourite – 'You just can't work with green in a living room' – and she was determined to design the sitting room to her own preferences.

The war over whether the chair could stay or go made the Battle of the Alamo look like a friendly tiff. The concession, ungraciously acceded to by both sides, was for the chair to go in the kitchen – as far away from the black leather suite in the living room as it could get without being dumped in a skip.

The arrangement worked out surprisingly well. Their mother liked to bake and their father liked to sit in the kitchen, where the two of them would chat while he half-read the paper and she sifted, mixed and kneaded.

'Ah, there you are, pet. Sit down there and take the load off. Gracious, the hours you work.'

Her mother bustled around her, ushering her into her chair. They all had their allocated chairs; only someone looking for an argument would sit in the wrong seat.

Laura's mother never considered for a moment that anyone coming into her kitchen might have already eaten.

She was of a generation that considered it a duty to feed anyone who crossed the threshold.

On this occasion, Laura realized she was indeed starving. The gruesome discovery this morning had dampened her appetite and she'd survived the day mainly on caffeine. She welcomed her mother's home cooking: moist roast chicken breast, buttery mashed potatoes and glazed carrots.

Laura liked the idea of cooking for herself. Maybe even adding such exotic ingredients as garlic or ginger to a dish. But on late nights like this, it really was nice to be handed a hot, home-made meal.

She poured gravy liberally over her dinner as her father inspected her over his newspaper, glasses propped on the end of his nose.

'Having some dinner with your gravy, are you?'

Donncha had followed her into the kitchen. 'Jesus, you can take the girl out of Kerry . . .' he said, watching her shovel the food into her mouth.

'That's just awful what happened today.'

Her mother, seamlessly moving from one chore to the next, now stood washing dishes at the sink, which sat conspicuously beside the brand new dishwasher Laura had bought her when they moved.

'Now, Kaye,' her father admonished.

'I'm just saying, Jim. I'm not asking for a detailed report. It's a terrible thing, when an old woman can't even . . .' Kaye paused to think what the woman might have been doing in the park before she was killed. 'Go for a walk . . .' She stopped washing the dishes for a moment and looked at her reflection in the kitchen window. 'It must be nearly time to get a Christmas tree.'

Nobody expected Laura to talk about what she did at work. Jim was a lifelong guard; they knew the score. But sometimes she wished she could come home to a boyfriend, or a best friend, and say 'I've had a rubbish day' and not get a lecture about professionalism.

She felt her phone buzzing in her pocket and cursed herself for forgetting to turn the bloody thing off.

She withdrew it discreetly and saw Bridget's number flashing. In their line of work, there weren't many females and Laura had been grateful to meet another young woman when she joined the NBCI. In her experience, there was a type of professional woman who liked to pull the ladder up behind her once she'd climbed it. Laura thought women were better uniting to support one another, and she was delighted to find Bridget shared that mentality. They became fast friends.

'I have to take this, sorry.' She excused herself from the table.

'I hope that's not work again . . .' Her mother's voice carried out to the hall.

'Bridget?'

'Hiya. You home?'

'Just in time for curfew. What's up?'

'Are you still interested in getting your own place?'

'It's like my thoughts are bugged. Of course I am. But I can't afford to rent on my own, and I'm not moving in with total strangers. Mad and all as my lot are, they are my lot.'

'What if I told you I was looking for a new place?'

'Are you serious?'

Bridget already had a set-up in a two-bedroom apartment with another woman and seemed happy enough.

'No joking. The lease is up here and my flatmate is moving in with her boyfriend.'

'I'd love to share with you!'

'Brilliant. I'll start looking at rental sites. Now, go to bed. And don't be having any naughty dreams.'

'Excuse me?' Laura responded, demurely.

'Don't take that tone with me, missy. I know.'

'Know what?' Laura said, blushing to her toes.

'I know who you've a crush on.'

CHAPTER 8

'. . . I'm pregnant.'

Maria said this in the same tone of voice she used whenever she had rehearsed bad news for him. She may as well have said, 'Now, don't be annoyed, Dad, but I've just failed maths.'

Tom's jaw dropped.

Nothing could be heard in the kitchen bar the ticking of the wall clock. Then both Louise and Maria spoke together.

'Tom, really, stop sitting there gaping like a fish. It's not the end of the world.'

'Dad, say something!'

Tom slowly closed his mouth and stared at his daughter. Was this really happening or had today just been a very long bad dream? His baby, his little girl, barely nineteen and just started in college . . . the girl who never talked about boys . . . pregnant?

'Did you just say you're pregnant? What? Who did this?'

'You don't know him, he's just a lad from her college,' Louise answered.

'Just a lad? What lad? You didn't even tell us you had a boyfriend.'

Tom was fuming.

Maria looked at him scornfully.

'He isn't my boyfriend. And last time I checked you didn't need to be married for ten years before you could have sex.'

There it was. The sex word. He cringed.

As did his daughter, evidenced by her clapping her hand to her mouth.

'I'm sorry, Dad.' Large tears welled in the corners of her eyes.

Tom wondered what he could do or say to stop the deluge from starting. Part of him wanted to comfort her. The other part wanted to go get a firearm and hunt down the man who'd stolen his daughter's virtue. He tensed his fists and felt the anger wash over him. Then he inhaled deeply and breathed out slowly.

He mustn't lose it. Not with her already crying.

'Maria, I'm just –' he had to choose his words carefully –'surprised. I need time to process this.'

He didn't ask her if she'd considered her options. He couldn't even deal with the fact she was pregnant, let alone have that conversation. He presumed that if she was at the point of telling him, she'd already made the decision to keep the baby.

He sat there, feeling like he'd been punched in the stomach. He and Louise loved children and had wanted more after Maria. But first money, then their careers, and finally nature had conspired to leave them a one-child family. So they had invested everything in Maria – her education, after-school activities, Disney holidays and the rest. Louise had taken a career break to be a full-time mother and had only recently returned to college to revisit her old love, English literature.

They'd done their best, and Maria had won a coveted place in Trinity College, studying medicine.

And now she was pregnant.

Maybe they'd overindulged her a little, as one-child parents are prone to do, but she'd turned out well. A little immature, maybe, but smart and beautiful. And kind. That's why her recent moody behaviour had seemed so out of character.

Tom wasn't worried so much about his daughter's studies. His main concern was that her life had just ended. There'd be no more nights out. No travel. No casual dating. No more being a young woman without a care in the world.

He was heartbroken for her. And that was why his anger dissipated so quickly. It wasn't his future that had been torpedoed. Even though he sensed he was being overly pessimistic – after all, many single mothers with less family support than Maria went on to achieve their dreams – he couldn't ignore the fact that this would make life tougher for her.

'She feels defensive,' Louise cut in. 'She was so stressed about telling you.'

Now he felt defensive. He imagined the two of them

having secret talks about how to manage the old man, the stuck-in-the-past prude who wouldn't know how to deal with the situation. That was the way of it when you lived with two women and had no other males in the house to back you up. At times like this, he felt like a hunted animal.

'I don't know why you would be afraid to tell me this,' he protested, puffing his chest out a little. 'I've seen a lot, you know. I'm a modern man.'

Louise and Maria snorted simultaneously, and he glared at them resentfully.

'When we go into the lingerie section of Arnotts, Tom, you act like a furtive pervert,' said Louise. 'You're as modern as my father was.'

He was about to object when he realized the futility. That was fair enough. He did think lingerie departments were the domain of women and should be kept that way. Maybe he was a little old-fashioned.

'How pregnant are you?' he asked.

Maria rolled her eyes. 'Have you never heard the saying "You can't be a little bit pregnant"?'

'I meant how many weeks, months? I do know a bit about pregnancy, Maria. I had some hand in your mother's.'

'Eughh, gross.'

'I think the fact we are having this conversation means we are beyond the point of you thinking your parents are gross, my dear.'

Louise stood up. 'Tom! Be the adult. I'm getting a glass of wine . . .' She paused. 'She's fourteen weeks.'

Tom's eyes flew to his daughter's stomach. Nothing had changed; no wonder he hadn't noticed anything. Yet he felt guilty. She hadn't been herself. Now he knew why. Some detective he was.

'Make it two glasses,' he said to his wife.

Maria sat there, chewing her nails. He looked at her, really looked at her for the first time since arriving home. She had bags under her beautiful brown eyes – her mother's eyes – her skin was pale and her usually glossy hair was lank. She actually looked thinner.

She must have been worrying herself sick.

Tom swallowed the lump in his throat. Standing up, he leaned over and wrapped his arms around his little girl. He said nothing, just held her.

They had a lot of talking to do, but not now.

She rubbed a runny nose on his shirtsleeve.

Time rewound.

Then he leaned down and kissed her head. 'It will be okay.'

She whimpered. 'Thank you, Dad.'

Louise cast him an approving look from the oak kitchen counter as she poured two large glasses of Barolo.

Day Two

Saturday, 11 December

CHAPTER 9

Sister Concepta was far younger than Tom had expected. Although she wore the clothes of an older woman – in fact, remarkably similar attire to their victim – she could only be in her mid thirties at the most. She wore a nun's headdress, but the hair peeping out from beneath it was dark brown. She was quite an attractive woman, with large intelligent blue eyes, a strong nose and full lips.

Right now, she looked anxious and he was pleased to see someone had fetched her a cup of tea.

'I'm sorry I could only come up today, Inspector. I had to wait for the morning bus. My sisters nominated me to make the trip. I'm the youngest in the convent, and they decided that must also mean I have the strongest stomach.'

Tom shook his head, indicating she did not need to apologize. Despite her apparent nervousness, the woman's voice was sensible and strong.

'I hope this is not too unpleasant for you, Sister.'

Tom pulled out a chair nearest to the nun for Laura. He'd brought her along to have a friendly female face in the room.

He and Ray sat down facing Sister Concepta.

'So, you believe the description of the woman we found matches the head of your convent, Reverend Mother Attracta. When did she go missing?'

The inspector tried to make his voice as kindly as possible, as though this was a routine missing person's case and they weren't discussing a woman who lay on a cold slab, just metres away.

'We think she went missing on Wednesday night. We only noticed her absence on Thursday morning. She's always last to retire, so I don't know for sure if she made it to bed that night or not. But I don't think she did.'

'We couldn't find a missing person's report that matched the victim, Sister. Didn't you alert anyone on Thursday?'

'We did. We told Father Seamus.'

Tom sat back, puzzled. 'Father Seamus? And did he inform the police?'

'Well, he must have, mustn't he? Why wouldn't he?'

Why not, indeed?

'Sister Concepta, what's your local police station?'

'Kilcross village.'

Tom nodded at Ray, who stood up and went to check if Kilcross garda station had received a missing person's report that had somehow not been added to the national listings.

'Tell me what happened on Thursday morning, Sister.'

'I got up at 5.30 a.m. and said prayers in my room. At 6 a.m. I went down for breakfast. The dining room hadn't been set. Normally, one of the other sisters does that the night before, but on Wednesday evening Mother had said she would set out the breakfast things before she went to bed.

'There had been a row. Sister Mary had smashed a plate and . . .' The nun's face reddened and she clasped and re-clasped her hands nervously. 'I apologize, you don't need to know all that.'

'Everything will be relevant if we are talking about the same woman, I can assure you. A minor tiff for one person can be the end of the world to another; someone can storm off in a fit of pique . . .' Tom held his hands out and shrugged.

'Of course. Sorry, I'm not telling you how to do your job. It's just those kind of . . . interactions . . . they're not out of the ordinary in an environment such as ours.'

Tom raised a quizzical eyebrow.

'A group of women living together, day in, day out. By choice, but not related.'

'You're not a closed order, are you?' Laura asked. She had heard of religious orders whose members didn't interact with the outside world.

'Gracious, no. We work closely with the local community. We do take solemn vows but we aren't strictly cloistered.'

Tom cleared his throat. If Reverend Mother Attracta wasn't their victim, they were wasting time. That morning's team meeting had proved fruitless, so a lot of hope was resting on a positive ID here.

Sister Concepta took the hint.

'Anyway, I thought I'd check just to see if she was ill or something before starting breakfast. I went to her room first. The bed was made but the room just didn't seem slept in, you know what I mean? Then I found it.'

The nun shuddered at an unpleasant memory.

Tom and Laura leaned forward simultaneously. 'Found what?' they said in unison.

'I found blood in the hall and the vase of lilies was smashed.'

'Blood? What are we talking about – a splash, a drop, lots?' Tom was suddenly very alert.

'Sort of a spray. Across the wall. The vase from the hall table was smashed on the floor and there was water splashed everywhere. If I'd gone into the hall first I'd have seen the mess, but there's another door leading to the kitchen and dining room from our quarters—'

'Let's backtrack for a moment,' Tom interrupted. 'You realized Mother Attracta was missing, you found a disturbance, including blood in the hall, and your first reaction was to tell this Father Seamus? Not the police?'

Sister Concepta's cheeks flushed. 'I know you might find our ways strange, Inspector. The other sisters were with me by then. We were very worried, but Father Seamus is our first point of call for most situations. From plumbing to finances to ... well ... a break-in.'

'Or kidnap and murder?' Tom shook his head.

'We didn't know what had happened to her. It made

sense to contact him. That was the consensus, anyway,' the nun added, defensively.

'Consensus? Did anybody think the police should be contacted?'

Sister Concepta met his eye. 'Maybe some of the younger sisters.'

He didn't need to ask; she meant herself.

The door opened and Ray came back in, shaking his head.

'Your local garda station has no record of a missing person.'

The nun looked dismayed. 'I don't understand.'

'Don't worry, Sister,' Tom said. 'I think it's time to confirm whether or not Mother Attracta is indeed our victim.'

CHAPTER 10

'I'm very sorry for your loss,' the inspector said, when they'd returned to the interview room.

The city morgue stood beside the garda station and it had taken barely a half-hour for them to bring the nun there, confirm the identity and return.

Sister Concepta shook her head vigorously. 'Oh, please, it's not my loss. I mean –' She took a deep breath. 'It's a terrible shock, but we weren't that close. I . . .' she trailed off, struggling to find the appropriate words.

'Still, it's upsetting to see someone you knew like that. It's an unnatural way to die.'

The nun clung on to her second cup of tea tightly, like a lifebelt.

'Sister, before we proceed, can you tell me, do you have contact details for the Reverend Mother's family? They need to be informed. Maybe you have already let them know that she is missing?'

'No,' the nun shook her head. 'She has no family, Inspector. Well, none that we know of. Maybe there are cousins or other relatives, but she had no siblings, you see. And her parents are long dead. We are her family, I suppose.'

'I see.'

'I could only see her face,' the nun said. 'What happened to her? Was she . . . was she strangled?'

'She was stabbed, Sister. I don't want to upset you with all the details.'

'I just don't understand how this could have happened. Who would have . . .? Why?'

The nun looked momentarily staggered. But then she took a deep breath, straightened up in her seat and leaned forward, resolutely.

'How can I help?'

'Just tell us as much as you can,' Tom said. 'Did anything out of the ordinary happen before Mother Attracta went missing? Was there anyone suspicious hanging around the convent or your village? What were her relationships like with the other sisters?'

Tom could see that the nun was concentrating hard on his questions. But when he asked the last one, a little twitch in her cheek told him what he wanted to know.

'For example, you mentioned a row with a Sister Mary. Did the Reverend Mother often argue with others?'

'I was always taught not to speak ill of the dead . . .'

There was a pause before the inspector continued the conversation.

'What is the name of your order, Sister?'

She looked startled at the change in questioning.

'The Sisters of Pity.'

The name jogged something in his memory. Like the vast majority of Irish people, Tom's entire family had been educated in religious schools. Maybe one of his sisters had attended a school run by this order.

Sister Concepta dropped her eyes to the floor. 'Mother is ... sorry ... she was ... a difficult woman.'

A sigh. Sister Concepta wanted to get this off her chest.

'You must understand, she was of her age. She grew up and lived in a society where religious orders were consulted, obeyed – even feared, in fact. They were powerful. When I joined the Church, it was a different time. I felt it was my vocation to carry out God's mission on earth. To serve people, not be served.'

Tom smiled politely. He didn't understand this strange compulsion of hers, but he respected it.

'I suppose a psychologist might look at me and say it was less a vocation and more me seeking to belong somewhere. My parents passed away when I was young and I'm an only child. The Church provided me with a family and a purpose.

'When Reverend Mother became a sister ... I don't know ... perhaps she was just like me. She's been in the convent since 1963. But sometimes, if you are left in charge of people and traditions for a long time, well ... what's that saying? "Power corrupts, but absolute power corrupts absolutely." Mother Attracta could be rude. And thoughtless. And vicious.'

Her last words, spoken quietly and calmly, were nonetheless loaded with hostility. Tom struggled to hide how taken aback he was.

Ray didn't win his struggle. 'You really disliked her,' he said.

'Most of the older sisters are used to her, but I could never –' Tears filled the nun's eyes. 'I'm sorry. It's wrong of me to say such things. Now . . .'

Tom inclined his head and spoke softly. 'It's crucially important we establish what Mother Attracta was like and how she lived her life, Sister. I can't have people sugar-coating her personality for me. If she had enemies, I need to know. And I appreciate your frankness.'

He could see the nun found solace in his words. She screwed up her eyes to think about his previous question.

'We're getting the convent ready for Christmas,' Sister Concepta offered. 'We do a lot of work with local schools and hospitals at this time of year. There hasn't been anything out of the ordinary that I can think of, though. Nobody hanging around. No strangers. No big rows.'

The pause before the last sentence was almost indiscernible, but there it was.

Something happened recently, but she wasn't saying what, Tom thought. Was life really that sedentary and unremarkable in the convent?

'I need to give it proper consideration, Inspector. I'm not sure I'm thinking straight at the moment.'

'All right, Sister. I think that's enough for now. You've

had a shock. Go back to the convent and give your memory of the last few weeks and months a proper going over. Try to remember everything, even things that may appear trivial or insignificant to you. I can't stress that enough. It's crucial that you and the other members of the convent realize quickly that nothing will be left secret in this murder inquiry. Nothing.'

His eyes bored into hers. She broke the connection first.

'We will have to come down to the convent, most likely before the day's end,' Tom said. 'Just one more thing. Were any of the other sisters missing on Wednesday or Thursday?'

The nun's eyes widened.

'I honestly couldn't say,' she replied. 'There are twenty-one of us . . . I mean, there were. We don't do everything together, and it's a large building. I don't recall seeing everyone. But I'd only notice if someone was missing when we are gathered for meals. Everyone was there for dinner on Wednesday night, but we didn't sit down formally on Thursday after our discovery. I'd have to think about that, too.'

Tom nodded. 'Please do,' he said.

Ray let out a low whistle when she'd left.

'For someone who's been taught not to speak ill of the dead . . .'

Tom nodded. 'It was a harsh view of our victim, but only one opinion. Even if she was . . . convincing.'

'Twenty nuns,' Ray said. 'And the priest. I can't see it being a woman, though. And surely a nun wouldn't be capable of such savagery?'

'Never underestimate a human being's capacity for depravity, Ray, no matter what their sex, profession or vocation. But yes, I'd be more than a little shocked if it turns out one of the convent's residents did this. What I can't figure out is why somebody would take her from Limerick and bring her to Dublin.'

'Unless the murderer wanted to get our attention in particular? Make a national statement?'

'It was still going to make a national statement and get our attention if it had happened in Limerick. The NBCI would have been pulled in no matter where in the country this had happened.'

'I don't think our colleagues down in Limerick have a lot of time for this Father Seamus character,' Ray said. 'They're en route to the convent now.'

'Who doesn't report someone missing in those circumstances?' Tom asked.

'Someone with something to hide?' Ray suggested.

The inspector stared down at his notepad. There was something gnawing at his memory.

'Sisters of Pity. It rings a bell. Remind me to look it up later.'

CHAPTER 11

Dublin's city centre was starting to fill up with Christmas shoppers moving in the direction of the capital's major thoroughfare, O'Connell Street. At the main bus terminal, across the road from the garda station, people were alighting from coaches arriving from towns and villages throughout Ireland. The year, like the one before, had been slow for the city's traders. The recession had long since decimated profits and many businesses, struggling for survival, were eagerly anticipating the seasonal boost in consumption.

Tom looked beyond the bus station to the beautiful facade of Gandon's famous Custom House. Behind its painted railings, away from the hustle and bustle of the city-centre traffic and the adjacent Financial Services Centre, the stately old building stood solidly, regal and calm. He admired its ornate roof for a moment before pulling his phone from his pocket.

It rang twice before his wife answered.

'Tom?'

'Hi. How are things?'

'Fine.' Louise was surprised to hear from him. 'Are you okay? Aren't you busy?'

'Of course. We just got our ID.'

Louise said nothing. She knew he wasn't ringing to talk about the case.

'Where's Maria?' He stifled a yawn as he asked the question.

Tom had slept terribly, his thoughts flitting from the new case to their daughter's bombshell. He'd spent most of the night staring at the back of Louise's head, wondering how she'd managed to keep it secret for so many weeks. That was new for him. He kept stuff from Louise all the time, because he had to. In his memory, it had never gone the other way. That he knew of.

'Where do you think?' his wife replied. 'Bed. No doubt she'll use pregnancy as a convenient excuse for not seeing this side of 12 p.m. most days.'

'No doubt.'

'Please don't worry about her, love. I'm here. You have so much on your plate.'

'How can I not worry? She's only nineteen.'

'Only nineteen? Tom, believe me, she's far from the youngest girl to face this. She's not even a girl. She's a woman.'

Tom bristled. He'd been deliberately ignoring the extra sets of sanitary towels in the airing cupboard for years. He still struggled to get his head around this tall creature who'd taken over his baby's pink bedroom and replaced the Barbies and teddy bears with black velvet cushions and middle-eastern throws.

He looked up and saw that Laura, who'd walked the nun to her bus, was coming back across the street.

'How are you handling this so calmly?'

Louise hesitated before replying. 'One of us has to.'

Considering what had run through his head when he'd first been told, Tom thought he was coping exceptionally well.

He took a deep breath. Louise was always wiser than him. This must have come as a huge shock to her, too, but she was already ten steps ahead, trying to be steady so he could be aggrieved. And he didn't even have the time to be frustrated right now. There was no head space to indulge in selfish and, quite possibly, irrational questions, such as: Why has she done this to us? How could she have been so stupid? And, the worst, if she can't even get through her first year in college, how will she rear a child? He felt guilty for even having the capacity for such thoughts.

'I'd better go.'

'Okay,' Louise replied. 'Will we see you later? I've started decorating the tree.'

'Try to remember, Santa has actual children to visit. Our house doesn't have to be the landing strip for his sleigh every year.'

'Bah, humbug!'

He rang off and greeted Laura.

'There's a bus in thirty minutes,' Laura told him. 'I left

her in the café. She's a little shocked but she'll be home in no time.'

'What's your take on her?'

'She seemed pretty genuine.'

All the members of the team were good judges of character. They had it instinctively, but their training enhanced it, as well as teaching them to be aware of their limitations.

His thoughts were interrupted by the sound of a car engine. Ray, who'd gone to get the car, pulled in beside his colleagues and wound down the driver's window.

'Blanchardstown?' he asked.

'Yes. I'll let you drive. Try not to kill us.'

'You'll let me drive? It's my car. By the way, when are you rejoining the world of motoring?'

'You'd have to ask my mechanic.'

'Are you still using the octogenarian under the bridge?' Ray laughed.

'Age isn't always an impediment, you know.'

'I bet you tell yourself that all the time.'

Laura banged on the car roof. 'Hey, Laurel and Hardy, are we getting a move on?'

Ray pointed to the passenger side and Tom, smiling, walked round to it while Laura slipped into the back seat. His phone buzzed in his pocket. Sean McGuinness's name flashed on the screen as he pulled the passenger door shut.

'Chief.'

'Got an ID, Tom?'

'Yes. She was the Reverend Mother of a convent in Limerick.'

Straight to the point.

'Jesus wept.'

'He's weeping now, for sure. So, a team will need to head down. I imagine you want me in charge.'

Since the establishment of the National Bureau of Criminal Investigation in the late nineties, specialized teams were routinely deployed to assist local squads with serious offences ranging from murder to organized crime.

'Absolutely,' McGuinness replied. 'There's no way the superintendent for the Midlands division will want this on his plate. They're up to their eyeballs already. Your body, Tom, your case. I'll make sure the local sergeant is ready for your team. Oh, and if you have to be down there overnight, see if they can put you up in the convent – save on expenses.'

Tom rolled his eyes but knew enough not to make a sarcastic comment. McGuinness was serious.

He hung up and looked at Ray. 'All your dreams are about to come true. I'm taking you on a trip where you'll be surrounded by women and perhaps even get to sleep in their midst.'

'Ah, for crying out loud, they want us to stay in the bloody convent, don't they?'

In the back of the car, Laura snorted. Tom turned and gave her a wink.

'I might have to leave you there to monitor events,

interview witnesses, you know,' he said to Ray. 'One of them might turn your head, and you'll forget you ever met any pretty girls in Dublin.'

Ray's cheeks flushed and he pressed down on the accelerator.

'We might be heading to a religious house, boss, but it'll be a while before you turn me into a monk.'

'Boom, boom,' Laura laughed.

'The media are in a tailspin looking for the name of the victim. Somebody let them know you got an ID at the morgue. And no, we don't know who,' Ian hastily added, in response to the look of fury on Tom's face.

Ray slammed Tom's office door, shutting the three of them in. 'Oh, this is going to be fun,' he said. 'Let me predict the headline: "Nun left hole-y after being nailed to tree".'

Tom and Ian stared at Ray.

'Don't you get it? A "holy" nun?'

Ray shrugged, while Tom placed his forehead in his hand.

'Holy nun,' Ian tutted. 'It's a superfluous use of words anyway. Can you be an unholy nun?'

'I guess if you're at a fancy-dress party. Then you can be a sexy nun.'

'Lads!' Tom banged his desk.

Ray and Ian jumped. 'Sorry,' they chimed.

'Right, we can't keep her identity a secret, but I'll ask Sean McGuinness to see if we can hold it back a little longer,' Tom said. 'That will give us a chance to get down to Limerick and get the lie of the land before the media hordes descend. Ian, will you fetch Laura and Michael?'

He shook off his coat, slung it on the back of his leather swivel chair and dialled Louise. Ray, who had no one to inform of his imminent trip, grabbed a newspaper from a table just inside the door of the office and settled down.

Louise answered eventually, sounding out of breath.

'Is everything all right?' asked Tom, anxiously.

'You'd think we were never apart, Tom. All is well. Maria hasn't gone into labour yet. Would you just relax?'

'Louise, I've to take a trip to Limerick. If I swing by the house, can you throw a couple of things in a bag for me?'

'Honestly, the schemes you come up with to get out of helping me prepare our home for Christmas.'

'So cynical. If it makes you feel any better, McGuinness has turned down my all-expenses request to book into a hotel with a casino attached. They're hoping I'll stay in a nunnery.'

There was a pause on the line. Louise knew there was no reason for him to stay in a convent unless the victim had originated there.

'No problem,' she said, her voice serious.

He was about to end the call when he thought of something.

'Louise?'

'Yes?'

'Don't let Maria pick up anything heavy.'

'And so it begins,' she sighed.

'Indulge me. She's my only child.' Tom turned to Ray. 'If you can just tear yourself away from the Premier League results . . .'

'When a man can't even read the sports page on a Saturday!'

His deputy threw his eyes to heaven and was just returning the newspaper to the table when the door opened and Laura crashed into him.

'We have to stop meeting like this. Though I have to say, you are looking very well today,' he said, and smiled.

Laura went a bright shade of red and pushed past him.

Ray looked at the back of her head, puzzled. He thought she enjoyed the banter. Then he cursed himself. Some female detectives hated having attention drawn to how they looked. They were working there because of their talent and skills, not their faces. He made a mental note to remember that Laura took issue with compliments – even if he had meant to be funny, not sexist.

As they were waiting for Michael, Tom decided to also include Willie Callaghan, his garda driver, on the trip. Willie had a good head, and Tom appreciated the older man's wisdom.

The Technical Bureau would have to send down a senior team; the local division had already been ordered to secure the presumed crime scene in the convent hall for the Dublin forensics team.

Michael joined them a few minutes later. 'We just need a dog now and we could be the Famous Five,' he joked.

'Which one of us is George?' Tom asked.

He left Michael to think of a comeback.

'I don't know how long we'll be down in Limerick,' he continued. 'Head home and grab what you need for a couple of nights. Ray, will you give Sister Concepta a ring and see if she's back in the convent? Maybe hint at a few empty rooms? I'm going to ask Willie to drive me down. I'm guessing two cars?'

The others nodded.

'Michael, you can come with us. Ray, you take Laura.'

Ray nodded. He'd use the opportunity of the car journey to impress on the younger detective that he wasn't a chauvinist.

Laura tried to keep her face composed. She wasn't sure how Bridget had figured it out, but she did have a thing for Ray – and it was growing by the day.

He turned to her now. 'Where do you live?'

'Clontarf.'

'I might need a street name.'

You're an idiot, her inner voice screamed.

'Sorry. St Paul's Avenue. Number thirty-four,' she said abruptly.

'I'll pick you up in a couple of hours.' Ray flashed his most winning smile, hoping he could charm her into remembering he was a nice guy.

That's a date, she replied, in her head.

CHAPTER 12

Tom met Willie at reception, which someone had tried to decorate gaily with a few tawdry strands of tinsel and fairy lights. Willie, in his late fifties, was one of the most relaxed people Tom had ever met. In fact, he gave the impression that if he was any more laid-back, he'd be asleep. His appearance didn't match his personality. Willie wore his uniform smartly, kept his thinning hair tightly cut, his moustache immaculately trimmed and always smelled of Old Spice.

'So I'm getting a junket to Limerick?' he said in his gravelly voice, as Tom approached.

The inspector nodded. 'If that's okay, Willie.'

'More than okay. The daughters are coming home from the States next week for Christmas, and the missus has the house cleaned to within an inch of its life. She wants to keep it that way until they arrive. I'm not allowed to walk on the carpet in the living room. She expects me to levitate to the couch.'

Willie's daughters had both made the all too familiar trip from college to a new country, along with thousands of other young Irish people forced to emigrate for work.

Christmas had become a bittersweet time for so many parents, not all of whom were lucky enough to receive a seasonal visit.

'I can't promise to keep you there for a week, but we'll see what we can do,' Tom said. 'Right, I need to call in at the house, but I want to check on my car first. I got a vague indication it might be ready today. You can drop me off, head to yours, then come back. And we'll collect Michael Geoghegan.'

'Is he coming?'

'Yes.'

'Right, so.' Willie stroked his moustache and said no more. 'Where's your mechanic? You're not still using that pensioner under the bridge?'

'Why is everyone so ageist these days?'

'Well, there might be a reason why you spend more time in other people's cars than your own.'

The two men left the warmth of the station and crossed the car park to Willie's gleaming vehicle. Tom opened the passenger door just as he felt icy drops on the back of his neck.

'Is that snow?' Willie asked, with all the giddiness of a schoolchild.

'It is,' Tom replied. 'They say it's going to be the coldest December on record. We could have snow right up to Christmas. If you're good, we'll stop on the way down and let you build a snowman.'

'Yippee,' the other man responded, dryly.

*

Ten minutes later they were outside the small garage where Tom's car remained hostage to the knowledge of a man infinitely superior to the inspector on all things motor-related. It was Tom's job to nod and agree with the garage's owner, Pat Donnelly. He had been servicing cars in Blanchardstown since the world was black and white, as Louise liked to say.

Pat was standing at the door of the garage in dirty overalls, looking at the sky, as they pulled up. Tiny white snowflakes were melting on the top of his balding head.

'He's looking for divine inspiration to fix your car,' Willie said.

'Pat!' Tom called, as he got out of the car.

'There you are.' The old man looked down from the heavens to his visitor, as if Tom had always been there but he'd only just noticed him.

'Any joy with the car?'

Pat shrugged. 'We'll get there. Found the problem. Common with Alfa Romeos.'

Tom braced himself.

'You wouldn't consider getting yourself a nice little German model? Or a Jap car? Can't stand those Italian ones. Must be the sun. Makes the engineers' brains funny, so they forget to put pieces under the bonnet.'

Tom had had this one-sided exchange with Pat many times. He nodded dutifully and assured the older man that he would indeed replace this car with a sensible, functioning model. Pat never tired of pointing out to him that his precious Alfa marque was owned by FIAT – which stood for, in his opinion, 'Fix It Again Tomorrow'.

'Well, I'm off to the country for a few days, Pat, so I won't need it today,' Tom said, loudly.

'Isn't it well for some. A holiday, is it? That's nice for you. And us old folks can't even go about our business without being murdered. It wouldn't have been fixed today, anyway. Snow coming.'

'Well, luckily I won't need it today,' Tom repeated, pretending he had some control over the timeline. He wasn't sure what the onset of snow meant for the prospect of his car being repaired. 'Okay, Pat, I'll see you during the week?'

'Enjoy your break.'

'Mad as a proverbial brush,' Willie pronounced, as he revved the engine.

Twenty minutes later they were at Tom's house, just as he got through to Emmet McDonagh on the phone.

'You've nothing more from the crime scene for me?' he asked.

'No,' Emmet replied. 'If you miss me that much, though, if you find the murder site I might pay you a visit.'

'What do you mean, if I find the murder site? Aren't you coming down to Limerick?' Tom knew he was chancing his arm.

'Sorry, Tom, that's just a kidnap site, by the sound of things. It's too busy in Dublin for me to wander off. I'll send you a senior team, but there's no "me" in team.'

Tom groaned. 'Yes, there is actually. There's no "I" in team. Right. Who's your best?'

'You met them – Ellie and Mark. I don't know about you having both, though . . .'

'Send both,' Tom said, hanging up.

'The house looks well,' Willie said.

Tom followed his eyeline. The Christmas tree stood behind the living room's French windows, lights twinkling, soft falling snow completing the Yuletide look. Just for a moment he allowed himself to daydream that he was going home to start the annual holiday. It was his favourite time of year – the rich succulent foods, the welcome visits from family and friends bearing brightly wrapped presents, the women getting tipsy on champagne while he puffed on one of the Cohibas his brother always gave him and enjoyed a tall glass of golden ale.

Paradise.

Louise opened the door as Tom's cold hands fumbled with his keys.

'Do you think it will stick?' was the first thing she said to him, referring to the snow still falling behind him.

'And hello to you,' he replied, kissing her on the forehead.

She had flour in her sideswept fringe, its whiteness in stark contrast to her dark hair, which she had tied back in a loose ponytail. She was wearing an apron over her jeans and red sweater. Good smells wafted from the kitchen.

She leaned around him to look into the garden.

'Honestly,' Tom said, shaking his coat off. 'You would

think this was sub-Saharan Africa the way Irish people react to snow. You know there'll be homeless people freezing to death if it comes down proper.'

'Tom!' She clipped him on the ear.

He pulled her to him. 'Sorry,' he murmured to the top of her head. 'I've only a half-hour. That's five minutes for tea and twenty-five minutes for being with my wife.'

He started walking her, crab-like, towards the stairs.

She laughed and pulled away. 'Twenty-five minutes? Are we talking an unprecedented twenty-three minutes of foreplay? Isn't it normally twenty-five minutes for the tea?'

'You keep up that cheek and I'll give you a caution.'

'You're a bloody caution,' she laughed. 'Your daughter's in the kitchen.'

He groaned. 'I could be away for days.'

'Yes, but you'll be in a convent so it will be the last thing on your mind.'

'Or the first, if what you read about these religious places is anything to go by.'

She tutted as she walked towards the kitchen. 'I was baking but I abandoned it to make you some sandwiches for the trip. I packed your clothes as well. Aren't you going to tell me what a good wife I am? I only leave one household chore to take care of another.'

'I can't think why you're bothering with a PhD in English, when you could be here, barefoot, fulfilling my every need,' he said.

She raised her eyebrows.

Maria was at the kitchen counter, attacking dough,

kneading it like it was some kind of wild animal she had to tame. She still looked peaky but less stressed. He stared at her, trying to see if anything else had changed in her appearance, anything to give away what was happening to her body.

'Dad . . . Mam wouldn't let me put the star on the tree until you came home.'

Tom looked incredulously at Louise.

'She shouldn't be stretching.'

Louise and Maria eye-rolled in unison.

'Don't worry, Dad, I'm starting my confinement any day now. Six months in a darkened room lying down so I don't strain myself. Come in here and help me with this star. I was thinking about running up the wall before somersaulting back to the ground and placing it mid-tumble. But perhaps you could just hold me steady on a chair.'

Tom followed her into the living room, Louise in his wake. This whole tradition was getting a bit absurd, particularly in light of the fact that his 'little' girl was now carrying her own baby.

He pulled out the footstool for her. Louise had been conservative this year; the conifer was lower than the ceiling, which still bore the scratch marks from the previous treetop.

Holding both Maria and the stool, Tom watched as his daughter placed the gold star on the top branch – the only one as yet unadorned.

'Just think –' Maria looked down at him innocently– 'this time next year, you'll be a grandad.'

CHAPTER 13

Ray pulled up outside Laura's house and hit the horn to announce his presence. The road she lived on was quiet; he nearly jumped himself at the sharp beep.

He'd just got off the phone with Sister Concepta, who'd arrived back safely at the convent.

He had been about to subtly hint at the possibility of accommodation for the detectives that evening, when she'd said, 'You'll stay with us of course? We've plenty of room.'

He'd feigned surprise at her offer before accepting with profuse thanks.

'The accommodation will be basic,' she'd said, 'but warm and comfortable. And you'll dine with the sisters.'

He looked at the clock on the dashboard: 2.30 p.m. Early, but he wanted to get the driving done in daylight.

He beeped again.

This time the door opened and an older woman looked out. Pulling her grey cardigan tight, she strode purposefully down the garden path towards the car.

Ray cursed. He must have the wrong house. She'd said thirty-four, he was sure of it. Was it the wrong street?

He hesitated for a moment before rolling down the window, in no humour to deal with a cranky housewife.

'Do you not know how to use a doorbell, young man?' the woman asked, in the thickest Kerry accent he'd ever heard. Thicker even than Sean McGuinness's.

'Er . . . sorry . . . I'm not sure I've the right house. I'm looking for Laura Brennan.'

'You can find the house but not the front door, is that it?'

Behind her, Ray could see Laura framed in the doorway.

'Mam!' she yelled out.

Her flushed face was trumped only by Ray's deeper shade of purple at being chastised by this Kerry matron.

Laura was coming down the path now, her curly copper hair a magnet for the falling snow, which seemed to be avoiding her mother.

Quite sensibly, in Ray's opinion.

He stepped out of the car, trying to appear cool and professional. 'I'm terribly sorry, Mrs Brennan. I didn't realize Laura lived with her parents. Sorry to disturb you.'

'Oh, my God,' Laura mumbled, mortified.

Her mother sniffed. 'Well, you've found your manners now. Lock the car and come in out of the cold. You might as well have a bite, too. Working on a Saturday and driving to Limerick, of all places.'

'Mam, we don't have time—'

'Hush now, that woman is not going to get any more dead while you finish your lunch.'

Mrs Brennan ushered the two of them up the path.

Laura stared straight ahead, unable to make eye contact with Ray, as he was frogmarched in the door.

A fire blazed in the old-style hearth against the back wall of the kitchen. An older man – Laura's dad, Ray imagined – sat in a comfortable-looking recliner beside it. He nodded to the visitor.

Ray sat across from Laura, who leaned forward and whispered, 'I am so sorry about this. She makes everyone eat. It's her thing.'

He whispered back. 'I'm just glad she didn't make me sit on the naughty step.'

The younger detective laughed, revealing two deep dimples in her cheeks.

Her mother conjured another plate on to the table, and Ray felt his stomach do a little dance. He hadn't realized he was so hungry. He'd grabbed some crackers in his apartment when he was packing. A home-cooked meal was a rare treat.

His delight must have shown because Mrs Brennan placed her hand on his shoulder and said, 'You can call me Faye.'

She pulled out a chair and motioned to Ray to start eating. Laura pushed her remaining food around with a fork until her mother chided her to eat.

'So, where's this place you're going to, eh?' she asked.

'Faye!' Laura's dad cautioned.

Ray realized the newspaper was a bit of a ruse.

'Take a puff of your pipe, Jim, and relax,' Faye answered him. 'Don't mind him,' she said to Ray. 'A permanent guard. He won't let Laura say boo in case they take her in under the Official Secrets Act.'

Ray looked at the man in the corner in a new light.

'It will be public knowledge soon enough. So, if you can keep it in confidence until then . . .' he said.

Jim lowered his paper, curiosity getting the better of him.

Faye nodded. 'We know how to do confidential.'

'We're headed to a convent down there. The victim was a nun.'

The colour drained from Laura's mother's face.

Ray was about to ask if she was okay when Jim interjected.

'Was she killed because she was a nun?' he asked.

'We don't know,' Ray replied. There was no need for spin here. 'We only got the ID this morning.'

Jim sat back in his chair and puffed furiously on his pipe.

Faye rose from her chair and walked to the sink, where she stared fixedly out the window. He'd only met her, but Ray sensed this reaction was uncharacteristically muted for her.

'What's the name of the convent?' she asked, as she twisted a dishcloth in her hands.

'Sisters of Pity,' Laura answered.

The woman visibly flinched.

Ray lowered his fork.

'Mam?' Concern and puzzlement filled Laura's face.

Her father stood up and walked to his wife, placing a comforting arm around her shoulders.

'What is it?' Laura asked.

Ray was alarmed to see Faye shaking as she turned to face them.

'Do you know the convent, Mrs Brennan?' he asked, gently.

After a pause, she replied.

'I know it. Oh, yes, I know it. And may God forgive me, but if that woman was a nun there, she deserved to die screaming.'

CHAPTER 14

Tom rang Michael's doorbell and waited, shivering.

It was Anne, the detective's wife, who opened the door. Tom was startled by her appearance. The Anne he knew was vivacious and lively. She kept her highlighted blonde hair cut in a neat bob and dressed in the latest fashions, flattering her slim figure.

The woman standing before him now had put on weight. Her hair was shoulder length and dull, her face bereft of colour. She wore a baggy grey tracksuit and looked utterly miserable.

'Tom,' she said, a strained smile on her lips. 'It's lovely to see you. He'll only be a moment. Will you come in?'

'Good to see you, too. I won't come in, pet. Willie's waiting.'

Tom was suddenly all too conscious that he hadn't seen the woman since she'd lost her baby. Louise had organized a card and flowers, of course, but they had wanted to give the young couple space to grieve. He had to acknowledge it, but how did you broach a subject that was months old? So he stood there, mute, trying desperately to think of something to say.

Anne was clearly more adept at dealing with the social ramifications of the loss.

'I meant to ring Louise and yourself to say thank you for the gift.'

'Not at all,' he responded. 'I'm . . . well, to be honest, I don't know what to say. I'm so very sorry.'

She nodded, and he could see from her expression that the miscarriage was far from dealt with.

'No one knows what to say.' She looked furtively over her shoulder and then said quietly, 'It wasn't the first time.'

He almost didn't catch it.

'Oh.'

Tom racked his brains for the right words and found himself wanting. Sensing that he could do no better than platitudes, he opted instead to place a comforting hand on her arm.

It was the right move. Anne didn't flinch or pull away.

'Thank you,' she said, eyes glistening. 'The worst thing is, it makes it scary to try again – for Michael, anyway. I can't give up hope. And now I think—'

She stopped short as Michael barrelled down the stairs.

'Sorry about the delay, sir,' he began, then noticed the look of concern on Tom's face, before turning to his wife. He looked back at his boss and his features hardened. 'I'll be off, then,' he said, coolly planting a peck on Anne's cheek.

He started down the path and all Tom could do was follow, giving Anne an embarrassed wave goodbye. She cut a lonely figure in the doorway but retreated inside before they were even at the gate.

At the car, Tom placed his hand on the door before Michael could get in.

'Michael,' he said.

The younger detective shook his head. 'She told you, didn't she?'

'It's nothing to be ashamed of.'

Angry red blotches broke out on Michael's cheeks.

'It's personal. She had no right . . .'

Tom hesitated. He needed to frame what he was about to say very carefully.

'Michael . . . for the most part, this is none of my business. But you've both been through something traumatic . . . and if it's something you're struggling to deal with . . .'

He held up his hands as Michael glared at him.

'You're an excellent detective,' he continued. 'I'm just asking if you need to be closer to home. You don't need to come on this trip. Others can take your place.'

He watched as the younger man went through a range of silent emotions – anger at having his private life exposed, followed by embarrassment, pain. Then he seemed to deflate.

Finally, he spoke.

'I need to go, sir. You don't understand. We've . . . we've lived with this for years. But this time is the worst. I've tried to be there for her. I've—'

His voice choked, and he stopped. Took a deep breath. Then the words spilled out of him in a great release.

'I've done as much as I can. The last few weeks she's been so moody. She's putting on weight, crying all the time. Sometimes she won't get out of the bed. When she does, she slopes around and says she's tired. You tell me it's nothing to be ashamed of, but that's how I feel. I don't know what I can do to help her. I don't know how to give her a baby that will stay.

'And she feels ashamed because she thinks she's failed. Our whole house is filled with shame.' He sucked in air. 'I love her but she needs help that I can't give. And, to be honest, I need a break. I really do. Nobody ever understands it from the man's perspective. It's my loss, too.'

Michael exhaled, and Tom could see he was relieved to have finally got the load off his chest.

They both looked up at the house, a little guiltily, as though Anne might have caught them talking about her.

'Look,' Tom said, 'I can't say I understand because I haven't been through what you have. But I know a man who needs a break when I see one. I had to ask, okay?'

Michael nodded. He brushed snowflakes from his spiky brown hair and shivered. He hadn't taken the time to put his jacket on.

Tom couldn't help but wonder about the vagaries of a universe that let his daughter conceive a so-far healthy pregnancy accidentally, when the planned pregnancies of this man's young family had ended so tragically.

'Let's go,' he said. 'I think the blood has stopped circulating in my feet.'

His phone rang as he got into the car.

'We're leaving now, Ray.'

'Sir, we just found out something important.'

'Go on.'

'The Sisters of Pity – remember the name rang a bell for you? Their convent in Kilcross is a former Magdalene Laundry. A notorious one.'

Tom sat in stunned silence.

'That's it,' he said. 'I read something about it a few months ago. I can't believe I didn't make the connection.'

'Sister Concepta wasn't in a hurry to point it out, was she? Anyway, Mrs Brennan almost had a heart attack when I mentioned the name of the order and Kilcross.'

Michael and Willie looked at Tom questioningly. He placed his hand over the mouthpiece.

'The nun was from a Magdalene Laundry,' he said.

The information didn't seem to make anything clearer for Michael, but Willie raised his eyebrows knowingly.

'Why was Mrs Brennan so upset? She wasn't in the laundry, was she?' Tom asked, indicating to Willie to start driving. 'Her sister was? We'd better get on the road, but let's say we meet and get a cup of tea? I bet it's quite a story.'

As the car pulled out, Willie mentioned a small service station about halfway down and suggested stopping for petrol there.

'What's the relevance of Kilcross being a laundry?' Michael asked. 'All the convents had them, didn't they?'

Willie shook his head. 'No, lad. There were ten or so big ones that operated for profit. Haven't you heard of the campaign groups out to get justice for the former inmates?'

Michael looked confused. 'Inmates? I thought the women just worked there? I haven't been paying much attention to it.'

'Well, you're about to get an education,' Tom said, gravely.

He had a knot in his stomach.

The case had taken a sinister turn.

CHAPTER 15

Over an hour later, Willie's car pulled off the motorway at their arranged meeting place. The 'services' were actually an old-fashioned two-pump petrol station with a small shop and coffee area attached. The shop seemed to be the bottom floor of a residence, judging by the lace curtains and flower boxes in the upstairs windows.

'I want you to give that car a ticket, Willie,' Tom said, pointing to Ray's vehicle. 'He must have broken the speed limit to get here ahead of us. Quite unusual for him, I can tell you.'

The snow had eased and the roads were still clear, but a dusting of white had settled on the surrounding fields. The dark clouds looked ominously heavy, and a greyish white light gave the early evening an oppressive feel.

Michael glanced up. 'If that's more snow in those clouds, we could end up getting stuck down here.'

Tom's brow creased with worry. Irish people were not used to dealing with inclement weather. Rain they could handle by the bucketload. Snow was a novelty and, when it did make a rare appearance, the resulting chaos made roads impassable across much of the country.

Ray and Laura were sitting on stools at a high table inside the window of the dimly lit coffee shop, the only customers.

There was no one behind the counter when they entered, but in response to the tinkling bell attached to the door, a little old woman, her short white hair standing on end, emerged through a curtain.

'Well, well,' she said. 'It's like Grand Central Station in here today.'

'Good afternoon, miss,' Tom said.

'More police,' she replied. 'I suppose you'll be wanting coffee. We don't serve doughnuts.'

Tom and Michael looked at each other, unsure whether she meant the confectionery or was calling them doughnuts.

Tom guessed the former.

'Three coffees would be great,' he replied. 'Would you mind terribly if we have our own sandwiches with the coffee?'

'Well, I'd say yes, but then you might arrest me. I don't want to end up a victim of police brutality. I know what goes on.' She touched the side of her large nose with her finger.

A young man emerged from behind the curtain.

'Nan, what are you doing down here? Go upstairs and watch the telly,' he said, trying to gently usher her away.

She glared at him. 'You're always trying to keep me out

of my own shop. Just like your father. Hoping I'll die of boredom up there so you can claim your inheritance.'

With one last glare at the two policemen, she left.

'Sorry about that.' The young man smiled at Tom and Michael. 'She ran this shop for forty years. Hard to break the habit.'

'She seems to have all her faculties,' Michael observed.

Their young server laughed. 'No, she's mad as a brush now. Thinks everyone's a copper. Go on, sit down and I'll bring your coffees. Three you said? Black, is it?'

'With a jug of milk,' Tom confirmed. 'The copper filling the car outside is with us.'

'You might have warned us,' Michael said, as they joined Ray and Laura at their table.

'It was funnier to watch your faces,' Ray replied. 'She asked us if we were here to interview her. I thought you'd phoned ahead as a joke.'

The woman's grandson arrived at the table with the coffees.

'So,' Ray said, turning to Laura. 'Do you want to tell them, or will I?'

'Well, I suppose I should tell the story. She was my aunt, after all.' Laura shook her head, still coming to terms with what she'd learned.

The absence of anyone else in the shop and the eerie quiet outside, despite the proximity to the motorway, put them all on edge. It felt like the right atmosphere for a chilling tale.

'I don't think I ever heard this story, growing up,' Laura began. 'It might have been referenced – poor Aunt Peggy, that kind of thing – but you know how Irish families are, though. Skeletons in every closet.'

Everybody around the table nodded sagely. So many Irish families had the uncle who added coffee to his whiskey every morning, or the child, raised by grandparents, believing its mother to be its sibling. Not hanging your dirty laundry out in public was a national pastime.

Laura took a deep breath.

'There were nine in my mother's family and she's the youngest. She had a special bond with her sister Peggy, because she was the only sister still living at home when Mam was growing up. Anyway, one night Peggy went to a parish dance, which was apparently as thrilling as it got back then. She was seventeen. My mother was eight, so this was around 1963 or '64.'

Laura took a sip of her coffee. Like most Irish people, she was a good storyteller and knew how to pace a yarn.

'Peggy was a real looker – dimpled cheeks, big blue eyes, that kind of thing. My mother remembers her that night as this vision going out in a cornflower-blue dress with a matching blue butterfly clip in her hair. Their brother Johnny was her chaperone and under strict orders to take care of her . . .' Laura paused.

The sense of foreboding was growing.

'My mother woke in the early hours to chaos. There was shouting and banging downstairs, so she got up and peeped into the kitchen through a crack in the door. She was young and probably only realized later what had happened that night, but she remembers seeing Peggy sitting in a chair, dress torn, her lip split. My grandmother had her arms around her and was trying to get Peggy to say something.

'The shouting had been between my grandad and Johnny and another brother, Kevin. Johnny had had a few drinks and left Peggy alone. Two local lads offered to walk her home, but, well ... I don't need to spell out what happened. They were brutal.' Laura flushed. 'Johnny found her where they'd left her, in a ditch at the side of the road. She was less than half a mile from home.'

Tom felt a ball of anger and compassion rise in his chest.

'The local priest got word of the episode and a few days later turned up at the house,' Laura continued, in a hushed tone. 'He told my grandparents that Peggy had led the lads on, they were good boys, one training to be a teacher, et cetera. Said Peggy would have to be packed off to the nuns in case she was pregnant. That's where single girls "in trouble" were sent. It seems the only thing worse than getting yourself assaulted, back then, was other people finding out about it.'

'And they just sent her off?' Michael asked, incredulous.

'Of course not,' Laura snapped. 'My grandmother was horrified. But the priest kept coming back and neighbours were starting to talk, saying that she left the dance with the lads, no decent girl would do that. None of us can imagine what it must have been like in rural Ireland in the sixties. Between the priests and the neighbours the pressure to send Peggy and her problems away would have been unbearable.

'I'm not long out of Kerry, and I can tell you there are still villages that could have leapt straight off the pages of *The Valley of the Squinting Windows*.'

Tom raised his eyebrows, surprised that someone so young was familiar with Brinsley MacNamara's classic and controversial tale about an Irish town torn apart by gossip and malice.

'It turned out the two lads were from prominent families,' she continued. 'They wanted her gone, and these people were used to getting what they wanted. Grandad caved first, but not because he didn't love Peggy. She had taken to her bed after the attack and wouldn't speak to anyone. Grandad thought that maybe the best thing for Peggy was to be away from the area for a while.

'So they let the priest take her to the Sisters of Pity convent in Limerick. She wasn't sent to one of the mother and baby homes run by the nuns, because they didn't even know if she was pregnant at that stage . . .' Laura paused.

Her listeners were enthralled and horrified in equal measure.

'The family was heartbroken. My grandmother kept sending letters to the convent but received no response. The priest had actively discouraged them from visiting. But after a month, Gran wanted to know if Peggy was expecting. She wanted to make sure the baby wasn't adopted. Mainly, she wanted Peggy home.

'My grandparents drove to the convent, but when they got there they had to fight with a nun just to see Peggy. When they did, she was unrecognizable. Her hair was shorn. She was covered in bruises and was half the size she'd been when she'd left Kerry. They wanted to take her out there and then, but Peggy started having some kind of fit. She just kept screaming, "You sent me here, you sent me here." But she wasn't pregnant.

'My grandparents went berserk with the nuns, wanted to know what had happened. The nuns told them Peggy was harming herself, because the "incident" with the two lads had sent her mad. They reassured the family that they would be better off leaving the sisters to deal with her, that they were professionals and could help Peggy.

'My grandmother never got over it. She kept going back to the convent, each time determined to put Peggy in a car and bring her home, but half the time the nuns talked her down, and the rest of the time, they wouldn't even let her in. Said it would just upset Peggy and the whole place. Grandad suspected the families of the two boys were pulling strings so Peggy would be kept in the laundry. They didn't want her back, walking about the village, making them uncomfortable. I never met Gran; she died two years after Peggy left, of heartbreak, Mam says.

'Years later, Mam went to look for Peggy herself. It wasn't until then she found out Peggy was dead. She'd hanged herself from the window of her dormitory.'

Everyone around the table winced.

'She'd died five years before Mam went looking. The nuns hadn't felt the need to inform her family. They wouldn't even say where she was buried. Said she had committed a mortal sin and didn't deserve to lie in a marked grave. She killed herself when she was twenty-seven, after spending ten years in the place.' Laura shook her head. 'That's everything.'

The story sounded completely incredible, and Tom knew he would have struggled to believe it if so much hadn't already come out about religious institutions. It was only in the last decade that the government had been forced to compensate victims who'd been routinely abused and tortured as children in industrial schools run by religious orders.

Now there was growing pressure from campaign groups to investigate the Magdalene Laundries and the role the state had played in their operation. The laundries had been originally conceived as charitable refuges for 'fallen' or abandoned women, but evolved into dumping grounds for all sorts of women regarded as 'difficult' by a judgemental society, heavily influenced by the Catholic Church. Some of the laundry inmates had had babies out of wedlock, others had reported abuse by a family member or neighbour; some just ended up there because they were homeless, had committed a minor crime or were moved from other institutions. The women claimed they were shamefully mistreated – forced to work from morning until night for no pay, underfed, beaten, abused and generally treated like prisoners.

The campaign thus far had been conducted largely under the radar. The government had managed to force the religious orders to provide a tiny portion of redress for the industrial school victims but, scorched by that experience, it was maintaining that the Magdalene Laundries were the domain of the Church, and families had sent their relatives there freely. The campaign groups, though, had ample evidence that the courts had sent girls to laundries for petty offences and that many young girls had been sent there directly from orphanages. All the institutions of the state, including the police, were implicated in sending girls to the laundries – and keeping them there.

Willie sighed.

'Your aunt's story isn't all that unusual,' he said. 'It was meant to be the case that the girls were released from the laundries if a family member came for them. But more often than not, they were worse than jail for people with no money or power. Slave labour for the nuns, that's what those girls were.'

'It's a heartbreaking tale, Laura,' Tom added. 'Your mother was very brave to share it.'

'It is horrific,' Michael said. 'I've heard of the laundries, I just don't think I ever realized what went on in them. But – and I don't want to take away from Laura's story – is it relevant to this case? Was Mother Attracta even in the laundry at the time? And was she involved with whatever went on?'

'I think it's significant,' Ray said. 'Sister Concepta said

Mother Attracta had been a nun since the 1960s, and she didn't mention her being anywhere other than at that convent. And it doesn't matter whether Mother Attracta was complicit in the bad things that happened in the laundry. A lot of people seem to have been damaged by those places. We have to at least consider the theory that somebody could be taking revenge, and Mother Attracta was a target just because she was there.'

Laura fidgeted in her seat.

'I'm not sure I'm comfortable with where that thought leads,' she said. 'My mother is full of rage at what happened to her sister. She wants justice for her. For Mam that means exposing the truth. Not murdering someone.'

Tom interrupted, before Ray could respond to Laura. 'We shouldn't jump to any conclusions.' For all his intelligence, the detective sergeant could be emotionally oblivious. 'It's important to know the background of the convent. That doesn't necessarily mean that the murder has any connection to the laundry. The laundries closed years ago. It's a very long time to nurse a grudge.'

'1996,' Willie said.

They all looked at him.

'That's when the last one closed.'

'I didn't realize it was that recent,' Tom said.

A clock chimed in the shop.

Darkness had fallen.

CHAPTER 16

Kilcross garda station was en route to the convent. It sat amid pretty, quaint houses, most of them shimmering with Christmas lights under freshly snow-topped roofs.

The sergeant, Ciaran McKenna, was a laid-back, friendly man in his early fifties. His youthful face was unlined, only his greying hair betraying his age.

Tom was relieved to note the man's relaxed demeanour. Some officers reacted badly to the Dublin-based murder team stepping on to their 'patch'. This sergeant looked like he would be a help rather than a hindrance to the investigation.

Ciaran told them that members of the divisional crime scene unit, an offshoot of the Technical Bureau, had attempted to isolate the scene in the hall where the nuns had found the blood and broken glass.

He paused before continuing, nervously. 'I don't know what you'll make of this. The nuns cleaned the hall.'

'Cleaned the scene?' Tom repeated, incredulously. 'What? Why? That's a criminal offence.'

'I don't think they realized that.' Ciaran shook his head. 'Said the glass and blood were distressing. It's just something they do – cleaning, I mean. Not much else to do up there. They've no television.' He pronounced this last sentence as if it was a crime.

Tom was flabbergasted. 'Well, we've senior crime scene investigators coming down tomorrow. Unless the nuns used industrial-strength bleach, the team will hopefully pick up something. I can't say it's not a blow, though. Can you come over in the morning and tell us what you know about the place and the victim?'

'Sure. You don't need me tonight?'

'Morning is fine. I want to see the nuns this evening. This Father Seamus . . .?'

'An obnoxious old fool – inflated sense of his own importance.'

'We have to talk to him, too,' Ray said. 'Does he stay at the convent as well?'

Ciaran snorted. Tom rolled his eyes.

'What?' Ray said.

'No,' the sergeant answered. 'He doesn't stay at the convent. They have this odd rule about "no men". You'll find him at the priest's house a few yards down from the church, in the village.'

'Well, we're staying at the convent,' Ray retorted, petulantly.

'I'm sure they'll be able to control themselves,' Ciaran responded, deadpan.

'The Reverend Mother,' Tom interjected. 'What was she like?'

The sergeant pursed his lips.

'Not pleasant,' he replied.

That made two witnesses with nothing nice to say about the victim.

The convent was a mile south of the village.

A glassy sheen made the narrow country road treacherous. Between concentrating on driving and the moonless dark night, they almost missed the left turn Ciaran McKenna had instructed them to take.

Once on the even narrower road, it was only minutes before the high walls of the convent became visible. They pulled through the tall, open iron gates into a large, gravel-strewn yard.

The convent was an austere and oppressive building, standing three storeys high. A few windows on one side of the lower floor were lit, but the upper two floors remained cloaked in darkness.

The front was coated in grim grey pebbledash. The bottom floor appeared to have been updated with modern window fittings, but the huge oak door looked like an original fixture. To its left ran a long, windowed corridor.

'It's scary, isn't it?' Laura came up beside Tom quietly.

She stared, wide-eyed and apprehensive, at the building in which her aunt had died.

'I'm sure it doesn't look so intimidating in the daylight,' he said.

'It probably looks worse,' she replied, and started towards the door.

Tom followed his team. He looked at the backs of Laura and Michael's heads and gave his own a quiet shake. Laura was mulling over her family history. Michael's focus was half at home with his wife. Add to that the niggling worries Tom harboured about his own daughter's news and really, out of the four detectives, only Ray could be said to have his mind fully on the case.

The large door opened before they had the chance to use the old-fashioned brass doorknocker. Sister Concepta stood in its frame, ready to greet them.

'Detectives, *fáilte*. I heard the cars. Come in out of the cold. *Tar isteach*.'

Fáilte and tar isteach – welcome and come inside.

They made their way into the impressive entrance hall. It had high ceilings and was brightly lit, with doors off to all sides. A broad staircase stood to their right and an overhead balcony faced them.

A rudimentary cordon had been set up in the left-hand corner of the hall around a door and a half-moon-shaped walnut table, upon which sat a large vase filled with red roses.

'Thank you for offering us refuge, Sister,' Tom said. 'I fear the weather is deteriorating.'

'It's our pleasure, really.' She lowered her voice. 'I told the others how Mother died. I hope that's okay.'

'Necessary, I imagine.' He looked around. 'The convent is bigger than I'd expected.'

'Yes, it used to service a far bigger community. What you see from the front is not even the full building. There are two more wings off to the back. We'd other buildings on the land but they've been demolished. Oh, look at me standing here talking and you only at the door. Would you like to leave your bags in your rooms and then I'll give you the tour? We're having a late dinner to accommodate you. You can meet everyone then.'

'That would be perfect,' Tom said.

He was eager to see the sisters at their most relaxed, and a dining setting suited that. They would all be on their guard during the interviews.

'So that is where you found the . . . disturbance?' He cocked his head, indicating the cordoned area.

'It is. I'm afraid Sergeant McKenna was very cross with us for cleaning up.'

'Why on earth did you?' Ray asked.

The nun shrugged. 'I can only apologize. Some of the sisters were very distressed. And when no guards came . . . well, we couldn't just leave it like that. There was glass everywhere. I should have told you earlier.'

'Nobody's been near it since the police team came?' Tom asked.

'Oh, no. Of course not. Shall we?' she pointed to the large oak staircase. 'Your rooms are just up on the balcony.'

The accommodation was as she had described it to Ray – basic but cosy. A narrow single bed filled one side of Tom's room, made up with freshly starched sheets and grey woollen blankets. A small locker with a basic reading lamp and a pine wardrobe completed the furnishings.

The only splash of colour came from the blue curtains drawn across the window.

He removed his suit jacket and opened his bag, from which he pulled out a dark fleece to throw on over his shirt and tie. A little note fluttered from its folds as he shook it out.

In case you're tempted to find warmth in the arms of one of the nuns – try this instead. Your long-suffering wife xxx

Tom smiled. He put the piece of paper back in the bag just as there was a knock on the door.

Ray came in. 'So you've no tea and coffee facilities either? I think we should complain.'

Tom ignored him and sat down to slide a spare pair of shoes under the bed.

Ray plonked down beside him.

'Are we getting comfy here?' Tom asked, amused.

'My room is as boring as this one.'

'The room you've been in for five minutes?' Tom sighed.

Ray was a complex character. He could be ferociously smart. He had insights that set him apart from other detective sergeants the inspector had worked with. He was kind-hearted and dedicated and loyal. But he could also be incredibly immature.

Sometimes it was like raising a second child.

Willie was on the landing when they emerged from Tom's room.

'Are you two bunking together? Top to toe, is it?' he chuckled. 'I might head back into the town and see if I can get a packet of cigarettes.'

'I doubt you'll find anywhere open,' Tom said.

'No matter, I'll just have a look,' Willie said. 'Unless you need me?'

'No, no, you give the car a spin. In case the engine cools down.'

Michael and Laura had just come out of their rooms.

'Right.' Tom rubbed his hands together. 'Let's get acquainted with this place.'

CHAPTER 17

A multitude of appetizing aromas hit the detectives when Ray pushed open the heavy kitchen door, from the savoury dishes bubbling on the cooker to the sweet, sticky cakes resting on countertops. Two middle-aged sisters moved to and fro between a centre island and a large range cooker, set amid the cupboards on the back wall.

The right side of the kitchen had been kept as an old parlour-type area. Here, there were three comfortable-looking armchairs and an old-fashioned dresser with an assortment of bottles and glasses on its shelves.

As Tom stood on the threshold, a door beside the chairs swung open and Sister Concepta emerged from what looked like the dining area.

'Inspector,' she greeted him.

Michael, bringing up the rear, let go of the door, which promptly slammed shut with an almighty bang, making everyone jump.

'Sorry,' he muttered.

The two cooks cleaned their hands on their aprons as they walked around the island to meet the new arrivals. Sister Concepta made the introductions.

'Inspector, this is Sister Mary.' She indicated the larger of the two women. 'And this is Sister Fidelma.'

'Pleased to meet you,' Sister Mary said, beaming. 'We don't get very many visitors here. It's wonderful to have new people to cook for.'

Tom could see now that the busy kitchen and all its wonderful smells were for their benefit. He found it slightly incongruous that they were being so well received, considering the circumstances.

As though reading his mind, Sister Mary's face flushed and she spoke again.

'I mean, if it wasn't for the awful event that has brought you here.' She cast her eyes to the ground and blessed herself.

'Well, I'm very pleased to meet you, nonetheless,' Tom said, smiling.

Laura displayed nothing but professionalism – Tom had to admire her restraint. He suspected she was mentally assessing each nun for any potential complicity in her aunt's death.

'There was a fifth in your group?' Sister Concepta said.

'My driver. He's in the village having a scout around,' Tom answered.

The nuns exchanged puzzled glances.

'There'll be nothing except public houses open at this hour,' Sister Mary said.

'I can't see that upsetting him too much,' Tom replied.

After establishing that dinner would be in forty-five

minutes, they set off on their tour of the convent. They started at the cordoned-off area in the entrance hall.

'That door behind the police tape opens on to the corridor you saw from the front of the house,' Sister Concepta told them.

Tom nodded. 'There was nothing disturbed in there?'

'Not that we could see.'

'Where does the corridor go?'

'Nowhere.' Sister Concepta shrugged.

'Oh?'

'It runs along the front of the house and then it just stops. We used to keep plants in it, like a sort of conservatory. It catches the sun beautifully. There were windows on the inside wall then as well, for the house, but they were knocked out and replaced with alcoves. It looks pretty, but it serves absolutely no purpose.'

'So why would Mother Attracta have been in this part of the hall late at night?' Ray asked. 'Was she at the coat rack, maybe?'

'We have a tradition,' Sister Concepta replied. 'Every evening candles are lit in each of the alcoves. It's to welcome lost souls, give them a guiding light. They're extinguished before we go to bed. That was Mother Attracta's task.'

'Where do the lost souls go after hours?' Michael mumbled to Ray, who smirked.

Sister Concepta heard Michael, and a hint of a smile danced on her lips.

'As I said, it's just a tradition. But don't worry, we leave the electric overhead light on for the lost souls.'

'So she could have been performing this task before she was assaulted?' Tom asked, ignoring Michael and Ray.

'I think so. The candles looked to have been put out.'

Tom tried to imagine the turn of events that night. Mother Attracta must have walked down the corridor performing her duty. When she arrived back at the entrance hall, she had been attacked.

Was she taken by chance, or did someone know that this was her specific nightly routine?

He examined the vase on the table, then the light switch and the wall surrounding it. To his left, just beside the front door, stood the huge old-style coat rack.

Something didn't fit.

If she'd been attacked coming out of the door, then why was the blow to the back of her skull? The door opened into the corridor, so she would have walked out to the hall without anything obscuring her view. There was no space to stand flat against the wall to the left or right. He supposed someone could have hidden behind or even inside the coat rack on the left. Unless she hadn't been alone in the hall and she had walked out ahead of her assailant.

'You said a vase had been smashed?' Tom asked aloud.

'Yes, that one's a new vase. We always keep fresh flowers in the hall. Oh!' Sister Concepta's hand flew to her mouth. 'Do you think he hit her with that, Inspector?'

Tom noted she used 'him'. Most people assumed the perpetrator was a man when faced with a violent murder.

'That morning, Sister; describe to me what you saw.'

'I don't need to describe it, Inspector. I can just show you, if you like.'

Tom cocked his head, puzzled. 'Show me how, Sister?'

He'd a daft notion when she said it that the sisters were going to re-enact the scene; a morbid take on a Christmas play.

'I took a picture before we cleaned up.'

He almost laughed.

The nun withdrew a mobile phone from her skirt pocket and scrolled through its photo album.

'It's not the best quality, I'm afraid, but you can probably load it on to the computer and enhance it.' She noticed the amused looks on the detectives' faces. 'We're not complete idiots.' She smiled and handed the phone to Tom.

The picture on her Nokia was small. Tom squinted at the image; it showed the door, coats and table. Blood was sprayed across the wall above the table, which itself was covered in strewn lilies and broken glass.

He looked down. They were standing on a multi-coloured but predominantly red carpet. It would be difficult to see a bloodstain, but fabric was less easy to clean than wood. Hopefully forensics would pick up something.

He looked at the picture again. He noticed one anomaly. In the photo, a candle in a clay dish also sat on the table.

'There's no candle on the table now, Sister. But there is in the photo.'

'We don't normally keep candles there. That was the candle from the last alcove. We put it back later that morning.'

'And do you know why it would have been on the table? It's not at the end of its wick. Would Mother Attracta have used it as a light to come back down the corridor?'

'She usually turned on the overhead light before she went into the corridor. Otherwise, as you say, she'd be in the dark on the way back. As I said, we leave that light on overnight.'

'Did you have a power cut that night, perhaps? Did anybody notice the lights going out?'

Sister Concepta thought for a moment. 'I didn't notice anything . . . and nobody has said anything.'

'Do you know where the fuse box is?' Ray asked.

'Yes, it's in the kitchen. The corridor light is that switch there.' She pointed to the wall behind Tom. 'Actually, now you say it, the fuse for that light did blow a few times in the last few months. I remember Mother Attracta complaining about it. Shall we, Inspector?' Sister Concepta indicated that they should move on.

Tom could see she was unsettled at their current location. That couldn't be easy, he thought. The main hall – no avoiding it.

The nun showed them the offices and the corridor that led to the kitchen. The inspector had decided to leave a detailed search of Mother Attracta's office and bedroom until the morning.

Sister Concepta had finished showing them the second floor when Tom lobbed the bomb.

'And where were the girls' rooms?' he asked, closely observing the woman in front of him. 'Sister, I wonder why you didn't tell us when we met earlier that this convent had originally been a Magdalene Laundry?'

Sister Concepta stopped short. The lighting was low but Tom could still see the glow in her cheeks.

'Why would I, Inspector? I went to Dublin to identify Mother Attracta's body. Why would the convent's history be relevant?'

'Mother Attracta was murdered,' Tom replied, evenly. 'And the laundries are gaining in notoriety.'

Sister Concepta chewed her lip. 'To be honest, it isn't something I would bring up willingly.'

Tom said nothing, waiting for her to continue. He sensed Laura had stopped breathing.

'What happened in the laundries is misunderstood and often miscommunicated. Not all servants of the Church have misdeeds on their conscience.' The nun held her head high, but her tone was defensive.

'Is what's being said about the laundries not true?' Ray asked.

She considered for a moment. 'I think there was a strict regime in the laundries that many might perceive as overly harsh. But talking about what went on then is out of context now. They were different times, and society had different norms. People forget that. Families sent their daughters to the laundries. Nuns didn't go stealing girls from their beds. They were sent here, or they came themselves as a last resort, seeking asylum.'

Laura bristled and gave a dismissive 'humph'.

Sister Concepta shot her a look and the two women locked eyes. Laura broke the contact first, giving Tom a sideways look.

'It's not entirely true, though, is it?' Ray probed. 'Not all families sent their children here willingly. In some circumstances they were encouraged to do so – by the Church. And even when it was unprompted, couldn't you argue that society was so conditioned and cowed by the Church's influence that many felt they had no choice?'

The sister bowed her head. 'I don't defend everything, Detective. But there are always two sides.'

'Will the Church let the other side be told?' Ray asked, refusing to back down.

Sister Concepta returned his gaze, unblinking. 'Maybe we can have a conversation about the history of the Church and the state before you go. In any case, in answer to the original question, the dormitories the girls slept in are on the third floor.'

Tom had tired of the sparring match. He felt sorry for the nun. She was young – probably the same age as Ray – and couldn't possibly carry the burden of responsibility for what had happened decades ago.

He was only a little sorry, though. Some of what she had said seemed genuine, and probably progressive for a nun, but mostly it had sounded like a message straight from a public relations manual. And she had been unconvincing in her delivery. He suspected the Church would be spinning some of those lines in the not too distant future.

'Can we see the dormitories?' Laura asked.

'If you like.' Sister Concepta's tone was clipped.

Tom sensed it was better to see the dormitories now.

Fascination with the convent's ghoulish history was understandable, but maybe viewing empty rooms would put their curiosity to bed.

CHAPTER 18

The third floor looked, to all intents and purposes, like the one they had just left, yet there was an atmosphere on the forbidding landing. Laura shivered when they arrived at the top of the staircase, and Michael felt goose pimples on the back of his neck.

'I'm sorry, the heating's never on up here, that's why there's a chill,' Sister Concepta said, as she flicked on the light.

A perfectly rational explanation, Tom thought, ordering the butterflies in his stomach to cease fluttering.

'This way, please.'

'When did the convent stop being a laundry?' he asked, as they approached the first room.

'In 1985,' she answered.

The nun withdrew a large ring, jostling with keys, from her pocket.

'Did you know the convent had been a laundry when you came here?'

She hesitated. 'Yes. I did,' she answered, before turning the correct key in the door.

'Why are the rooms kept locked?' Ray asked.

Sister Concepta cocked her head, as though asking herself the same question.

'They just are,' she finally answered, with a shrug.

She opened the door, and the hall light spilled into the darkened room.

They walked into the first dormitory.

The tension among the detectives was palpable, but it quickly dissipated. The room was completely empty.

'Sorry, I should have remembered, this room has been cleared,' Sister Concepta said. 'You want to see what the dormitories looked like when they were in use.'

The tone of her last sentence was deliberately sharp, calling out their morbid fascination for what it was.

Did the dormitories pertain to the investigation? Tom mused. Perhaps, if the killer's motive were retribution.

He looked at Laura. The strain on her face was evident. The rest of them might be indulging in gratuitous macabre curiosity, but this was very real for her.

The nun opened the next door.

As they stepped over the threshold, it felt as though the temperature dropped further.

Time stood still.

Along the walls on either side, the bare metal frames of beds stood where they had always stood. Between each one sat a tiny locker. This was all the personal space afforded the young women in which to store their worldly belongings. At the end of the room a long washbasin sat atop a wooden cupboard, between two windows. A thick layer of dust covered everything, and cobwebs glistened silver in the corners of the room.

The nun flicked the light switch. Nothing happened.

'Bulb must be gone . . .' She shrugged.

Tom suspected the light just refused to shine in this crypt-like space.

He kept an eye on Laura, trying not to react when she moved hesitantly to the windows at the end and peered downwards. He watched the back of her copper hair, caught in the glow of the unnatural light that streamed in through the window, and shuddered, imagining her walking in the ghostly footprints of her aunt, who had made her way to such a window decades before.

The inspector turned to Sister Concepta, who was openly staring at Laura.

'Where are the toilet facilities?' he asked.

'Oh, I'm sorry, do you need to . . .?'

'No. I mean, where did the girls go? In this room and the last, between them there must have been sixteen beds. I see a washbasin, but no toilets.'

'Oh.' She was embarrassed. 'There are toilets at the end of each landing.'

'But weren't the girls locked in at night?' Tom asked.

He didn't know this for sure, but something told him that was the case. If the nuns were in the habit of locking the rooms, that habit had come from somewhere.

'Yes, I suppose they were.' Sister Concepta pursed her lips. 'I imagine they used chamber pots in the evening.'

'As recently as 1985,' Tom observed.

She looked up at him and he saw defiance flash in her eyes.

'I feel like you want me to apologize, Inspector, for something that happened, as you know, long before I became a nun.'

He felt the force of her words. It was the first time he had seen her angry.

As quickly as it came, the seemingly uncharacteristic fury was gone.

'I'm sorry,' she said. 'I'm being too sensitive. May I ask you a question, though?'

'Of course.'

She fixed him with a stare.

'Do you think there's a connection between Mother Attracta's murder and the laundry?'

He looked at her. 'It's highly unlikely,' he said, eventually.

Sister Concepta's shoulders sagged in obvious relief.

'In my experience,' Tom continued, 'when a murder's committed, it's usually by somebody close to the victim.'

Michael had followed Laura to the end of the room and was hunched down, examining the side of the wooden cupboard.

'What are you looking at?' Tom asked.

'There are initials scratched here.'

Laura abandoned the window with lightning speed.

Tom joined them. He didn't know what Laura's aunt's surname was, but he fervently hoped they didn't see the initial P for Peggy. All he saw, though, were the initials MM, carved repeatedly in the wood.

He ran his fingers over the amateur grooves. 'MM. That was on the back of Mother Attracta's cross. It's Mary Magdalene, isn't it?'

'Yes. Many of the older sisters have the same crucifix,' Sister Concepta replied.

'Why would someone carve that here?' the inspector asked.

She shrugged her shoulders. 'I don't know. I suppose we have to remember that some of the poor souls who stayed in this place wouldn't have had their full mental capacities. Repetitive behaviour can be a sign of an unsettled mind.'

'Do you have a list of the women who stayed here?' Laura said.

'Many of the girls who came here were given house names to protect their privacy,' Sister Concepta replied. 'Are you looking for someone in particular?'

Laura nodded.

There was no denying the look of compassion on the nun's face in that instant.

Tom observed her with interest.

'Would you like me to look for a record?' Sister Concepta asked Laura, her voice gentle.

'Very much. Please,' Laura answered, taken aback.

For crying out loud, Tom thought. An investigation within an investigation. It was time to call a halt to this distraction.

'Sister, perhaps we should see the rest of the house?' he said.

'Of course. Follow me.'

CHAPTER 19

As they left the room, Tom felt a shift in the mood. Sister Concepta appeared relieved to have left the dormitories. Before they went back downstairs, she brought them to the end of the building, where a large window gave them a view of the land beyond the house.

'You can't see them at night, but there are some foundations still behind us from the buildings that were knocked down. They would have housed part of the laundry and the orphanage.'

'Orphanage?' Tom and Ray repeated in unison.

'Yes,' Sister Concepta replied. 'It was very common for nuns to run orphanages before the state took over. There was a separate mother and baby home up in Limerick City, but it didn't have the capacity for all the babies. Some of them were sent here, and the convent also took in pregnant girls from the surrounding rural areas. Shall we move on?'

The detectives reflected on the additional information.

'So, how long was Mother Attracta in charge?' Tom asked, as they walked back down the flights of stairs.

'Twenty years, I think,' she replied.

'Meaning she wasn't in charge when it was a laundry?'

'No. But she was here. The Reverend Mother before her had been in charge since the late sixties. Her name was Mother Theresa.'

'What was she like?' Ray asked.

'I never met her. I believe she was very strict.'

On the other side of the house was the nuns' main sitting room, where they encountered more sisters. The nuns were relaxing and enjoying the warmth of an open fire. Most of the rooms in this wing had been used as classrooms and were empty.

Their final destination was the chapel.

There were six wooden pews on each side of a centre aisle, in front of a compact altar. A crucifix hung on the back wall, to its right an image of the Holy Ghost, portrayed as a dove. On the left was an icon of the Virgin Mary.

'Would you mind if I left you for a few moments so I can check if we're ready for dinner?' Sister Concepta asked Tom.

'Not at all. I don't want to keep everyone up too late but I'd like to speak to the sisters individually after dinner.'

'Whatever we can do to help.'

When the nun left, the detectives sat down on the hard wooden pews.

There wasn't a sound to be heard from inside or outside the house. The silence was unsettling.

'So, what do we think?' Tom asked.

Ray rubbed his chin, now coarse with stubble after the long day.

'I don't like this place; I'm used to working out of a station. I'm just wondering what the hell we do if we get snowed in here.'

'I know. This place gives me the heebie-jeebies as well,' Michael said. 'The whole Magdalene thing is creepy – locking girls away from the world like that – but I still think that's just a distraction.'

'Go on,' Tom said.

'Those empty rooms,' Michael continued. 'It puts it in perspective. It's ancient history. How likely is it that someone who was in the laundry came back decades later and battered Mother Attracta over the head? The laundry closed in 1985, twenty-five years ago. If our victim was as unpleasant as Sister Concepta made out to you earlier – an opinion the local sergeant seemed to share – I think our suspect could be one of the other nuns in this house, or someone from the village. I know it's unlikely to be a woman, but . . .'

'I agree, up to a point,' Tom said. 'We should start with those around her. But so far, other than our gracious host who seems young and fit enough, we've seen a group of nuns ranging in age from their late forties to their seventies. I haven't seen anyone I'd suspect would have the strength to do what was done to Mother Attracta.'

Ray shrugged. 'She was an elderly woman, though, and didn't weigh much. I can't imagine a middle-aged nun killing someone, but if we're talking trumps here, that heavyweight sister in the kitchen could take Mother Attracta every time.'

Michael snorted.

'Jesus, Ray.' Tom shook his head.

The image Ray had conjured broke the tension for most of the detectives, but Laura didn't smile. She had been twisting a curl earnestly with her finger and now looked up.

'How could one of the nuns have killed her?' she asked. 'They'd have had to take her on Wednesday night, and the pathologist said she wasn't killed until Thursday, sometime around 11 a.m. She was hardly brought to the park in daylight, which meant waiting until four-ish at least to move her. A nun from here would have been gone a whole day. Surely they'd have been missed?'

'Well, we've to establish that, but they might not have been gone a whole day,' Tom said. 'We know she was taken on Wednesday night, but if she wasn't killed until the next day, the killer could have moved her somewhere close to the convent, stayed with her that night, murdered her in the morning, then come back here, before leaving again later that day and bringing her to Dublin.'

Laura raised her eyebrows in a way that implied she found the idea far-fetched, but couldn't yet rule it out.

Tom continued. 'It's possible, but not probable, I know. We'll need to ascertain in the interviews if everybody has an alibi for those twenty-four hours.'

'How are we going to organize the interviews?' Ray asked.

'Let's pair up, Laura and I in one room, you two in the other.'

'Any word from Dublin?' Michael asked.

Tom fished his phone from his pocket. It had been so quiet that he wondered if they had no network coverage. But no, the signal was strong and the phone fully charged.

'No missed calls,' he said. 'I'll phone them in a moment.'

'The park thing really confuses me,' Laura said.

'Maybe the killer wanted her as far away as possible to throw us off the scent?' Michael suggested.

'Myself and Tom discussed this earlier,' Ray said. 'She wasn't left in a way that destroyed any hope of us identifying her. The killer might have delayed us finding out where she was from, but didn't prevent it. I have this feeling that our murderer was, as Sean McGuinness puts it, depositing her in our back garden. But as Tom points out, we'd have ended up on the case, anyway.'

Tom inclined his head.

'I suppose we've no way of knowing if they knew that, though. Would they have assumed detectives from Limerick would be sent to Kilcross? The general public is not that familiar with garda structures, or how the National Bureau of Criminal Investigation works.'

'What if they didn't want a Limerick team because they might have more local knowledge?' Laura mused.

Tom stood, massaging the backs of his thighs. The numbness in his buttocks summoned memories of enforced attendance at Sunday Mass as a child – which, he knew, had lasted no longer than an hour each week but at the time had felt like endless purgatory. How many hours had the Magdalene girls been forced to sit and kneel at these pews praying for forgiveness for imagined sins?

'Let's join the suspects for supper,' he said, drolly. 'Otherwise, we'll be here speculating all night. Go on ahead. I'll ring Dublin.'

He walked with them as far as the end of the corridor before stepping into the large living room where they'd seen the nuns relaxing earlier. It was empty now. Sinking gratefully into one of the comfortable armchairs by the open fire, where peat briquettes glowed invitingly, he dialled Ian's number.

'How are the sticks?' Ian answered. 'Any fear of you getting snowed in?'

'There's every chance, but I'm pretty sure Ray would walk ahead of the cars shovelling snow to get back to the comforts of the capital. Have you got anything for me?'

'I was rather hoping you'd have news for us.'

'Wishful thinking. Anything from the park?'

'We've had a few calls that we're checking out. A higher than usual number of cranks.'

'I can well imagine. Is it out that she's a nun yet?'

'Surprisingly, no. The hacks are in a frenzy trying to get an identity. RTÉ is looking for an update. McGuinness has decided to keep them in the dark until the morning. He says he'll do a presser then. He's channelling obstructive in a big way – hoping you'll get it solved before he has to do media.'

'I was planning on sleeping at some point, but I'll postpone,' Tom said. 'Anything more on Gerard Poots?'

'He is who he says he is. Lovely house, not too far from you – Luttrellstown. Wife. Nice career. When are you getting your forensic scientists?'

'In the morning. They'll have their work cut out for them – the nuns cleaned everything up.'

'You're joking?'

'I wish I was.'

'Who gave the order to clean? If someone down there committed the murder, it would be very handy to have every trace removed before you arrived, wouldn't it? It's not like they'd have had time to do it while they were kidnapping her.'

'Good thinking,' Tom said. 'We're about to have dinner.'

'Well, let Ray taste it first. If they're planning to bump you off, he's more expendable.'

'I won't tell him you said that. Speak tomorrow.'

Tom hung up and surveyed the room. There was no television – the local sergeant had been right – but the bookcases along the wall were crammed. A small unit in the corner contained board games and boxes of playing cards. At his feet there was a basket of wool, knitting needles poking out here and there.

The room reminded him of his grandmother's house years ago, before mod cons became the norm. It was restful. He wouldn't miss a television in a room like this. Then he smiled and shook his head. Who was he kidding? A nice cigar, though, and maybe a good book.

His musings were interrupted by the banging of the heavy brass doorknocker – a sound that echoed throughout the convent. Someone was impatient to come in out of the cold.

Tom arrived in the main hall in time to answer the front door.

Willie was back, stomping his feet on the light layer of snow that now covered the ground.

'Making yourself at home, I see. They have you doing doorman.'

'You couldn't find a nice country pub for a sup, Willie?'

'I'm shocked you have so little faith in me. I'd sniff out a pub in the desert. I'd a half-pint and, I don't mind telling you, a very interesting conversation with some locals.'

Tom lifted his eyebrows inquiringly, but just then the door behind them opened and Sister Concepta looked out.

'I thought I heard the door. Ah, your colleague is back. Would you like to join us for dinner?'

'Lovely,' Willie and Tom said, a look passing between them that said they would talk afterwards.

CHAPTER 20

When Sister Concepta opened the door to the dining room, the murmur of conversation died down and the rest of the convent's inhabitants turned to look at the additional guests. All the nuns wore veils, but only some of them were in full habit. The rest wore a mixture of navy, brown or grey skirts and white blouses, topped with V-neck woollen pullovers.

Two long tables were laden with steaming tureens of stew and woven baskets spilling over with bread rolls. Ray, Michael and Laura sat at the end of one long table, so Tom and Willie joined the other, greeting the nuns on either side, as Sister Concepta took her seat at the top.

The two tables were full, but there were others on either side that sat empty, reminders of a busier convent. The walls were painted a warm beige, and heavy cream curtains gave the room a comfortable feel on the cold winter's evening.

Tom was wondering why nobody had started eating when Sister Concepta joined her hands in prayer.

'In the name of the Father, the Son and the Holy Spirit.'

Of course! Grace before meals. He made the sign of the cross and, momentarily ignoring his lapsed Catholic status, dutifully hung his head as the nun intoned the familiar prayer.

When Tom thought it was safe to look up, he saw that the sister seated beside him was holding a ladle of beef stew and pointing at his plate.

'Shall I serve you?' she offered.

'Please, Sister. This smells divine.'

'I'm Sister Gabrielle,' she said. 'Sister Concepta said we should all introduce ourselves to you.'

'Detective Inspector Tom Reynolds,' he replied.

Sister Gabrielle looked roughly the same age as Tom. The small glimpses of hair under her headdress were strawberry blonde, and she was pretty – in a farmer's daughter way, with a plump round face, large blue eyes and dimpled cheeks.

He smiled as she generously spooned the thick meaty mess on to his plate.

'Help yourself to the rolls,' she said. 'Sister Fidelma makes the most beautiful bread. If you snooze you lose. Some of the sisters can't help themselves. These are like apples in the Garden of Eden.'

As she talked, she placed three rolls on her side plate, held one up to her nose, broke it apart and inhaled the rich doughy smell.

'You're lucky to have such gifted cooks,' Tom observed.

He turned to thank the nun on his other side, who was brandishing a decanter of deep red wine with intent. He nodded to her to pour but held up his hand to indicate a half-glass was sufficient.

'We tend to break out the good stuff coming up to Christmas – and especially when we've guests,' Sister Gabrielle said. 'There are many periods in the year when we're either fasting or limiting ourselves, so I suppose we appreciate our treats all the more when we do indulge.'

'Fasting?' Willie chimed, from her other side, as he helped himself to a roll. 'Now, why would you do that to yourselves?'

The nun Tom recognized as Sister Mary tittered like a schoolgirl, then clamped her hand over her mouth as though shocked that the sound had escaped.

Tom liberated a roll from the rapidly depleting pile and, following Sister Gabrielle's lead, broke it in two. The warm aroma that rose to meet his nostrils made him salivate, and he placed one half in his mouth. It was delectable. Crisp on the outside, soft and hot on the inside. The bread tasted sweet and sour simultaneously. He'd have to sneak some of these home for Louise; he wouldn't be able to describe how good they were and do them any justice. He washed the tasty mouthful down with a sip of the rich wine, guessing it was a Bordeaux.

The sacrifices I make for this job, he reflected, contentedly.

The inspector was abruptly roused from his bread-and-wine-induced reverie. An elderly nun on the other side of the table suddenly bellowed at him, as though seeing him for the first time.

'What are you doing here? You men can't be in here!'

Tom froze, mid-chew.

The nun beside her placed her hand firmly on the older sister's arm.

'Gladys, hush now. This is our guest. He's a policeman, here to see what happened to Attracta.'

'What?' the nun roared back at her. 'Speak up. Stop mumbling. Why does everyone mumble these days?'

The nun beside her raised her voice further, though she'd been pretty clear the first time. 'He's here to find out about Mother Attracta.'

'That bitch? Why?' The elderly nun sat back, tore off a piece of bread with her teeth and chomped noisily, a mischievous look on her face.

Tom nearly choked. Sister Gabrielle gasped and blessed herself. The nun sitting beside Sister Gladys groaned and placed her head in her hands.

A shocked silence descended on the room.

All eyes turned to Sister Concepta as she slapped the table and glared at the older nun.

'Sister Gladys, you cannot use that kind of language. May God forgive you for speaking ill of the dead.'

Tom waited to see how the chastised nun would react. She seemed belligerent, and up for a fight, but after Sister Concepta spoke, the elderly woman just bowed her head.

Tom looked around discreetly. Sister Concepta was the youngest nun there, easily by ten years; yet she had assumed authority in the absence of Mother Attracta.

The buzz of conversation struck up again.

'I apologize for that little outburst, Inspector,' Sister Gabrielle said quietly. 'Gladys is our oldest sister. She's in her mid-eighties and stroppy with it. We're so used to hearing her ripping at one thing or another we barely notice any more. She suffers from a rare form of straight-talking. She has no politeness filter.'

Tom laughed. 'Isn't that a great way to be, Sister? We spend so much time thinking about what we shouldn't say, it's a wonder we ever say anything at all.'

'But can you imagine the chaos if we went around saying what we really thought about people all the time?'

'Perhaps,' Tom replied. 'I suppose it depends on your nature. If you're the sort of person who only thinks the best of people, it wouldn't matter how honest you were.'

'If you were the sort of person who only thought the best of people, you'd soon be dissuaded of that notion if everyone went around saying what they thought,' the nun retorted.

'You have me there, Sister. And what do you really think of people? What did you think of Mother Attracta, for example?'

Sister Gabrielle smiled as she toyed with her food. 'I should have realized you were leading me there.'

He took a mouthful of the stew, savouring the delicious flavours. The beef was tender, the stew flavoured with bay leaf and thyme and fresh root vegetables. Paprika and black pepper gave it a subtle edge.

'If you are asking me to be honest,' she replied, 'I have

to say I found Mother Attracta to be a difficult woman, as did most of us.'

Tom kept his face neutral.

'I'm deeply shocked and saddened at the manner of her passing, but Mother Attracta was a hard, overbearing woman. If Sister Gladys had roared at you like that while Mother was at the head of the table, she'd have been on basic rations in her room for a week.'

Tom looked around the table. Each nun was deep in conversation with those around her and he could see smiles, although there was the occasional nervous glance in the direction of the detectives. Or rather, every nun bar Sister Gladys, who was busy chewing her food with a force that could only mean she had all her own teeth.

The atmosphere was very relaxed for a group of people who'd only found out that day that one of their members had been brutally murdered.

Ding dong, the bitch is gone.

Tom turned back to his neighbour.

'Was there anybody here who liked Mother Attracta, Sister?'

The nun bowed her head, embarrassed. 'Of course, Inspector.' She indicated the table behind her.

Tom glanced over his shoulder.

The table was largely abuzz with chat, but three of the nuns appeared to be absorbed in their meals. They weren't engaging with the wider group.

'That must be hard,' Tom said, turning back. 'To all live together, but in separate camps.'

'It isn't that black and white. We all have our confidantes. I can tell you what Sister Concepta would have done if she hadn't become a nun. I can tell you which actor Sister Mary has a crush on. I know Sister Bernadette is afraid of the dark. I didn't have that sort of relationship with Mother Attracta.'

Several large platters of dessert treats were carried in after dinner. The tables heaved under the weight of apple strudel, Black Forest gateaux, pavlova with fresh cream and winter berries, and small mountains of cinnamon raisin cakes, glazed with syrup.

Willie nearly expired with excitement as he helped himself to a little of everything. Tom, uncomfortably aware of an expanding midlife midriff, limited himself to a sumptuous cinnamon cake.

'Don't worry, Inspector,' Sister Mary told him. 'Nothing goes to waste. We bring all of our Saturday leftovers to the church hall on Sunday, and anyone from the parish can join us for lunch after Mass. It's usually just our elderly parishioners but sometimes we have special community lunches.'

Tom nodded pointedly in Willie's direction. 'I'd be less concerned about food going to waste and more worried about those old folks going hungry.'

The nun gave another of her high-pitched giggles. She was evidently starting to relax around the officers, as were the other women. Sister Gladys kept winking at Willie, causing him to chuckle, until Sister Gabrielle explained that the elderly nun had a tick in her left eye that flared when she was stressed.

As the meal came to a close, Tom found himself in the unfortunate position of bringing the new-found camaraderie to an abrupt end. He asked Sister Concepta if it would be possible for them to begin their interviews.

'And could you possibly allocate us two rooms, Sister?'

A nervous quiet greeted the inspector's request. The nuns had been reminded that their unexpected guests weren't there solely for the good food and company.

Tom stood up and addressed the room.

'Please don't worry, Sisters. These interviews are routine. My colleagues and I will split into two groups, and perhaps you will decide amongst yourselves the order in which to come to us . . .' He paused for a moment to observe the room. 'We would like to express our condolences to you on your loss. I hope that we can return Mother Attracta to you for burial as soon as possible. Right now, we need to concentrate on finding her killer.

'With that in mind I would ask that you use the opportunity of our time with you to tell us anything – and I mean anything – that you think is relevant to our investigation.'

The nuns nodded their heads obediently.

CHAPTER 21

The detectives left the dining room and followed Sister Concepta through the kitchen into the corridor beyond.

'I turned the heating on in a couple of the offices earlier, Inspector.'

'Very thoughtful of you, Sister. Would it be possible for us to use one of the rooms as a base for our duration here? It might only be until tomorrow.'

'Yes, of course, whatever you need. I'll give you the key so you can lock it when you're finished. Actually, you might like to have Mother Attracta's office. I can have the radiators turned on in there for the morning, and you'll have a computer at your disposal.'

'Thank you. We'll need about fifteen minutes to get ready. Oh, and Sister, please don't forget to call in to see us yourself at some point.' Tom smiled apologetically.

Her return smile was less enthusiastic.

'I fear it won't be long before we start putting a strain on the hospitality,' Tom said, when she'd gone. 'Michael, could you get the tape recorders from the car? Now, Willie, fill us in on what you picked up in the village.'

'What's this about the village?' Michael asked, clearly aggrieved at missing out.

'You'll catch up if you hurry, Michael,' Tom said. 'It's just Willie's adventures down in the local pub.'

'I've always thought drunks make the best witnesses,' Ray quipped.

Michael gave Tom a rueful look, then, taking Willie's keys, left to get the interview equipment.

'Let's step inside one of these offices,' Tom said. 'No point standing out here in the cold.'

The blast of heat hit the four officers as they entered the first room. Tom wondered why such a small group of nuns continued to rattle around a house so large they couldn't afford to heat it. Were they hoping for a resurgence of applicants?

The overhead light didn't work but Laura found a corner lamp and flicked the switch, illuminating the room with a dimmish glow.

The office was of moderate size and plainly decorated. A large crucifix hung between the two windows, behind the desk, and a small statue of the Virgin Mary stood on a chest of drawers in the corner.

The desk had one chair behind it and two facing it. Two more straight-backed, functional chairs were stacked in a corner. There were few home comforts here.

Ray arranged the chairs so there were two behind the desk and one facing, while Willie took another chair and sat to the side.

The wood-framed windows here did not have their

curtains drawn to hide the frigid night. Snow was falling heavily now on to the still landscape. Grey clouds loomed low and heavy overhead, giving everything an artificial, daylight-like glow. Tom sincerely hoped the weather wouldn't impede the arrival of the crime scene technicians in the morning.

The inspector sat down. 'So, Willie, what did you find?'

'Well, a lot of tumbleweed to begin with. There wasn't a newsagent's to be found.'

Laura threw her eyes to the ceiling.

'He's a city boy, Laura,' Tom said, and the young detective laughed.

The inspector was Dublin born and bred himself but didn't have the same ignorance about rural life. Willie seemed to spend more time exploring holiday resorts in Spain than his own country.

'Anyway,' Willie continued, unperturbed, 'there's more that unites our counties than divides them. Like any good village, there was a pub – more than one, in fact. It even had a shop in it. Brilliant, isn't it? Shops in pubs!'

'Okay, Willie, so we've established you're in a scene from *The Wicker Man*, but can you get to the point? We only have about ten minutes.'

'I'm getting there. Strange you should mention that movie, because I tell you, when I walked into the pub, every head turned. They don't get too many strangers here.'

'Willie, we're just off the main road to Kerry,' Laura exclaimed.

'And who goes there?' Willie retorted, triumphantly. 'They were a friendly bunch in spite of it all. I didn't say who I was or the reason we're here. Just said my boss had business in the convent. Apparently, they've a couple of "newbies" in the village at the moment, as they put it – a man who was born here but left years ago for America, and some writer woman who's renting a house. It's becoming almost a tourist hotspot.

'I bought a couple of pints for the old-timers at the bar, and that loosened their tongues enough to get them talking about the convent. Let's just say there are mixed emotions about this place. The lads had some unpleasant tales. Thinking about what they said now, well, it wouldn't surprise me if this place was haunted.'

Willie's usually cheerful visage had grown serious. His voice was grave and low. He looked around him shiftily, as if he expected a headless spectre to swoop down from the ceiling or through the door at any moment.

It didn't help that the combination of the dim lamp and the ethereal glow from the window gave the impression that a seance might be on the cards.

Tom was happy enough to humour Willie's dramatics. But even he felt the hairs on the back of his neck rise as the door handle creakily began to turn.

The door opened and Michael barged in, breathing heavily, dusting white flakes from his shoulders and carrying the box from Willie's car.

'What have I missed?' he asked.

The tension was broken.

'An ill-informed attack on rural dwellers, but aside from that we're just starting,' Tom replied. 'Go on, Willie.'

Willie resumed.

'On the one hand, there was this old man singing the praises of this place,' he said. 'Talking about how great the nuns are, and all they've done for the parish over the years. He holds Mother Attracta in high regard. Reckons she had to be tough because of what she had to deal with.'

'Meaning?' Tom asked.

'Meaning the wayward sinners the nuns were kind enough to take in, back in the day. He was in the minority, mind,' Willie said, apologetically, glancing in Laura's direction. 'Two of the other locals near howled him down. They think this place is a stain on the town and they'd like to see it knocked down, even though they admit the nuns do good work in the community nowadays.'

'Did they say why they hate it so much?' Tom asked.

'One of them, Henry Flannery, used to do all the deliveries to the convent for the village grocer. He said the girls were treated terribly. Said he saw things on occasion that made his blood run cold – girls down on bleeding knees scrubbing floors with toothbrushes; girls who'd been beaten black and blue. He also said that, despite the generous amounts of food he delivered, the girls he saw were skin and bone. They were all forced to wear these shapeless grey smocks so they wouldn't be a "temptation" to men.

'The other chap was more measured. He said the girls

were supposed to follow convent life, and it wasn't meant to be a holiday camp. But he agreed there was an awful coldness about the place. I suspect the truth is somewhere in the middle because it seems some of the girls were treated better than others, and some of the nuns were nicer than others. The ones in charge seemed to be the worst.'

Willie sighed. 'Flannery also said that when people refer to the Magdalene "girls", they have a notion in their head that they were young women. But, according to him, they were often children. Said he saw some as young as thirteen transferred directly from the orphanages to the laundry.'

'Good God.' Tom felt an unbearable weight settle on his shoulders.

'There's more,' Willie continued, shifting in his seat. 'Flannery said this one girl, who used to work in the kitchen and take the deliveries, started showing she was expecting. After a while she disappeared and he never saw her again. But his point was, she'd been in the laundry two years straight and couldn't have been more than fifteen when she arrived. If she was never out and she was never around boys, how had she gotten pregnant?'

Laura shook her head, confused.

Tom had a sinking feeling he knew what was coming next.

'He suspects someone in authority was abusing certain girls. Apparently, there were a number of priests living in the parish house at the time, and one of them was moved suddenly in the sixties. But he reckons it happened again a few years later ...'

Willie took a breath. 'Both men believe a lot of the nuns were intimidated by the sisters in charge and were afraid to challenge their brutal regime. Guess who was the worst of the lot? Mother Attracta. Or Sister Attracta, as she was then.'

The inspector grimaced. 'So, if she was like that to the girls in her care ... after the girls stopped coming, did she stop being vicious? Or did she start directing it at the other nuns?'

The sound of a door opening and closing in the distance alerted them. The inspector glanced at his watch; it was 8.45 p.m.

'You better go in,' Tom said to Ray. 'See you in a couple of hours. Find out who drives. And who suggested they clean up the mess in the hall.'

CHAPTER 22

Sister Concepta ensured trays of hot drinks were brought to both rooms. Tom took a long sip of his strong, creamy coffee as he surveyed Sister Bernadette. Willie had ushered their first interviewee in, before braving the glacial air outside for a cigarette.

The nun straightened her skirt and smiled nervously. Sister Bernadette was a kind-looking woman with the leathery face of one who has been exposed to a lot of sun, large brown eyes and a broad smile. She looked in her late forties, but the hair peeking out from under her headdress was as white as the falling snow.

She started talking before Tom could swallow his coffee.

'This is all very *CSI*, isn't it? Imagine, a team of detectives in our little convent!'

Tom was struck by her remark.

'I'm surprised you're familiar with *CSI*, Sister. I didn't see a television here.'

She looked flustered as she tried to find her voice.

Tom and Laura had seen this many times – perfectly innocent people, with nothing to hide, became quivering wrecks when put into a room with the police. Some people had to resist the urge to confess to crimes they hadn't committed, such was their sense of misplaced guilt around the guards.

'We used to have one,' Sister Bernadette said. 'Before, I mean. Not that I watched it a lot. I mean, I wasn't addicted to *CSI* or anything. I don't know anything about police procedure, really.'

She clamped her hand over her mouth and looked at Tom, mortified.

'I'm just curious, Sister,' he said, kindly. 'I can't say I've come across too many murders committed by people using American cop dramas as their style guide.'

The nun lowered her hand, the tension broken by Tom's attempt at humour.

'So, you used to have a television. Why don't you have one now?'

The nun chewed her bottom lip. 'It seems so silly now. In light of . . .'

Tom sighed. This merry dance again.

'Sister, if you're worried about telling us something because it shows Mother Attracta in a bad light, I'm afraid you're going to have to get over that. Mother Attracta is the reason we're here, and we need to know everything about her – warts and all. You were saying?'

Sister Bernadette looked chastened.

'Of course, of course. Well, we had a telly, but Mother Attracta got rid of it.'

'Why?' Laura asked.

'One night, a few months ago, she barged into the sitting room and started ranting and raving that someone had been in her office without permission. We hadn't a clue what she was on about. She said if whoever had been in her office didn't confess, there and then, there would be consequences. Obviously, nobody confessed because nobody had been in her office. I mean —' Sister Bernadette leaned forward conspiratorially— 'I think she was going a bit doolally these last few months. She seemed on edge, even snappier than normal.

'In any case, that night Mother Attracta blew out the candles as usual after we'd all gone to bed, then she hoisted the television from the sitting room into her office and locked it. *On her own.* She eventually sent it up to the old folks' home. We found out what had happened very quickly the next morning, because Sister Gladys used to watch this talk show every day. She went in with her cup of tea and the next thing we heard this shriek. We thought she was being murdered. Then we thought she was going to murder Mother Attracta.'

As soon as the words left her mouth, Sister Bernadette gasped and blessed herself.

'I'm sorry,' she said, hurriedly. 'I shouldn't have said that. Of course she wasn't going to actually murder her.'

Tom held his hand up to quieten her. 'It's just a turn of phrase.'

The woman in front of him exhaled. She sat back in her chair.

'Is this very formal, inspector?' Sister Bernadette asked,

inclining her head towards the tape recorder at the edge of the table.

'Not so formal that you have to be worried. We're recording the interviews in case we miss something, or need to come back to something that could be helpful.'

'Oh, of course,' she smiled.

'Or in case one of you confesses,' he said, with a small laugh.

The nun's jaw dropped.

'So, Sister, are you in this convent long?'

'I'm here just over five years,' she replied, after a few seconds had passed and she'd regained her composure.

'Have you only been a nun for five years?'

'No. I entered the novitiate when I was eighteen. I worked abroad. The order has always had missionary sisters.'

'Where did you serve, Sister?' Tom asked.

'Latin America. For over twenty-five years. Bolivia and Ecuador, but mostly El Salvador.'

'Really?' He sat back and absent-mindedly picked up a pen to tap on the table. 'You must have tales to tell. You were there in some troubled times, no doubt?'

'I could tell you stories that would make your hair stand on end. Stories of poverty and cruelty you can't even imagine. But I could also tell you of the wonderful people I met and all the good we did there.'

Sister Bernadette's face glowed as the pleasant memories resurfaced.

'It must have been strange returning to Limerick after such an experience, Sister. Why did you come back?'

She held her palms outstretched and shrugged.

'My family. I was abroad when my father died, and then my mother got cancer. She's passed now, God rest her, but I was here for her final few years.'

'Here, as in Limerick? Is this where you're from originally?'

'Yes. I asked specifically to be transferred here so I could be close to her. We grew up in the village just beyond this one.'

In different circumstances, Tom would have enjoyed hearing the nun recount her exploits in Latin America. The tumultuous political period she would have witnessed first-hand had always fascinated him, as it had many Irish people in the eighties.

He wondered, though, how a woman who had lived so independently and seen so much could have put up with the old-style authoritarianism of Mother Attracta.

'You must have been very restless to begin with when you returned?' Tom posed the question innocently.

'My mother was sick, as I said, and I spent a lot of time running back and forth to take care of her. After she died, well, yes, I found everything strangely routine. But I can't say I didn't find it challenging. The Lord tests us in different ways.'

'You felt tested here?'

She nodded.

'In what way?' Tom continued.

'I found the systematic nature of the convent difficult

to get used to. And Mother Attracta had her quirks. I couldn't quite see the point of them.'

'So you didn't get on with her?'

'No, I wouldn't go that far. I got on with her fine. I knew how to handle her. I just didn't like her.' She squirmed in her seat.

'I appreciate your candour,' Tom replied. 'You said Mother Attracta had been . . . acting differently in recent months?'

'Yes. There was that episode when she accused us of being in her office. I'm not sure I can point to another specific incident, but there was a general edginess about her.'

'Did you have any run-ins with her, or did you notice anyone else arguing with her?' Tom asked.

Sister Bernadette paused to think. 'Some of the other sisters might have.'

'Like who?'

Tom watched as the nun sucked in her cheeks and weighed up the loyalty she felt for the other nuns against the obligation to tell him what he needed to know.

She clearly came to the conclusion that he would probably find out from one of the other sisters.

'Herself and Sister Concepta had a huge row at Hallowe'en. The others will tell you, anyway. There were some other altercations, but nothing noteworthy that I can think of.'

Tom was surprised. Sister Concepta hadn't mentioned any recent rows with Mother Attracta.

'What was the row at Hallowe'en about?' he asked.

Sister Bernadette blushed. 'Mother Attracta had seen fit to discipline a sister for something trivial. Concepta confronted her, and there were fireworks. But you need to know, Mother Attracta could pick a fight with a wall, and there's not one of us who'd hurt a fly, especially Sister Concepta.'

Tom tapped his pen on the table. Some nuns were well capable of inflicting pain, if the Magdalene stories were to be believed.

'Did anything else happen out of the ordinary in the days immediately prior to Mother Attracta going missing?' he asked.

Sister Bernadette shook her head. 'Not that I recall, no.'

'What time did you go to bed the night she went missing?'

'Just after dinner. I had a headache and felt like I was coming down with something. Some of the sisters have had bad colds recently. I read for a few minutes and fell asleep with my book in my hand.'

'You heard nothing that night?' Tom asked.

'I might have heard the sounds of the other sisters going to bed. I know I woke up at one point when I dropped my book on to the floor.'

'And the next morning, Thursday morning, what happened?'

'The first thing I remember is being woken by a rapping on my door. They'd found the mess in the hall.'

'And when you'd all seen it, you decided to report it to Father Seamus?' Laura offered.

'Yes, Sister Clare rang him. She's a close friend of Mother Attracta.'

'Was it her idea?' Tom asked.

'No. Sister Gladys's.'

Tom looked puzzled. 'Sister Gladys is the nun who roared at me earlier?'

Bernadette smiled again. 'Yes. She says what she thinks, and her age incapacitates her. But her mind is sound.'

'And when the police didn't come, what did you think?' Tom asked.

'I was concerned. Everything indicated something bad had happened. Some of the sisters thought she might have cut herself and gone to get help, but that didn't add up. I started to get worried. It wasn't until yesterday evening, when we were listening to the news and heard the description of the woman who'd been found, that we put two and two together.'

'In the meantime, you cleaned up the hall,' Tom said.

Sister Bernadette looked down, shamefaced. She nodded.

'I'm sensing you didn't think that was a good idea, Sister,' Tom said.

'No, I didn't. But Concepta took a picture before we touched anything. She's clever like that. To be fair, it really was very distressing.'

'Whose idea was it to clean in the first place?' he asked.

The nun closed her eyes and furrowed her brow in thought. When she opened her eyes, she looked at the inspector blankly, honestly.

'I really don't know. All I can tell you is that Sister Gabrielle saw me in the chapel and told me the plan.'

'What did you do all day Thursday?'

'Let me see. I spent most of the day in bed. I felt quite weak. I read for a while but in the afternoon I slept. I fetched some soup from the kitchen later on.'

'Did you see other sisters that evening?'

'Oh, of course. Sister Gladys is in the kitchen most nights. There are generally a couple of us congregating there or in the sitting room at any given time.'

'Tell me, Sister,' he said. 'Do you drive?'

'Yes. I never would have managed abroad if I didn't. We covered great distances.'

'I saw some cars in the garden. Do they belong to the convent or individual nuns?'

'To the convent.'

'Did you know, Sister, when you came here, that the convent had been a Magdalene Laundry?'

Sister Bernadette hesitated before she answered. 'No, inspector. I didn't even know what a Magdalene Laundry was. I'd lived abroad from a young age.'

'Do you believe the things former inmates of the laundry are saying now?'

'Yes.' She nodded her head. 'I discovered very soon after I arrived what the convent had been and how it was run.'

Tom was surprised. She hadn't given them the line.

'And yet you stayed,' he said.

'Why wouldn't I?' She shrugged. 'Inspector, when I came home to Ireland it was for family reasons. By the time my mother died, I was settled. The Magdalene Laundries are history. Negative history. I never saw anything but good in the religious people I worked with abroad. What happened here in Ireland was inexcusable and can never happen again. But I'm sure you'll find it wasn't just the religious institutions that have something to answer for.

'I guarantee the Garda Síochána would not come out of any objective study of the Magdalene era covered in glory. Didn't they drag the girls back when they tried to escape? Why don't you leave the force because of that, Inspector?'

Tom sat back. She had a point. He suspected she had a good grasp of socio-political nuances and was well able to articulate them. This was a woman he could spend some time talking to. He dipped his head, acknowledging that she had won that bout.

Tom looked at Laura to see if she had any further questions.

She indicated she didn't with a faint shake of her head.

'That's all for now, Sister,' he said, pushing his chair back off the ground slightly with his feet.

'What do you think?' he asked Laura when she'd left.

'I think the reasons for topping the old dear are mounting,' the younger detective replied.

'Because she took the telly?' Tom teased, with a grin. 'Sorry, it's getting late. Do you think Sister Bernadette could be a suspect?'

'I don't know. Here's a woman who obviously became a

nun for very different reasons than Mother Attracta's. She comes home to nurse a sick mother and ends up being stuck under the authority of a woman who sounds more like the second coming of Bloody Mary Tudor than the Virgin Mary. And she has strong views on the laundries.'

Tom was mulling over the interview. He rubbed his tired eyes. There was something she'd said that he'd meant to return to.

He'd have to listen back to the tape.

CHAPTER 23

They discovered little of any value in the hours that followed.

At least half of those interviewed had been in the convent long enough to know it as a Magdalene Laundry. Virtually everybody said they had seen other sisters throughout Thursday, but none of the nuns could say if anyone had gone missing for any length of time.

No one had noticed a power cut the night before or heard anything out of the ordinary. Nobody remembered hearing a car engine outside the convent, leaving Tom to wonder how the killer had removed the victim. Nor could anyone say for sure who had been behind the decision to clean up the blood and glass in the hall.

They all agreed that Mother Attracta had been generally 'unsettled' in the last few months. It looked like she had good reason to be, Tom thought to himself.

The inspector found Sister Ita – a friend of Mother Attracta – a particularly unpleasant character. After stating that the laundry had been 'an asylum for penitents', the nun then launched into a character assassination of Sister Concepta, implying the woman wanted to be the new Reverend Mother and mightn't be afraid to kill to realize her ambition.

Their final interviewee was Sister Concepta herself.

'I appreciate it's been a long day, Sister – for you, especially.'

She smiled. 'I think you may be suffering a little more than me, Inspector. I'm very fond of my sisters, but sitting in a room at this hour of the night listening to them describe their daily routines one after the other, well . . .'

'All part of the job, I'm afraid.' He shrugged, as jovially as he could manage. 'There are just a few little things I need to clarify. You came up to us this morning on the bus, but the convent has cars. Don't you drive?'

She shook her head. 'Not to cities. I'm too nervous. But I can drive.'

'Couldn't someone else have driven you?'

'I didn't want to drag the others up.'

'Hmm. I asked you earlier if there had been anything out of the ordinary in recent weeks, any big rows. You never mentioned that you had a serious run-in with Mother Attracta at Hallowe'en.'

Sister Concepta looked at Tom blankly. Then she furrowed her brow as if trying to remember the incident to which he was referring.

It was an act. He could see her fists clenching in her lap.

'Oh, yes, I remember. We did have a disagreement but, to be honest, we were always arguing. I think because I am the youngest we clashed more often.'

'What was that row over?'

'Well, the laundry, as it happens. Sister Bernadette answered the phone one day to a journalist. He asked her opinion of the women who had gone to the papers with their stories. All Bernadette said was that she felt sympathy for them. Mother reacted like a crazy woman. She ordered Bernadette to pray for forgiveness and locked her in the chapel.'

Tom now realized what he'd forgotten to ask Sister Bernadette during her interview: which nun the Mother had been disciplining.

Why the hell hadn't Sister Bernadette told them that she herself had been at the heart of the fuss?

It was almost midnight. Somewhere a boiler was chugging away, struggling to send hot water through the building's creaky pipe system as the temperature outside dropped further.

'Why did you get involved?' Tom asked.

'I had to. Sister Bernadette was so distressed. She was screaming and banging on the door of the chapel. I felt sick listening to her.'

'A locked door for a grown woman seems unusual. Not pleasant, even. But wasn't that a disproportionate reaction?'

'It wasn't just the locked door.' Sister Concepta placed her elbows on the table edge and laced her fingers. 'Attracta turned off the lights.'

The inspector was puzzled. He was expecting something more sinister than 'Attracta turned off the lights'.

Then he remembered his conversation with Sister Gabrielle earlier.

'Sister Bernadette is afraid of the dark,' he said.

'Yes,' Sister Concepta replied, surprised he knew. 'She's afraid of the dark for good reason. Sister Bernadette had only recently arrived in El Salvador when the village she was staying in was raided by a pro-government militia. Most of the inhabitants were too terrified to leave their homes, but there were men and women there from the guerrilla movement. When the militia started burning the houses, with the people inside, the guerrillas went out to fight. They were hopelessly outnumbered, and were all slaughtered in the village square.

'Sister Bernadette was hiding in a roof space in one of the houses that wasn't set alight. She was in the pitch black and heard everything. The owner of the house wouldn't let her out because she was a nun, and the militia would have raped and murdered her.

'Our sister sleeps with a night light. When she talks about what happened, she says all she can remember is the darkness, the smell of burning and the screams of people being massacred. We all know that story. We all know she's afraid of the dark. For Mother Attracta to do that . . .' Her face screwed up in distaste.

Tom's expression mirrored hers.

'Sister, from what we've heard tonight, Mother Attracta had few friends in this convent.' He said this evenly. 'She seems to have been quite a malicious woman. Why did you put up with it? Didn't anybody resist?'

'Of course we did.' Sister Concepta raised her voice. 'Why do you think I confronted her when she did what she did to Bernadette? But look at it from our perspective. Mother Attracta, whether we liked it or not, was the head of our convent. We elect our heads democratically, but we don't stage coups and we don't have elections every couple of years. Convents like ours are changing – they have to change – but Mother Attracta was clinging to the old method of doing things, a method that was on its way out. She dug her heels in, but she was fighting a losing battle and she knew it. Sometimes we challenged her. Mostly, though, it was easier to try to ignore her. For a quiet life.'

Her voice was so lacking in conviction, Tom sensed that she would have fought Mother Attracta every day had it been left to her. The other nuns had obviously kept Concepta on the proverbial leash.

No wonder, with Attracta dead, she had become their de facto head. She had been their leader-in-waiting all along.

'Sister, have you thought any more about whether anybody was missing on Thursday for any length of time?' he asked.

She nodded. 'I've been thinking about it all day. Now you've seen the convent, you know how large it is. Throughout Thursday, we were in a tizzy. Some of the sisters spent a good deal of time in the chapel and others went out looking for Mother.'

Tom sighed. It would be easier to turn water into wine than to get these nuns to verify one another's whereabouts.

'One more thing. The decision to clean up the mess in the hall: who first suggested it?'

Sister Concepta pinched the top of her nose with her thumb and forefinger and closed her eyes in concentration. When she opened them, her mouth formed a ghost of a smile.

'I think I know why you're asking. But I have to tell you it's highly unlikely this is the breakthrough you're looking for. It was Sister Gladys.'

Tom did indeed find it difficult to imagine Sister Gladys in the role of a murderer. But he now had two things to consider.

Sister Gladys had also been the one who determined that Father Seamus be contacted, rather than the police, when they discovered that Mother Attracta was missing.

CHAPTER 24

The inspector shivered as he hung his suit in the wardrobe. The rattling wooden sash windows on the upper floors did little to retain the heat.

They'd agreed to meet at breakfast to go over the interviews. The nuns ate at 6.30 a.m., so he'd asked Sister Concepta if they could have the dining room at eight. He'd assured her they could serve themselves tea and toast. Father Seamus was due to say Mass for the nuns in the chapel at 9 a.m. and Tom would speak to the priest afterwards.

He dialled Louise's number on the off chance she was still awake.

She wasn't, but she still answered the phone, her voice sounding sexy and sleepy.

He imagined her cosy in their bed, her dark hair tousled on the pillow, her skin soft from her lavender night cream.

'Dragged yourself away from the party, huh?' she yawned.

Tom could hear her propping herself up on a pillow.

'It was getting pretty wild,' he said.

'Don't tell me anything,' she commanded. 'What happens in the convent . . .'

He laughed. 'Sorry for ringing so late. I got this crazy idea to do all the interviews tonight.'

'So you kept those poor detectives and all those nuns up with you. Shameful, Tom.'

He sighed.

'You sound exhausted,' she said.

'I am. How's Maria?'

'This is going to be a long six months if you're going to ask that several times a day, every day.'

'I'm going to worry.'

'Well, feel free to keep that to yourself. She's got enough to concern her without worrying that you're worrying. She's already convinced you'll be harassing the baby's father.'

He stayed quiet. Those very thoughts filled his head every time he remembered his daughter was pregnant.

'You're so predictable,' Louise said, reading his silence. 'What's happening there?'

'You've heard of the Magdalene Laundries?'

'Um, yes. You're not thinking of sending Maria to one?'

He blinked.

What a thought!

And yet that was exactly what had gone through many fathers' heads in the not so distant past.

'You know, I've been thinking about the Magdalenes for hours. And not once did I consider that, back in the day, Maria could have ended up in one of those places,' he said.

'Over my dead body. Have I fallen back asleep, Tom? You're making no sense. I thought you were joking.'

'This place, Louise. It used to be a laundry.'

He could hear her pulling herself up in the bed properly, more awake now.

'Is that woman's death some kind of revenge killing, Tom?'

'It has crossed my mind,' he replied. 'But to be honest, after tonight's interviews I sense she made enemies easily. I'm starting to wonder if there wasn't a gang of nuns in it together. What was that book? The one on the train where they all take turns to stab the victim ...'

'*Murder on the Orient Express*. Agatha Christie.'

'That's the one. Here we all are in a convent in the middle of nowhere, looking like we'll be snowed in, the murderer quite possibly among us. All we need now is for the lights to go out.'

'You're giving me goosebumps,' she said. Then, 'Are you okay? You sound a little traumatized.'

'Just tired.'

'Me, too.'

This time he could hear her sliding back down into the bed.

'What are you wearing?' he said, in his best seductive voice, which he suspected made him sound like a middle-aged pervert.

'My red check pyjama bottoms and your old red sweater.'

The thought of her sleeping in his sweater made him

love her more than if she'd said she was wearing a see-through negligee.

'Oh, I have some good news,' she said, suddenly. 'Well, I think it's good news. I expect you to as well.'

'I need some enforced good news,' he said.

'The dad is coming over for dinner. With his parents.'

'The chap who knocked Maria up?'

'Lovely, Tom. Things seem to be all right between the two of them.'

'What do you mean by all right? Is he going to marry her?'

'Jesus, there's you giving out about how medieval the laundries were. No, they're not a couple. But he's recovered from his jaw hitting the floor. If he's willing to come over with his parents it shows he's taking this seriously.'

'Dinner, though?'

'What's wrong with dinner?'

'You have to be polite for hours. Can't they just come over for a drink? I'll need a drink.'

'Nobody in this family will be drinking. It was alcohol that set these events in motion, from what I gather.'

'Like mother, like daughter.'

'Tom, if you were here I'd give you a smack in the chops for that remark.'

'There, I've given myself a mental slap for you. As I recall we were both intoxicated. But we were also newly married.'

'Yes ... well ... you may be right. I blame the drink for

that, too. His parents know who you are, and that you're busy right now, but I suggested over Christmas.'

'Anyway, you need to get some sleep. I love you.'

'I love you, too.'

He would have been happy to sleep with the phone to his ear, just listening to her breathing. Instead, he waited for the click.

He was taking one last look out the window when he spotted a light in one of the nuns' rooms in the adjacent wing. Just as he noticed it, he saw that someone was standing at the window looking out. No, they weren't looking out. They were looking over at his window. After a moment, the curtains were pulled.

He counted the windows. It was the fifth room.

A cold feeling settled in his stomach. He wasn't easily spooked – but it was late, and this place unnerved him. And he still had the image of Mother Attracta crucified to the tree, fresh in his mind.

There was a rudimentary bolt just over his door handle. As soon as he came back from the bathroom, he used it. All the detectives had brought their firearms down with them – his was a Walther P99c. Tom had never had to fire it, or the Smith & Wesson he had been issued previously, and he wasn't sure if having a gun made him more comfortable or less.

The Garda Síochána was typically an unarmed force, but guns had become more of a feature in Ireland in the last decade and most detective units were issued with sidearms. The pistol was in the drawer now, left slightly ajar so he could reach it in a hurry, if he needed to.

Absurd as it might seem to be worried about being attacked by a nun, there was no escaping the fact that a woman had been kidnapped from this house a couple of days ago and brutally murdered.

He settled into a restless slumber, filled with disturbing dreams of long corridors and locked doors.

And all the while, the feeling that somebody was watching him.

Day Three

Sunday, 12 December

CHAPTER 25

Ray was the first officer to wake the following morning. He emerged from a deep sleep, sweating and disturbed. He'd had a strangely erotic dream about Ellie Byrne, but halfway through she'd been wearing a nun's habit. Then, just as they were about to get serious, her face had contorted into mad old Sister Gladys.

He tried to shake the image from his head. He needed a scalding hot shower and a loofah.

In the next room, Michael was rousing from his most peaceful sleep in months. As he came to, it slowly dawned on him that he'd slept well because he didn't have to be conscious of someone else in the bed. Someone who was so fragile she might break if he touched her.

As soon as the thought articulated itself, he was racked with guilt. It was as if thinking it gave birth to an idea – that this is how he would sleep all the time if Anne and he weren't together. How could he think that about his beautiful wife? How could he imagine being separated from her when she had done nothing wrong and needed him?

He put the back of his arm over his eyes to dry the tears that sprang so easily these days.

He would phone her today. He'd tell her how much he missed her after just one day. He didn't know what he could say to make things right, but he couldn't even consider the alternative. If she missed him too they could start with that.

Meanwhile, untroubled by fantasy or reality, Willie turned over on his back contentedly and resumed his enthusiastic snoring.

Next door, the not-so-gentle rumbles of his driver infiltrated Tom's dreams. He fought opening his eyes and, pulling the covers over his head, tried to find sleep again.

In the room furthest from Tom's, and on the other side of Ray, Laura lay still, staring at the side of the chest of drawers and wondering where she was.

When she realized, she turned and looked at the wall. On the other side, the man she'd been fantasizing about for months was sleeping. She didn't know if his bed was the other side of the partition or on the far side of the room.

She placed a hand on the wall. The thought that he might be lying inches away turned her stomach to butterflies. She heard a movement which, unknown to her, was Ray getting up. Her hand automatically flew back and her heart thumped. What was she like! She knew teenagers less lovesick than she was. She pulled the blankets over her head and groaned.

A beep on her phone alerted her to a text message. It was Bridget checking in. Laura unlocked her home screen.

How's it going there? Frustratingly slow here. Wish I'd gone down. Up since dawn checking out apartments. Settled in for the New Year, maybe?

Laura smiled. Then the memory of what she'd found out about her aunt yesterday flooded her consciousness. She sat up straight in the bed. She was still holding the phone, squeezing it so tight it hurt her hand.

She wished Bridget had come down in her place. Then she felt guilty. Bridget was adopted. The other detective had talked about looking for her birth mother. Considering how much they'd learned in the last twenty-four hours, she wasn't sure it would be any healthier for Bridget to be in a place like this. Being here could send anybody with questions about an adoptive background into a tailspin.

Willie's discordant trumpeting finally proved too much for Tom. He opened his eyes blearily. Grabbing his phone, he hit the flash display for the time. 7.29 a.m. God Almighty!

Willie's snoring stopped abruptly as his alarm launched into a full-scale symphony of noise.

Tom sighed. There was no delaying the day. A shower would wake him.

He emerged from his room to find that Ray and Michael had nabbed the two bathrooms first.

As Tom waited on the landing by the banisters, Laura's door opened.

'Did you sleep well, sir?' she asked, clutching a large towel and a flannel bag.

'I'd have slept better if I wasn't in a room beside Puff the Magic Dragon,' he replied grumpily, then wondered if Puff was known for his snoring at all, or where he'd got the saying from.

As they stood there, Willie emerged, yawning and fully dressed.

'Did you sleep in those clothes?' Tom asked.

Willie looked at him, puzzled. 'No. Did you sleep in your clothes?'

Tom looked down at his pyjama bottoms and fleece. 'Clearly not. I thought I might grab a shower before I got dressed, that's all.'

'Is that why you two are standing here?' Willie asked. 'Did ye not wash yourselves yesterday?'

'This is how he behaves when he gets more than thirty miles away from the wife,' Tom said to Laura. 'Personal hygiene out the window, smoking like a trooper. He probably has a flask of whiskey in his room and a Nintendo.'

Laura wasn't listening. An Adonis had just materialized and was walking towards them.

The two men turned to see Ray coming down the hall from the bathroom with only a towel around his waist, his chest glistening.

'Jesus, Ray, you do know these nuns aren't used to

seeing any men in this house, let alone half-naked ones?' Tom said. 'Are you trying to drive them to distraction?'

'Well, I wasn't expecting a welcoming committee when I got out of the shower,' he retorted, as he closed his door firmly behind him.

'Ladies first.' Tom stood back to let a wide-eyed Laura past him to the now vacant bathroom.

When she'd left, Willie turned to Tom.

'You see that?' he said, meaning Laura's reaction.

'I saw it.'

'Ray didn't, though.' Willie smiled.

'Ray's an idiot.' Tom shook his head.

'Well, I just need to empty the old bladder, so I'm going to pop in here before you, if that's okay?' Willie nodded towards the bathroom at the other end of the hall, which Michael had just left.

'Just be sure that's all you're emptying. I want to enjoy this shower, and I can't do that if I'm holding my breath.'

Willie chuckled.

By the time Tom joined the others in the dining hall, his brain was functioning. He'd found the shower old-fashioned – a hose attached to the taps and run up the wall – but the water pressure was good and the temperature hot. It had done the job.

The nuns had left out a cold spread. Just before Mass they had turned on the modern coffee machine in the kitchen, and it was now emitting a wonderful aroma.

Tom helped himself to a cup, while taking in the impressive array of pastries, breads, jams and cereals.

He helped himself to a bowl of granola, spooning yoghurt into the mixture of grains and berries. Willie, eagerly piling his plate with Danish pastries and croissants, looked at him aghast.

'I'm just hazarding a guess we will eat again today,' Tom said, eyeing Willie's plate.

'Fail to prepare, prepare to fail,' Willie threw back.

'Give us the highlights of your interviews last night, Ray,' Tom said, as he took a seat.

'Well, to start with, I think this woman is lucky she wasn't killed until now. I know you told us to be careful not to make rash judgements, but after our interviews last night it's clear she had no shortage of enemies. That mad nun who roared at you last night – Gladys? Well, she actually said, and I quote: "If I'd known someone was going to smash her head in, I'd have held her still." '

Laura almost choked on a mouthful of brioche.

'She was the most forthright of the lot,' Ray continued, 'but she wasn't the one who disliked her the most.'

'Who was that?' Tom asked.

'Sister Clare. It's strange – she described herself as a good friend of Attracta, but the animosity was coming off her in waves.'

Michael nodded in agreement. 'Turns out she was in line to succeed the last Reverend Mother, and Attracta managed to somehow overtake her.'

'That is interesting,' Tom said.

'Why would she pretend to like her?' Laura asked.

'Keep your friends close and your enemies closer,' Michael answered.

'Nearly three hours of interviewing bloody nuns, and all we've established is that Attracta was an old bag,' Ray moaned. 'Should we seriously consider the nuns as suspects?'

Tom half smiled. 'Not prime suspects, but they did know her better than anyone, so we can't rule them out. I'd like to know more about this Sister Clare. Several decades – that's a long time to stew. Then there's Bernadette leaving out her role in the Hallowe'en row. But we need to look at the villagers and dig more into Attracta's past.' He sighed. 'We don't have much. Hopefully, forensics get here quick and find something.'

'Or the priest admits to it,' Michael suggested.

'Or another nun gets murdered,' Laura said.

They all turned to look at her.

'What?' she said innocently. 'You know as well as I do that, in a situation like this, if the killer strikes again there'll be a better chance of more evidence.'

'Yes,' Ray replied. 'Let's hope for a serial killer. That will solve all our problems.'

Laura flinched at his sarcasm.

'She's right,' Tom said. 'And, I'm a little concerned she could be prophetic too. This place is all honey on top and vinegar beneath.'

'But still, a nun wouldn't commit murder, surely?' Ray repeated.

'There was a laundry in Dublin.' Willie put his pastry down.

It was this simple act of abandoning food that made the others realize he was about to say something serious. It was almost funny.

'Rossa Abbey,' he continued. 'When the nuns sold the land for housing, the developers were excavating and found the remains of one hundred people in unmarked graves. Only sixty of them had death certificates recorded. There was even a body with missing limbs. Most had been cremated, leaving no way of discovering the causes of their deaths.

'Maybe they were all natural deaths, but still – to bury remains in an unmarked grave . . . that takes some coldness. Religious garb doesn't mean being free from sin.'

'This happened in Ireland?' Laura asked, her voice full of disbelief.

Willie nodded solemnly. 'In 1990.'

'I can just about imagine one of the nuns here snapping and lashing out at Attracta,' Tom said, shaking his head. 'Maybe killing her accidentally. I don't understand the theatrics, though – the inscription and the crucifixion.'

'Unless the killer was trying to make her look like a religious martyr,' Ray offered.

Tom turned to look at him. His deputy had articulated the germ of an idea that was floating around his own consciousness.

Willie had resumed eating and was now on his third croissant. Where did he put it? Tom wondered. The man was as thin as a rake, and the only exercise he seemed to take was moving his feet between car pedals.

'Willie, could I force you into some detective work?' he asked. 'Will you check to see if the electricity was cut off on Wednesday night?'

The older man nodded, just as the door opened and Sister Concepta looked in.

'There you are, Inspector . . . officers. I hope breakfast was satisfactory. Did you sleep well?'

'Breakfast was delicious,' Tom said. 'There was no need to make a fuss for us.'

She shook her head. 'Not at all. Father Seamus is almost ready to meet you. I've told him you'll see him in the main sitting room, if that's all right?'

'That's perfect, Sister. I wanted to ask you if we could have the keys for the rooms, to go over the convent more thoroughly.'

The Sister nodded and reached into her pocket. She was wearing her full habit today.

'You can have mine,' she said. 'I trust you. I'm leaving most of the doors open, anyway. To aid your investigation. It's silly to have them locked all the time.'

Another Mother Attracta rule had just bitten the dust, thought Tom.

CHAPTER 26

Michael perched awkwardly on the edge of one of the sitting-room couches. His pose reminded Tom of a teen-age boy on a forced visit to an elderly relative's house.

The door opened, and Willie popped his head in.

'Just spoke to a mate in the Electricity Supply Board. He did a quick check for me, said he couldn't see anything off the grid on Wednesday night in this area.'

'Thanks for that, Willie.'

The other man nodded in acknowledgement and closed the door.

'I'm starting to wonder if someone turned off that light switch,' Tom said.

They could discuss his theory no further, though, because at that moment Father Seamus entered the room. The inspector stood to shake the hand offered regally by the priest.

Father Seamus was in his early seventies. The sparse tufts of hair dotting his head were a dirty grey. Thin-framed glasses rested on the tip of his skinny, hooked nose; the tilt of his head as he looked through them added to a general air of superiority, while also giving him an unfortunate mole-like quality. He was dressed simply, in a dark pullover with a light grey shirt and black trousers. The clothes hung lankly on his thin frame.

'Inspector,' he said, in a nasal tone.

His grip was bony, but strong. It was strong enough, Tom mused, to wield a weapon.

Father Seamus settled imperiously into one of the armchairs beside the fireplace.

Tom seated himself in the second armchair, crossed his legs and steepled his hands, resting his chin on the tips of his fingers.

He said nothing. First impressions counted, and he hadn't been won over by Father Seamus.

The priest shifted in his chair. After another moment, uncomfortable with the silence, he spoke.

'So, Inspector, you asked to see me? I am quite busy today. I've to be at the church for eleven.'

'I suppose we're all busy today, Father,' Tom replied. 'You've to say Mass, and we have to solve a murder. But thank you for taking the time to see us.'

The priest studied him. He was unused to anything less than fawning respect. At least to his face. He evaluated Tom and changed tack.

'I'm happy to help however I can, Inspector. Unfortunately, I don't have the assistance of another priest at the moment. I did have a younger man, Father Terence, but he's been away for the last six months covering another parish. I'm hoping he can return soon. If I don't say Mass, no one will.'

He bared yellow teeth in a smile that looked more like a grimace.

'I understand, Father Seamus,' Tom replied. 'I imagine as the only priest in the parish you're under a lot of pressure at the moment, which might explain why, after the sisters here reported to you that Mother Attracta was missing, you didn't convey that message to the police.'

'Ah,' the priest said. 'I suspected you might be wondering about that. It's straightforward, really. You see, they left me a voice message.'

'A voice message?' Michael parroted.

The priest nodded emphatically. 'Yes. If I had actually spoken to one of them, of course I would have contacted the local gardaí and told them Mother Attracta was missing. But instead I got this garbled message on my home phone about smashed glass in the hall and Mother Attracta not being there.

'Well, you know what women can be like when they get carried away . . .' He gave Tom a knowing look. 'And in any event, I didn't even get the voice message until Friday.'

Tom uncrossed his legs and sat forward.

'Let me get this straight, Father,' he said. 'Are you telling me that none of the sisters spoke to you directly on Thursday?'

The priest nodded.

'Who left the message?'

'Sister Clare.'

'And why didn't you hear it until Friday?'

The priest shrugged. 'I didn't check the phone. Thursday was a busy day for me. I wasn't in the house much. It wasn't until Friday, when I picked up the landline to dial a number, that I found out I had a message.'

'Don't you have a mobile phone?' Michael asked.

'Yes. But she didn't ring that.'

'So,' Tom said. 'You got the message on Friday. But by Saturday you still hadn't contacted the police. Why not?'

Father Seamus shifted in his chair, before removing his glasses and cleaning them with the end of his pullover.

'Now that we know what happened to poor Attracta, clearly I should have informed Sergeant McKenna,' he conceded. 'But I really didn't understand the import of the message when I heard it. I had a lot on my mind this week, and I thought it was something or nothing. I can only offer my sincerest apologies.'

The line was utterly rehearsed.

'What were you doing on Thursday?' Tom asked.

The priest raised the tips of his fingers to his temples and affected a look of deep concentration.

Michael and Tom exchanged a sceptical glance. It was only three days ago.

'A lot of overdue errands, really,' Father Seamus responded, eventually. 'I took a walk through the village at one point to call in on some parishioners. That can take some time. They like you to stop and chat. I did some work in the church because my cleaner, Mrs Guckian, has a twisted ankle. I followed up on some correspondence, and I took a trip in the car. I wanted to visit Father Terence, to see if he'd be returning.'

Tom fidgeted impatiently in his seat. His and the priest's definition of busy varied wildly.

'I'm afraid, Father, we're going to need you to be more specific. I need to know the times you took these excursions. And can you remember where you were on Wednesday evening?'

The look the cleric gave Tom was a sight to behold. His face turned purple, and he swallowed several times.

'What are you implying?' he blustered, his tone rising. 'Are you accusing *me* of something? Do you understand that I have known Mother Attracta for over forty years? This is ludicrous. I hope to goodness you haven't being asking the sisters to account for their movements. You do realize we are servants of God!'

Tom sat back and let the priest vent. The man was a beat off apoplectic. It had taken only the merest poke to infuriate him. While Father Seamus ranted, Tom focused on a vein that pulsated on the side of the man's forehead.

After more indignant protestations, the priest belatedly sensed that the man opposite him was unmoved by his outpouring. His voice trailed off and he stared at Tom, clearly deliberating whether it was worth storming out and what the ramifications of such a move would be.

'You should calm yourself, Father,' Tom said, softly. 'We are asking everyone who knew and lived with Mother

Attracta to detail their whereabouts on Wednesday and Thursday. It's standard procedure in a murder investigation.'

The priest swallowed, and the livid purple in his face started to recede. Seeing that his overreaction had not achieved the desired effect, he straightened the knees of his trousers and had the good sense to look shamefaced before he started backtracking.

'I apologize. I'm not myself since getting the terrible news. Could I have some time to recall the exact details of my movements during the week? I'm getting old; the brain doesn't work as well as it used to.'

'Please. Take some time. I would rather you remember correctly than unwittingly give us inaccurate information. Michael here will call to the village later and collect your statement from you.'

The priest nodded. Tom noted him surreptitiously checking his watch.

'We won't keep you much longer,' he said.

The priest looked up. 'You miss nothing.'

'Not much. In recent weeks, months even, had you noticed any incidents in the convent or village that gave cause for concern?'

'Nothing. We have a peaceful community here, Inspector. Nobody from Kilcross would ever commit such a terrible crime. Is it not more probable that some passing deranged soul committed this heinous act?'

'Anything is possible. But I wouldn't be doing my job if

I didn't rule out the people in closest proximity to the victim. Even if she was left in Dublin.'

It was only minor, barely perceptible, but something flashed across the priest's face when Tom mentioned Dublin. The inspector waited to see if the priest was about to offer anything.

When he didn't, Tom moved on.

'You say you knew Mother Attracta for forty years. Did you have a good relationship?' he asked.

'I had the utmost respect for Attracta, and she for me. She was a woman of exacting standards. She knew her place in the world and the place of those around her. A very Christian woman.'

'As part of our inquiries, Father, it has come to our attention that this convent housed a Magdalene Laundry. There is much being said about those laundries to imply they were not run in a very Christian manner. Would you contest that?'

The priest sniffed. 'I will contest any vicious untruth that is spread about my parish until the day I die. There's a modern element in society and, yes, even in the Church, that is trying to revise history. Of course, it's important that we in the Church listen to the people who claim they were unhappy in religious-run institutions. There are always two sides.

'But I saw how the Magdalene Laundry here was administered. The sisters took care of those poor souls when the rest of the world shunned them. They took in wayward girls and unwanted girls and shared the word of the Lord with them, helped them find the right path in life.' The priest shook his head. 'This violence these . . . people . . . speak of, it's out of context. You're not that old, Inspector, but you're also not so young that you don't remember a world where it was acceptable to smack a naughty child, to discipline with a hand when a word would not suffice.'

'You seem quite defensive,' Tom said, quietly.

Inwardly, he was simmering. The reports into the abuse of children in industrial schools revealed cruelty far in excess of harmless smacks. Broken bones, scaldings, starvation and manslaughter . . . Tom wondered if the priest would describe that violence as 'out of context'.

The same accusations were now being levelled against the Magdalene Laundries.

'One can appear that way when one is being unjustly accused,' the priest replied, tartly. 'The laundries were set up to help pay for the nuns' charity, and also so the girls would have good, honest work. The Devil makes use of idle hands. And the work was symbolic – in washing the dirty linen, the women were washing away their sins.'

'The women who were in these institutions seem to have other recollections.'

The priest gave the inspector a withering look.

'It's amazing what people will say when they think there's money on the cards, Inspector. Many of those women were deranged when they went in and, no matter what the nuns tried, they were mad coming out as well.

They had sinned and been rightly ostracized by their families and communities. Truly repentant people accept their guilt and try to live the rest of their life with dignity. They don't go shouting to the gutter press—'

Tom held up his hand and signalled for him to stop. The priest reacted as though he'd been slapped. He was used to preaching from the pulpit. He wasn't accustomed to being silenced.

The inspector was done with this odious man and his pious claptrap. Something told him that if he'd met Mother Attracta alive, the conversation would have gone pretty much like this.

What did that mean for Father Seamus as a suspect? The priest considered the victim a friend, and they were obviously alike. Had their mutual hateful personalities made them allies or enemies?

The man's demeanour made Tom certain he was hiding something, but what?

'I will let you get to your next Mass, Father,' he said, and stood up.

The priest looked surprised, then grateful. He stood up, too – though he was slower getting to his feet.

'Thank you, Inspector. I wish you every success in your investigation.'

As though his part in it were over.

CHAPTER 27

When Father Seamus had left, a small laugh escaped Michael's lips, releasing the tension that had built up during the interview.

'He's a piece of work,' he said.

Tom stared at the closed door. 'Did you see that look, Michael, when I mentioned Dublin?'

The other detective paused and considered. 'Yes, I did. It felt like he wasn't telling us something.'

Tom nodded grimly. 'I think that, too. When you get his alibi details, check them thoroughly.'

'He lives alone,' Michael said. 'The woman who cleans the church probably did his house, too. He could have been gone all Wednesday night and nobody would have noticed. And if he had taken Mother Attracta, he could have brought her back to his house. He'd know the routines here, be able to get into the convent. I'm sure Mother Attracta would have been more comfortable turning her back on somebody she knew – that's how she could have been hit from behind, when she came out of the corridor.'

Tom nodded again. 'But does he have motive? In any case, he has something to hide.'

'He's not too old, is he?'

Tom shrugged. 'Early seventies? He's slight of frame but he's able-bodied, and his handshake was firm. And the victim was an elderly woman.'

They watched from the window as the priest got into his car, reversed over the deepening snow and turned out the gates.

Seconds later, a white jeep, embossed with a Garda Síochána logo, drove in.

'I hope this is Ellie and Mark,' Tom said.

They arrived in the hall just in time to see Sister Mary open the front door. She must have been passing through right at that moment, because her girth indicated that she rarely moved anywhere at speed.

'Come in, come in,' she greeted the new guests. 'My goodness, what an awful day. Are the roads bad?'

'Not the worst,' Ellie Byrne replied.

A red-haired man followed her in.

On cue, Ray and Laura emerged from the doorway across the hall. Ray's face lit up. Laura, catching sight of this, looked crestfallen.

Tom felt sorry for the young female detective. She didn't stand a chance against this black-haired beauty. Laura was a good-looking woman, but Ellie was stunning. And Ray was smitten.

C'est la vie.

'Good morning,' Ellie smiled.

'Ellie, thanks for coming.' Tom shook her extended hand. 'I was expecting Mark as well?'

Ellie shook her head. 'No luck, I'm afraid. We're too stretched. I do have a very enthusiastic helper, though. Sorry, have you met? This is Jack Doherty, another of our technicians.' She indicated the man beside her.

Jack nodded at Tom, sullenly. He looked to be in his thirties but with his shaggy beard and lined face, he could pass for older. Tom suspected the man was none too happy to be dragged down to the middle of nowhere in the freezing cold on the brink of the Christmas holiday.

Ellie caught sight of the cordoned area to her left.

'Is there something behind that door?' she asked.

Tom cocked his head. 'Something and nothing. We believe the victim was attacked at that spot.'

Ellie's eyes widened. She'd cottoned on. 'The nuns cleaned up?'

Tom nodded.

Ray nodded.

Michael nodded.

Laura just glared.

She'd have to learn to stop broadcasting her emotions, Tom thought.

'Divisional crime scene technicians came in yesterday and secured as much as they could,' Ray said.

'Right,' Ellie said, with a bemused smile. 'Hopefully the good Sisters didn't use too much bleach, but there's a reason our hospitals were cleaner when the nuns were in charge.'

'Do your best,' Tom said. 'Let's get you both a cup of tea, and then you can begin. I want you to have a look in the vehicles out front as well. Specifically the car boots.'

'We'd better get started, so,' Ellie said. 'That's a day's work.'

'A full day, I'd imagine,' Tom said. 'I doubt you'll get home tonight. We can arrange rooms for you here . . . there are plenty.'

'That's okay,' Ellie smiled. 'We had a notion we'd not get home. I'm booked into the B&B in the village. Jack's from Limerick originally and has family a few miles north.'

Just then, Sister Concepta arrived in the hall and polite introductions were made.

The nun turned to Laura and said, quietly, 'I wondered if you'd like to help me look for that file you wanted? It's been playing on my mind, and I've time to spare before we head to the village.'

Laura cast Tom a pleading look.

What could he do but nod?

'Just don't take too long. And while you're there, get a feel for the number of women who were in the laundry.'

Tom gave Ellie final instructions and went with Ray and Michael to Mother Attracta's office.

The room was decorated far more opulently than anything they'd seen so far. The desk was large and ornate, with a comfortable and expensive-looking leather chair behind it. The other furniture looked equally tasteful and of antique value. Bookshelves covered the walls.

The Apple Mac that sat on the desk was incongruous amid the old-fashioned, library-style setting.

'Can we get that picture on Sister Concepta's phone uploaded on to that?' Tom asked, pointing to the computer.

'Already done,' Ray said. 'She did it for us while you were with the priest. Anything of use from him?'

'He's not telling us everything,' Tom answered.

Ray looked thoughtful. 'Right . . . well, there's nothing of any import in this room. We checked the safe, just money and chequebooks. There's nothing missing and, according to Sister Concepta, nothing has been moved.'

The inspector walked behind the desk. He touched one of the keys, and the photo filled the screen.

Tom studied every detail, hoping something would jump out at him. It wasn't great quality, but in the bigger picture he could see the vivid red of the sprayed blood, and the smashed glass on the table and floor. As he examined the image, it occurred to him that none of the sisters had said they heard glass smashing the night the nun was taken.

He absent-mindedly pulled out the chair and sat down, still staring at the photo.

Mother Attracta had hit the vase with her hand. That would explain the glass shards Emmet had found in her skin. The heavy vessel must have smashed against the wall. He closed his eyes and imagined the nun holding her hand up to the light switch and then bringing it down, hitting the side of the vase. It smashes against the wall. The plaster and water muffle the sound of the glass, but shards fly everywhere.

Opening his eyes, he pored over the photo again.

Mother Attracta's hand had been cut. But had the glass hit her killer? Had he or she raised a hand to protect face and body?

Tom sat back.

'Michael,' he said. 'Tell Ellie to look for two types of blood. I think the glass from the vase may have hit Attracta's attacker.'

Michael headed out.

'The light in the corridor was turned off on purpose, Ray.'

'What do you mean?'

'The killer turned it off when Attracta was in the corridor. She picked up the candle to guide her back to the door. The fuse had already blown a couple of times, so she knew what to do.'

Tom closed his eyes again, imagining the scene.

'When she came out of the door, she turned and placed the candle on the table. She lifted her hand to the switch – because you switch off a light before you replace a bulb or fuse. That's when she was knocked out.'

He opened his eyes. Ray was staring at him.

'But wouldn't she have turned the light off, anyway?'

'No, Sister Concepta said they left it on at night.'

'So, you think the killer tripped the fuse previously to see how she'd react?'

'Exactly. Everything about this murder was planned with careful precision. There was nothing random about it.'

CHAPTER 28

Laura watched as Sister Concepta gingerly pulled out boxes from tall stacks.

It was like witnessing a giant game of Jenga.

'You're sure it was around 1964?' the nun asked, opening first one box, then another, shaking her head when she failed to find what she was looking for.

'Or 1963. Isn't there some kind of system?' Laura was perched on a couple of boxes in the absence of a seat. There were so many files. How could they ever establish how many women had been through the laundry?

She felt entirely unprofessional. Here she was investigating her own family history while her colleagues were focused on finding Mother Attracta's killer. She couldn't shake the feeling, though, that she had found out about Peggy for a reason. It couldn't just be coincidence, she reasoned.

Sister Concepta tucked a stray hair back under her headdress.

'This is the system,' she replied. 'These rooms are the only ones in the house that Mother Attracta left alone. All these folders used to be kept in filing cabinets.'

Concepta shrugged. 'I suppose at some point it was decided they were historical documents, and they were boxed up and left to gather dust.'

They had turned on the light to illuminate the windowless room. On the wall, a bricked-up alcove stood where once there had been an opening to the glass corridor and garden beyond.

'Why did you fill in the window?' Laura asked, puzzled. 'It seems so strange – to block out the natural light.'

Sister Concepta stopped what she was doing and stood up straight, placing her hands on her hips and stretching her back.

'I really don't know what was going on in Mother Attracta's head. I think she considered knocking down this wall completely, and enlarging the rooms out to the front, when we stopped using the corridor as a conservatory. We didn't have the money to do it. But she wasn't happy with the windows remaining, and had them bricked up.'

'When did she have all this done?'

'It was just after I came here. To be honest, I got the sense she just didn't like the windows. I know ... it sounds peculiar.'

'What issue could she possibly have with windows?'

'I can't explain it. Maybe she saw something through one of them? Ridiculous, huh?'

'Maybe she just didn't like her reflection, and you've a vivid imagination,' Laura said.

Sister Concepta smiled and resumed her search.

The detective shifted uncomfortably and got up off the hard boxes she had been sitting on. 'May I?' she asked Concepta, indicating the top box with her hands primed to open it.

The nun nodded distractedly.

The first folder Laura took out was dated February 1975 and was the file of a woman named Sheila O'Neill.

Laura scanned through the details. Sheila had been seventeen when she entered the laundry for a period of 'reflection and prayer', after having a baby out of wedlock. She had been given the house name 'Bridget'. When Laura read the name she felt a lump form in her throat, thinking of her own friend back in Dublin.

Someone had written in pen, in long sloping handwriting, that 'Bridget' had:

> . . . kicked and screamed, even biting one of the sisters who restrained her, and threatened more violence and to run away. It was explained to her that as her father had brought her to the house there was nowhere for her to run away to. In the words of her own kin, nobody has room for a slut like her.

The detective's stomach tensed as she read the offensive word. She imagined Sheila, frightened, abandoned, pining for her baby, and being told nobody wanted her any more.

She flicked through the next few pages and saw a litany of punishments recorded in ledger style as 'Bridget' adjusted to her stay. In the middle of the file, in different handwriting this time, someone had written:

> Despite being here for six months now with no word from her mother or father, Bridget still asks daily when she will be allowed to go home. It has been explained repeatedly to Bridget that this is not a prison but somewhere she can earn the forgiveness of her family for the grave sin she inflicted on them. The girl's repetitive questions can only stem from some kind of mental handicap.

Towards the end of the file, Laura noted a decline in punishments. She had almost reached the end, dated 1977, thinking that maybe Sheila had adapted to her circumstances. But the final page filled her with joy. In March 1977, Sheila had escaped from the laundry. A note said her family were contacted but hadn't heard from her.

The detective hoped that life had worked out well for the young woman. Sheila must have realized that the best way to break free was to keep her head down and then seize whatever chance made itself available to her.

Laura replaced the file. Her hand was on the next one, ready to take it out, when she hesitated. They wouldn't all have happy endings.

She was flicking idly through the remaining files when something caught her attention. The bottom of the box was white, not brown cardboard, as she would have expected. She reached in and pulled out a photograph. On the back, a list of names was written along with the date: 1976. A group of about thirty women of all ages was pictured standing outside the front door of the convent. There was the large oak front door. Adjoining the outer wall of the room in which she now stood was the glass corridor, filled with large palm plants and other greenery.

Two nuns stood in the middle of the group, and another at either end. The photo was colour but it had faded, and the individuals in it looked drained. The girls' grey smocks looked dreary, and most of them wore their hair short and clipped to the side. Some of them were smiling, but most stared at the camera without expression.

Laura brought the picture closer and studied the nuns.

Even though it was thirty-four years old, she thought she could identify Mother Attracta standing on the edge of the group. She was younger and her figure was rounder, but she had the same harsh features with which she had aged. Her thin-lipped smile was broad. There was nothing forced about it, but it didn't make her look any more pleasant.

Laura was examining the other nuns when Sister Concepta exclaimed, 'I think this could be the box.'

For just an instant, Laura had felt a flicker of recognition at something in the photo. She stared at the picture, casting her eyes up and down the windows behind the group, trying to see what had jumped out at her. She didn't know what had aroused her subconscious, however, and the appeal of the nun's find won her attention.

'This is from the second half of 1964,' Sister Concepta said, lifting a file from the box.

Laura replaced the photo and walked over. Her stomach felt queasy with anticipation.

'You said her name was Peggy Deasy, didn't you? Would it have been Margaret, and she was Peggy for short?'

Laura nodded uncertainly. 'Yes, I suppose it could have been.'

'Margaret Deasy, September 1964,' Sister Concepta said. 'There's nothing else here close to that name, but the address should confirm if this is your aunt.'

The atmosphere was electric as Laura held out her hand for the file.

Tom and Ray were examining the wing that housed the nuns' bedrooms. In the empty corridor that ran along the length of the cell-like bedrooms, the inspector knocked on, then opened, the door of the fifth room – he had counted the windows last night.

Ray waited silently in the hall, as Tom stepped inside.

The room was minimalist but not entirely bare. On the chest of drawers beside the bed stood a photo of a man and a woman on either side of a young Sister Bernadette.

A brief glance around the room was sufficient.

'What was that about?' Ray asked, when they had moved on.

'I saw someone standing in that window last night looking over at our wing.'

'And whose room is it?' Ray asked.

'Sister Bernadette's.'

Ray whistled. 'I slept with my door locked last night. Never thought I'd be spooked by a bunch of nuns.'

Tom smiled. 'Me, too.'

They walked further down the hall, their shoes echoing on the hard wood.

'Why would she have been looking over?' Ray asked.

'Nosiness? Guilt? Planning her next kill?'

Mother Attracta's bedroom was next.

Tom and Ray turned over every inch of the spartan room. Like her office, it revealed nothing of any interest.

There were few personal items. No family pictures. Her wardrobe consisted of grey, blue, black and brown skirts – some tweed, some pleated, some plaid – with blouses of varying bland colours and cardigans. Three full habits hung on the rail, at a slight remove from the other clothes. It was a depressingly minimalist collection for a lifetime.

'What has made you suspicious of the priest?' Ray asked, as he flipped through the nun's bedside Bible.

'I can't put my finger on it. He's hiding something, I'm sure of it. He said they were friends, but given what we've learned about Mother Attracta, I can't help but wonder if she was capable of blackmailing him over something she'd discovered.'

Ray looked around the tiny room and sighed. 'It's dismal, isn't it? These bedrooms – they're like cells.'

Tom stood still.

If he'd been a larger man, he could almost have reached both sides of the room with his arms outstretched. And yet . . .

'Compared to the dormitories, I suppose these rooms were five star,' he replied.

Ray raised one eyebrow. 'Really?'

'It's a sanctuary, isn't it?' Tom continued. 'Having your own room. Somewhere private. Imagine those girls locked in those dormitories every night, forced to use chamber pots with seven other people in the room. The nuns really did everything to deny them a little dignity.'

'When you put it like that.'

Tom shook his head. 'I have this feeling that the laundry is somehow connected to the nun's death. I don't want to talk about it too much in front of Laura, but if I'd been her aunt's father, and I'd found out what happened to her, I'd have been tempted to make her tormentors pay.'

Ray nodded. 'I'm just playing devil's advocate here, but couldn't it also be the case that a nun who came here later found out what happened in the laundries and wasn't happy about it? We've already met two who fit that description – Concepta and Bernadette.'

'Yes,' Tom replied, thoughtfully.

An idea was scratching at the edges of his brain.

It was just a wisp, but there it floated.

He'd ruminate on it for a while.

CHAPTER 29

Sister Concepta handed the file to Laura. Her hands shook ever so slightly as she took it.

'I am sorry for the things that went on in the laundries. You can put some of it down to the times, but not all personal responsibility can be abdicated.'

Laura bit the inside of her cheek, and nodded slightly. Sister Concepta was too young to be seeking absolution for acts committed in the past, but the gesture was appreciated.

'Do you mind me staying here and putting some of these boxes back?' the nun asked. 'I've left it all a little precariously balanced. I can let you make copies of that, but I need to keep the original. If there is to be an investigation, we'll need the files.'

Laura indicated she didn't mind. She placed the file on a box and turned to the front page.

She braced herself when she saw her aunt's name written beside the date: 9 September 1964. That was the day Peggy had entered this place. The address underneath confirmed it was the correct file. Laura recognized her mother's old homestead.

What Mrs Brennan would give to be reading this file.

Everything else in the room receded as Laura turned the pages slowly.

Peggy had entered the convent in a state of trauma. Her given house name was 'Annette'. She had been examined for pregnancy and, when none was found, was told she should thank the Lord for her good fortune and repent of her sins.

The young woman was assigned a bed and told her job in the laundry would be to repair clothes. The priest who had driven her there had informed the Reverend Mother that Peggy was an excellent seamstress.

Laura could feel her heart thudding. She turned the page and swallowed as she saw the lists of 'infringements' Peggy had been accused of in her early days and weeks. Continuously breaking silence in reflection time, being aggressively disobedient, refusing to eat, causing damage to the door in her dormitory, spitting at a sister, deliberately ripping garments she had been assigned.

The list was endless.

Laura was torn between pride at her aunt's blatant disregard for the nuns' authority and horror at what she must have endured.

Beside each transgression, a punishment was listed. Sent to bed without dinner, kneeling in prayer for three hours, cleaning blocked toilets, five lashes on the back of the legs, washing sanitary towels, hair cut. As she read each sanction, Laura winced, as though it was her own flesh being slapped, her own hair being pulled and shorn.

On the fourth page she found a handwritten note among the typed words. From the previous file, she knew there was a disturbing dichotomy between the meticulously typed log of details and disciplinary actions and the malicious, hurtful tone of the handwritten notes. She cast her eyes over the writing with trepidation.

Despite repeated efforts to settle Annette into life here at the convent, she may not be suitable to our peaceful ways. This young woman has displayed signs of a troubled mind, which is beyond our assistance and may require professional treatment. She has accused several sisters of unkindness towards her, ranging from imaginary pinches and smacks to spiteful words that cannot be either repeated or written by a person of good conscience. We can expect nothing more from a girl who made up such vicious lies about two upstanding young men because she had no self-control.

She has started to harm the body God has given her in the most disgusting form of self-mutilation. We have removed everything we think she could be using for this, yet she still finds ways of tearing the flesh from her arms. We hope the good medical people can remove Annette, but we will persist in our endeavours to help her find inner peace.

Laura blanched and felt bile rise in her throat. She stepped away from the file momentarily and placed her hand on her stomach.

There was a quick movement behind her, and Sister Concepta grasped her elbow.

Laura pulled away roughly, and looked at the nun accusingly.

'Are you okay?' the sister asked, concerned. 'You're very pale.'

'I'm fine,' Laura snapped. Then, gathering herself, she asked, 'Could I possibly have a glass of water?'

'Of course.'

Sister Concepta left the room hurriedly.

Laura returned to the pages. Each visit by her grandparents had been noted, until they stopped coming. No details were recorded, however, about the traumatic nature of these visits.

Laura estimated from the dates that the visits had ended when her gran had died. She didn't know why her grandad had ceased his efforts. Maybe he was just a man of his time, unknowing of the ways of women, in thrall to the Church, and unable to see how he could help his daughter. Laura feared he might have also blamed Peggy a little for his wife's premature death.

She came to the last two pages of the file. There were no disciplinary actions listed towards the end of Peggy's life in the convent. According to the notes she had become almost catatonic. She didn't speak, barely ate.

In September 1974, Peggy's suicide was recorded. Almost ten years to the day after she had been admitted, she hanged herself. The entry was stark – just a date and the fact that it was suicide.

On the next page, a final handwritten note:

Father Patrick has kindly allowed us to bury Annette in the village cemetery in an unmarked grave. She cannot, for obvious reasons, be buried within the convent's walls. The violence against her body that she exhibited in life eventually led to her death and she must face an uncertain eternity as punishment for this unholiest of sins.

Garda Barney Kelly has been in to see us again. This young man appears to have an unnaturally active imagination for a police officer. Despite there being no sign of foul play and the fact that Annette was clearly disturbed, he continues to query what led her to do this. I have had to ask Father Patrick to intervene because the officer's visits to us have become a cause of upset for the other girls.

There were no further entries. Laura flicked back through the file to see if she had missed anything.

She was staring at the last page again when the door opened and Sister Concepta walked in, followed by Ellie.

The sister placed a glass of water on the old window sill beside Laura, then left the room without saying anything.

Ellie, still in her white forensic gear, looked at Laura with a mixture of awkwardness and compassion.

As the heat rose in the detective's cheeks, she turned and grabbed for the glass of water, but she fumbled and sent it flying to the floor. The glass didn't smash but the water fanned out around Laura's feet.

She groaned.

Ellie crossed the room and picked up the glass before Laura could even bend her knees. She placed it back carefully on the sill and stood beside the detective, clearly unsure of what to say.

'What did she tell you?' Laura asked, irritable in her embarrassment.

Ellie bit her lip. 'Just that you were in here looking at a personal file. She thought you might need someone, other than her, for support.'

Laura threw her hands out to her sides.

'Amazing how supportive nuns are nowadays, isn't it?' she said. 'All things considered.'

Ellie looked at the file still sitting on the box.

'A relative?' she asked.

Laura nodded.

'I'm sorry. Were you close?'

'Not close at all. She was my aunt, but I never met her.'

'But she was in the laundry here?' Ellie asked. 'Tell me to shut up if you want. Jack told me on the way down what this place used to be and . . . what happened here.'

'Yes, she was here.'

'For long?'

'From 1964 to 1974.'

Ellie shook her head in disbelief. 'Ten years? That's awful. What happened when she got out?'

'She died here. She was sent here, utterly traumatized, and never recovered. She wasn't allowed to recover.'

The other woman looked horrified.

'I'm so sorry,' she said, eventually.

'Do you know something?' Laura said. 'The nuns who ran these places were absolute bitches. All of these boxes contain pages and pages of misery.'

She felt a ball of rage building and roughly shoved the side of the box nearest her, sending it crashing to the floor and into the wet puddle she'd made.

Ellie jumped back, startled.

Laura clasped her hand to her mouth.

'Oh God! Oh God!' she repeated, lifting the box to safety as if it were a baby.

She grabbed the hem of her cashmere cardigan and attempted to dry the cardboard, getting more frustrated as the unabsorbent material proved useless.

Ellie gently took the box from her and sat it back on its pile.

'Hey, it's just a splash of water,' she said.

Laura nodded, feeling numb. 'I know. I'm okay. I just want a minute. You need to get back to your work.'

'Are you sure? Can I get you anything?'

'I'm fine.'

Ellie gave her an uncertain look but let it go.

Laura watched her retreating back, and wondered why the other woman had to be so beautiful and so bloody kind too.

It really was very inconsiderate of her.

CHAPTER 30

The hall was in complete darkness when Tom and Ray arrived back downstairs. Ellie had sealed the windows to keep out the light. She was working with luminous light sticks, attempting to detect vestiges of blood.

When they could see that she was finished, Tom flicked the lights back on.

His hopes were dashed as Ellie rested back on her heels and shook her head.

'Nothing so far. Not even a fingerprint. And there should be plenty, given the number of people who live in this house.'

'It's something the Church seems to excel at,' Ray said. 'Cleaning things up.'

'Not a Catholic, then, Detective?' Ellie raised her eyebrows, interested.

'Begrudgingly,' he conceded. 'I'm hedging my bets with the big man.'

'What next?' Tom asked.

'I'm going to move into the corridor. But if you are sure she was attacked out here, I don't know what that's going to reveal. Jack is fingerprinting the doors and windows.' She shrugged her shoulders. 'We've a lot of fingerprints to eliminate for the outside exits.'

Tom felt his shoulders sag.

How the hell could Attracta have been bludgeoned and kidnapped from this hall without any forensic evidence being left behind? Sister Concepta had told them it was Sister Gladys who suggested the area be cleaned. Was it possible, though, that whoever had killed Mother Attracta had put the idea into the elderly nun's head?

Seeing his disappointment, Ellie filled the silence.

'I'll keep going,' she assured him. 'Hopefully something will turn up. You think she could have been taken up to Dublin in one of those cars outside?'

'It's one possibility.'

She nodded slowly, her face clouded in thought.

'It's probably a stupid question, and I'm sure you've done it already, but . . . have you asked the toll company for CCTV footage from when she went missing?'

Tom looked puzzled. 'Toll company? We didn't come through any toll booths on the way here.'

Ray frowned. 'Really? We did. Which way did Willie take you?'

'The usual way – the dual carriageway and then off at Rathspillane.'

Suddenly it dawned on Tom. 'They've opened the new motorway section. Of course. That's how you and Laura got to the petrol station before us.'

Ray chuckled. 'Trust you old men to stick to the tried and tested. You added about twenty minutes on to your journey there.'

Tom turned to Ellie. 'Well, I didn't think to check because I didn't realize there was a toll plaza. It's lucky we have you here, and we don't have to wait for that idea to occur to Ray.'

Ellie smiled. Ray glared at Tom.

'I'll get the licence plates outside, then, shall I?' he said, his voice petulant.

'If you'd be so kind.'

Ray opened the front door, to be greeted by the Kilcross sergeant.

'Ciaran.' Tom strode over and shook the other officer's hand. 'Good to see you.'

The sergeant cast an appreciative eye over Ellie, as she made her way into the corridor.

'Anything from forensics?'

Tom shook his head.

'Those bloody idiot nuns. Oh! Whoops. Good morning, Sisters.'

The sergeant dropped his head respectfully, hiding his blushes, as the nuns trooped into the hall from the kitchen, carrying baskets and flasks. Most of them ignored him as they filed out the front door.

'We're heading down to the village now, Inspector,' Sister Concepta said. 'We don't want to let this tragedy or the weather come between us and our duties. Will we see you down there for lunch?'

'Possibly, Sister. There are a couple of things I need to follow up on after last night's interviews. Please take care driving, there's a lot of snow on the ground.'

'We will. Are we to keep quiet about Mother? It's just, I'm not sure I can guarantee it.'

'I don't expect you to, Sister. We'll be releasing her name today, and you can expect the media to descend. They've been clamouring to know the identity of the victim since we found her. They will come to the convent, I'm afraid.'

'We'll close the gates,' she replied, and then added, 'though the horse has bolted.'

'Down to the village,' Ciaran scoffed, when the nuns had left. 'Geographically, the village is "up". It just shows you how their minds work.'

'Exactly what I wanted to talk to you about. Shall we?'

They made their way to the sitting room. Inside, Ciaran took up residence in front of the fire, his hands clasped behind his back to warm them.

'I've more time for the nuns than I'm letting on,' Ciaran said. 'Some of them, anyway. They do great work in the village. Visit the nursing home every week. Take care of some of the folk not yet in the nursing home.

'They run little allotments for the kiddies in the school – teach them how to sow vegetables, that kind of thing. There's a genuine goodness in some of them. Sister Concepta is a lovely woman. Would have made a good wife in another life. Attracta was a different kettle of fish, Inspector.'

'No need to stand on ceremony, Ciaran. Tom's fine.'

This was technically the sergeant's patch, and Tom wanted the other man to see him as an equal.

'Well, to be honest, Tom, dreadful and all as it sounds, there'll not be many people around here who'll miss the Reverend Mother.'

'Last night we interviewed the women who lived with her, and virtually all of them said the same,' Tom said.

'I didn't have a lot of dealings with her personally, because she didn't throw her lot in with the other nuns in their community work. But when I did run into her, well, she was as condescending as that other old blowhard, Father Seamus.'

'Should we be looking at any of the villagers?' Tom asked.

'No one springs to mind. She kept to herself – and whatever routines they have here. Praying and the like. But this village is not a haven of godliness just because it has a big convent on its doorstep. Fifteen years ago, I had a local fellow – as normal as you like – worked his small bit of land all day, down the pub twice a week for two Guinness and a Jameson. One day, he went home, shot his wife in the head and then put the gun in his own mouth. No explanation.'

Tom had a vague recollection of the tragedy.

'Nobody has been acting strangely over the last few days,' Ciaran continued. 'I don't think anyone even knows she's missing. I do know one person who'll be happy to hear that she's dead.'

'Who's that?'

Ciaran hesitated before replying. 'My old boss, Barney Kelly. He was the sergeant before me. He hated her. But he's in the old folks' home now. I call in once a week. Some of the younger lads do, too. His wife died a few years ago. No kids.'

'Do you know why he hated her?'

'Not the specifics. But he had no time for the place when it was a laundry, that's for sure. He would have been ahead of his time like that. The lads in our station would have been more likely to send their shirts down for cleaning than to give out about how the place was run. I suppose that was how it was then. Nobody knew.'

Tom had heard the phrase 'nobody knew' about many situations and on more occasions than he cared to remember. When you scratched the surface, most people usually did know.

But it was easier to pretend they didn't.

'Would he mind having a chat with us?' Tom asked. 'His mind is still intact? I want to dig into Attracta's background.'

'He'd enjoy it. The old beggar's not in the home because he's lost it. He signed himself in. He likes being taken care of. There's a little Filipino woman in there, I think he has her in mind as a second wife,' Ciaran chuckled.

'The priest claims he was out all day on Thursday,' Tom said. 'One of my detectives is picking up exact times from him later. Would you be able to give us a hand checking the priest's alibi? I imagine it will require some local knowledge.'

'Not a problem. Is Seamus a suspect?'

'Would you suspect him?'

A log crackled on the fire and spat a shower of tiny sparks. The fireguard did its job; nothing broke through.

Ciaran cocked his head sideways.

'On the one hand, I'd say he got on better with Attracta than anyone else. On the other, the man makes my skin crawl. I wouldn't have had him down as the murdering type. He's what I'd describe as all mouth and no trousers, hides behind the cloth. But maybe I have him wrong.'

'We'll add his to the list of car registrations to check with the toll company. I can't imagine that whoever did this was stupid enough to get caught on CCTV, but maybe we'll strike lucky. Anyway, it's time to start questioning the locals to see if they saw anything suspicious on Wednesday.'

'I have two lads helping me in the station. They've started making general inquiries about strangers in the village in the last week or two. It's the kind of thing that's noticed.'

'You should know something else about Attracta's murder . . .' Tom lowered his voice and told him what had been done to the nun's body. 'The ultimate cause of death was cardiac arrest,' he concluded. 'But it was horrifically violent. Before and after.'

Ciaran was visibly shocked. He blew out air from his cheeks.

'I'd no idea.'

'The nuns aren't aware of it. I wanted to see if anyone gave anything away. You know, Father Seamus never asked me.'

'Asked you what?'

'How she died. He was more concerned with getting out of here. I didn't give Concepta the details, and most of those we interviewed last night tried to get us to hint at what had happened. But Seamus never asked.'

Ciaran absorbed the information, nodding.

'Considering what was done to the body, you'd lean towards a man, wouldn't you?' he mused. 'I guess that places Seamus high on the suspect list.'

Tom checked the time on the clock over the mantelpiece.

'I think we can make Mass. Fancy hearing the word of God?'

'I'm not sure that's what comes out of Father Seamus's mouth, but sure, let's give it a whirl.'

CHAPTER 31

'If you ask me, the snow and ice probably make these roads more passable. The council is happy to leave bloody potholes large enough for sheep to drown in. They let Dublin grab all the road maintenance money.'

Ciaran kept up his running commentary on the inadequacies of rural local authorities the whole way into Kilcross.

By daylight, Tom could see how picturesque the village was. The Christmas season suited it. Most of the houses had small, gated gardens and, even covered in snow, the neatly pruned bushes and winter border plants were visible. Lights twinkled again this morning in the decorated windows, and most of the front doors were adorned with holly wreaths, replete with red berries and gold painted bells.

The various pubs on either side of the road revealed an impressive ratio of drinking houses to residential homes, unique to rural Irish towns and villages. An attractive olde worlde sweet shop lay incongruously between two pubs named, bizarrely, for their original respective owners, Smith's and Smyth's. Tom wondered whether both pubs had loyal, exclusive customers, or whether the punters flitted unfaithfully between the I and the Y, perhaps pausing en route for a quarter of humbugs.

The road led to an open triangular green, on the north side of which stood the church. Its stone spire soared into the leaden grey sky. In better weather, it would cast an oppressive or comforting shadow over the village, depending on your religious views.

Ciaran parked his squad car irreverently on the footpath below the steps leading up to the main church door.

Inside, there were roughly two hundred people gathered. It wasn't a huge number, but Tom knew this was probably most of the village.

The sergeant indicated the back row. Three young boys and one deck of Top Trumps were its only other occupants.

The boys' faces exploded into red blotches when they realized they were being joined by the village's most senior policeman and another official-looking man.

At the altar, Father Seamus coughed loudly to remind the congregation he was the most important person in the building.

When Mass was over, the cleric cleared his throat again.

'Now, before we go, I have an announcement,' he said, solemnly.

The crowd sat up. This was the most engaged they'd been in an hour.

'You will have seen the dreadful news concerning the poor woman who was found, murdered, in the Phoenix

Park on Friday. I am sad to say that the victim was, in fact, our own Mother Attracta from the convent.'

Father Seamus paused to let his words sink in. There were several gasps from the congregation, followed by shocked mutterings.

The priest held up his hands for silence. The last voice to be heard was the little chap sitting to the right of Tom, who hadn't realized a hush was descending and chose that moment to say, excitedly, 'Does that mean we're getting a day off school?' to his friends.

This innocent remark earned him a clip around the ear from his mother. Turning from the row in front, she reacted with impressive speed to his embarrassing faux pas.

The sharp sound reverberated in the silent church.

Noticing Ciaran and Tom had witnessed the slap, the mother blushed furiously and spun back round in her seat, no doubt mentally adding her humiliation to the list of things she would chastise her son for later.

Father Seamus cleared his throat impatiently.

'This is clearly traumatic news for all of us. A very senior investigation unit has come down from Dublin. They have assured me personally they will do everything in their power to ensure whoever committed this heinous act is brought to justice. When we have details of Mother Attracta's funeral I will inform everyone, as I'm sure you will all want to attend.

'I must also tell you that the sisters will be organizing lunch as usual after Mass. They are undeterred in their duties, and for that I think we must, as a community, honour their bravery and dedication by gathering in the parish hall.'

The woman directly in front of Tom leaned across to the slapped boy's mammy.

'I've a bloody roast beef in the oven. What am I supposed to do with that?'

'May you go in peace, to love and serve the Lord.'

With this phrase, the priest signalled they were free to leave.

Ciaran turned to Tom. 'Is he growing on you yet?'

'Like fungus. I've lost my appetite. But let's head to that lunch, anyway, will we?'

Outside the church, Willie had just pulled up with Ray, Michael and Laura. A second car parked behind with two uniformed guards inside.

Laura looked pale. The inspector made a mental note to ask her about her aunt's file.

'Most of the villagers are heading round to the nuns' lunch,' he told the team. 'The priest just made the big reveal from the pulpit. Michael, I want you to pull him out of that hall and get his alibi for the twenty-four hours in question. Ciaran will help you. Ray, can you head up to the nursing home and talk to a Barney Kelly there about Mother Attracta? He's the old Kilcross sergeant.'

'Did you say Kelly?' Laura interrupted.

Tom raised his eyebrows quizzically.

'I saw his name written down earlier,' she said. 'There's something I wanted to ask him. It relates to the laundry.'

She directed this to Ray, hoping he'd let her go in his place.

Ray shrugged. 'No problem with me, Laura.'

'Right,' Tom said. 'Well, it might do no harm for him to know you had a relative in the place, Laura. Ray, are you okay to talk to those in the village who aren't at this lunch? Use one of Ciaran's lads for guidance on who will be at home. By the way, did you talk to the toll company?'

'I did. They're going through the CCTV footage from the booths. But it's a lot of hours' worth, and we gave them several registrations. It could take a while, but HQ is helping.'

'Okay. Keep me posted. Willie, I can hear your stomach from here; you'd better come to this lunch.'

The large parish hall was square with a stage at one end, stacked with plastic chairs. A long trestle table ran down one side, and it was here that the sisters had laid out the afternoon's repast. Villagers sat in groups at circular tables dispersed around the hall.

The nuns were wearing aprons and dishing out hot lunches, while children greedily and impatiently eyed the delectable sweet treats that awaited them for dessert.

A door at the end of the hall led to a kitchen, where food could be prepared for dances and other events. It was from this door that Father Seamus now emerged, having changed out of his official vestments.

Ciaran tapped Michael's shoulder, and nodded towards the cleric.

The priest had armed himself with a plate, and was making a beeline for the roast chicken and honey-glazed ham, when they approached.

'Can I help you?' he asked, without taking his eyes off the food.

'I'm afraid lunch will have to wait, Father. We need to get that list you promised Inspector Reynolds.' This was Ciaran.

Father Seamus looked incredulous.

'Really? You need it right now? I haven't eaten since breakfast.'

'I'm sorry, but this takes precedence.'

The two men stared at each other.

Father Seamus broke first.

'Oh, very well. We'll go across to the house. I need to check my diary.'

'After you,' Ciaran offered politely, holding his hand out in the direction of the front door.

'May I at least get my coat?'

'Of course. We'll wait for you here.'

Leaving Ciaran and Michael to shepherd the priest, Tom went into the kitchen in search of Sister Clare.

There, he found several nuns. Sister Gladys sat snoozing in the corner, her feet elevated on a stool and a newspaper propped on her lap. A half-cup of tea was perilously balanced on the arm of her chair.

Another sister was sweeping the floor vigorously around Gladys, uncaring as to whether her chore woke the woman.

Tom rapped on the open door to get their attention. He couldn't be sure, but he thought he saw Sister Gladys's eyelids twitch.

'Good afternoon, Sisters. I wonder, is one of you Sister Clare?'

The tall nun drying dishes placed her hand on her breast.

'I'm Sister Clare,' she said.

She was an older woman, perhaps in her late sixties. She had been good looking in her youth, and her features were still strong, her cheekbones quite elegant. Her forehead, however, was creased with worry lines, and an unfortunately placed wart dominated her chin.

'Could I have a quick word?'

The nun nodded and followed him out.

Tom had noticed a stack of fold-up chairs in an adjacent dressing room. He pulled out two chairs and opened them, chivalrously offering the nun the first.

She collapsed with a sigh, and tried to make herself comfortable.

'It's good to get a rest. I'm getting too old for all this work,' she said.

'Forgive me if I'm being impolite, but how old are you?'

'I'll be seventy in January.'

'Positively sprightly compared to Sister Gladys, eh?'

She smiled. 'Oh, I wouldn't underestimate her, Inspector. She plays her age very well. Like now, for instance. She's in the back there pretending to be asleep so she won't be asked to do anything. But if someone decided to throw an impromptu party and produced a drop of Jameson, she'd be up on a table doing a jig.'

Tom smiled at the image.

The nun looked around at the costumes. 'This is Sister Concepta's favourite room, Inspector. She loves performing in plays. Quite the little actress.'

Tom frowned.

Seeing he'd no intention of responding to her poisoned arrow, Sister Clare spoke again. 'I told your officers everything. I don't think I've anything to add.'

'If you remember anything else, of course, that's important. But actually I want to pick up on something you said last night. I believe you were good friends with Mother Attracta?'

'I knew Attracta for a long time.'

'Yes, you were both in the convent when Mother Theresa was in charge. Was it the case that you were originally meant to succeed the Reverend Mother, Sister?'

The nun looked down, straightened her tunic. 'That's hardly relevant now, Inspector.'

He waited.

She made eye contact and smiled, bitterly. 'What is it? Do you think I was passed over and have nursed a grudge for twenty years? That I decided this week I'd had enough?'

When Tom said nothing, she laughed. It was a thin, unpleasant sound.

'Isn't it funny how people call it the past and yet nobody lets it go? Could I really have been Mother Attracta's friend if I'd been angry for that long? Yes, I should have been the next Reverend Mother. I was the more popular. I was the more learned. But you know what they say. Pride always comes before a fall. Attracta won the vote. Was I happy then? No. Did I learn from it? Yes. I had to accept that decisions are always made by a higher order. Attracta won, fair and square. Despite what some may say . . .'

Tom was impressed at the subtle and innocuous delivery of the final killer sentence.

'What might some say, Sister?'

The nun sighed, as though he had pressed hard for the information and she would now have to unwillingly divulge it.

'Some of the sisters believed Mother Attracta fixed the vote. It was nonsense. They only said it because her victory was unexpected. Attracta had been charged with bringing the ballot box to Father Seamus – perhaps because, as many of us thought, she hadn't been in the running. As it turns out, she had.'

'Is there a suggestion she interfered with the ballot box?'

'Only from those who supported my candidacy. But I put it to bed. I consulted with Father Seamus, and he assured me categorically that the seal on the box had not been broken. It was wrong of me to even think such a thing, but there were so many rumours. Once I, the expected winner, had endorsed Attracta's victory, no one else challenged it.'

'It was magnanimous of you to support Mother Attracta

and to become good friends with her after such an episode,' he said.

'Oh, we were friends before, Inspector.'

Sister Clare's voice was cold. Tom understood immediately what Ray and Michael had meant. This woman had hated Mother Attracta.

'Will you be the new Reverend Mother?' he asked.

'These days the job suits a younger woman. There will be a vote, of course. I will probably be asked to go forward. But I have no interest in it now.'

Tom believed her, if only because he knew she realized she didn't have the popular support among the other nuns to win. So the theory that she might have killed Mother Attracta to take over her role didn't stand up. But as they say, revenge is a dish best served cold.

'Sister, I believe you were the one who rang Father Seamus and left a voice message for him on Thursday. May I ask why you left a voice message when your call was so crucial?'

Sister Clare frowned. 'I'm not an idiot. I must have rung Father Seamus more than a dozen times – on his home phone and on his mobile. When he didn't answer, I left a message.'

'You rang his mobile and he didn't answer?'

'It was turned off. That voice came on, the one that tells you the user doesn't have a mailbox set up. So I couldn't leave a message, but I left one on the home phone. And I called to his house. But there was no answer. I assumed he'd pick up the voicemail soon enough.'

Tom didn't let anything show on his face.

'Thank you, Sister. I should let you return to your duties.'

He stood up, extending his hand to support her as she rose.

'I really do hope you find the person who killed her, Inspector. No matter what anyone has done, no one has the right to play God and take someone before their time.'

He stood in the doorway of the small room, looking at her retreating back.

'No matter what anyone has done . . .'

That said it all about Sister Clare's view of Mother Attracta.

CHAPTER 32

Ciaran and Michael were waiting impatiently and uncomfortably on dated, course-fabric armchairs when the text message alert came from Tom.

Ask him why his mobile was turned off Thursday

The detective leaned across and showed the phone screen to Ciaran, who raised his eyebrows.

The room had a general unlived-in feel. A light sheen of dust coated the unimaginative furnishings, a sure sign the priest was not coping too well without his cleaner. The heavy curtains may once have been burgundy but were now mottled and faded. A hard-backed scratchy green couch made a set with the two armchairs, and a shabby old sideboard was heaving with unappealing religious texts.

Father Seamus had directed them into this room. After the priest had gone upstairs, Ciaran told Michael that the comfortable sitting room was across the hall, available to a better class of guest.

They could hear his footsteps above them.

He'd been up there for ten minutes already, supposedly checking his diary.

Ciaran sighed loudly. 'Think we can arrest him for time wasting?'

'I'm not sure ten minutes qualifies . . . I think this is him, at last.'

'I hope this is satisfactory,' Father Seamus said, entering the room. He oozed irritability.

Michael cast his eyes over the sheet of scrawled handwriting.

The priest had followed his instructions to the letter and provided a full itinerary of what he had done over the twenty-four hours in question.

Thursday seemed to be accounted for by a drive to his former colleague Father Terence and numerous visits to residents in the village. The declaration that he 'watched television' on Wednesday night was the only uncorroborated period in the priest's alibi.

He handed the sheet to Ciaran, who read it slowly, then glanced up at the priest before looking down at the sheet again. When he lifted his head, Michael expected him to say something about the list.

Instead, the sergeant just nodded and said, 'Thank you, Father Seamus. Can you tell us why you had your mobile phone switched off on Thursday?'

The priest blinked furiously, his body tensed.

'I didn't —' he started, and then stopped. He waved his hands dramatically. 'Oh, yes, I remember now. The battery died.'

'Earlier, you said the sisters hadn't rung you on your mobile,' Michael said.

'Well, that's correct. No one rang me – they obviously couldn't get through.'

'All right, then. That's all we need for now,' Ciaran said.

The priest looked relieved.

'Good,' he said, rubbing his hands together. 'I've a little bit of work to do here now I think of it, so I won't go back to the hall.'

The two men struggled into their coats while the priest held open the front door, anxious to be rid of them.

Michael noted three locks on the inside of the door, and wondered why the priest needed so many.

Father Seamus saw him staring. 'You've noticed my little bit of security. Unfortunately, I have to be cautious. I keep the money from the parish collection in the house until it's lodged in the bank. There's always a chance of it proving a temptation for some desperate soul.'

'Has it happened before?' Michael asked.

Ciaran raised an eyebrow, and shook his head dismissively.

Feeling the need to justify himself in the face of Ciaran's obvious scepticism, the priest jumped straight back in.

'There's always a first time. Isn't prevention better than cure? I'm sure the sergeant would rather I kept my doors tightly locked than turn up at the station with a bloody nose and an empty collection bag.'

Neither man spoke until they were out the gate and Father Seamus had shut the door.

As they started to trudge through the snow, Michael turned to Ciaran. 'What's really with the locks?'

'No idea. We have petty crime from time to time. It's usually a teenager acting up, and I generally know the bad apple. But this parish is neither rich enough to have a big offertory on a Sunday nor blasphemous enough to break into the priest's house to steal it. It's a security measure, all right – just not for what he says. My guess? He's been siphoning off the collection plate for the last few years and has a big stash of coins in the attic. He's up there every night counting them like Silas Marner.' Ciaran chuckled at his own joke.

'His statement,' Michael said. 'He seems in the clear on Thursday, anyway. Aside from the drive, he spent most of the day in the village.'

'Yes. Even with people who weren't here.'

Michael stopped dead in his tracks. 'What do you mean?'

Ciaran pulled out the list. 'He said he called in on Larry O'Farrell. Well, Larry's sister was taken into Limerick City General on Wednesday evening. Larry was in the pub when he got the call. He dropped into the station and asked me if he had drunk too much to drive himself up. He'd had seven pints at that stage, so I advised him to go home and sleep it off. To the best of my knowledge he drove up there on Thursday morning and hasn't been back since. It'd be very rare for him to leave the village, mind, but he did this week.'

Michael's eyes widened. 'So Father Seamus has given a false alibi? We should go back.'

'And do what? Arrest him? Let's not be too hasty. We'll check Larry's house just in case – and then the rest of the list. If it's just Larry, the priest will claim he got confused. But if he's made another little mistake . . . well, then Father Seamus has some explaining to do.'

Michael looked back at the priest's house. A movement in one of the upstairs windows caught his eye.

The priest must have been looking out at them.

'If you're sure,' he said, uncertainly.

'He's going nowhere, lad. Don't worry. It will take us less than an hour to get this checked.'

They walked deeper into the village.

'Aren't most of the villagers in the hall?' Michael asked.

'Not the ones on this list,' Ciaran replied. 'Father Seamus only makes house calls to incapacitated and lost souls. We've a couple of houses and the pubs to drop into.'

Michael tried to bury a sense of foreboding. If the priest had given them a false alibi, maybe he would take this opportunity to flee the village. He could be packing even now. The detective withdrew his phone from his pocket.

'Hold on a minute,' he said to Ciaran, before typing as fast as his freezing fingers would allow. He sent the text to Ray.

Priest's alibi looks suspect. Keep an eye on house if possible. Worried he'll do a runner.

The phone beeped almost immediately.

Heading back that direction. Will do.

Michael returned his phone to his pocket.

At least there'd be no issues with the priest's where-abouts for the next hour or two.

CHAPTER 33

Darren, the fair-haired Kilcross guard who drove Laura to the nursing home, could have passed for sixteen. He spent the short few minutes of the journey subjecting her to cheesy chat-up lines.

Laura rested her forehead against the cool glass of the window. Darren had the car heating on full blast and between that, his incessant nattering and what she'd uncovered in her aunt's file, her head was pounding.

'Here we are,' the young guard said, pulling into a driveway.

The sign on the gate said 'Autumn Oaks'. Laura hoped that when she got old any family she had would either take her in or shoot her. She hated the thought of ending up in one of these places, which invariably boasted the most clichéd, patronizing names imaginable.

'Are there many elderly people from the village here?' she asked Darren. 'Don't they have families to care for them?'

The guard's face only registered confusion. He had a Dublin accent, and Laura supposed he considered nursing homes the most normal thing in the world. They didn't have the same sense of family in the capital, from what she could see.

'This home serves most of the south of the county,' he replied. 'I guess some of them don't have families, or the families have left the area. I'd rather my parents were in a place like this than rattling around on their own in a lonely house, wouldn't you?'

She made a non-committal murmur.

The snow lay mainly undisturbed in the car park. She'd have thought Sunday would be the busiest day here, but the weather had evidently given family members a convenient excuse to abdicate their visiting duties and stay at home.

They entered the building to a blast of hot air that made the inside of Darren's car seem like the North Pole.

Laura immediately removed her coat and cardigan.

'Are they roasting the old people?' she exclaimed. She could already feel tiny droplets of sweat start to form on her brow and under her arms.

Darren laughed. 'It's like this all year round. The elderly feel the cold more. Luckily, most of the nurses are from warmer climes.'

Bereft of her outer layers, she caught Darren taking in her figure appreciatively. Laura wished she hadn't undone that extra blouse button for Ray's benefit this morning, especially as it was now apparent he'd look through her if Ellie were standing on the other side.

'Do we wait here?' she snapped at the unfortunate

Darren, the only man within snapping distance. 'Will someone come out to us?'

'Oh. No,' Darren answered, bruised by her sharp tone. 'Barney's room is down there.' He pointed to the end of the hallway.

'We can just wander into his room? Not very safe, is it?'

Darren shrugged. 'What's there to fear?'

'Indeed. Who'd kidnap and murder an old person?'

The young guard shrank farther into himself.

Laura started to feel a little ashamed. She fanned herself with her hand.

'Shall we?' she said, straining to find a kinder tone.

Down, but not out, Darren reacted like a puppy offered a doggy treat. He bounded ahead, stopped at the last door on the corridor and knocked.

The door was opened by a short, dark-skinned woman, about Laura's mother's age. She had a round pudgy face with smiling eyes, and smelled strongly of clean cotton and fabric conditioner.

'Hello, Carla, is the patient receiving visitors?' Darren said.

'Patient, my eye,' Carla scoffed, with an accent that held a touch of the exotic but had been corrupted by the broad flat brogue of the Irish Midlands. 'You're just in time. I'd like him arrested for pinching my bottom. Randy old man.'

'Consider it done,' Darren replied. 'Carla, this is Detective Brennan.'

Laura held out her hand, and the other woman shook

it firmly. The detective was surprised by the strength of her grip, until she remembered that this woman lifted people in and out of baths and beds, dressed them and did all the other tasks their daily routine required.

Carla looked her up and down. 'Hmm, he'll like you –' she picked up a basket from beside the door – 'I'll go do his laundry and see to my other dears. You can have him.'

The room was cosy, made all the cosier by the dialled-up heating. A large bay window revealed a spectacular view of the rolling hills behind the nursing home. Today, their usual forty shades of green had been reduced to a simple palette of white.

A large mahogany bed covered with a patchwork quilt sat between two bedside lockers and facing a wardrobe large enough to host Narnia. An old television sat atop an ornate map chest that looked like it had been liberated from a pirate ship.

There were large comfortable leather armchairs on either side of the bed. Laura imagined they were there for visitors of residents confined to their beds.

Barney Kelly was not in that category.

He was leaning forward eagerly in one of the chairs as they entered, and when he set eyes on Laura, his face lit up.

'Well, well, am I dreaming or have my dreams come true?' he said, rising from his chair. 'Fáilte.'

Barney Kelly was Santa Claus.

That was Laura's first impression as she took in the

tall, stout man standing in front of her, with his rosy cheeks and full white beard and moustache.

She shook his bear-like hand.

'You're real,' he said, his eyes glinting as he wrapped his other hand around hers, so she was trapped in his grip. She felt like replying: 'You're real!' And maybe tugging his beard for good measure.

'I'm Detective Sergeant Laura Brennan from the National Bureau of Criminal Investigation,' she said. 'The murder squad.'

Barney raised his eyebrows. 'I don't get too many visitors as beautiful as you, Laura. May I call you Laura? You're a picture of an Irish *cailín* . . . Darren, if you'd be so kind?' He indicated the chair on the other side of his bed while sitting down and making himself comfortable.

Darren, who'd been marvelling at the elderly man's ability to speak to a beautiful woman with such confidence, sprang into action. He fetched the chair and placed it in front of Barney.

'I bet if you chase Carla, she'll get us a cup of tea,' the old man suggested. 'It's Sunday; she shouldn't be doing laundry, anyway.'

'No, just catering to all your other whims,' Darren retorted.

Barney ignored him and, resting his elbows on the sides of his armchair, gave Laura his undivided attention.

'How do you take your tea, dear?'

'Milk, no sugar,' Laura replied, her eyes not leaving his.

'Carla knows my order, Darren. See if you can get her to

give you a few biscuits, as I've visitors. She might let up on the regime.'

Darren sighed but went to do Barney's bidding.

The old man's face was one of the kindliest Laura had ever seen, but when they were left alone, the jocularity was replaced by a keen interest in what she had to say.

'It's been a good while since I talked to someone from serious crimes. I can't see what you'd need from me. Ciaran's a good lad. You've met Ciaran, haven't you?'

'He's helping our team right now. I'm here for your recollections more than anything,' Laura said. 'I'm assuming you won't have heard this yet, but Mother Attracta from the convent was murdered on Thursday. She was kidnapped, tortured and stabbed. Her body was left in the Phoenix Park in Dublin.'

Laura cut to the quick. She addressed the former guard as she would her dad – no sugar-coating necessary – but she hadn't realized how she was expecting him to react, until he did the opposite.

Instead of being shocked, Barney just shook his head incredulously and said, 'So, it's true. God does move in mysterious ways.' He sat back. 'Sorry, I don't mean to sound unsympathetic. It's an awful way to die. But Mother Attracta and I go back a long way, and I'd be a fraud if I sat here and pretended to mourn her.'

'Sergeant McKenna suggested we speak to you,' Laura said. 'When we found the body, we couldn't imagine who would kill an old woman so violently, but she seems to have made enemies easily.'

'That's putting it mildly. Mother Attracta, in my opinion, was downright evil. More like a bride of the Devil than a bride of Christ.'

The words 'Satan's whore' flashed in front of Laura's eyes. She looked at the old but still powerfully built man in front of her. When he mentioned Attracta's name, his whole body tensed. She mentally shook herself. It wasn't possible.

Barney laughed. 'I can see you, you know. Sitting there, wondering if you should add me to your list of suspects because I hated the old bitch. Well, do. But it'll be a waste of time. I had an epiphany a long time ago – that woman would answer for her sins to the man below, but she wouldn't meet him through any act of mine. I'm old and I'll be meeting my own maker soon enough, but I won't be bringing the baggage that woman had.'

Laura shook her head at the notion that Barney was on his last legs.

But the old man nodded. 'I may look hale and hearty, but I have lung cancer. Forty cigarettes a day will do that to you. Not everyone knows, but the nurses here do. I can't win this fight.' Barney smiled resignedly. 'I'm happy. You get to my age, you've no family left and really, you just get tired. I'm tired.' His shoulders sagged.

Laura was overcome with sympathy. She'd only met him minutes ago, but the genial old man seemed like such a life force.

'I'm really sorry to hear that, sir. Are you up to this?'

'Absolutely. I'd welcome a break from obsessing about mortality.'

'Well . . . if you're sure. You said something about an epiphany?'

'Indeed. I was driving home one night in this terrific storm and I saw her – Mother Attracta – ahead of me on her bike, wobbling all over the road in the wind. She must have been out in the village for something and got caught. She looked like that witch out of *The Wizard of Oz*. You know, the one who steals the little girl's dog? For just a moment it crossed my mind – a cloud of madness – to run her over! Turn the wheel and knock her off the bike. It would have killed her for sure. Thankfully, sanity prevailed. Why would I commit a sin for her sake? No, she would get hers. People always do.'

He leaned back and sighed, evidently relieved to have got his confession, for what it was worth, off his chest.

The door opened and Darren came in carrying a tray. He placed it on the locker beside Barney.

'Ah, Jaffa Cakes and Jammie Dodgers. Lovely. Now if you two young people will do me a favour and try not to scoff the lot, I've found a new hiding place. My belly. Carla will never know.'

Laura took the hot cup, wondering what she'd been thinking agreeing to drink tea in temperatures akin to the tropics. There were no other chairs, so Darren perched on the side of the bed nearest Laura. They had to wait for Barney to down four biscuits before they could resume.

'But why did you dislike her so much?' Laura asked, as

the old man slurped his tea. 'I'm also curious about something of a more personal nature.'

'Start with the latter. I'm intrigued.'

'Well, my aunt was sent to the convent when it was a Magdalene Laundry in 1964. She died there. Her name was Peggy Deasy. Sorry, are you okay . . .?'

The colour had drained from Barney's face, and his teacup clattered noisily against the saucer. Both Darren and Laura jumped forward, concerned.

'Did you say Peggy Deasy?' The old man's voice was barely audible.

'Yes, she was my aunt. I think you looked into her death . . .? Do you need me to get someone?'

Laura was alarmed. Barney was slumped in his chair, his breathing shallow. She turned to Darren, who was hovering nervously, deliberating whether or not to run for help.

Before either one could act, Barney banged his fist on the armrest, startling them.

'I knew it!' he roared. 'I knew it! I knew that girl's death would come back to haunt Attracta. And there she is – murdered – and Peggy's niece is sent down to investigate. That's no coincidence.'

'I don't understand.' Laura shook her head, confused. 'What does Mother Attracta have to do with my aunt's death?'

Her quiet words had the effect of calming the old man. He returned his teacup to the tray and, edging forward, took Laura's free hand in his.

'Everything, dear. You asked me why I disliked that nun. Your aunt is the reason why I hated her and all those dried-up old shrews in that convent.'

Laura glanced at Darren, who looked as confused as she was, and back at Barney.

'You don't understand,' the old sergeant said. 'Let me tell you the story. Drink your tea . . . good girl . . . you see, I was only a young officer when I was sent from Dublin to Kilcross. A little village like this held no appeal for me, I can tell you. It was the late sixties and Dublin was starting to come to life after the misery of the fifties, but I was sent to the back of beyond. I mean, what kind of crimes would be committed in a place like this? Ha! I wasn't long finding out that even the tiniest village can harbour the deepest wickedness.

'A place this small is like a microcosm of the world. Every emotion is heightened. Everyone knows your business. What might be a short-lived squabble among neighbours in a city can turn into a century-long feud here. There's nowhere to go, you see.

'It was worse, back then. If a lad went through a rough patch as a kid, he was marked for life as the bad 'un. If a girl got in the family way before she was married, well . . . that's where the laundries came in . . .'

Barney paused to sip his tea. Laura waited, spellbound.

'I didn't interact much with the convent at first. It was the big house outside the village, somewhere you heard about but didn't see. I didn't buy into the notion, though, that the laundry was heaving with wanton women. I knew it wouldn't take much more than a kiss down the lane and maybe letting a lad have a fondle for a girl around here to be described as "loose".

'My first real encounter was when one of the girls was reported missing. The nuns rang us and said the girl was simple-minded, that her family had entrusted her to their care and she'd wandered off. You can imagine, I was happy to take part in a search party. My partner and I found her walking on the road to the city. She started running when she heard the car – I don't know why she didn't keep to the woods, where we might not have seen her. Maybe she was so frightened she wasn't in her right mind. But we caught her.

'I tell you, it took me all of five minutes to realize that girl was not some simpleton. And it took me less than that to realize that the bruises on her arms and head were not caused from running into tree branches. She sobbed the whole way back and begged us to let her go.'

Barney's face darkened as he replayed the scene. 'I was torn. My sergeant had told me to find the girl and bring her back to the convent. My gut said there was something very wrong. But I was afraid to disobey an order. I gave myself the excuse that I would find out exactly what had happened to get her in that state, and I drove her back.'

He shook his head angrily. 'I listened to that girl sobbing with a knot in my stomach that I thought would make me sick, telling myself all the while that it wouldn't be anything the nuns had done. We pulled up and I helped drag her into the house. Mother Theresa was in charge then, and she met us at the door with two of the other sisters, who took the girl off with them.

'I'm not such a coward that I didn't ask questions. I asked had the girl been in a fight. I asked why she had bruises and what she'd been running from. I asked everything but I didn't ask why one of those sisters clattered the girl around the ears before pulling her through the door that led off to the dormitories.'

Barney looked shamefaced. 'I listened to their excuses. Then I left, patting myself on the back because I sounded very stern and refused a cup of tea. I left her there and went home and made myself a lovely supper that I couldn't eat a scrap of. But I made it my business after that to keep an eye on the place. I'd call up on the pretext of seeing how things were going. I was hoping to catch a sight of the girl, so I could reassure myself she was all right.'

'And did you?' Laura asked.

Barney sighed. 'Sometimes. But in trying to look out for her I saw so much else that disturbed me. I started making notes. Those girls were treated disgracefully. They were slaves to those nuns. Then your aunt died . . .'

Barney stopped. The room was silent, bar his ragged breathing.

Laura was frozen, afraid to move or speak.

Can they see me? I'm looking out at them, looking in.

People rarely see me. They see the surface. What I want them to see. A normal, functioning person. My superficial self.

They don't see me. They don't see my soul and all the badness that lies within. The rot. The thoughts that consume me. The vengeance I must seek.

It's not my fault. I am what God made me. What this world made me.

If I could have chosen something different, I would have. What I wouldn't give to love and be loved. To be happy. To be free of the rage that courses through my every vein and the sadness that can be found in every fibre of my being.

I refuse to carry guilt. I refuse to be shamed – I have nothing to be ashamed of.

The people I hurt are entitled to nothing better. I am superior to them in every way. I used to fear such people, feel redundant in their presence, but I have turned my fear into strength.

I no longer quake when I see their faces, shiver when I hear their voices.

That first blow, to the back of Attracta's head, simultaneously smashed through all my anxieties and doubts and released in me the determination I need to get this done. It set free what has bubbled inside me for so many years.

On the outside, I look and sound the same.

If only they knew.

The detective is looking over at me, can probably see my outline through the net curtain. But he knows nothing; he sees nothing.

I had to wait for the others to leave, off on their wild goose chase to see if the alibi stacks up.

It won't, but that hardly matters now.

I must get out of here. Before they come back and find out what I've done.

Before they discover that I've killed.

Again.

CHAPTER 34

Michael was vexed. After an hour of crunching around the snowy village, Father Seamus's alibi had so many holes a bus could be driven through it.

They had banged on Larry O'Farrell's door for five minutes before his neighbour let them in with the spare key. The house was empty. O'Farrell didn't have a mobile phone, but a call to the hospital revealed that he had been at his sister's bedside almost constantly since Thursday morning. When a nurse put him on the line, he informed them that he was staying in his sister's house and hadn't had a visit from Father Seamus before he left.

Mrs Guckian confirmed that Father Seamus had indeed called in on her, but it had not been in the early afternoon, as he had claimed. She was sure she had seen him late that evening.

Two other elderly residents in the village asserted that they had seen the priest on Thursday. They were so old and forgetful, though, that it struck Michael they could have seen the priest at any time on any day and been prompted into believing they'd seen him on Thursday.

One of them had mistaken Michael for his own brother and was quite clearly suffering from dementia.

To save them a cross-country drive, Ciaran phoned Father Terence. After his initial shock at finding out that Mother Attracta had been murdered, the priest told them he hadn't seen Father Seamus on Thursday.

Not only had he not seen him, but he hadn't been expecting him either.

None of the bar staff in any of the public houses remembered seeing Father Seamus, though he had written on his list that he had called into 'the pub'.

'It's not looking good, is it?' Ciaran said.

'We need to question him again,' Michael replied. 'He sent us chasing our tails. I think he might be planning a runner.'

'I don't think he'll be running, lad. But let's go back, all the same.'

Ciaran's words were calm, but Michael detected a hint of anxiety.

He was glad he'd asked Ray to keep an eye.

Ray stood beside one of Ciaran's squad cars, stamping his feet on the kerb to keep warm. Pure boredom had driven him to get out of the vehicle and walk around. He'd sent the uniformed guard off to get coffee. Ray wasn't pulling rank. The man was glad to go for the walk, and he knew where to buy a hot drink.

The temperature had fallen again. Ray fervently wished he had a hat, or anything more substantial than a buzz cut. His ears were freezing. The world was still, the snow dulling what sound there was in the sleepy village. Even the wind had dropped. Ray couldn't shake a disquieting feeling that this was the calm before the storm.

He stared over at the priest's house. It had been a half-hour since he'd seen movement behind the curtains in one of the downstairs rooms. A ten-foot-high wall enclosed the priest's and his next-door neighbour's back gardens. The only exits were gates to the side of either house, both clearly visible from Ray's vantage point. He wasn't worried that the elderly priest would scale the back wall.

Ray kept checking the reception on his phone; he was still waiting for the toll company to get back to him. The phone had lost signal a couple of times already. He'd texted Dublin to see if there had been any developments at that end. Ian replied with a sad smiley face, which Ray found strangely unprofessional but highly amusing.

An oncoming white jeep drew his attention. He hadn't seen any cars go by since they'd arrived, and he squinted now to see who was driving. As the vehicle approached, the driver's dark hair and red lips gave it away. He felt his stomach do a little dance.

Ellie pulled up slowly behind the squad car.

'Well, fancy bumping into you here,' she smiled, as she got out. 'Where's your boss?'

'He's in the parish hall, enjoying a nice lunch, I reckon,' Ray smiled back.

'And poor you stuck out here in the cold. What are you doing, anyway?'

'I'm on priest watch.' Ray nodded over to the house. 'He's rapidly rising up our suspect list. Actually, he's probably our only solid lead at this point. I'm here to make sure he doesn't make a run for it.'

'I have complete faith in you being able to catch and take the old man down.'

'What brings you here?' he asked.

'Don't worry, Jack's still hard at it. He sent me out to get his lunch. He claimed I needed a break, but I sense he wanted to get rid of me. I'm under strict orders to bring him back a McDonald's. I don't know who he thinks he is – I'm the boss.'

She cast her eyes around the green. 'I don't think he'll be getting that Big Mac. You'd think, being from near here, he'd know what's available.'

'The pubs seem to do food.'

'Have you eaten?'

'Not yet. I'm stuck here until Michael gets back.'

The disappointed look on her face would have been enough to make his day, but the sight of Michael and Ciaran rounding the corner had him nearly leaping for joy.

Michael speeded up as they approached, outpacing the older officer, who was getting more red-faced with each passing yard.

'Did he try to leave?' he asked Ray.

'No one in or out. Are you going in?'

'Not yet. I just called Tom; he told me to hang on for

himself and Willie. He's talking to the villagers and doesn't want us moving too fast, but this is our man. I know it. He gave us an alibi that wasn't worth the paper it was written on. Better to have all our ducks in a row, though. Still no word from the toll company?'

Ray shook his head. 'If you're hanging on here, do you mind if I nip into one of the pubs for a bite?'

Michael raised a knowing eyebrow.

Ray flashed a toothy grin. 'Shall we?' he said, turning to Ellie.

The local guard had just returned with Ray's cup of coffee.

Ciaran took it off him. 'Waste not, want not.'

Michael was warm from the brisk walk back through the village and refused Ciaran's offer of the guard's other cup. The poor chap looked relieved, and started sipping immediately.

Still feeling the hint of love in the air, Michael pulled out his phone to text Anne.

Miss you down here. Hope you're okay. Case moving fast, please God home soon. Love you.

It took a few minutes but the return text was worth the wait.

Love you too. Miss you so much. Want to talk to you but nothing to worry about.

All they had needed was a little break, he thought. By Christmas they'd be back to themselves.

Ray ordered lunch at the bar and returned to Ellie, who had settled into a seat beside a blazing turf fire.

He joined her, breathing in her perfume.

'Coco Mademoiselle,' he observed.

Ellie looked at him, surprised. 'Are you re-enacting scenes from *Scent of a Woman*? That was impressive.'

Ray stared at the table, mortified. 'No, it's my sister's perfume. She orders it every Christmas. She reached a point where she got fed up with my lame efforts at gifts and started giving me orders.'

'So, I remind you of your sister. Interesting.'

He could see the playful smile on the edge of her lips. Lips he'd like to kiss. And now he'd introduced his sister into the conversation.

Ellie laughed. 'Don't worry, it's not my favourite. I'll wear something else next time we meet. Bombshell, perhaps. Unless your mother wears that one?'

Ray laughed. He wasn't imagining her flirtatious tone.

'It's nice to take a break from it all, isn't it?' Ellie said, serious now. 'It gets very intense.'

Ray nodded. 'The best advice Tom ever gave me was to switch off. Some of your best ideas come when you've taken a breather.'

'He knows what he's talking about, your boss.'

'You seem fairly comfortable in your job,' Ray said. 'You don't seem fazed by all the death you see. I worry I'll never get used to it. I'm eight years in the murder squad and my stomach still turns if it's particularly vicious.'

She shrugged. 'To be fair, I think your reaction is normal. It's horrible when you see people become blasé about death. I've always had the advantage of a more scientific brain. I can walk into a crime scene and just see the evidence, switch off from the gore . . .'

She paused. 'Sometimes it's hard. You get an old man found dead at home, and they need to check it's nothing suspicious. Doesn't bother me; he's old. You get the young lads who've been shot by some rival gang member, and it's not pleasant; but you know they chose a certain life.

'Sometimes, though, you get a child. That's unbearable. I can't stand seeing them hurt. Death in children – it's unnatural.' Ellie shuddered. 'But even when it's tough, you know that by doing your job you're trying to get justice for that person. Am I making sense?'

'Perfect sense.' Ray sipped thoughtfully, then asked, 'What do your family think of your career choice?'

'They're proud. I'm an only child, so they would have been supportive whatever I did. You?'

'My mother's family is proper working class, so it took them a while to accept me joining up. They wouldn't be into anything dodgy, they're just suspicious of authority in general. Nowadays, they see it as a plus. Keep asking me to help with things. Especially passports.'

They both laughed.

Their food arrived, and there was silence for a few

minutes as they tucked in. Ray had ordered the roast lamb, Ellie the salmon darne.

'How's your fish?' he asked.

'They killed it twice. Your lamb?'

'It's mutton dressed as . . .'

She forced down another few forkfuls then pushed the plate away, checking her watch as she did.

'You in a hurry to get back?' Ray asked.

'Yes and no. I'm wondering if Jack found something while I was out; I've never seen a site so clean. And I really want to impress your boss.'

'You can only do what you can do. If we can find the murder site, then we're sure to pick up DNA. Surely the killer won't have done as good a job of cleaning up as that team of nuns did?'

'I think you're right,' she snorted. 'Have you any clue where she could have been killed? It's a long way from here to Dublin.'

He shook his head. 'I wish I knew. It looks like we could identify her murderer before finding the site, though. That's why the lads are watching the priest's house.'

'You're not serious. You think the priest killed the nun? Jesus, the papers would have a field day. Why would he kill her?'

'Tom thinks he has something to hide, and maybe the nun was blackmailing him.'

Ellie shook her head. 'I guess everyone always thinks the impossible can't happen – until it does.'

She sipped her orange juice while he finished eating.

'I enjoy your company,' she said, nodding as if to give him a stamp of approval.

Ray was taken aback by her directness. But before he could say anything, his phone rang.

'That'll be Tom,' he said, pulling it from his pocket.

But it wasn't.

He listened patiently to the man from the toll company.

'That's perfect,' he replied. 'Can you text those times through to me? Thanks.'

He hung up and looked at Ellie, apologetically. 'I need to find Tom.'

She stood, pulling on her coat. 'Good news?'

'The best. We have him. And you can take some of the credit.'

CHAPTER 35

'You know how your aunt died?' Barney asked.

'She hanged herself,' Laura said.

'She did. The doctor rang the station and the guard on the desk knew I'd been taking an interest, so he gave it to me. I remember driving in through those gates.' He half closed his eyes, recalling images long burned into his memory. 'They hadn't cut her down. She had attached the rope to a bedstead in her dormitory. It shouldn't have worked. The rope was too long. She should have crashed on to the roof of that corridor running along the front of the house. She might have died from the impact but not from hanging.

'But it was the window she'd chosen. A month before, there'd been a huge storm and a tree had fallen on to the corridor just at the spot under her dormitory, collapsing part of it. The local roofer hadn't got around to reslating but had covered the hole with a piece of tarpaulin. It was only held in place by a few bricks. The weight of Peggy's body meant she plummeted through the covering and swung into a downstairs window, feet first.

'When we arrived, she was dead. Her neck had been broken but I remember her feet ... her poor feet ...' The corners of Barney's eyes filled with tears.

Laura felt her chest constrict as the horror of how her aunt had suffered hit home.

The old man coughed and withdrew a large handkerchief from his pocket, blowing his nose noisily into it.

'I'm sorry,' he said. 'As if I have the right to be sitting here blubbing like this, when she was your kin.'

Laura was lost for words.

'There's more,' Barney said, his voice almost a whisper.

Only the sound of a clock ticking in the corner of Barney's room could be heard – that and Laura's heart – until the old man started speaking again.

'You know who was standing in the downstairs room when Peggy's feet came crashing through the window? Mother Attracta. She was showered in glass. They thought the old witch was going to lose an eye. And she deserved it. What's it the Bible says? An eye for an eye.'

Despite the room's heat Laura felt chilled to her bones. She recalled the conversation with Sister Concepta in the records room earlier, about how Mother Attracta had inexplicably ordered the windows bricked up.

The thought that their victim had known her aunt – had somehow been connected to her aunt's death – was both terrifying and exhilarating.

'Why do you say that? An eye for an eye? What had Mother Attracta done?' she asked.

Barney hesitated, but the young woman's pleading expression was too much.

'Attracta tormented that girl. I told you, she was an evil woman. Many of the Magdalenes were just young girls, but there were a lot of older teenagers and women in their early twenties who would have gone there straight from the mother and baby homes. Their families didn't want them back after they'd had their children.

'Attracta would torture the ones who'd had to give up babies – tell them how great the tots were doing with their new mammies, how in God's eyes the adoptive mothers were the real parents because they hadn't sinned. It used to drive the girls mad; you can't imagine how traumatized they were after losing their little ones.

'But Peggy seemed to particularly irritate her. Peggy went into herself. No matter what Attracta said to her, she had the blinds down, so to speak. So that twisted nun tried harder with her. She'd beat her for the slightest thing. Whisper in her ear all the time about how her family didn't want her, how she should be grateful that the lads who'd raped her – oh yes, I found out why Peggy had been sent to the place – had paid her any attention because she was an ugly thing. I never spoke to Peggy; the other girls would tell me this.'

Barney took a deep breath. 'I tried to do little things for her, and for the other girls. I smuggled little packages of sweets in, and the older women would make sure she got them. I talked to the local doctor to see if she could be released back to her family. But by that stage, the nuns had medical advice saying Peggy needed to be institutionalized. Bad and all as it was in the convent, she was probably fortunate they never managed to get her committed to an insane asylum, given the times. Then I discovered her family had stopped visiting anyhow, so they mustn't have wanted her back.'

'My grandmother died a couple of years after Peggy went in,' Laura said, defensively. 'She died from a broken heart. She never wanted her in there. My mother was very young when Peggy entered the laundry. She went looking for her later, but Peggy was already dead.'

Barney's mouth formed an 'O' of regret.

'I didn't know,' he said. 'I thought her family had abandoned her.'

They sat silently for a moment, absorbing the tragedy, before Barney continued.

'Whatever I thought about her family, it was Mother Attracta I blamed for what happened to Peggy. The girl might have placed that noose around her own neck, but by God, that woman drove her to her death. I hope she rots.'

Barney spat out the last few words with a contempt that echoed how Laura felt.

'Why didn't you arrest Mother Attracta for assaulting the girl?' Darren asked, shocked by what he'd just heard.

Barney sighed. 'Lad, you didn't arrest a nun. You wouldn't understand – the Catholic Church ran this state back then. Even the government was afraid of them. But I did everything to investigate that girl's death. I wanted those bitches put under pressure, even though it was a suicide. I wanted them to know that I was watching them. I felt responsible.'

Laura was gripping the sides of the armchair so hard her knuckles had turned white.

'Why did you feel responsible? You looked out for her,' Darren interjected.

Barney closed his eyes. 'I tried to look out for all the girls, but I was looking out for Peggy in particular. She was *the* girl, you see. She was the girl I dragged back when she tried to escape all those years before.'

Laura felt the room closing in on her. Her head started to spin. She could vaguely hear Darren asking her if she was okay. It sounded like he was in a different room, his voice muffled.

'I need a bathroom,' she said, leaning forward as the bile rose.

Barney stood up, alarmed.

'Just over there,' he said, pointing.

Laura swayed as she stood, and Darren grabbed her elbow to steady her.

She just made it. It took all her willpower to close the door behind her before she emptied the contents of her stomach into the toilet bowl.

When the retching subsided, Laura flushed the toilet and propped herself over the sink. Her reflection in the mirror was frightful.

She ran the cold tap and splashed her face before squeezing a sliver of Barney's toothpaste on to her finger and rubbing it around her teeth. Then she patted her eyes with wet tissue to reduce the puffiness. Finally, Laura took her phone from her pocket and texted Tom.

She felt stupid. She had never met her aunt. Why was this affecting her so much? And she was mortified. Why hadn't she sent Darren out of the room? She'd only met him, and now he knew her family history and had witnessed her humiliating reaction to it.

She steeled herself to return to the overheated little room where Barney was waiting for her.

The old man was exhausted, sunk in his chair, head in hands.

The young guard made to help her, but she shrugged him off.

'I'm fine,' Laura said, facing Barney. She couldn't sit down. She had to get out of here.

He looked up. 'I am so sorry, girl. What happened to your aunt has haunted me for a very long time.'

Laura bit her lip. She closed her eyes and took a deep breath.

'I can't say I understand why you brought her back. I became a police officer because I wanted to help people, not deliver them to harm—'

She stopped. Considered the dying man in front her. He had shrivelled from the bombastic, cheerful presence she had first encountered. It took everything she had to utter her next few sentences.

'I wasn't around, back then. I don't know what the world was like. I can see what happened to my aunt has preyed on your mind, and you've spent enough time dwelling on it. It wasn't your fault what happened to Peggy. You did what you could.'

She just about got the words out. Any pang she felt at saying them was alleviated by the look of pure gratitude on the man's face. Her forgiveness had lifted a great weight from his shoulders.

'Look, before I go, can you tell me who might have hated Attracta enough to kill her? Is anyone in the village capable of it? Could it have been one of the sisters in the convent? Or Father Seamus?'

Laura robotically asked the necessary questions, conscious of the fact that right now she didn't give a hoot who had killed the nun.

Barney rubbed his beard. 'I don't know what life was like in that convent in recent years, so I can't speak about the women who lived with her. Father Seamus? Yes. The man is capable of anything. There were ... incidents. Two or three of the girls in the laundry got pregnant in the seventies. They never saw boys, and the only men ever about the place were the priests. It happened once or twice in the sixties, too, but a priest was moved that time.

'I made it known I was keeping an eye on Father Seamus, and I think one or two of the nuns cottoned on as well. Nothing else happened after that. But I've always had my suspicions – and I wonder if Attracta did, too. Would she be capable of blackmail? Yes, very much. And if she confronted him about it, well, there's no saying how he'd react. Why she'd do that now, after all this time, I don't know.'

Laura and Darren exchanged an appalled look.

Barney balled his fists and banged them on the side of the armchair. 'If Father Seamus killed her, well, she had it coming. But if you ask me, so does he.'

As soon as the anger came, it was gone, and Barney was diminished again.

Laura turned to leave the room.

'Laura?' The elderly man's tone was pitiful.

She looked back at him.

'If you visit your aunt's grave, will you ask her to forgive me? I shouldn't have brought her back. I'll never forgive myself.'

Laura started to well up. She had to get out of this room. She had never visited her aunt's grave and probably never would, if it was unmarked.

Darren had the good sense to say nothing as they walked back to the car. When they got in, he turned to her.

'What you said in there to Barney – at the end – it was very good of you. He'll die with an easier conscience because of it.'

Laura didn't respond.

CHAPTER 36

A pattern was emerging of how Mother Attracta was perceived in the village. Some of the elderly matrons had good things to say about her, but most people found her stand-offish and haughty. None of them struck the inspector as potential killers.

Tom had received a text from Laura twenty minutes previously saying she needed to see him urgently.

When he met her outside the parish hall, he was shocked by her appearance. As pale as a ghost, she looked to have aged in the couple of hours since he'd seen her last.

'I can't do this, sir. I have to excuse myself from the investigation,' she blurted, before he could say anything.

Tom took a deep breath. 'Why? Is it about your aunt? Something that Barney Kelly told you?'

'Yes, it's about my aunt. But it's also about that woman. After what I just heard, I'll sum it up like this. I don't care who killed her. Whoever did it deserves a medal.' She slumped back against the church wall and brought her hands up to her face. 'I have to go back to Dublin,' she mumbled from behind her fingers.

He said nothing for a moment but silently cursed. He needed to get a job done here, not solve the mysteries of Laura's aunt's past.

'All right. I can see you're very upset. What did Barney Kelly say?'

Laura blew out the breath she'd been holding in and relayed, as calmly as she could, what the retired sergeant had told her about his interactions with the convent and her aunt's death.

'There's more. Something Barney said about Father Seamus. He thinks the priest might have sexually assaulted some of the girls. And he says Attracta would have been more than capable of blackmailing him.'

Laura threw her head back. 'You see why I can't stay on this case. That convent – it's evil.'

'You don't have to stay, Laura. I won't make you.' Tom was appalled. 'It's entirely up to you. I want you to consider one thing, though. Your aunt's story and the other things we've learned paint a picture we cannot ignore. It's clear the cause of this murder may well lie in the past. Michael and Ciaran are standing outside the priest's house right now, waiting for us. He gave us a false alibi for Thursday. I know he has something to hide. What Barney Kelly told you could be crucial.'

He gave Laura a minute to process the new information.

She chewed her bottom lip. Then she asked, 'So he's our man?'

Tom shrugged. 'I don't know. Maybe. Do you want to see this through?'

She stared at the ground. 'All that stuff I said ... about not being able to arrest her murderer ...'

'Pretty understandable, I'd say. Look, when we discovered Mother Attracta's body, my notion of what kind of woman she was involved grandkids and bingo. It was human to make those assumptions, but they were wrong. Just because somebody is elderly doesn't mean they are good, or innocent.

'Mother Attracta was not a good woman. But that doesn't mean we shouldn't pursue her killer. It's our job, Laura, to enforce the rules. See this through. Arresting her murderer won't make her any less bad, but it will make you a better detective.'

Laura considered her boss's words. He had made her see sense.

She felt calmer. And grateful. Here they were in the middle of a murder investigation, and he still had time to help her deal with her personal problems.

'I'd like to stay on, if that's okay. Thank you, sir. For understanding and for giving me a chance.'

Tom nodded. 'Right, then, let's head round to Father Seamus's house.'

They arrived at the priest's residence just as Ellie was dropping Ray off on her way back to the convent. Willie and Michael were already there.

Tom's entire team was now assembled, all hoping that this was the break they'd been waiting for.

He sighed. 'We won't be storming the building. We

can't pull him in for murder on the basis of a dodgy alibi. We just need to ask some questions.'

'Boss, I've something that changes things,' Ray said. 'I got a call from the toll company. Father Seamus's car was recorded on CCTV going through one of the booths at 10 p.m. on Wednesday and coming back at 7 p.m. on Thursday. He went to Dublin. We have him.'

Nobody breathed for a moment, then Tom spoke.

'Well, why didn't you say so? That puts things in a new light. Right, Ciaran, can you get an arrest warrant sorted? At best, he's obstructed a murder investigation by lying. That alone could be enough to bring him in. But let's see if he has a plausible explanation.'

'I'm on it,' Ciaran said. 'Under no circumstances are you to bring him down to the station on your own. I want to be the one to handcuff him.'

'Ray and I will question him in his house for now,' Tom said. 'There's no need for five of us. Michael and Laura, send out an alert to all the garda and petrol stations adjacent to that motorway route to check CCTV in their towns and villages for sightings of his car. If he's our killer, we might discover where he brought her. Willie, drop the lads down to the convent, will you? We'll keep you posted.'

The inspector looked over at the priest's house. He'd had a gut feeling that Father Seamus was going to play more of a role in the investigation.

Could they have cracked the case in such a short period? He was afraid to hope.

*

Ray pressed his finger against the priest's doorbell and they waited.

A minute passed. Ray rang again.

Nothing.

They looked at each other.

What was Father Seamus playing at?

Tom knelt down and looked through the letter box. He could see nothing in the hallway, and all the doors were closed.

'Is he asleep or something?' Ray wondered aloud.

'Father Seamus?' Tom called into the letter box. 'It's Inspector Reynolds here. We need to ask you some more questions. Can you come to the door, please?'

There was no movement and no sound.

Tom stood up and looked around. Willie had turned the car round at the church and was driving back towards them, with Michael in the passenger seat.

The inspector walked to the garden gate and waved him down, while Ray pressed the bell again and followed it up with three heavy knocks.

Willie pulled up and rolled the window down.

'Michael, did Father Seamus say what he was going to do after you left him?' Tom asked.

'He said he had work to do.'

'There's no way out the back?'

Michael shook his head, frowning.

Willie turned off the engine, and the two men got out of the car.

'He could be sitting upstairs hoping we'll go away,' Willie suggested.

Tom shook his head. 'The man's not an idiot. He's probably been watching us watching him.'

Michael frowned. 'I was worried he'd do a runner, but what if he's done something stupid, like top himself?'

'He'd need a really guilty conscience to do that,' Tom said. 'Do you have his phone number?'

Michael punched in the priest's number. Ray hunched down and placed his ear against the open letter box.

'No answer.'

'I heard it ringing,' Ray called.

'We'll give the back a go,' Tom said.

Willie rang Ciaran and told him what was going on.

'Ciaran says the cleaner has spare keys,' he told Tom, resting the phone against his collarbone.

'Tell him to pick them up. We'll try the back entrance in the meantime.'

Michael climbed over the gate at the side of the house and unlocked it. He and Tom made their way along the side of the building, pausing to peer in a side window. Tom could see the outline of furniture through the net curtains but could discern no movement.

The side passage led out to a large square lawn. A small fence separated the priest's garden from that of his neighbour.

When they reached the back door, Michael placed a

gloved hand on the knob, preparing to shake it. To his surprise, the door opened.

He looked at Tom, who shrugged.

'It can be common in the countryside to leave back doors unlocked.'

Michael shook his head. 'No, he has three locks on his front door. Doesn't strike me as someone who'd leave the back door open.'

'That gives us reasonable cause to enter, then.'

Michael stood back and let Tom step into the house before him, directly into a large kitchen.

'Father Seamus?' Tom called out. 'It's the police. Your back door is open. We're coming in to make sure you're all right.'

There was no response.

Tom crossed the kitchen and opened the door cautiously. He looked out and, seeing nothing amiss in the hall, strode to the front door and opened it, turning the three locks.

Ray, Willie and Laura stepped in from the cold.

'Father, there are a few of us in the hall now. We're going to check the rooms. If you're here and you can, please make yourself known to us,' Tom called out again. He leaned over to Michael. 'Ciaran didn't mention anything about the priest being a rabid firearms collector or anything?' he whispered.

Michael shook his head.

'Well, take it easy, anyway,' Tom said. 'The man might

be completely unstable. Laura, Michael, take downstairs. Stay together. Ray, you come up with me. Willie, keep an eye on the front of the house in case he tries to jump out a window.'

Ray followed Tom upstairs.

They found themselves on a U-shaped landing, with a choice of rooms to their left and right, all doors closed.

'Which way?' Ray asked.

'I always veer left. Like my politics,' Tom replied.

'Well, if that's your logic, I believe in the death penalty, so I may as well start on the right.'

The bedroom and study Tom checked were empty. He made his way round the landing until he and Ray met back where they had started, in the middle.

A bathroom lay behind the final door. Ray yanked back the shower curtain dramatically, but found nothing.

The two men stood, puzzled, at the top of the stairs.

'Where the hell is he?' Ray asked.

Tom leaned over the banister. 'Michael, Laura, anything?'

Laura's face appeared at the bottom of the stairs. 'Nothing, sir.'

'Try calling his mobile phone again.' The inspector looked overhead. 'There's an attic . . .'

An open padlock hung from the door above them, the key still in the lock.

'Brilliant,' Ray muttered.

'What's the matter?'

'All the horror movies have attic scenes.'

'You big baby. I'll go up, then, shall I?'

Ray looked dubious. 'How are you going to manage that?'

Tom pointed to a string dangling from a long bamboo stick affixed to the side of the attic door.

'Behold this magical contraption,' he said.

He pulled the string, which released the stick. A little hook at one end of the stick fitted into a twin hook on the attic door.

Ray looked at Tom approvingly. 'I can see how you made inspector.'

'Stand back,' Tom said, serious now. He called out again. 'Father Seamus, This is Inspector Tom Reynolds. I'm about to open the attic door. I'm armed and there are other police officers with me.'

When there was no response, he pulled on the stick.

A set of collapsible stairs descended softly to the landing.

Tom placed his foot on the first step.

Ray grabbed his arm. 'Maybe I should go up.'

'Touching,' Tom said.

The inspector always advised caution – and he showed it himself – but when they were forced to undertake something reckless, he preferred to be the one taking the risk.

He could only hope he wouldn't be confronted by a madman at the top of these stairs.

He started up the steps and paused.

'That switch on the wall there, Ray – no, the one in the middle – flick that.'

Ray turned on the switch.

Suddenly the dark opening overhead was filled with bright light.

Four . . . five creaky steps . . . and Tom's head was through the attic door. He had held his breath all the way up, and he resisted the urge to duck now. As it turned out, he had been worrying about the wrong thing.

Father Seamus was not lurking in the attic. There was something much worse.

'Ray?' Tom croaked.

'What is it?'

Ray charged up the stairs behind him, forcing Tom to climb into the attic proper.

The room had been converted, and Tom was able to comfortably stand upright.

'Shit!' Ray exclaimed.

The detective sergeant's face was a mixture of horror and revulsion.

Almost every inch of every wall was covered in pornographic photographs of women. Young women mostly, in various lewd and graphic poses. Pictures, pulled from the wall in haste, lay scattered around the floor.

A television and DVD player sat on a table across from a small couch. Another table held a desktop computer. Both tables were stacked with DVDs, their indecent covers revealing their content.

It was a museum of depravity.

'Get your gloves on,' Tom said, moving closer to look at the images properly. 'This is all evidence.'

The girls were very young. Not quite children, but borderline illegal.

'The sick bastard,' Ray said.

'I guess this is why he has three locks on his front door,' Tom replied.

Ray pulled a pair of disposable gloves from his jacket pocket and approached the computer. He pressed a key, and the screen came to life. The computer was on standby; the priest must have been near it recently. A still from an adult video appeared.

Ray sat in front of the computer and pulled the image to the side of the screen.

'He was deleting downloads,' he said.

Tom shook his head; the attic made his skin crawl. 'He knew we'd discover he lied about his alibi. He was up here trying to hide his tracks and get rid of this stuff before we got a search warrant. Probably didn't know where to start. He must have been disturbed and hurried down, which would explain why the padlock was open. But where is he now?'

'Tom . . .' Ray's voice was flat and disbelieving.

'What is it?' Tom walked over to the desk.

Ray had opened a folder beside the keyboard.

It was full of old photos, one or two already ripped up. These weren't like the ones on the walls. Some of the girls were actually children, and they were all semi-naked. In each of the photos, they were trying to hide the exposed parts of their bodies, mainly their barely formed breasts. Their eyes looked away from the camera, towards the floor in most cases. In one picture, tears lined the face of a girl who looked no older than thirteen. The background was the same in every photo – a seventies-era sitting room, replete with garish floral drawn curtains and a patterned sofa.

It was the hair that confirmed it. Each of the girls had identical tight bobs, swept to the side. Tom had seen that style before in photos of Magdalene girls.

'They're laundry girls,' Tom said, feeling nauseous.

'There are seven different girls, even without the torn-up photos,' Ray said. 'That'll be his sitting room. He must have brought the girls up here on some pretext the nuns were okay with. Probably let them think they were his favourites.' He slammed the folder shut in anger.

'Holy crap!'

The surprised yell rang up the stairs, making them both jump.

'What now?' Tom exclaimed.

CHAPTER 37

Ray made it down the attic staircase first.

'What is it?' he yelled, rounding the landing.

'You've got to see this,' Michael shouted back.

Willie hurried in the front door just as Tom and Ray reached the bottom of the stairs.

Laura was backed flat against the wall beside the kitchen, her mouth hanging open.

Michael stood at the side of the stairs by an open door that Tom hadn't noticed when he'd crossed the hall minutes earlier. The door was made of the same wood as the panelling under the staircase, providing a discreet storage space.

But it didn't contain the usual bric-a-brac.

On the floor, having just tumbled out, lay the prone figure of Father Seamus, curled into a foetal ball. His dead eyes bulged wide in horror, his face blue.

'I just rang his mobile, and Laura heard it behind that door,' Michael said. 'He fell out on top of her.'

Tom stood over the priest.

He had no obvious injuries. There was no blood seeping from any wound. No bruising was apparent.

After seeing the contents of the folder upstairs, the inspector found it hard to summon any compassion for the man who lay dead at his feet. He hunched down and stared at the priest's neck to see if there were any marks that would indicate strangulation. The skin was unblemished bar one possible contusion.

Tom stood up.

'I can't see an obvious cause of death, but I can only imagine it's not natural – unless he was hiding from someone in the stair cupboard and had a heart attack?'

'I nearly had a bloody heart attack,' Laura said. 'That's his mobile on the floor – it must have been in his pocket.'

'Ray, get Ellie on the phone,' Tom said. 'Tell her we need her up here immediately. We have to work on the assumption this isn't accidental, and secure the scene. He died in the last couple of hours. If someone was audacious enough to murder him under our noses, then they could be insane enough to hang around and watch the aftermath. So let's get Ciaran and his lads back here, too. Michael, Laura, we need to check the nuns' alibis for this afternoon. I'm going to ring headquarters. And somebody call an ambulance.'

The detectives engaged in a flurry of activity, as Tom pulled his phone from his pocket.

'I guess this rules out the priest for Mother Attracta,' Ray said, as he pulled his own phone out.

'If he's been murdered, and if it's the same killer,' Tom cautioned.

'Sir,' Laura said, 'it's something Barney Kelly said to me when I was up with him.'

'Yes?'

'He said the priest had it coming, just as Mother Attracta had. He was angry. And he's dying. He has nothing to lose.'

'You're only back from the nursing home a short while, though. How fast can he move?'

'You can get down here in ten minutes in a car.'

'Okay. Confirm he didn't leave the home.'

Tom's first call was to Emmet McDonagh.

'Who's dead now?' Emmet said, wearily.

'The local priest. I can't confirm it yet, but I'm pretty sure this is a murder scene, Emmet. Now will you come down?'

There was silence down the line.

'It's starting to get very *Da Vinci Code* down there, isn't it? I'll be lucky to make it down tonight in this weather. Get Ellie and Jack started, and make sure the scene is well photographed.'

Emmet hung up, and the inspector dialled his boss. It was Sunday afternoon and Tom guessed McGuinness would be at his grandson's weekly football match. They played every Sunday, hail, rain or shine. Or in this case, snow.

Sure enough, when the phone was answered Tom could hear the determined cheering of half-frozen parents and grandparents in the background.

'Tom. Good. What's the latest?' McGuinness' voice stuttered in the cold.

'I have another body, sir. It looks like murder.'

A noise halfway between choking and outrage barrelled down the line.

Tom held the phone away from his ear. He considered not saying who the latest victim was.

'You can't be serious? Is it related?'

'Well, up to about ten minutes ago he was my main suspect, so you could say that.'

'Who is it? Where are you?'

'I'm with the victim. It's the local priest.'

The line fell silent. Silence from Sean McGuinness was always worse than ranting.

'I don't know what's more upsetting, Tom – that a priest is dead, or that a priest was your chief suspect in the murder of a nun.'

Tom said nothing.

'If the priest was a suspect, why wasn't he in custody?' McGuinness demanded.

'He only became a suspect proper in the last hour. He gave us an alibi and when it was checked, it was full of holes. His house was being monitored. His and the immediate neighbour's houses are surrounded by a ten-foot wall, and he was an elderly man.'

'Is McDonagh on the way down?'

'Yes.'

'Good. The Deputy State Pathologist is in Limerick, so you're in luck. I'll ring him. I'll speak to the assistant commissioner for the region and get some extra manpower sent in to assist you. You're working with the local sergeant already, so Limerick will be happy to leave our bureau in charge. A man was shot dead in Limerick City last night, so that team has its hands full.'

Two vehicles pulled up outside the house. Ciaran emerged from one, and Ellie and Jack from the other.

'I'd better go.'

'Get me regular updates. And tell me if you need anything. I mean anything at all, Tom. I'm not having the media claiming we haven't devoted sufficient resources to this.'

Michael came up the drive. He'd gone next door to check if anybody was in.

'No one there,' he said.

'Where's the body?' Ellie asked, as she approached.

'In the hall. Emmet McDonagh is on his way down, weather permitting, and we'll have pathology here shortly. Can you tell if it's murder? It's not obvious to me.'

She shrugged and walked in ahead of the two men. Jack emerged from the back of the van, carrying the forensics equipment.

'We didn't find him straight away,' Tom said to Ciaran, as they stood at the front door, looking in. 'I was starting to wonder whether he'd done a runner or if someone had kidnapped him, too. Wait until you see what we found in the attic.'

'Not another body?'

'Lots of them. Mainly naked, in pictures.'

Ciaran blessed himself as he took in the lifeless body on the floor.

'Is there an actual doctor on the way?' Ellie asked. 'To confirm he's dead?'

'His own doctor is coming,' Ciaran said.

'And we've rung an ambulance,' Tom added. 'You don't think he's in some kind of coma or something?'

'Wouldn't be the first time. You know they've excavated coffins and found nails embedded in the lids from people trying to scratch their way out.'

Tom shuddered. 'I'm hoping if he's still alive we'll establish it during the post-mortem. Does it look natural?'

She threw her hands out as if to say 'I'm not psychic'. She checked for a pulse before peering closer.

'There's no obvious sign of struggle. All I can see without removing his clothes is this mark on his neck. It's not symptomatic of strangling. This could be a puncture wound from a needle, but I can't be sure. I'll try and do a bit more with the body without disturbing too much.'

Tom noticed Jack standing beside him. He was staring at the priest as if this were the first dead body he'd ever seen, his nose wrinkled in disgust.

'Can you take pictures, Jack?' Tom asked, distracting the man from his reverie.

Jack turned, suddenly realizing Tom was there. 'Sure. I'll get started.'

Ray came down the stairs and ushered Tom and Ciaran out to the garden.

'You find something?' Tom asked.

Ray nodded. He looked disturbed.

'I found plenty. I've figured out where Father Seamus was overnight on Wednesday. Are you ready for this?'

'Where was he?' Tom asked.

'His computer has contact details for brothels in Dublin and emails to several of them. He was due to visit one in the city centre on Thursday morning.'

'You are joking me!' Ciaran exclaimed. 'Thursday morning? You're telling me our priest was visiting ladies of the night, in the morning?'

'I don't think they have set opening hours in brothels,' Ray replied. 'I guess he went down late on Wednesday night to avoid the drive up and down on the same day. He was booked into a hotel on the Wednesday night. Easy enough to check if he was there, they'd remember checking someone in that late.'

'Ciaran, Barney Kelly made a serious statement to my officer Laura earlier,' Tom said. 'He implied the priest could have been involved in getting some of the women in the Magdalene Laundry pregnant. Now we've found explicit photos of underage girls, probably from the laundry, in the priest's possession. Is this something you've heard before?'

Ciaran hesitated before replying. 'As a rumour, speculation, nothing more.'

Tom nodded. 'I suspected he was hiding something. We were starting to wonder if he killed Mother Attracta because she had been blackmailing him.'

Ciaran's face paled.

'What is it?' Tom asked.

'Will we head back to the convent?' Ciaran suggested. 'I can fill you in there.'

'Sure,' Tom said, scrutinizing the other man. 'Let's check around the back first. Laura, Michael and Willie are going to be checking the nuns' whereabouts this afternoon. We need to do another door to door, at least in the immediate vicinity, to see if anybody saw anything in the last two hours. There are more guards being sent in from Limerick city.'

'Good,' Ciaran replied. 'We'll cover the village by the end of the day.'

Tom looked across at the small green on one side of the priest's house, the next property being the church. On the other side, he saw large semi-detached houses stretching back to the road on which they had entered the village.

Tom pointed to the empty house next door. 'Who lives there?'

'It's a rental. There's a woman leasing it at the moment. A writer. She only comes down occasionally. An old woman used to live there; her family have her in a home now. They've been renting out the house the last few months to pay the medical bills.'

They made their way round to the rear of the priest's house.

'I feel a bit guilty,' Ciaran said. 'Michael had a notion we should pull the priest in for questioning. I disagreed and said we should verify his alibi first. I regret that now.'

'There wasn't enough to pull him in for questioning at

that point. Ray was keeping watch, and I was in no hurry to come over from the parish hall.'

'Monitoring the house was also Michael's idea,' Ciaran replied, glumly.

They arrived at the wood behind the priest's house and stood back so they could see the top of the garden wall. It was covered in pristine snow except for one spot, which had been disturbed.

The two men examined the ground underfoot. They saw the footprints almost immediately, etched into the snow, leading to and from the trees.

'How far back does this wood go?' Tom asked.

'About five minutes' walk to a road,' Ciaran replied.

'That's where the killer came from. The tracks have to be recent, or the snow earlier would have covered them,' Tom observed.

'They look like men's boots,' Ciaran said. 'You didn't see any prints in the garden?'

'I have to admit I wasn't looking for any,' Tom said. 'I was focused on the back door rather than the garden. I was still assuming that the priest couldn't have exited the property via the back. We weren't thinking that anyone had broken in, at that stage. There were definitely no signs of wet footprints in the kitchen, anyhow. So if someone did enter, they took off their boots beforehand.'

Even as he spoke, the snow started to fall again, flakes landing in the incriminating bootprints.

Tom pulled out his phone and rang Ray.

'Tell Jack to get round here pronto. We've found footprints.'

'Personally,' Ciaran said, as Tom took photos of the prints on his iPhone, 'I'd have used that tree to hoist myself over.'

Branches hung over the wall from a large horse chestnut on the priest's side of the garden.

'That's how our killer got over, all right,' Tom said, standing up, but not before placing his jacket over a set of footprints to protect them. He started shivering almost immediately. 'The branches look sturdy enough.'

They could hear the sound of an ambulance making its way through the village, siren blaring, its frantic wailing too late for Father Seamus.

The pathologist and doctor arrived at the same time as the ambulance. Tom had worked with the pathologist before and greeted him with a familiar handshake. Then he introduced himself to the doctor.

'Mulligan's the name. I'm the village GP,' the other man said. 'I've been Father Seamus's doctor for nigh on thirty years. Is it a suspicious death?'

'I'm pretty sure, but the pathologist will confirm that,' Tom said.

The doctor looked like he should have retired some time ago. He was frail and his glasses seemed too big for his ageing head. But his eyes were lively, and he seemed pleasant enough.

'Is it okay for us to come in?' Tom asked Ellie from the front door.

The crime scene technician was back on her knees beside the dead priest, carefully checking his hands and fingernails.

'It's okay now. There were so many of you in here when he was found, we'll have to check everything against your samples, anyway.'

She stood up and introduced herself to the two new professionals, running through the preliminary work she had already done.

The two paramedics had discreetly brought a wheeled stretcher up to the front door of the house and were awaiting a signal to remove the body. The snow was falling heavily now, swirling in the air like a scene in a snow globe.

The pathologist assumed control over the examination of the corpse.

'He had a heart condition, Inspector,' Doctor Mulligan said. 'If there's no obvious injury, what makes you think something sinister happened?'

'He was in that cupboard.'

The doctor looked at the cupboard door and raised his eyebrows.

The pathologist knelt down beside Father Seamus and performed the same ritual as Ellie, carefully moving clothing aside and then focusing on the mark on his neck.

'What was wrong with his heart?' Tom asked the doctor.

'Arrhythmia. It was weak and prone to irregular heart-beats. He needed surgery, but he was a stubborn man. The necessary recovery period bothered him. He would have needed somebody to move in and take care of him.'

'If you ask me, he's been injected with something right here.' The pathologist straightened up from his appraisal of Father Seamus's neck. 'It was sudden and it was jammed into him hard, hence the discolouration and slight swelling. I've seen something similar before in the murder of an elderly woman in Louth. Her son finished her off.'

'A poison of some sort?' Tom asked.

'We'll need an autopsy for that kind of information. Luckily for you I plan on being in Limerick city for a day or two. I've just completed one post-mortem there but haven't written anything up yet. I can do this poor man today.'

As the pathologist resumed his examination of the body, Tom turned to the GP.

'I haven't encountered this outside of films and books, Doctor. What kind of poison would you inject into some-one to kill them?'

The doctor scratched his head. 'There's a long list. From arsenic – I know, a bit dated – to air. Yes, a good deal of air in someone's veins can kill them. Not a small bubble, mind. If it were me and I knew Father Seamus's medical history, I'd use some sort of adrenalin shot to give him a massive heart attack.'

The pathologist stood up slowly, rubbing his knees. He circled the body and stared into the cupboard.

'I'd work on the assumption that this was murder,' he said. 'If he'd had a heart attack while in that cupboard, for whatever reason, his instincts would have been to push the door open and seek help. It's more likely his dead body was placed in there and the door shut. I'm happy for the body to be moved to the mortuary now.'

Tom nodded. 'You've known Father Seamus for a long time, Doctor Mulligan. Did he ever confide in you about anything? Was he afraid of anything or anyone?'

The medic scratched his head. 'I guess you're asking me if he believed his life was in danger. No, we never had those sort of patient-doctor sessions. I don't know who could have done something as . . . clinical as this. Now, had somebody strangled him, I could have given you a list of suspects.'

'I did get the impression he was quite disliked. How did you get on with him?'

The doctor smiled grimly. 'I got on with him fine, Inspector. But I'm a Protestant, so I didn't have to listen to him pontificating every week.'

'Thank you, Doctor. I'm sure pathology will want to see his medical records, if you can help with that.'

They all watched as Father Seamus departed his house for the last time, on a stretcher between two paramedics.

Tom noted Ellie, standing silently behind them in the doorway as a mark of respect. Jack, as usual, was nowhere to be seen.

'We'll be lucky to get more personnel down here

tonight,' Ciaran said, as the ambulance doors swung shut. 'Weather's getting worse.'

Tom looked up at the oppressive sky. The clouds hung low and heavy. He brushed snowflakes off his face with a hand that was already starting to lose feeling. He'd retrieved his jacket, but even that couldn't keep the heat in.

'It's starting to feel like we'll never get out of this village,' he lamented.

CHAPTER 38

Driving conditions were becoming next to impossible. On the car radio, the weatherman was advising people to stay indoors and only travel if necessary.

As Ciaran's tyres struggled to gain traction on the icy road surface, daylight began to fade. 'Haven't seen snow like this in a long time,' the sergeant said, squinting at the road ahead.

The five-minute drive took over twenty, and the inspector breathed a sigh of relief when they reached the convent safely.

Sister Bernadette opened the front door. Tom and Ciaran stepped in gratefully, shaking their overcoats and wiping their feet on the doormat.

'That's a fierce storm blowing up out there,' the nun said. 'Almost everyone is back, and the rest are en route. Your detectives told us what happened to Father Seamus. Is there any more news?'

'No more news other than the man is dead, Sister,' Tom replied.

'Do you know how he died? Was he murdered?'

'It looks like he was.'

The nun's eyes widened. 'Lord save us. You need something to warm you up. I'd offer tea, but I think a couple of Irish coffees might be in order.'

Tom could have kissed her. There were few things he liked more in the world than a strong Irish coffee. The whiskey, black coffee, brown sugar and fresh cream combined to make a drink that acted as a stimulant, relaxant and dessert.

'That's the best offer I'm going to get today, Sister.'

'I can make you a better offer again. I know you're using Mother Attracta's office as your headquarters but we have another sitting room that we don't use much, and there are the makings of a fire in the grate. It can be lit in minutes. I just need to get Sister Gladys sorted first. I left early to get her home.'

'Thanks for that, Sister. Actually, before you go, there is something I need to ask you following our conversation last night.'

She raised her eyebrows.

'You told me that Sister Concepta and Mother Attracta had a huge argument at Hallowe'en. But you didn't mention that you had played a part in that altercation.'

The nun dropped her gaze to the floor. 'I wasn't deliberately trying to hide anything. It was partly embarrassment and partly me not seeing that it mattered. I wanted to forget about the whole silly affair but Sister Concepta insisted on fighting my corner. She would have reacted in the same manner no matter who was involved, Inspector. Concepta rarely missed an opportunity to clash with Attracta. Sometimes she's just so fiery.'

Tom looked at the nun for a moment, before nodding. 'That's fine, Sister.'

Tom filled Ciaran in on the Hallowe'en episode as they walked.

'Bernadette was a missionary nun, wasn't she?' the sergeant said, thoughtfully. 'Strange that someone who has seen so much would stand back and let someone else get stuck in on their behalf.'

'I think the point she was making there is that she is more careful about choosing her battles.'

'Fair enough.'

In the sitting room, a couple of couches were positioned around a grate, expertly laid in the old-fashioned manner with screwed-up newspapers, sticks and peat briquettes. No cheating with firelogs here.

Ciaran took matches from his trouser pocket and shook them.

'Boy scout,' he said.

He hunched down and lit the base of the fire. Tom crossed to one side of the room and rapped on the wall. The dull thud confirmed its solidity. He'd imagined so, but wanted to check.

'No one will hear through those walls,' Ciaran commented. 'This building is sturdy.'

Tom murmured in assent before reminding the sergeant, 'You said there was something you had to tell me.'

The sergeant raised himself awkwardly from the floor and plonked himself on one of the sofas. 'I'm worried you're going to go away from this place with a bad impression of me. First leaving Father Seamus in the house this afternoon, and now this.'

Tom waited. It depended on what 'this' was.

'There was something, a few years ago, to do with Father Seamus. A woman rang the station. I didn't take the call. There was a young lad on the desk at the time, he's moved on since. She was barely coherent but she made allegations against the priest. Claimed he was a rapist and that he'd been interfering with the girls in the laundry, even got a few of them pregnant. She gave her name but didn't say if she was one of the women who'd been assaulted, or if she'd even been in the laundry.'

'What was her name? What did you do about it?' Tom asked, sitting up straight.

'I can't remember the name. I'm sure we've a record of it. But the guard who took the call said she sounded stark raving mad. She didn't leave a number. I did send one of my officers down here to ask if any woman of that name had been in the place. Attracta denied it and said the records had been destroyed so she couldn't check.'

'Did you raise it with the priest?'

Ciaran fiddled nervously with the pin on his uniform tie. 'No. What could I say? A woman rang in, there's no trace of her, mind, but she's accused you of rape. To a priest?'

Tom shook his head. 'Ah, Ciaran.'

The other man's shoulders drooped. 'I know, I know. But without a proper witness statement, how were we supposed to pursue it? I'd already had a few run-ins with Seamus. For even the slightest reproach of his "authority" —' Ciaran made quotation marks with his fingers, 'he would bring a world of trouble to your door. Sometimes it just wasn't worth it.'

'I get it, I just wish you'd told me earlier. This woman who rang in – we have to get her name. Was she young? Was she old? Did she have an accent? Where's the guard who logged the call?'

Ciaran shook his head to all of the questions. But on the last, he had an answer of sorts.

'When he left us he was headed to Dublin. The garda database will tell us where he's stationed. I'll get on it right away.'

He made to leave the room. At the door he turned.

'I should have taken it more seriously.'

Tom shrugged.

Nobody could have predicted what had unfolded since.

Minutes later, Willie, Laura and Michael found the inspector. They were accompanied by Sister Bernadette, who was armed with a typical, tall Irish coffee glass, complete with handle to protect the drinker's hand from the heat.

'I met Sergeant McKenna in the hall,' she said, by way of explanation for the lonely coffee.

'Drinking on the job, sir?' Michael nodded at the cream-topped concoction.

'I'll be back with the one you asked for in a minute,' Sister Bernadette playfully scolded Michael.

'*Sláinte!*' said Tom, sipping blissfully.

He never stirred. He liked the flavours to blend themselves as the glass was tipped. After another mouthful, he filled them in on Ciaran's story.

Laura tutted. 'No wonder so few women report rapes. How calm and collected should she have sounded? "Stark raving mad" – who wouldn't be?' The detective shook her head angrily. 'By the way, Barney Kelly didn't budge from the nursing home. His nurse had to give him some medication after we left.'

'There wasn't much the Kilcross guards could do with no proper statement and a caller they couldn't trace,' Michael said, risking Laura's wrath but stating the facts anyway.

Before she could jump back in, Tom intervened.

'The rape allegations and what we know about Father Seamus from his attic add a new dimension,' Tom said. 'But before we get into that, did you confirm where all the nuns were this afternoon? For a start, we can absolutely rule out Sister Gladys as a suspect. The killer got into the priest's back garden by climbing over a wall. That elderly nun might be sprightly for her age, but she's not defying the laws of logic.'

'We can rule her out, anyway,' Laura said, pulling out her notebook. 'Sister Gladys was in the kitchen with two other nuns for the entire time in question. We've others who are accounted for, too.'

She read out more names.

Five nuns left the parish hall at different stages during the afternoon – Sister Concepta, Sister Bernadette, Sister Ita, Sister Clare and Sister Mary.

'To do what?' Tom asked.

'Sister Concepta and Sister Mary were delivering food parcels to villagers, separately. Sister Ita started cleaning the church on her own, but Sister Clare followed her over and helped her finish up – shortly after you talked to her, it seems, so she probably wanted to have a moan. Sister Bernadette went for a walk, but she did return later to take Sister Gladys back to the convent.'

'Sister Bernadette went for a walk, in these conditions?' Tom shook his head. 'A walk to where?'

Laura shrugged. 'I know. We weren't convinced.'

Tom pictured the five nuns. He couldn't imagine Sister Mary harming a fly. And Sister Ita, for all her bitterness, seemed to be Attracta's one true friend.

'Let's cross-check what they were all doing on the day of Mother Attracta's murder,' Tom said. 'I don't want to jump to any conclusions but I've a headache just considering the possibility we could have two separate killers operating in this tiny place, or a pair working in tandem.

'Now, though, it's crucial we identify Ciaran's mysterious caller. We're going to have to find out how many women went through the laundry, what the age demographic was, if there are records of where they are now and, most importantly, if any of them have been in this area recently.'

The others looked at him, disbelief spreading across their faces.

Laura was the first to speak. 'Seriously, sir, I've been in one of the rooms where those records are held. There are boxes upon boxes of paper files. There doesn't seem to be a digitized record –'

She was interrupted by a light knock on the door. Sister Bernadette had fulfilled her promise and came in bearing a tray with three more Irish coffees.

Willie thanked her profusely as the nun left the room. None of the others spoke. They were all wondering if she'd killed Father Seamus.

Tom ran his tongue over his teeth, wondering if it had been a good idea to drink the coffee, considering the latest victim may have been poisoned. He shook his head to dispel the notion, and turned to Laura.

'I know this throws the case wide open, and it's going to take a massive amount of work to go through those files. I'll ask for the rest of the team to be sent down from Dublin. In the interim, we can get local guards to help. I'd be just as happy as you to conveniently tie this up with one of the nuns, but we have to investigate every avenue.'

'Jack says those footprints were made by size ten men's wellingtons,' Michael said. 'You'd pick them up in any shoe store. And it wouldn't have to be a man wearing them. I have to say, though, I'm finding it hard to imagine a woman, let alone a nun, committing these murders.'

'Wouldn't it be nice if all killers were men,' Laura snorted. 'It would narrow suspect lists greatly.'

'Most killers are men,' Tom said. 'And that could still be the case here. We can't confine our investigation into who was held here to the women themselves. We could be looking at a male relative, or a boyfriend whose girlfriend was forced to give her baby up. Somebody like that, seeking revenge, could be living right here in the village. None of the nuns said they heard any vehicles arriving or leaving the night Attracta was taken. That means her killer carried her from the house to a car that was probably parked outside the gates. A strong, fit woman could do that, but it would be easier for a man.'

The door opened, and Ciaran came back in.

'I've tracked down that guard. He remembers the name the caller gave. He always had a brilliant memory. Liz Downes. Unfortunately, he couldn't tell if she was young or old because she was hysterical. But he does recall something – the woman said she knew for certain that Father Seamus had raped a woman between 1973 and 1974. She said "a woman" but I'm willing to lay money on her being that woman.'

Everyone in the room sat up. 1973 was thirty-seven years ago. If Liz Downes had been a young girl then, she'd be middle-aged now.

'Good work,' Tom said, standing up. 'Okay, Willie, could you lend us a hand until I can get the rest of the team down? Will you get the names of the parishioners Concepta and Mary say they delivered food to, so Ciaran's lads can confirm what times the nuns were there. And see if Bernadette met anyone on that "walk".'

Willie nodded, happy to throw his lot in.

'Right, everyone else, we need to get stuck into some old-fashioned police work with the records. Ciaran, I want us to establish how many women went through this laundry and where they are now.'

Tom cast a wary eye out the window. He was relieved to see the heavy snow had stopped, but travelling conditions would be atrocious. It was Sunday – he very much doubted if there would be sufficient snowploughs out to clear the major roads, let alone the minor ones.

If they couldn't get more personnel, the workload for the team would be overwhelming. Despite it, or maybe because of it, he could feel a sense of enthusiasm in the room.

They had something new to go on, and that was always a good thing.

CHAPTER 39

Ray felt like he needed a long, hot shower after viewing the pornographic material Father Seamus had collected. Such a desperate addiction in anyone would have disturbed him, but seeing it in a priest felt more than unnatural. It was abhorrent. The man had been lecturing people for years about sin, sitting in judgement in the confessional box, all the while hiding his own very sordid secrets.

And hide it he had. Ray had searched through the house while local gardaí bagged the pictures and files in the attic, after extensively photographing the room. He found nothing else that offered any clue to the priest's double life.

Ray had spent as much time in the priest's hidden den as he could stomach. The DVDs appeared to be legal pornography, though most of them skated close to the wire.

As well as the films, there were magazines, erotic novels and the multiple images on the walls, which looked to have been painstakingly pinned up over years. There was nothing else resembling the material he had found in the folder containing the photographs of the Magdalene girls.

Ray was adept with computers and was prepared to do an extensive search on the priest's, but there was no need. The history had never been cleared and he could see every filthy site ever visited, every movie downloaded. Father Seamus's attempts to delete the files had been amateurish – they were easily retrievable.

Ellie was working alone downstairs, focusing on the inside of the stair cupboard. The other police officers were now searching the woods for other signs of the killer.

'Find anything?' Ray asked, coming down the stairs.

She jumped and banged her head.

'Sorry,' he winced.

She rubbed her temple. 'My fault. I forgot you were here, you've been up in the attic so long,' she said.

'Longer than I cared to be. Is there anything in there?'

'Yes, no, maybe. I don't know. I could really do with Mark right now. There's nothing obvious. I've picked up lots of fingerprints. We'll have to run them against our own people who were in the house. If he was murdered by lethal injection, I honestly don't think the killer would be stupid enough to break in and not wear gloves.'

She held up her latex-encased hands and wiggled her fingers. 'There's no blood, no sign of a struggle. Maybe something will show up on the body.'

'We've our work cut out for us,' Ray said. 'I've got to make a call. Do you want me to make you a coffee or something? I don't think that's contaminating the scene, is it?'

'I think we should err on the side of caution,' she smiled. 'Jack will be back soon, I'll ask him to bring some.'

Ray left to ring Father Terence, thinking that Jack seemed to be more use to Ellie as a messenger boy than an assistant.

The priest answered after a couple of rings, and Ray introduced himself.

'I believe you were talking to Sergeant McKenna earlier and he informed you we had cause to be in Kilcross?'

'Yes, he rang. How can I help, Detective?'

Father Terence's voice sounded like that of a young man.

'I'm afraid I have to impart more bad news. I'm sorry to do this over the phone but, with this weather, it's the only option. Father Seamus died this afternoon.'

There was an audible intake of breath on the other end of the line.

'Pardon me? I thought Mother Attracta had been murdered.'

'Yes, Mother Attracta is dead – and so is Father Seamus. We suspect foul play in his death, too.'

'I don't understand.'

There was a tremor in Father Terence's voice. He was either an excellent actor or truly distressed.

'I know this must be very hard to get your head around, and I don't have all the answers. I can imagine you're very shocked but I really must ask you a few questions to try to help our investigation along. Is that okay?'

The priest swallowed and cleared his throat. 'Of course; ask me anything.'

'How long did you live here for?'

'Over two years.'

'And you lived in the priest's house?'

'Where else?'

'Father, when you were here, did you ever notice anything unusual about Father Seamus?'

'Unusual how?'

'Did he have any strange habits? Was he away much? Did you notice him spending much time in the attic?'

The priest let out an involuntary laugh. 'In the attic? I shouldn't say so. We had a lot of damp in that attic because of a leaky roof, and I'm severely asthmatic. Seamus kept it locked.'

Crafty old devil, Ray thought.

'As for habits . . . well, not many, really – and none that were "strange". He was very much into old movies. He used to travel up to Dublin every now and again for showings in the Irish Film Centre.

'To be honest, Detective – and this might seem like I'm fobbing you off, considering I lived with the man for two years – but it wouldn't be an understatement to say we were like ships in the night in that house. When I arrived I was still tied into my last parish, and I wasn't long in Kilcross before I was called upon to provide cover for other parishes around the county. Seamus had his own parish under control and was very accommodating.'

'I understand,' Ray said. 'Did Father Seamus ever talk

about the past, specifically the period when the convent in Kilcross housed a Magdalene Laundry?'

'Not that I recall.'

'Did he have any run-ins with anyone that you know of? What was his relationship like with the nuns in the convent? Do you know if he had any enemies? Please, think hard.'

As he was speaking, something occurred to Ray. He pulled out his notepad and jotted it down.

'There is something . . .' said Father Terence.

'Yes?'

'It was just after I arrived in Kilcross, so about two and a half years ago. Father Seamus got a call very late one night. He never said who rang. I heard shouting and went to see what the problem was. He had just hung up and he was shaking. He said it was a hoax caller. He was nervous for weeks after, I recall. That was around the time he got the extra locks fitted on the door. It seemed to me to be an overreaction to a prank call.'

'Yes, indeed.' Ray could feel the excitement of a lead developing. 'And he didn't say who had called him, or what they'd said?'

'No. I tried to bring it up the next day. He was, let's say, adamant that I was not to raise the topic again. So I let it be.'

'There's nothing else you can remember, Father? No other arguments? Nobody coming to the house?'

There was silence for a moment, as the priest searched his memory.

'No, Detective. I'm sorry, I can't think of anything else.'

'If you do, will you ring us straight away?'

'Absolutely. Detective?'

'Yes?'

'Should I be taking precautions?' There was a note of fear in Father Terence's voice. 'Is this some kind of maniac killing religious people? I lived in Kilcross – do they know who I am?'

'No, Father. We suspect whoever did this specifically targeted Mother Attracta and Father Seamus. By all means take due care, but don't worry unnecessarily.'

Ray rang off and immediately dialled Tom's number.

'I have something,' he said when the inspector answered, relaying details of his conversation with Father Terence and the late-night phone call to the dead priest.

'Hmm. That fits with something we've just found out from Ciaran.' Tom told him about the woman caller to the police station. 'I'll find out exactly when the call was, and see if it was around the same time.'

'I was thinking,' Ray said. 'Father Terence said Father Seamus made the odd trip to Dublin, but he didn't mention any pattern. What if our killer planned on taking both victims on Wednesday but Father Seamus was gone?'

Tom mulled it over. 'You could be right, Ray. It would explain why our killer was desperate enough to kill him under our bloody noses.'

'So, if it's not one of the nuns, has the killer been in the village since Thursday night waiting for an opportunity? Why leave it until now?'

'Maybe, despite his false alibi on Thursday, the priest

was actually busy on Friday and Saturday, and the killer couldn't get him alone?' Tom mused.

'Not even at night?'

'Well, if it was a nun she mightn't have felt secure sneaking out immediately after Mother Attracta was abducted. Then we arrived down yesterday. She could have been waiting for an opportunity.'

Ray nodded, but didn't speak. There was something niggling at him. He looked down at the scrawl on his notepad.

'What is it?' Tom asked, intuitively.

'Assuming for a moment we're dealing with a single suspect, I feel like the killer wants to make a point, to show us that he or she can act with impunity. A woman was taken for twenty-four hours, tortured, killed and displayed in a public park. Our killer then broke into the priest's house while it was under surveillance and murdered him. And the carving on the nun's body – 'Satan's whore' – is this some sort of crusade? Is the killer punishing religious people who have done wrong?'

Tom fell silent as he considered.

'It's plausible,' he said, eventually. 'I have the others looking at the women who went through the laundry. One of them could be on some sort of mission to avenge a perceived wrong. Of course, one of the sisters could be, too. What's your take on that priest you were talking to? He lived with Father Seamus for a while. Does he know more than he's letting on?'

Ray rocked on his heels. 'It sounded like this was all news to him. And he was pretty convincing.'

'Okay, well, check him out, anyway. Then try to get back here. We're going to need all hands on deck to go through these files. How are Ellie and Jack getting on?'

'Jack is useless, and Ellie's dog tired.'

'Wrap it up for the day, then.'

No sooner had Tom ended his phone call with Ray than Ian rang him from Dublin. The sergeant had news for the inspector.

'We tracked down the young man Gerard Poots was with the night they discovered the body,' the Blanchardstown sergeant informed him. 'He confirmed the story. The lads in vice know him well. Sad case . . .'

'Go on.'

'A couple of teenagers have come forward. They were in the park that night but didn't want their parents to find out. The girl cracked in the end – reckoned she should try to help, and to hell with the consequences. The bad news is they didn't see anything resembling your priest's car.'

'Don't worry about that. He's dead. I'm pretty sure he didn't kill Mother Attracta.'

'What!' Ian exclaimed. 'What happened?'

Tom gave him the short version.

'Shit,' Ian said. 'Well, the couple said they were sheltering in the little glen – you know, the one with the duck pond? They saw a vehicle turn off the road and follow the track through the field towards the woods where the nun was found.'

Tom straightened up. 'And?'

'Well, unfortunately, they both hid. They thought it was a park ranger or someone. So they can't give us details. But they can confirm it was some kind of 4x4 and that it was light in colour.'

Tom had a clear view of the convent's front yard from where he was sitting. Of the five cars owned by the nuns, two were SUVs. One was silver, the other light gold.

'That's very interesting,' he replied.

'Glad to be of help. The bad news is the media have the victim's ID. They'll be descending on you as soon as the weather permits. It's snowing pretty heavily up here.'

'Same here. Don't worry about the media. They haven't got anything else yet, have they? Like the carving?'

'No. Is there anything else you need from me here?'

'Yes, check out the brothel that Father Seamus was visiting. I want to rule him off the suspect list for Mother Attracta entirely. Ray can give you the details.'

Tom rang off as Ian was repeating the word 'brothel?' and steeled himself before dialling the superintendent's number.

McGuinness was sticking to his usual Sunday routine. He was at home and Tom could hear the strains of Rachmaninov in the background. He had been in McGuinness's house often enough for Sunday lunch to know that his boss's favourite pastime after watching his grandson's match was to have a hearty meal and then relax with a cognac and some classical music. Those who only saw the brusque, stressed side of the man at work would be amazed to see how cultured and laid-back the superintendent could be.

Tom filled him in on the latest turn in the investigation and made his request for the rest of the Dublin-based team to be sent down.

In the background he could hear the Rach 3 piano concerto, until McGuinness turned it down. Now all Tom could hear was his boss's heavy breathing.

'Tom, I have no problem with your team going down. I'll tell you what I do have a problem with – how the public is going to react if it looks like the police's main suspects in a double murder are former Magdalene Laundry inmates. Have you any idea how that would be received? If some priest gets killed in a hit and run in Galway, should we start pulling in and interrogating men who were in Letterfrack?'

Letterfrack was one of the notorious industrial schools for young boys run by the Christian Brothers.

'I know how it sounds, but I'm afraid the priest's predilections are sending the investigation in that direction.'

McGuinness sighed heavily. 'I hope you're wrong, Tom. The laundry issue is political dynamite at the moment. Between you and me, I suspect the government are playing silly buggers with this because they're terrified of how much they might have to pay in compensation claims. The bottom has fallen out of the economy; they've enough on their plate with the bloody IMF on their case.'

'I've no doubt they would rather it all went away,' Tom agreed. 'I've had my eyes opened over the last few days. Between this place and the mother and baby homes . . .'

'I know. Disgusting,' McGuinness said.

It was one word, but it was potent.

Tom knew McGuinness was a practising Catholic. For him to be critical of the Church's history was a damning indictment.

After the call, the inspector left the sitting room and found Ciaran in the hallway, just finishing a call on his own phone.

'Ciaran, when did that call come into the station from the Downes woman?'

'It was two and a half years ago – summertime.'

'That fits,' Tom said, and told him about the call to the priest's house. 'Is there any word from the canvass of the villagers? Is the weather slowing things down?'

'That's what I was just checking. The team have made good progress. People are slowing them down by inviting them in for hot drinks. Those they've spoken to are shocked about Father Seamus but there's no indication anyone saw or heard anything. The woman renting next door to the priest's doesn't seem to be down this weekend.'

'Do you have much of that in the village – people taking holiday-type rentals?' Tom asked.

'Not particularly,' Ciaran responded. 'We're too small: no sea, no lakes, no quality restaurants. No real attractions except isolation.'

'Does anybody know this writer woman?'

'I'm sure someone does. I caught a glimpse of her one time, on her way into the house. Red hair. The curtains are always twitching here, though, so someone will give you a proper description.'

'Is there any chance your lads can ask about her while they're doing their rounds? And can they come to the convent when they're done in the village?' Tom filled Ciaran in on his plan for the systematic search of the records.

'If the road is still passable, they should be able to. I might get off now and help them finish up.'

Tom left to find Sister Concepta. He found Sister Gladys instead, and realized she was the very person he wanted to talk to.

The nun was sitting in her armchair in the kitchen, both hands cupped around a mug of tea. She was lost in thought. It took a moment for her to notice he'd come into the room.

'Can I join you?' he asked, indicating the armchair beside her.

She sniffed. 'I can't stop you.'

Up close he could see the depth of the wrinkles on the woman's face – deep grooves etched into the skin that spoke of great age and experience. Her white hair was receding at the temples, and the hands that clasped the mug were bony, fragile and covered in liver spots. Her eyes, though, when she looked directly at him, sparkled with intelligence. He suspected, too, that the lines around her mouth weren't merely the wrinkles of old age but indicated a person of good humour – which made her apparent permanent crankiness all the more intriguing.

'You're a bit young, aren't you, to be heading up an investigation like this?'

She spoke with the same clear, loud voice he had heard her use at the dinner table last night. A schoolteacher's voice.

'I presume they're sending someone more senior down to take over, now the priest has been whacked as well.'

She sniffed again, and took another sip of her tea.

He sat quietly for a moment, his chin resting on his hand, his arm in turn resting on his knee. It had been a long time since he'd been told he was too young for anything, and he quite enjoyed it.

He edged forward ever so slightly and spoke softly. 'I know, Sister, that most of the women in here see you as some kind of demented old bat who's on her way out. I think you might play up to that. It probably suits you to have them ignore you and say what they like – thinking you'll forget it, anyway. You probably also like being able to say whatever the hell you want and get away with it.

'But I have a sneaking suspicion that your brain works just fine, Sister. I'd really like to have an honest conversation with you. And I think you want to have that conversation with me, too. So what do you say?'

CHAPTER 40

The nun said nothing for a few moments.

Tom sat back and looked at the clock on the wall. It was after six. This time yesterday the kitchen had been buzzing with activity, but now there was just himself and Sister Gladys.

It was pitch black outside, but nobody had pulled the curtains across the back door or windows. Tom could see snow falling again. There'd be no reinforcements coming from Dublin this night.

'Let me compliment you back.' Sister Gladys broke the silence. 'You're not as stupid as you look, either.' She rested the tea on her lap, a hint of a smile tweaking the corners of her lips. 'What do you want to talk to me about, Inspector? If it's about Attracta being murdered, your young men got everything out of me last night. I'm a murderer by proxy, if not by fact. In my fantasies I've strangled that woman, shot her in the head, buried her alive, you name it. Call it my religion, call it being sane, call it being too bloody old, but I would never actually carry out any of my rotten thoughts.'

He noticed she'd lowered her voice. He couldn't hear

anyone in the dining room, but still she was conscious of potential eavesdroppers.

'Why did you hate her so much?'

Sister Gladys placed her tea on the table, and picked up a ball of wool and knitting needles. He watched as the hands he had considered frail moved with incredible dexterity, crossing each stitch with speed and accuracy.

The clock ticked and the needles clicked, and all was quiet apart from that.

'The list of reasons I had for hating that woman is as long as the wool in this ball,' the nun said. 'In most recent times it was the fact she spoke to me like I was the village idiot. Patronizing, condescending old witch.

'She punished me, do you know that, Inspector? At least she thought she was punishing me. She'd send me to my room if I said something she didn't like.' Her tone was incredulous. 'There isn't enough respect for elderly people in this country. You go past a certain age and people think they can speak to you like you've regressed to being a small child again. Shouting in your ear and speaking in baby language. So I shout back. I speak to them like they're idiots. They usually are, mind.'

'I agree,' Tom said. 'You didn't hate her because she treated you disrespectfully, though.'

Click, click, click.

The nun paused to switch the needles between hands and started again with the next row of stitches.

'No, I didn't. I hated her because she was evil.'

Tom wasn't as shocked as he suspected he should be. 'To the girls in the laundry?' he asked.

Gladys looked at him over the needles. 'No. She was an evil bitch to everyone.' She resumed her knitting. 'You're fascinated by the laundry. People always are with tragic tales from the past, aren't they? How come it was acceptable, and why did people just stand by and let it happen? It's never how you think, though. Back then, the laundry was just a way of life.

'People are very moralistic about history but very few of us analyse what we contribute to the horrors of the present. Look at the way poor refugees are treated in this country right now – set up in direct provision centres, their children denied basic rights. Look at the refugee children who go missing from the system, kids trafficked into all sorts of diabolical situations. Oh, I read the papers.

'And then there are those small, inconsequential acts, when we sin by omission. How often do neighbours ignore the sounds of violent fighting in the house beside them, even when they know there are children in the home? How often do people walk past a homeless person like they're not there? Humans aren't saints. Not now, not then.'

Tom closed his eyes for a moment and rubbed his brow. She was right, of course.

'You, though, Sister. You have a conscience. You weren't happy with the laundry?'

'No. The laundries weren't meant to be holiday camps,

mind. This country was austere and grey for most of my life. Poverty everywhere. We were supposed to take in the charity cases, the ones no one else wanted. If you want to provide charity, you need money. The state gave us some funding, but we had to source the rest. So we worked – and the girls had to work, too. Sewing, selling vegetables, laundering.

'For some, it wasn't sufficient to make enough to run the place. Certain individuals were greedy. And they worked the girls hard. They stopped working themselves. They turned an act of charity into an act of profit. They forgot what we were meant to be about and the vows we took.

'Some sisters were brutalized by the regime and became as bad as the worst offenders. Other nuns came here and you knew, just to look at them, that they weren't Christians to begin with. They sought power, and there was nothing more powerful than the Church for a long, long time.'

Tom released the breath he had been holding.

Sister Gladys leaned down and picked up a small pair of scissors from a basket on the floor. Sitting back up with a wheeze, she snipped the wool she had been using and picked up a different ball, knotting the new wool on to the old. She seemed to be knitting a long, multicoloured scarf.

'Some people like to inflict pain. Sadists, I think they call them. Well, we had a couple of them here. Not all of us –' she stopped knitting and looked him directly in the eye to impress her point – 'not all, Inspector. But often, when behaviour is acceptable, people follow it like sheep. There are a couple of sisters here who did things in the laundry that I'm sure they've been praying for forgiveness for ever since, even if they won't admit it.'

She resumed knitting. 'Others, however . . . well, they don't think they've anything to ask forgiveness for. You tell me, though – is it right to beat a young woman to near unconsciousness for not starching a shirt properly? To make girls work six days a week from early morning to late at night – hard, backbreaking work? To give them barely enough food to live, let alone thrive? Is it right to stand back when you know that girls in your care are being interfered with, and do nothing?'

A tear appeared in the corner of Sister Gladys's left eye. It grew bigger and bigger until it spilled over the eyelid and rolled, slowly, down her cheek.

She sniffed, placed the needles in her lap and pulled a scrunched-up tissue from inside her sleeve.

'I don't like remembering,' she said, wiping her cheek and her chin, before dabbing her eye.

Tom placed a comforting hand on her arm. 'It can't have been easy to have those feelings and witness others' suffering. What did you do?'

'I stayed. That was all I could do. When I wasn't that long in the place, I wrote a letter to the Minister. I was trained as a teacher but none of those girls ever got an education. Do you know what the government did?

Nothing, except report me. I got a dressing down I wasn't going to forget in a hurry.

'I nearly left. I took my vows seriously but I thought, "This isn't for me." Already, though, some of the girls clung to me. I was one of the few who showed them kindness. So I couldn't leave, do you understand? I had to stay.' More fat tears spilled down her cheeks.

Tom found the sight pitiful.

The loud, abrasive, slightly mad Sister Gladys was easier to take than this old lady, crying silently inside and out. How tough her life must have been – so clever and compassionate, and yet she'd been helpless to stop what was happening around her. By the time the laundry closed, she would have been completely institutionalized and unable to leave.

Sister Gladys sniffed and wiped her eyes roughly. 'I wanted to stay in the end, Inspector. I . . . I saw some girls go through something, and I swore to God I would help them afterwards. As much as I could.'

'What did you see, Sister?'

Tom could hear his heart thudding.

'You know we had an orphanage at the back of this building?'

'Yes.'

'It was run well. I will say that for the sisters who worked in it. None of the children in their care ever came to harm. You see the stories now of babies being allowed to die from neglect in those homes, children buried in mass unmarked graves, the government using the kids for vaccine trials . . .' The nun shuddered. 'But we also had a hospital wing for pregnant mothers. That wasn't usual, as you probably know. Mother and baby homes were generally separate from Magdalene Laundries. But we ended up taking some girls in, and then some of our own girls ended up pregnant.

'Their babies were forcibly taken from them. They were single mothers. They had no rights. The adoption law enacted in the fifties should have made it harder for the infants to be taken from the girls. But it didn't. The sister in charge of the pregnant girls ensured the adoption papers were signed. That sister was Mother Attracta.'

She started knitting furiously again.

He waited a minute.

'Sister?'

She kept clicking the needles. Eventually, she put them down, irritably.

'What did it do to the girls?' he asked.

'What do you think it did to them? I sat with some of them and tried to bring them solace. But you cannot comfort a woman who has had her baby taken from her against her will. I saw girls go mad from the grief. I saw babies ripped from their mothers before they even knew if they'd given birth to a girl or a boy. They weren't even allowed to hold them.

'And the worst was that there were sisters who thought they were doing the girls a favour. Inspector, most of society agreed. Single women with children? Not unless they were widowed. No one wanted to see young girls

parading around the streets with babies in perambula-
tors and no rings on their fingers. A lot of these girls were
working class. There was an elitism there that believed
the children were better off with a certain type of
family.'

Her voice broke. 'Babies were stolen from their mothers
with our blessing. The politicians can try to pin all this
on the religious orders but it was with their blessing, too.
And then those babies were sold.'

'Sold?'

'That's what I said. You think money didn't change
hands when adoptions were arranged? The best were the
American couples. It wasn't that lucrative for this convent; we weren't a full-blown mother and baby home. For
those institutions, there was a rare old trade going in
babies. Three thousand pounds would have been the
norm in the sixties for buying a nice little Catholic Irish
baby. That was a lot of money, back then.

'They never even checked what happened to those little
angels when they went abroad. Never checked if the parents were suitable. I've heard such horror stories!

'But even here in this laundry a few pounds could
grease the wheels and get you ahead of others on the
adoption list. Well-to-do people always managed to get
the youngest babies, the healthiest babies – and yes, even
the babies the girls didn't want to give up.'

Tom physically flinched. How much deeper and darker,
he wondered, could the history of this place get?

The nun picked up her cup and spat hard into it, then

dropped her head and wiped her eyes again. Tom felt the venom in the act.

'You say you suspected the girls were interfered with?' he asked, after a minute had passed. 'By whom?'

She stared him straight in the eye. 'By the man who's answering for it in hell this very day. Not that anybody in charge believed the girls. I did, though. When I found out, I did all I could to make sure he wasn't allowed to bring any more girls up to that house for special "lessons".'

Tom nodded. She'd confirmed what the detectives suspected.

They sat there in silence for a few minutes.

After a while, the side door to the kitchen opened and Sister Concepta came in.

'Inspector, your detectives are going through the records room, but I'm not entirely sure what they're looking for. Can I talk to you?'

'One moment, Sister Concepta.'

Tom waited until the nun had stepped outside before turning back to Sister Gladys.

'Why did you suggest cleaning up the hall and ringing Father Seamus when it was discovered Mother Attracta was missing? Why not phone the police?'

The nun puckered her cheeks in amusement. 'Do you think I was trying to cover my tracks, Inspector?'

'No,' he smiled. 'I'm curious, though. You know, cleaning a crime scene could be considered an offence?'

'Only if you knew it was a crime scene. Well, let's speak

hypothetically. Imagine I suspected something had happened but I just didn't care. That I was sure whoever took Attracta had a very good reason, and I wasn't going to be complicit in their discovery. Maybe I'd just clean up, tell the old git up the road and get on with things. Would you arrest me for that?'

Tom nearly fell off his seat. He stared at the little old lady and shook his head. When he'd recovered, he stood up.

'Hypothetically, there would be some charge there,' he said. 'But I've a lot on my plate at the moment. Sister, aren't you afraid that if someone wanted to punish Attracta for something she did in the laundry, they might be willing to lash out at any of you?'

The nun's eyes brimmed again. 'Maybe some of us deserve it.'

Tom was speechless. He struggled to find something to say that could alleviate the nun's pain. Then it came to him.

'There's something I need you to do, which could help someone whose family suffered because of this laundry.'

The nun's eyes widened.

'Do you remember Peggy Deasy? She was here from the mid-sixties. She hanged herself.'

'Yes, I remember her, of course I do. That was a dreadful tragedy.' She shook her head sadly. 'You know her family?'

'That young detective I have with me, Laura Brennan; Peggy was her aunt.'

Sister Gladys placed a hand to her breast, and gasped.

'Is there any chance you could talk to her about Peggy? I don't mean the bad stuff. Did the girl have any good times? Can you tell Laura anything to make her feel better?'

The old woman scratched a mole on her chin, her eyes half closed. Then she opened them, and nodded eagerly.

'She was a beautiful girl, Peggy. Even with her head shorn and all the weight she lost. When her hair grew back there was another sister here, Sister Clarence – she's dead now – who used to brush it for her and plait it. Peggy never said anything, but I think she enjoyed it. We did our best. There are little things like that.'

'Tell her, Sister.'

The inspector's phone rang, as he went to join Sister Concepta in the hall.

It was Ray.

'Sir, I'm having real difficulty getting back to the convent. Ciaran just got here and says he nearly came off the road in parts. There's a B&B in the village, the one Ellie is staying in. Should I stay there tonight?'

'Sounds like you found a silver lining, Ray. This reception is terrible ... are you still in the priest's house?'

'Yes, but we're finished for this evening. We're bracing ourselves for the walk across the village.'

Tom wished him luck and hung up. He signalled to a patient Sister Concepta that he had one more call to make.

He got through to Emmet's mobile on the first ring.

'I don't think I'll ever forgive you, Tom Reynolds. I'm in some bloody godforsaken hole outside Roscrea in the dingiest B&B you've ever come across. My car is being slowly buried in snow outside. The landlady – and believe me when I tell you she could be rocking in a chair in the attic of the Bates Motel – has offered me a snifter of *poitín* and a midnight visit to her room. She's offered me everything except a damn sandwich. A few snowflakes, and the country comes to a standstill . . .'

Tom let Emmet rant on for a bit longer.

'You won't be down tonight, then?' he asked.

He had to hold the phone away from his ear as Emmet let rip anew. A minute or two later, the head of the Technical Bureau ran out of expletives.

'No, I bloody well won't be down tonight, Tom. If they get the salt and the snowploughs out, I'll be down in the morning. Do you think you can keep the body count down to single digits until then?'

'I can't promise anything, but I fervently hope so. The way things are going, I'll be sleeping with one eye open tonight.'

CHAPTER 41

'Sorry about that,' Tom apologized to Sister Concepta for keeping her waiting. 'This weather is playing havoc with the investigation.'

'It doesn't seem to be causing any difficulties for the killer,' she replied, tartly.

'Hmm. Willie Callaghan spoke to you about the people you visited this afternoon, I imagine?'

'Yes. I've told him there are several villagers who can vouch for my whereabouts when Father Seamus was murdered in his house – which, I believe, your officers were watching at the time.'

It didn't take a mind-reader to tell that Sister Concepta was not happy.

Tom sighed. 'I know you are really putting yourselves out for us here. I can see that you, in particular, are trying to keep the routine going for everyone, despite all that's happened. I think you know, though, that we are just trying to do our job as thoroughly as possible.'

She looked slightly mollified.

'What are you doing in the records rooms?' she asked.

'Checking every avenue. Actually, we could do with

your help. More of my team are due down but probably won't arrive until tomorrow. I need to find out about former residents of the laundry, Sister. How many there were, their names and where they are now.'

He continued speaking, even though she looked on the verge of collapsing with disbelief.

'I'm particularly keen to find a woman we believe was here in the mid-seventies. In the absence of computerized files, I think we're going to need all the help you can give us.'

'Are you serious? You think the person who killed Mother Attracta could have been a woman from the laundry? That was all so long ago. I don't understand why you keep dragging it up.'

'There might be someone who isn't happy to let it lie in the past, Sister.'

The nun looked unconvinced.

'I really think you're clutching at straws, Inspector,' she said. 'But if you insist on pursuing this, I will help in any way I can. We're meant to be gathering for prayers, but I'm sure the Good Lord can spare me this once.'

They made their way to the first of the records rooms, where the team had started sifting through files already. Even though the room itself was relatively small, Tom felt his whole body grow weak as he stared at the piles of boxes.

'Is there not some kind of master index, even on paper?'

The nun chewed her lip.

'Sister?'

She hesitated.

'I'm so used to keeping it secret.'

'Keeping what secret?' Tom asked.

His senses prickled. What was she hiding?

'What we've been doing.'

Sister Concepta blew out her cheeks.

'I suppose there's not much point in keeping it to ourselves any longer. Especially if it can speed things up and end this madness . . . It shouldn't exist, but it does,' the nun continued. 'There's a master file that contains a partial index of the records.'

It was a little bit anticlimactic. This might be a huge secret for Sister Concepta, for whatever reason, but Tom was just relieved to know there was some sort of key to help sort through the stacks of files that lay before them.

'Why shouldn't it exist?' he asked.

'Because nobody sanctioned myself and Sister Bernadette to start it.'

'Ah!' Tom exclaimed, as the penny dropped. 'You and Sister Bernadette were compiling the laundry's records behind Mother Attracta's back.'

Sister Concepta nodded.

'I thought you were quite circumspect in your opinions about the laundry when you gave us our tour yesterday,' Tom said. 'Are those your real views?'

The nun blushed. 'I think there are two sides. Some women quite obviously suffered in the laundries, and their suffering has been dismissed. That doesn't mean the laundries didn't perform a necessary social function, or that everyone in them had only bad experiences. When the industrial schools' history came out, I knew the laundries would be next. I had seen some of these files. Pure curiosity, I'm afraid. Nosiness, Attracta would call it. I knew after reading them that their stories couldn't stay hidden.

'A few of us talked about it several years ago and decided we needed to do something to save these records. We were . . . afraid, I suppose, that Attracta would decide to get rid of them. The Vatican has instructed us not to, but I had heard Mother Attracta tell relatives of laundry girls that the files no longer existed.'

'Who amongst you decided to save them?' Tom asked.

'Myself, Sister Bernadette and Sister Gladys. Only two of us could do the actual physical work. We began collating key facts. Names, their ages, how long they were here and when they left. We've covered from the year the laundry closed, in 1985, back to 1965. Kilcross became a laundry at the start of the last century, though there are no files from the early years. Progress has been slow enough, given the difficulty in accessing the rooms without Mother Attracta finding out, and having to cover for one another. We thought it best to start with the most recent years – those women are most likely to still be alive.'

'So it was you who was going in and out of her office and getting Mother Attracta all wound up? Were you using her computer?'

Sister Concepta shook her head adamantly. 'No, Inspector. I really don't think it was us she was suspicious of. We were at pains not to leave anything amiss, and we never went into her office.'

'Then where did you compile your work?'

'I have a small laptop. I keep it in my room. I didn't even connect it to the internet because I was afraid Mother Attracta would see the computer's name pop up on the server.'

Tom shook his ahead, astonished. 'What you did was very brave, Sister, and it's going to save us a lot of time. Can you fetch your computer for us now?'

As the nun turned to leave, Michael spoke.

'Sir, I just found a Downes, 1973.' He pulled out the file.

Tom's heart skipped a beat. Had they struck lucky?

'Crap. This is Margaret Downes.' Michael put the file down, disappointed.

Tom allowed himself to breathe again.

'It's still important. If the name is Downes, we'll have to go through it. But it's a common enough name, so keep looking for a Liz. I'll go check out this master file.'

Tom waited for Sister Concepta in Mother Attracta's office.

She returned promptly, and they watched as the laptop booted up.

'I asked Sister Bernadette this afternoon about the incident at Hallowe'en,' Tom said. 'She hadn't informed us that she was the one Mother Attracta locked in the chapel. Do you think that odd?'

Sister Concepta sighed. 'No. She was probably embarrassed. They fought a lot when Sister Bernadette came here first, but Mother Attracta ground her down. She knew how to press a weak spot. It was a special skill of hers but Bernadette was never able to rise above it, so Attracta could always get to her. The woman thrived on discord, you see. Despite what she's been through abroad, Bernadette was no match for Mother, and she felt humiliated because of it.'

'Did Attracta find your weak spot, Sister?'

A shadow crossed the nun's face. 'No. We had our clashes, but she couldn't get under my skin. I can be very resolute when I have to be.'

The screen of the old laptop flickered to life at last.

'We didn't record this data very professionally, Inspector, but it's some sort of spreadsheet format. Scroll down for the names.'

She clicked the file open, dragging the arrow over a number at the top of the sheet: 500.

'Is this the total number of women who were here from 1965 to 1985?' he asked.

'Yes. They say the average stay was seven months, but a lot of women stayed longer. Those who left but came back are counted as one entry. There's a rumour that thirty thousand women went through the laundries in the last century. I don't know if that's true.'

Tom stared at the three digits. It could be worse. It was a large number of women to get through, but it was manageable.

'Forgive me for asking this, Sister, but how reliable is this data? Given that you had to undertake this work in difficult circumstances, might you and Sister Bernadette have missed a box or two?'

She looked him straight in the eye. 'Please don't underestimate for a second the importance we attached to this task. We were methodical. We went from January to December in every year. There's an average of four boxes per year. You can trust this information.'

He hoped she was right. It occurred to him that if she or Sister Bernadette had wanted to remove all traces of a laundry inmate, they had been excellently placed to do so. But then he had to ask – why would two women dedicated to preserving the laundry's history want to cover something up?

'May I?' he asked, indicating her seat.

'Please.'

She stood up and let him sit at the computer.

Five hundred women, an average of forty to sixty each year.

The departure dates for the first few names were all around the same time – the middle months of 1985. But their dates of entry to the laundry varied wildly. The first woman had entered in 1982, aged twenty. The second woman had entered in 1983, aged twenty-four. The third woman had entered in 1969, aged seventeen.

Beside each of their names 'living' had been typed.

'What does this mean?' Tom asked.

'Some women died while they were in the laundry.'

'Died how?'

'Old age, illness, accidents.'

'You didn't fill in that kind of detail, just "living" or "deceased", am I correct?'

'Yes. All the personal information is still in the original files.'

'This woman who entered in 1969 . . . what's that, sixteen years? Where would she have gone when the laundry closed?'

'That was the problem, Inspector. A lot of the women became institutionalized. When they decided to close the laundry, places had to be found for the women. I remember what was in that woman's file. It traumatized me because it was the first time I'd seen it. She was transferred to a psychiatric hospital.'

Tom blanched.

'The first time?' he parroted. 'There were more, then?'

'Many.'

'What of the other women who left?'

'Out into the world. We've no way of knowing what happened to them, though I suppose you could easily track them. I suspect many left for England. Many of them wouldn't have seen returning to their home places as an option. Of course, some entered religious life themselves.'

'Really?' He was taken aback that anyone held in a laundry would choose to become a nun. Perhaps it was a form of Stockholm syndrome.

'Are any of the nuns here . . .?' he tailed off.

'No. There used to be one. She entered the laundry in the forties and became a sister in the fifties. She's dead now. You're surprised, but it's not unusual for someone who has spent years in a religious institution, be it a laundry or an orphanage, to become religious themselves. Exposure to God's teachings doesn't always turn a person off religion.'

'I'm just not sure it was God the laundry girls were being exposed to,' Tom replied.

He scrolled down the columns until he reached 1974. He skimmed the names of that and the preceding year. He only saw one Downes – the Maggie Downes whose file Michael had found. He'd have to check with Ciaran to make sure he hadn't got the name of the caller wrong. There was no Liz Downes, which could mean one of three things: Liz had been lying or not using her real name; Ciaran's officer had got the name wrong; Sister Concepta's master record was incomplete. Or, Tom considered, Liz hadn't been an inmate at all, but knew someone who had.

'Can we connect your computer to the internet and email this file?'

'I think so. The computer's a couple of years old but I'm pretty sure it's suitable for internet access.'

Sister Concepta sat back down in the seat vacated by Tom. Within minutes she'd hooked up the computer and opened a Google search engine.

'I have an old email address,' she said. 'Will I email from that or from yours?' she asked.

'I'll put mine in,' he replied, and took the chair again.

As he pressed send, he dialled Ian.

'Ian, are you still in the station?'

'No. I sent the team home before the storm got too bad. I can go back in if you need me to.'

'Don't do that. I'm sending you a file with a list of names. I was expecting the rest of the team down tomorrow, but this is work you can do better there. I need you to get background on the names – find out where they are now, family details, et cetera.'

'How many people?'

'Five hundred, but we already know some of them have passed away, and their deaths are marked on the list.'

'No problem. Send it on.'

Tom hung up and turned to Sister Concepta.

'Right, I think it's time to call it a night. If we keep going like this, someone is going to fall down with exhaustion. And it just might be me.'

'Let me get some supper sorted for you all. I'll leave my laptop here for you,' the nun said. 'There's no need to hide it now.'

CHAPTER 42

Michael and Laura had been joined by Willie. All of them looked up, bleary-eyed, when Tom opened the door to the records room.

'Let's call it a night, lads. Go get some air, a wash – whatever you need – and grab a bite to eat.'

'We haven't found another Downes,' Michael said, getting up from his cross-legged position.

'Nor did I on the master record,' Tom said. 'Have you got Margaret Downes's file to hand?'

'It's right here,' Michael said, handing it over.

'I'll call Ciaran and double-check that the caller was Liz Downes.'

Tom stayed behind as the others left. He had to dial Ciaran's number twice before he got through. He opened the first page of the file, which he'd rested on a box, while he waited for the other officer to pick up.

'Ciaran?'

'Tom? Can you hear—'

'Just about, Ciaran. Are you finished?'

'Oh, I can hear you now. The lads finished their rounds

of the village before it got too bad, but the ones sent in from neighbouring stations will have to stay in the B&B. They can't get home. Miley Duignan, the owner, thinks all his birthdays have come at once.'

'Anything come up on the doors?'

'No witnesses to anyone going into or leaving the priest's house – though one allegation from someone . . . Hello? It was just . . . and Michael leaving . . . put us on your suspect list.'

'Ciaran, you keep breaking up. What about the woman renting the house next door? Any more information on her?'

'Well, here's the funny thing. Nobody has met her properly. We know her name, Catherine Farrell, but I . . . no record . . . no . . . doesn't exist.'

'What? Ciaran, you're gone again.'

'I said—'

The dial tone sounded loudly in Tom's ear. He looked at the phone. He didn't have a single signal bar.

'God damn it!' he exclaimed.

He was staring at the file in front of him. On the first page was written: Margaret Catherine Downes.

Was it just a coincidence that the woman next door to the priest was called Catherine?

He scanned the pages of the file. Margaret had been given the house name 'Maggie', which seemed unusual. From what Tom had learned, the girls were normally given different names altogether. A vague memory surfaced . . . weren't the girls in the Magdalene Laundries called 'Maggies'? Did the nuns think they were being clever, giving her that anonymous name?

Maggie had entered the convent in 1973, aged seventeen. There was very little personal information, but a handwritten note stated that she had been moved to the hospital wing of the orphanage in mid-1975 to give birth. Tom frowned. If she had been in the laundry since 1973, how had she become pregnant in 1974? He flicked to the back of the file but there was no final entry indicating when Maggie had left the laundry. That was strange.

He squinted at one of the staples on the last page. Was that a tiny piece of paper on its edge? Had the last page been removed?

All thoughts of tiredness and hunger left him. He headed back to Mother Attracta's office and dialled Ciaran from the landline. The sergeant answered, but he had barely said hello when the connection was broken.

Tom groaned and picked up his mobile again. The snow was wreaking havoc with the reception, but one bar had returned.

He typed a text hastily.

Are you positive the woman who rang two years ago was called Liz? Could the officer have been mistaken?

He pressed send and prayed the signal would hold. When the little whoosh sound indicated the text had been sent successfully he nearly whooped. He stared at the screen, willing Ciaran to respond.

A response popped up seconds later.

Absolutely. Excellent memory. Adamant about the name.

'Shit!' Tom banged his expensive smartphone a little too hard on the desk.

Ciaran had said that the woman who had rung the station had been hysterical, and the sergeant seemed to think that she had been one of the women raped in the laundry in the early seventies. Margaret's surname and circumstances seemed to fit the criteria. Liz could still be a relative – but could it be the case that Margaret was actually Liz? But why use her real surname if she was hoping to stay anonymous?

He was heading out the door when he thought of two potential answers. What if the trauma of her life as 'Maggie' in the convent had made her change her first name? The second possibility was more daunting. What if Downes was her married name and Liz her first name? Then they needed to find a Liz in the convent in 1974, with a different surname.

He turned to the laptop. It had gone into sleep mode and he needed a password to open it. He would get something to eat and retrieve the password from Sister Concepta while he was at it.

Michael had been looking forward to talking to his wife, but as he dialled her number he suddenly felt nervous.

He felt his heart leap when she answered.

'Michael. Are you okay down there? The weather is awful.'

'I'm fine, Anne. We could be cut off at any time. The reception here is atrocious. We're snowed in but the investigation is picking up pace.'

'It's . . . they're saying . . . news.'

As her voice faded in and out, Michael felt panic rise. He'd waited all day to make this call.

'Anne, the line might go – what was the news you had to tell me?'

'What? I can't hear you. Can you . . .? Weather . . . I didn't leave the house today . . . afraid I'd fall on the ice.'

He sighed. 'Anne, what's your news?'

'. . . didn't want to . . . on the phone . . . can wait.'

'I can't wait,' he exclaimed, almost laughing. All bloody day and now he could barely hear her.

'Anne, listen, I want to tell you something. I love you. I'm sorry everything has been so hard.'

'. . . you.'

'What?'

'I love you, too. I'm pregnant—'

The line went dead.

Michael sat, dumbstruck. His palms began to sweat, and the phone fell from his hand.

Did she just say she was pregnant?

He racked his brain. Yes, they'd had sex, just once, shortly after she'd lost the baby. A brief, emotional encounter. They'd both cried and she'd moved as far as possible from him in the bed afterwards, as if they'd done something dirty and wrong.

But the doctors had told them, and they knew from bitter experience, that it was almost impossible to conceive straight after a miscarriage.

The phone rang, startling him out of his reverie. He fumbled for it on the floor.

'Did you hear me?' Anne said.

'Yes, yes, I heard you. Did you say you were . . .?'

He could barely breathe.

'Twelve weeks,' she bellowed, as if by shouting she could surmount the space between them. 'I took the test last night. Michael?'

'I can't believe it,' he responded, shaking with emotion. 'Are you all right?'

'Yes. Are you happy?'

'I . . .' He almost wished the reception would go again. He didn't know what to say. Was he happy? He was bloody terrified, that's what he was. He couldn't bear the thought of going through it again. They had suffered too much to hope that this time would be any different.

'Michael, it's okay. I know what you're thinking. This is a gift. It will work this time. I feel it. I never felt like this on the others.'

He choked back the ball in his throat.

'I love you,' she said, before the phone went dead.

I love you too, he thought. *But I can't endure this again.*

Twelve weeks. If they lost this one, he would get a

vasectomy. He wouldn't even tell her. He'd just do it. Her capacity for optimism was clearly greater than his.

He fell back on the bed and looked at the ceiling. Then he started thinking of all the girls who'd looked at ceilings in this building in years past, the laundry girls, those who had been forced to give up their babies. Wasn't he in an enviable position by comparison? Wasn't it better to have a shot at being happy?

He put his arm across his eyes and cried, quietly, tears of anguish etching their way down his cheeks and along the curve of his neck on to his fresh shirt collar.

The lodgings in the B&B were far warmer and cosier than Ray's room in the convent. Several guards from the next village had also sought refuge, and Jack had also decided to play it safe rather than risk the roads to his family home.

Of all of them, Ray was the most content. He was still stuck in the middle of nowhere, but at least now he had a room with a television and a kettle.

The cherry on top was that Ellie had agreed to have a drink with him in the bar that evening. True, everyone else would be having a drink there too, but that was just detail.

He splashed hot water on his face in the en suite and made his way downstairs. The owner of the B&B – a small, elfish-looking man – was on the phone and writing in a large guest ledger.

'Yes, yes, I have a room. It's the last one, mind. No,

there's no other B&B in the village. Nor a hotel. Well, now, that I couldn't say, but it would be about a half-hour drive from there to here. In that awful weather, too.'

He hung up, smiling, but composed himself when he saw Ray. He had the guilty air of a man caught capitalizing on a misfortune.

'It's awful, Officer, what happened to that poor nun and priest, isn't it? I hope you catch the fella who did it. Terrible, altogether.'

'Not bad for business, though,' Ray said pointedly, eyeing the ledger.

The other man looked at him uncertainly, unsure whether Ray was being genuine or baiting him.

Ray's face was open and honest.

'Well, I won't lie now, I have the whole place booked out for the next two nights. The press.'

Ray grimaced at the B&B owner and shook his head. He'd be running some kind of macabre tour by Easter.

He glanced at the ledger. Even upside down, he could see a name written there. A woman's name.

Ray snorted. McGuinness must have told her to come down. When Tom found out, there'd be another murder.

He laughed all the way out the door, much to the B&B owner's bemusement.

The entrance to the pub next door was mere metres away, but the ends of Ray's trousers still got soaked as he slipped and slid through the crisp, deep snow. He noticed that the night sky was not as overcast, and hoped this boded well for a better day tomorrow.

It was the same pub he and Ellie had lunched in earlier, but now it was heaving. The comfortable fireside seat had been colonized by two old men, who were playing dominos and salaciously dissecting the events of a day that would go down in village folklore.

Ray admired the villagers' dedication to alcohol and gossip – even the bitter cold couldn't keep them at home.

He spotted Ellie and Jack at the bar. She was wearing a long-sleeved pink cashmere polo-necked sweater that clung to her body as though it had been designed purely for her. Every man in the pub was casting appreciative glances at the exotic stranger.

A pint of Guinness sat beside her glass of white wine.

He pushed through the bustling bar, avoiding chinking glasses and swaying customers. As he approached Jack from behind, he overhead the tail end of the man's conversation.

'I'm just saying, if one of my relatives had been in a place like that, I'd kill the bastards, too.'

'Ray,' Ellie said, and Jack turned round, startled at the interruption.

'We were just talking about Laura's aunt. We took a guess.' She indicated the pint and the extra stool on which she had deposited her bag and coat.

'Good choice,' he said, raising the pint glass to his lips and savouring the creamy head of the black stuff.

'I'm going to try and ring home again,' Jack said. 'See you later.'

Ray stood up to let the other man pass. He sensed that

Jack wasn't best pleased by his arrival. Perhaps he wanted Ellie to himself.

'Any news?' Ellie asked, as Ray sat down.

'It's moving along. I had an idea earlier that could be another direction for us to look at.'

In one corner of the pub, two fiddlers and an accordion player had struck up a reel. Ellie leaned closer, tucking her hair behind her ear so she could hear him. It was very distracting.

'What's your theory?' she asked.

'Mother Attracta and Father Seamus both appear to have done their religion a disservice. So I wonder if someone religious is punishing them.'

'Like one of the sisters acting as some kind of avenging angel?'

He nodded.

She leaned her head to one side. 'It's plausible. A true Christian would surely be horrified by what went on in those laundries. But that poses a bit of a problem for you.'

'What do you mean?'

'Well, there are plenty of nuns in that convent who would have been around during the laundry years. If you have someone exacting revenge on people of the cloth for besmirching it, why stop with Attracta and Seamus?'

'It's definitely crossed our minds, but I hope you're wrong.'

'Does your boss have any theories?' Ellie asked.

'He's looking at the women who went through the

place. Thinks someone directly affected by the laundry might have come back.'

'When did the laundry close?'

'In 1985.'

'Surely they'd have done it before now. Twenty-five years! I prefer your theory. Someone who had to put up with Mother Attracta every day and knew what Father Seamus had done. Maybe one of the nuns has cracked.'

She took a long sip of wine. When she put down her glass, she smiled and changed the subject.

'We shouldn't be talking about work. The whole point of me staying in the B&B is to clock off.'

Ray was happy to switch to a more pleasant topic.

'Tell me a joke,' she said.

He cocked his head, amused.

'A joke? I don't think I know any.'

'Everyone knows a joke!'

'The only funnies I know are my chat-up lines,' he quipped. 'They normally get the ladies rolling in the aisles.'

Ellie, who'd just taken a sip of her wine, snorted and nearly fell off her chair.

They chortled to themselves, drawing curious looks from their fellow patrons.

'I can't imagine that's true,' Ellie said. She was still smiling but her voice was serious.

Ray blushed.

They sat in companionable silence for a few moments.

'The press will be in the village tomorrow,' Ray said,

WITH OUR BLESSING | 360

suddenly remembering. 'You won't be able to stay in the B&B.'

She shook her head. 'Well, there's no way I'm staying up in that haunted house. I'm hoping to head back to Dublin. I just need to check I haven't missed anything at either site.'

Ray looked at her over the top of his pint and felt a surge of disappointment.

It must have shown on his face, because she placed her hand on his knee and leaned forward.

'Don't worry. When we get back to Dublin, maybe I'll let you take me some place where the choice of wine extends beyond red or white.'

Tom had eaten with indecent haste the thick chicken and vegetable soup provided by the nuns. He couldn't shake the feeling they were on to something with Liz Downes.

As soon as he finished his meal, he found Concepta and requested her computer password.

Back in the office, he reopened the master file.

He scrolled back through the years, starting from 1976. Tom thought there had been an Elizabeth, but he wasn't sure in what year.

His heart skipped a beat when he found one in 1973. Elizabeth Carney.

His eyes scanned the entry. She was thirty in 1973. That would make her sixty-seven now. The age made him uneasy. Sixty-seven was hardly ancient, but surely too old to be scaling walls? She had left the convent in 1976.

Tom searched the records rooms until he found the 1973 files. Michael and Laura had marked the sides of the boxes with the relevant years, making his job easier.

He found Elizabeth's file. But as he skimmed it, hope faded.

Elizabeth Carney had entered the convent voluntarily. She had worked as a prostitute in Limerick city and was destitute when she came to the nuns asking for charity. The file remarked on Elizabeth's obedience, and on how determined she was to atone for her sins.

The description did not fit that of a woman who might have gone on to seek revenge. There was no report of any pregnancies. The last entry showed that Elizabeth was moving to another laundry, to assist the nuns there, and would be going forward as a novitiate.

The inspector slammed the file shut.

Margaret Downes had to be the woman who'd made the calls.

Hopefully, tomorrow would bring clarity.

Day Four

Monday, 13 December

CHAPTER 43

Tom slept easier his second night in the convent. The bed was more familiar but the real explanation probably lay in the fact that he was dog-tired. The first thing he did when the alarm went off at 7 a.m. was check his phone.

The reception bars were all there, climbing happily up his little signal icon. He had no missed calls – his wife obviously hadn't been that worried about him. His 3G was also working, and he pulled up the news headlines.

The main story reported how the weather had brought the country to a standstill. The government and county councils were blaming each other for a lack of preparedness; the councils didn't have enough salt for the roads, the government had issued no severe weather warnings. Farmers were furious at being unable to access their livestock; children were thrilled because nearly every school in the state was closed.

The headline that stated councils were out in force expending their limited salt supplies to clear roads reassured Tom. The local authorities were to be assisted by the army in isolated rural areas. He laughed to himself.

An ordinary winter's day for anywhere in Central Europe was an epic weather event by Irish standards.

The second headline concerned the two murders. The state broadcaster was covering the story conservatively – the woman discovered in the Phoenix Park on Friday morning was a member of the Sisters of Pity order in Limerick. Her murder had been followed by what appeared to be another suspicious death, this time of the parish priest in her home village, Father Seamus McGahan. The police had made no comment following the second death, but the two appeared to be linked.

The rest of the article was just trying to fill in the gaps, carrying outraged quotes from members of the Church and politicians. He sighed and put the phone down. Presuming the roads were made passable, the media would descend on the area like flies today.

What an economic boost for the little village of Kilcross.

He met Michael on the landing. Despite being the first officer to bed last night, the detective looked shattered. His eyelids drooped and his hair was dishevelled – the look of a man who had tossed and turned for a good many hours.

He muttered a good morning as he stumbled past Tom on the way to the bathroom.

The inspector put a hand on his shoulder. 'Are you all right, Michael?'

The detective started nodding but then shook his head

and visibly crumpled. Leaning against the wall, he rubbed his eyes as if tiredness were now his master.

'I couldn't sleep.'

'Why not?'

Michael shrugged.

Tom made a decision. 'Put on something warm and come outside with me for a quick walk before breakfast. You can catch up on some hours this afternoon, if need be. But there's no point in going back to bed now. I'll wait for you downstairs.'

Michael nodded dumbly.

Willie emerged next, yawning and stretching sleepily in his doorway as he surveyed the landing.

'I could get used to being down here,' he said to Tom. 'The wife normally wakes me by leaning over and telling me what she wants me to do before I leave for work or when I get home. Thirty years. I'd have been out already if I'd done her in.'

Tom tutted.

Willie and his wife bickered relentlessly. But if something happened to one of them, the other wouldn't be able to function.

'I'm going to get some air,' Tom said. 'By the way, did you get talking to Sister Bernadette about her "walk"?'

'No. When I went looking for her, she'd gone to bed. And I had no desire to follow her up. I'll find her this morning.'

'Do that. Let's pull together at breakfast.'

While waiting for Michael in the hall he met Sisters Mary and Gabrielle coming back from morning prayers.

'Are you ready for breakfast?' Sister Mary inquired, cheerfully.

'I'm actually going for a short walk. Work up an appetite.'

'Oh, but you'll freeze out there, Inspector. Are you going on your own?'

'No, one of my detectives is joining me.'

She placed a hand on a rotund hip. 'Wait there,' she commanded.

She swished into the kitchen. When she emerged, a couple of minutes later, Michael was coming down the stairs.

'Hot chocolate,' she said, handing them an easy-sip flask each. 'I put a nip of brandy in it.'

Tom, bemused, thanked her.

They stepped out the front. The flasks steamed in the cold air.

'Shall we walk round the back of the house and check out the ruins of the laundry and orphanage?' Tom suggested.

Michael raised his eyebrows in assent, not really caring where they walked.

The snow was still deep, but the morning was clear and crisp. The clouds weren't as laden as they had been the previous day. It didn't look like the government would have to declare a state of emergency, after all.

They walked in silence. Tom realized if he didn't start the conversation, nothing would be said.

'What is it, Michael? I'm guessing it's not the case. Are you still worried about Anne?'

When the young man maintained his silence, Tom ploughed on.

'Michael, you will get through this. You're a strong couple. Children aren't the be all and end all, you know. And if being parents is so important to you, have you considered other options?'

'We know there are options,' Michael said. 'It was too soon, but I was going to raise it with Anne. Children are everything to her. That's why we tried so many times. But the last time, it just did it for me. It's like something snapped. This is killing us. It's become like the third part of the marriage, you know? Like that empty space in the bed between us is actually filled with all the dead babies we should have had.'

Tom was dismayed to notice tears starting to form in Michael's eyes.

'And what's changed?' he asked the young detective. 'You can give it time and have that conversation, surely?'

'What's changed is she's pregnant again.'

Tom felt his head spin. Feeling completely inadequate, he racked his brain for the right thing to say. He considered himself fairly progressive for a man when it came to discussing emotional matters, but the last few days had been a stretch. There was a reason men didn't engage too often in conversations about feelings.

'How far gone is she?'

'Twelve weeks.' The detective kicked at the snow.

'Michael, this is going to sound as clichéd as it gets, but you can't spend every second worrying about this. No, listen to me; I know that's harder than it sounds. But if something is going to happen, it will happen. Is she happy right now?'

'Sounds delirious. She was miserable when I was leaving on Friday, then she did the test.' He smacked his forehead with his hand. 'Of course! She's been in and out of that bathroom every hour for the last few weeks. She's been a wreck, hasn't looked herself at all. I thought she'd just given up, was depressed. It must have been the pregnancy.'

'Didn't she have those symptoms on the other pregnancies?'

'She never had any symptoms with the others. We wouldn't have even known she was pregnant half the time, except she stockpiled pregnancy kits.'

Tom had a vague memory of Louise telling him once that sickness in the early stages of pregnancy was generally a good sign. He said nothing, not wanting to get the young man's hopes up.

'Let her have this, Michael. Don't worry her because you're worried. What good will come of that? And if it doesn't work out, give it some time and then tell her you can't do it again.'

Michael sighed.

Tom reckoned his hot chocolate might have cooled

enough to drink by this stage. He took a sip. The brandy, poured with a generous hand, delivered a surge of heat down his throat. The breakfast of kings, he thought, as his eyes watered.

'Jesus,' he said. 'Drink your brandy. There's some chocolate in it.'

They started walking again, Michael gingerly sipping from his flask.

'I wonder what McGuinness would say if he knew we were having alcohol for breakfast,' he said, when he could use his tongue again.

Tom smiled. McGuinness kept a bottle of Jameson in his office.

'Can I let you in on a secret, Michael?'

The younger man nodded, curious.

'My Maria is expecting.'

Michael did a mental double take. 'That's fantastic. She's your only child, isn't she?'

'She is. But she's only nineteen. First year in college.'

They were at the back of the convent now. The ruins that Tom had seen from the upper floor the first night lay in front of them. Only the tips of some of the snow-covered stones were visible, and the two men had to be careful where they placed their feet. In other places, parts of the walls were still intact. Both of them shuddered as they walked between the old stones, and not from the cold.

'Do you like Maria's boyfriend?'

'She doesn't have a boyfriend.'

They stopped and looked around, taking more sips from their flasks.

'Last night, sir, after Anne gave me the news, I started thinking about the girls who'd ended up in this place after having babies, or for even looking like they might have kids out of wedlock. I was thinking they'd have given anything to have my problems.'

'I know what you mean,' Tom sighed. 'It's been playing on my mind, too. The thoughts of Maria being sent to a mother and baby home for being single, then ending up somewhere like this. It breaks my heart.'

'Do you think any of the sisters were affected by what went on here?'

'I know it. I spoke to Sister Gladys last night. She saw some awful things. She said that the only thing she could do for the girls was stay. That was her sacrifice. And she'll probably never be recognized for it.'

'The women she showed kindness to will never forget it.'

Tom knew Michael was right.

'Are you ready to go back in? There's something I want to follow up on.'

They turned back towards the convent.

'What's on your mind?'

'The woman who's renting the place next door to the priest's house. Ciaran is struggling to track her down. I could barely hear him on the phone last night, but he mentioned her name – Catherine Farrell. I happened to be holding Margaret Downes's file in my hand when I was on the phone. Guess what her middle name was?'

'Catherine?'

'Correct.'

'Same woman?'

'Her file says she entered the laundry in 1973. But she had a baby in 1975.'

'That fits perfectly,' Michael exclaimed. 'If Margaret Catherine Downes is Catherine Farrell, she could have been watching the priest's house the whole time and checking out the convent.'

'Right again. We need to find out what became of Margaret, asap.'

Tom's phone rang as they arrived back in the front hall. It was Emmet, back on the road.

'Good to see you're up and at it, Tom. This case must be killing you – 8 a.m. starts, is it?'

'I'll have you know I was up with the lark. I suppose you couldn't wait to get out of the charming B&B. Leave the luscious landlady sated in the bed, did you?'

'I didn't even stop for breakfast. The good man who runs the garage on the main street was open; he served me a hot sausage roll and a coffee. There's barely a car on the road. It's like the 1990 World Cup again; people have abandoned work.'

'How's the driving?' Tom asked.

'Slow but steady. I'll head straight to the priest's house

then up to Limerick HQ to make sure their lab is running the scene evidence properly. Where is Ellie, by the way? I couldn't get through on the mobile.'

'She's staying in a B&B in the village. With my deputy, as it happens, who's planning a proposal. There's terrible phone coverage here, that's why you can't get her.'

'Ha!' Emmet snorted. 'I wouldn't worry about your deputy. Ellie has that effect on all men.'

'If you're up in the city anyway, will you check in with the pathologist? He's working out of Limerick hospital. Father Seamus's GP said the priest had heart trouble and reckons he could have been given some kind of injection.'

Tom could almost hear Emmet's brain whirring in the background.

'Hmm. From what I know, Tom, it's a bit difficult to inject someone using the element of surprise – unless they're in a deep sleep, or they've let you come up close enough. If you tried to stick a needle in someone, approaching from behind, for example, one quick movement and they'd have it out before you could inject all of whatever you had in the syringe.'

'What are you getting at?'

'Did he know the person injecting him, is what I'm getting at. People have used syringes as murder weapons, but it's usually on victims who have no means of getting away.

'You say he'd a heart condition. There was a nurse in

the States – Gilbert, I think she was called – who was injecting her patients with epinephrine. It caused them to have heart attacks. They had heart conditions, anyway. So the other staff in the hospital didn't think too much of the unusual number of deaths in her care, until there were too many to ignore. I think they referred to her as "the angel of death". Any chance your priest was having an afternoon nap?'

Tom paused before replying. 'There weren't any obvious signs of struggle, so perhaps. The beds were all made, though, and we got the impression he'd just come down from the attic.'

'Well, if that's not the case, then you need to focus on who knew him – who would he not be surprised to see, and who would he let get close enough to empty a syringe into him.'

'Would they need medical training?'

'It would certainly help. But you could have somebody who has just done his research. Tom?'

'What?'

'McGuinness hasn't tried to take the investigation in any funny direction, has he?'

'What do you mean?' Tom knew exactly what Emmet meant, but he wanted him to say it.

'You know full well. He hasn't asked you to consult the quack?'

Tom smiled. 'No.'

Emmet breathed a sigh of relief. 'Well, just do me a

favour. Solve the bloody thing quickly, and let's keep it all scientific and medical. I do not want to have to encounter she who I will not name while I'm down here.'

Anyone listening in on their conversation would have thought the Technical Bureau head was talking in tongues. Emmet had a long history with the woman in question, and putting the two of them on the same investigation would be an incendiary proposition.

Luckily, McGuinness hadn't mentioned her.

Yet.

CHAPTER 44

The sisters had kindly left breakfast out again, this time a mixed grill. Willie was already in situ, loading his plate with large pork sausages flavoured with herbs and pepper, slices of crispy bacon, spoonfuls of buttery scrambled eggs and boxty, the traditional Irish potato pancake.

Even Laura seemed to have regained her appetite and was helping herself to toast and eggs. Her hunger noticeably diminished, though, when she overheard Michael telling Willie that Ray had slept in the village B&B last night, where Ellie had her lodgings.

Tom joined them and began ladling spiced sausages on to his plate.

'How about a slice of tomato there, Willie, to curb the cholesterol? Maybe some mushrooms?'

Willie's withering look indicated that adding vegetables to his plate, even fried, would constitute a crime against breakfast.

They had no sooner sat down than Tom's phone rang, the screen flashing Ciaran's number. He put him on loudspeaker so the others could hear.

'Glad the phones are back, Tom.'

'I have you on speaker, Ciaran. We're all here. You were trying to tell me last night about the woman in the house next door to Father Seamus.'

'Yes. Catherine Farrell. This has me perplexed. The nosiest woman in the village – that's Mrs Guckian, Father Seamus's cleaner – couldn't tell me anything about her. She has seen her but says Catherine was wrapped up for the weather, so all she saw was a woman of average height, with red hair and glasses. She couldn't guess an age except to say she didn't look old. Mrs Guckian did say Father Seamus had conversed with the woman a few times and appeared to like her.'

'What about the agent who rented the property?'

'She dealt with the letting agent by email, so he never met her. Paid everything through an account – rent up front until the end of the year, that's this month. The fella said she was looking for a property in a rural village where she could write in peace. She suggested a couple of villages but, given her budget, she could only really afford the property in Kilcross.

'I tried to follow up on the references she provided – a former employer and a publishing company. Neither number is in service. I suspect the agent didn't bother checking when she paid up front and in full. We tried the contact number she provided, but it rang out.'

'What about the bank account?' Tom asked.

'It's in her name. But if Catherine Farrell is a pseudonym, she could easily have forged documentation to set up an account. If I want more details from the bank, I'll have to get a warrant.'

'Hmm. This is bothering me too, Ciaran. Do you think the agent might come to the house and let us have a look inside? Can he do that if he can't get hold of her – check the property?'

'If he has legitimate concerns I think he can, yes. I'll ask, but he's based in Dublin so it mightn't be until tomorrow. The old lady's family all live in the capital, so they didn't use a local agent.'

'Well, see what you can do. Listen, I was just speaking to Emmet McDonagh, the head of the Technical Bureau. He suggested that if the priest was injected with something, he was either asleep or sufficiently comfortable with the person to let his killer get that close.'

'But we think he had just come down from the attic, don't we?' Ciaran asked.

'Yes. The attic door was shut, but not locked. He wouldn't have let anyone up there with him. And I doubt anybody could have surprised him, coming up those creaky steps.

'I have this feeling he was attacked downstairs. All of our suspects at the moment seem to be female, and no woman would have the strength to carry him downstairs after he was dead. If they dragged him down the stairs, his body would have had more marks.'

'The back door was unlocked, as though he'd let somebody in,' Michael interjected. 'That also implies he knew his killer.'

'If we're certain the killer didn't have a key, or Father Seamus hadn't left it unlocked,' Ciaran said. 'Wouldn't he be surprised, though, at someone calling to the back door?'

'If he was in the attic, they could have said they'd tried the front and then gone round the back. Maybe he thought he'd left the side gate open? And his cleaner has keys, doesn't she?'

'Yes, but she also can't walk at the moment.'

'Could she have loaned her keys to anyone?' Tom asked.

'I don't know. We'll check that out at our end.'

'Might the neighbour have popped in the odd time over the back fence?'

Ciaran thought about this. 'Possibly.'

'Keep looking into that Farrell woman, Ciaran,' Tom urged before ending the call.

The inspector was about to start tucking into his breakfast when the detectives were disturbed by the sounds of doors banging and a commotion in the kitchen next door. Tom pushed his chair back and hurried towards the noise, followed by the others, in time to see Sister Concepta and Sister Gabrielle carrying Sister Gladys between them.

For one horrible moment, the inspector thought the old woman had become the latest victim. But her eyes were open and filled with pain.

'Give her space,' Sister Concepta said to the five or six nuns fussing around, as they gently lowered her into her usual armchair. 'Mary, get her a whiskey.'

'Make it a large one,' Sister Gladys said, weakly.

That brought a smile to everyone's lips.

'Make way.' Sister Bernadette pushed through the room, carrying an ancient leather medical bag.

'What happened?' Tom asked.

'She went out for a walk,' Sister Concepta answered. 'The snow has covered some of the low walls out the back and she fell over one. What possessed you to go out in that, Sister? You're lucky it's just your ankle and not a hip. If people insist on walking out there, we'll have to cordon off those ruins so nobody else tries to kill themselves.'

Sister Gladys accepted a glass spilling over with whiskey from Sister Mary.

'Maybe I just wanted to start drinking early today, Concepta.'

She was putting a brave face on it but winced as Bernadette, now sitting in front of the older woman, carefully lifted the ankle and rested it in her lap. She unlaced the older woman's shoe and peeled down a long black stocking.

'I can't have those men standing there looking at my legs,' Sister Gladys said, cocking her head at the male detectives, although barely an inch of flesh was visible.

'Don't be silly,' Sister Bernadette said. 'You've nothing they haven't seen before.'

'They haven't seen mine before.'

'We'll spare your blushes and leave the kitchen, Sister. It's not too badly damaged, I hope?' Tom addressed this to

Sister Bernadette, who was manipulating the ankle tenderly.

'Just a sprain, thank God. If it was a break we'd have to go up to the hospital, but I can deal with this.'

The police officers left the kitchen, accompanied by Sister Concepta.

'She was out at the orphanage ruins. Said she was "remembering". Honestly! If she'd been out there for any length of time she would have caught pneumonia.'

'You're lucky you have Sister Bernadette,' Tom said. 'Does she have medical training?'

'Bernadette? Oh, yes. She was trained as a nurse. That's how she ended up with the missionaries.'

'Is she your only nurse?'

'Fully trained, yes. We'd be lost without her. I have a little knowledge, but not enough for all eventualities. If you don't mind, I'd better get back in there.'

'Of course.' He held the heavy door open for her.

When she was out of sight, the detectives exchanged looks.

Michael was the first to say it. He counted out each point on his hand.

'Medical training; unaccounted for yesterday afternoon; hated Mother Attracta and had a run-in with her she didn't tell us about; was a familiar presence to Father Seamus; wasn't happy that this place was a laundry and had started compiling its records—'

'And she's not that old,' Laura added.

Tom nodded. 'I think I'll follow up with Bernadette

about yesterday myself, Willie. Let's listen to her initial interview again.'

Grabbing some toast on the way, the two men went to Mother Attracta's office to get the tape recordings.

Tom rewound to the point where he'd asked Bernadette what she had done on Thursday, the day after Mother Attracta had been kidnapped.

'What did you do all day Thursday?'

'Let me see. I spent most of the day in bed. I felt quite weak. I read for a while but in the afternoon I slept. I fetched some soup from the kitchen later on.'

'Did you see other sisters that evening?'

'Oh, of course. Sister Gladys is in the kitchen most nights. There are generally a couple of us congregating there or in the sitting room at any given time.'

'Did you hear that?' Tom asked.

Willie nodded. 'The "oh, of course". It's not that convincing when you think about it. And "Sister Gladys is in the kitchen most nights"?'

Tom nodded. 'I'll talk to her. You grab Michael and Laura, and the three of you start asking the other sisters if they saw Bernadette that day.'

Back in the kitchen, the nuns were busy making tea and buttering warm scones.

Sister Bernadette was packing up her medical bag; the patient was reclined in her chair with a smile indicating the prescribed alcohol was having the desired effect.

'Sister Bernadette, may I see you?' Tom asked.

'No problem, Inspector. Do you want to go somewhere quieter?'

'Please. Mother Attracta's office?'

Willie hung back as Tom left with the nun.

Once inside Mother Attracta's office, Bernadette filled Tom in on the elderly nun's condition.

'If she keeps the leg up for a few days, she'll be fine. She's very lucky it wasn't worse.'

'She's lucky you were here, Sister. Did you train for long as a nurse?'

'I worked in Limerick General for five years. I had a special talent for it. One of the consultants said I should have trained to be a doctor, but my peers would have frowned on that. It was nursing or midwifery for the likes of me. It stood me well in Latin America, I can tell you. I had to have a strong stomach at times.'

'I don't doubt it. You can save lives, then? You'd know all about heart attacks and strokes and such?'

Sister Bernadette looked at him, amused. 'Well, that's what the training is for, Inspector. I'm sure you don't want to talk to me about my prowess as a medical practitioner.'

Tom paused, then exhaled loudly. 'Sister, you informed members of my team yesterday that you had gone for a walk around the time we believe Father Seamus was murdered. I need to follow up on that. Why would you go for a walk in these dreadful conditions, and did you meet anyone while you were out?'

The sister crossed her arms defensively. 'Why does

anyone go on a walk? Sister Gladys just went on one. Why are you asking me in particular?'

Tom sat back, resting his hands on the sides of the chair. His body language was open, unthreatening.

'In a double murder investigation, Sister, it's normally me asking the questions.'

'If this was a proper interrogation, though, wouldn't I be entitled to a solicitor?'

'Of course. And if you want to go down that route, that is absolutely your right.'

She cast him a frightened look. 'Do I need to go down that route?'

He shrugged. 'I need honest answers. You can choose to have that conversation informally, like we're doing now. Or we can head to Kilcross station and have it formally.'

She blinked twice. 'No, I don't want to do it formally.' She bit her lip before speaking again. 'Inspector, I spent a long time dealing with very corrupt police forces, and I saw too many young men and women forced into false confessions behind closed doors. So I get a bit jumpy when someone is asking me a question with a subtext that implies yesterday afternoon I might have murdered a man.'

'I think you're a few skips ahead, Sister. I'm not going to be forcing any confessions out of you. I'm just asking questions. When you were walking, did you see anybody?'

She looked over his shoulder and out the window.

Something had changed in her face. The usual trace of

good humour that resided in her eyes was gone. A melancholy had descended.

'In 1980, when I had just started working in El Salvador, there was an incident. Three nuns and another woman travelling with them were raped and executed by the National Guard. You might have heard of it. I'd never met the women, but they were heroines to all of us who worked as missionaries. That was the same year that Archbishop Romero was assassinated.

'The reason I'm telling you this is because we lived in fear. We ministered to the poor people of the countryside, and every day was one of anxiety. I'm not making myself out to be a hero. That kind of experience exposes you to the truth about yourself. Have you ever wondered how you would respond in certain situations and convinced yourself that you would respond bravely? When I left Ireland, I thought I was the bravest woman in the world. Then I was confronted with real situations – and every time I froze. I was petrified. It was quite a coming of age.

'But I did learn to live with myself and my limitations. And maybe I was courageous, because I stayed. By the time I came home I had learned how to handle fear, not in a confrontational way, but by making myself invisible.

'Isn't it amazing to think that while nuns were being raped and murdered in El Salvador for trying to help an impoverished, frightened people, nuns like Mother Attracta were lording it over people in Ireland as if the clergy inhabited some kind of moral high ground?'

Tom shifted in his seat. His mind raced as he wondered whether Sister Bernadette was trying to make some kind of indirect confession.

'The point is, Inspector, I learned to disappear. Sometimes, when I'm around the sisters here, I just go off and find my own space. I often walk, or pray or read in my room. I enjoy the solitude. And yesterday I went for a very long walk around the back paths of the village, snow and all. Silly, I know, especially when you see what happened to Gladys this morning. I just needed fresh air and peace. I met no one.'

Tom cupped his chin in his hand. 'Sister, you told us you slept for a period of time on Thursday and that you then went down to the kitchen for supper. How many hours were you asleep? What time did you go to your room?'

She shrugged. 'Three, four o'clock? I didn't check. I woke at 7.30 p.m.'

'And when you went to the kitchen, who did you see specifically?'

'I'm not sure I saw anyone.' Her voice was low.

'You said, Sister, in your interview—'

'I know what I said.'

'Were you lying?'

She shook her head. 'Not intentionally. I knew you were trying to establish if I had an alibi. It turns out I hadn't.'

Tom sat back and observed the woman, wondering what other deceptions she was capable of.

'You're not always afraid, though, are you?' he said. 'It was audacious to start compiling the laundry records with Sister Concepta.'

Sister Bernadette sat up a little straighter in her chair. 'So you know about that. I'm not sure how much daring I showed. Running around at night, hoping we wouldn't be caught. Real courage would have been doing it openly, surely?'

'You did what you could. I just have one more question. The first night I stayed here, I looked out my window and thought I saw you looking over at me. Were you?'

She blushed. 'I thought you'd seen me. I wasn't looking at you. I was looking out at where the foundations stood for the laundry and the orphanage. I couldn't sleep for thinking about those girls. Then I saw you at your window, and I pulled my curtains.'

She sounded plausible, though the fact she was dwelling on the laundry's past gave him pause for thought.

'I think that will be all for now, Sister.'

A few minutes later, Michael stepped into the room to find his boss staring out the window, deep in thought.

'Well?' Tom asked.

'No one remembers seeing her on Thursday. For most of the day. Do you have enough to take her to the station for formal questioning?'

Tom shook his head. 'Not yet. Not having an alibi does not a murderer make.'

'What does your gut say?'

Tom looked out the frost-covered window for another moment before he answered.

'I have a feeling she's keeping something from us. We need to start looking into her background. Discreetly. She's been looking at those files for years – it can't have escaped her attention that girls got pregnant while they were in the laundry.

'Religion is an honourable vocation for her, and Ray suggested our killer could be on some kind of holy mission. I've been pondering another direction altogether, involving one of the laundry girls. But if Bernadette was that badly affected by what happened when she was abroad, maybe a few screws have come loose and she's on a crusade against members of the Church here.'

He sighed. 'I'm going to ask some more questions about those rape allegations. Maybe Sister Clare this time. Her memory seems pretty sharp.'

CHAPTER 45

Tom was on his way to interview Sister Clare when he met Ray and Ciaran coming in the front door.

'We've something interesting, boss,' Ray said. 'I found these on the priest's computer.' He held a sheaf of print-outs in his hand. 'I gave the computer a cursory going over yesterday but I had a proper go at it in the station this morning. We've moved all the evidence there, by the way. It took me a while but I searched through the priest's emails from the last couple of years.' Ray's face was grim. 'Wait until you see this.'

There were twenty emails in total. Tom scanned their contents. The first one read:

You are not fit to call yourself a man of God.

Each email got progressively angrier until the last:

How many children did you father, you evil man? You will rot in hell for what you did. Do you think about all the poor girls you raped when you stand at the pulpit moralizing? Do you remember their suffering? Have you ever imagined their anguish when their babies were torn from them? There is a circle of hell

that Satan created for people like you. I hope you die screaming. You will never
be forgiven for what you did.

EVIL EVIL EVIL EVIL EVIL EVIL EVIL EVIL EVIL EVIL EVIL EVIL

The venom of the last line was visceral, as though the writer had wanted to carve the words onto the screen.

Tom felt a shiver run down his spine.

None of the messages were signed. The email address was a letter and a series of numbers, R1219, at a Yahoo! address.

'Is this just a random combination, or does the address mean something?' Tom asked.

'I thought at first it was an anonymous jumble,' Ray said, 'but the writer was sending him another message. I was thinking about that whole religious mission angle, so I looked up biblical references. It's Romans, Chapter 12, Verse 19.'

'What's the quote?' Tom asked.

Ray produced another sheet and handed it to the inspector.

Tom read the fiery exhortation: *Avenge not yourselves, but rather give place unto wrath: for it is written, Vengeance is mine; I will repay, saith the Lord.*

His eyes widened as he read the words. 'Good work, Ray. Can we source the origin of the emails?'

'I don't have the expertise,' the detective replied. 'In the absence of someone from our own IT department sitting down at the computer, we're a bit stuck to get it done in a hurry. Ciaran says there is a guy in the village who is a techie genius, but we didn't want to ask him for help without clearing it with you first.'

'You've a computer whizz in the village?' Tom asked Ciaran.

'Yep. The chap has just come home from the States. He was working in California, Silicon Valley. I think his roots were calling him and back he came with a shedload of money.'

'And a fabulous American wife?' Tom asked.

'No, but he has had quite a few visits from a tanned young man. I don't think it's his son.' Ciaran raised his eyebrows knowingly.

The man's love life was probably the talk of the village. Up until recent events, anyway.

'Is he trustworthy?'

'I think he's well used to discretion.'

'Then get him in. Ray, contact the phone company and get the priest's call records for the last couple of years.'

Tom looked back down at the quotation he was still holding in his hand.

'What is it?' Ray asked.

'It's this quote. It's about the Lord avenging wrongdoing. It's specific that those on earth are not supposed to take vengeance into their own hands.'

'So? Maybe the person who chose the quote just wanted something about vengeance.'

Tom shrugged. 'Maybe. There are better quotes. Anyway, I take it people are able to travel again now?'

'It's better, but not great,' Ciaran replied. 'I put chains on the tyres.'

'Being able to move again is going to bring its own problems,' Ray said.

'What do you mean?' Tom asked.

'The B&B in the village is booked out with media and ... er ... at least one other interesting character. I told Ellie and Jack they'd have to move down here, unless Jack can get to his family. Ellie said they might be heading back to Dublin tonight, though.'

Tom looked at him strangely, wondering who could be more noteworthy than the media. 'Tell Ellie and Jack to get down here. I think Emmet will stay the night, and he'll want his team. I'm going to find Sister Clare.'

As Tom turned away, all business, he missed the huge grin of pure happiness spreading across his deputy's face, as Ray anticipated another night chatting up Ellie Byrne.

Tom found the nun in the sitting room. Sister Clare was alone, a book in hand. While he'd been searching for her, he'd found the other nuns making up Christmas gift baskets for children in Limerick hospital. He wondered why she wasn't helping. She didn't even appear to be reading the book she was holding, just staring at the page, her thoughts elsewhere.

'May I disturb you, Sister?' he asked.

She looked up. 'Please, Inspector. I was just trying to distract myself from the awful events of the last few days.'

'What's your chosen diversion?' he asked, pointing at her hand.

'Oh, this?' Sister Clare closed it and showed him the cover.

It was a copy of *Wuthering Heights*. Tom couldn't hide his surprise.

She smiled. 'You thought it would be a copy of the Bible? This is my favourite book. Yes, I know, one of the most romantic novels of all time. And I a nun.' She placed the well-thumbed novel in her lap.

'My wife claims it's romantic as well,' he said. 'She's studying English at the moment. But I read it in school and thought it was downright disturbing. That section when Heathcliff digs up Cathy from the grave . . . that's a strange kind of love.'

'Oh, you're wrong, Inspector. It's love in its absolute form – obsession. Your wife is correct, and I know most people enjoy the book solely for Heathcliff and Cathy. I, however, have always been interested in the other Brontë characters. They may be just obstacles to the star-crossed lovers' lives, but they are fascinating. Such wrongs are inflicted on them. Yet, look at Cathy's husband – he remains a good man.'

So said the nun who had spent her life relegated to the role of a bit player in the convent after Mother Attracta had usurped her rightful place as its head.

'Anyway, it's surely not literature you need me for. We do have book club on Tuesday nights, if you care to join us tomorrow.'

'I wanted to talk to you about the orphanage that was attached to the convent. When did it cease to exist?'

The nun frowned. 'Around the same time as the laundry. Why?'

'Where are the records for it now?' He ignored her question.

'We gave them to the Limerick adoption authority. They decided to gather adoption records for the county in 1999.'

'Were all of the babies in the orphanage put there willingly?'

'Of course, Inspector. It was not the done thing back then to have a child out of wedlock.' She pursed her lips. 'Looking around the country now, you can see why.'

Tom was careful not to react to her words. This was not about his daughter.

'You also dealt with pregnant girls, didn't you? Did you build a hospital ward specifically for that purpose?'

'We had an infirmary already in the orphanage. When any of the children or the laundry girls got sick, that's where they'd go. We added a delivery room.'

'Who assisted the girls in labour?' he asked.

'There were two sisters who were fully trained midwives, and some others who were partially trained. One of the midwives died years ago. You must be aware who the other was.'

'No. Who?'

She looked at him, surprised. 'The other was Mother Attracta.'

'Mother Attracta delivered the babies?' Tom repeated.

'Yes, for decades. There weren't many deliveries, though. Most unwed women went to the mother and baby home up in the city. We got maybe one girl a month.'

'Sister, it appears that some girls got pregnant after they had entered the laundry. Given their seclusion from the world, can you explain how that happened?'

She looked at him haughtily. 'I'm sure I can't. Unless you're looking for some kind of lesson on the birds and the bees.'

He leaned forward. Making his voice low and dangerous, he fixed her with a look that warned: Be careful how you reply to this.

'Sister Clare, I looked at the file last night of a woman who entered this convent in 1973. In 1975 she had a baby. Now, were you taking the girls out to discos? Were they allowed to have young men over? Could lads have been hopping the gate and having secret forays with the girls in the fields?

'You see, I find it hard to understand, Sister, how girls whose physical and moral care was entrusted to yourselves could end up pregnant under your watchful eyes. And I cannot imagine that, when it did happen, there wasn't a furore and questions weren't asked.'

She couldn't meet his eyes when she replied. 'Of course questions were asked, Inspector. It was outrageous. But the girls weren't monitored twenty-four hours a day. We weren't running a prison. Sometimes they walked around the grounds. They would work in the vegetable gardens. Boys must have got in. I assure you that such pregnancies only happened a few times in my memory.'

'Did you ever wonder whether the girls were being taken advantage of by someone closer to home?'

The colour rose in the nun's cheeks.

'Before you answer me, Sister, I want to tell you that I do not appreciate being lied to. I have a good idea what was happening to those girls. Now, I can only assume that those who knew about it did not actively facilitate it but must have found it beyond belief. Or they were too cowed by the person who was perpetrating the offence to confront him. Because if anything other than that is the case, then we are talking about complicity in an unspeakable crime. And I can assure you, there is no statute of limitations on that.'

He could see he had made her revisit something so unpleasant that every fibre of her being was reacting against it. The battle raged on her face.

Eventually, she spoke.

'There is no conspiracy here, Inspector,' she said. 'Yes, there was a certain suspicion at the time you speak of. If you think for one moment any one of us would have stood by if it turned out those allegations were true—'

'What allegations?'

She caught herself, realizing she'd gone too far. There was no way back now.

'The allegations against Father Seamus. The three girls who got pregnant claimed that he ... had been improper in his behaviour towards them. Well, it was vindictive, of course. They cooked it up amongst themselves. As if ... as if a man of God would do such a thing.

'Some years earlier, a similar allegation had been made about another priest and he had to move from the parish. Not because he did anything, but because of the hurt those accusations caused. That's clearly where the girls got the idea. It was easier than owning up to what they'd done. It was all lies.'

She nodded her head to emphasize her point. To convince him or herself, he wasn't sure.

He observed the nun, disappointed. 'Sister, things are going to be reported about Father Seamus that prove your version of him wrong. I would like to know exactly who made the accusations against him, and what happened to their babies. They may be needed for DNA testing.'

'But you can't!' she shrieked, jumping up from her chair. 'Do you hear what you are saying? The girls didn't want the babies. Those children are adults now and probably don't even know they are adopted. They will never have seen their original birth certificates. And you'd approach them – pull apart the lives they have lived all this time – and claim they were the result of rape? Are you mad?'

'If justice demands it, Sister, that is what I will do.'

Tom knew that was something he'd avoid at all costs. But he felt so angry it was easy to make the threat.

He pulled a notepad from his pocket. 'Your memory seems to be excellent. Could you please write down the names of the women who claimed that Father Seamus had fathered their babies?'

Sister Clare gave him one last imploring look, but saw only resolve in his eyes. She snatched the paper and pen from his hand with bad grace.

When she returned it, she had written three names.

Bríd O'Toole

Noreen Boyle

Margaret Downes

'Thank you,' he said curtly. 'That will be all.' Tom dismissed her from the room, though she had been sitting in it first.

He exhaled loudly when the door closed, glad to see the back of her.

CHAPTER 46

Tom rang Ian at the station, scanning Sister Clare's list as he waited for the sergeant to picked up the call.

He wasted no time giving his instructions. 'Ian, I'm going to read you three names, and these are the ones I want you to prioritize while you're doing background checks on the master list,' he said.

Ian took the names down. 'I can give you an update already,' he said.

'Go on.'

'Well, of the five hundred names, the nuns had already listed fifty of the women as deceased. That's correct. We also found death certificates for another eighty. There may be more than that, but if they got married it will take us a little longer to find the certs. I've a few officers using online search facilities here; the bulk of the team is down in the General Register Office. We're checking which surnames changed before we move on to emigration records. If you've narrowed it down to these three women, I can't tell you how much easier this is going to be.'

'I can't categorically say it's one of these three women

I'm looking for, Ian, so you'll have to press on with the rest. We'll dig out their laundry files here; we already have Margaret Downes's. This is a real can of worms. I'm not going to let up until I get to the bottom of it.'

Tom hung up and remained in the sitting room, quietly watching the wood hiss and spit as the fire burned merrily in the grate. Through the lace curtains in the window he could see the grounds at the front of the convent, covered in white, bereft of movement except for the clumps of snow that periodically fell from the trees and landed, silently, on the virgin snow beneath.

He picked up his phone.

Maria answered after a couple of rings.

'Mam said you were mounting "Maria-watch" from down there.' She yawned.

'I'm only ringing to tell you I love you and I'm thinking about you,' he said.

He knew she'd been expecting a smart remark but his heartfelt words disarmed her. Their relationship nowadays was characterized by witticisms and sarcasm, emotions evident but left unarticulated. It had been that way since she entered her teens.

There was silence for a moment and then a surprised, 'I love you, too.'

He could hear a catch in her throat.

'Dad? You're not disappointed in me, are you? I'm planning to stay in college. I mean, I'll try to. It might be better if I get a job and pay my way.'

He shook his head vigorously. 'I could never be

disappointed in you, Maria. Don't even think it. Whatever you do, I'll support you. But don't imagine for one second you're facing this on your own, or that we won't be there for you every step of the way. We're your parents; that's our job.'

A vehicle pulled slowly into the drive.

Maria was silent on the other end of the phone, and he knew she didn't want to say anything in case it came out with a sob.

He lifted the smartphone and pressed its cool glass against his forehead. 'Hug, pat, kiss,' he said.

She laughed, the tension broken.

'Hug, pat, kiss,' she said back.

It was the routine they had played out every evening for years. He would arrive home from work and call up to say goodnight to his little girl. Louise called it their OCD routine – a hug, a pat on the back and a kiss on the lips.

'See you when you're home, Dad,' she said.

She ended the call, and he stood up.

The vehicle was Ellie's. Tom met her at the door and helped her carry her equipment case back into the convent.

'Déjà vu,' she said. 'Emmet was with us earlier, but he's in Limerick city now.'

'I'm just about to ring him. He won't be happy in someone else's lab – he gets crankier the further he gets from home.'

'I find that hard to believe,' Ellie replied. 'I'll give everything a quick going over. Emmet has a habit of finding things even when you think you've covered every millimetre.'

'It's all part of his God complex. Where's your sidekick?'

'Still up at the priest's house. I get the sense he's reluctant to come down here. Between you and me, I think this place gives him the creeps.'

Tom left her to get settled. On the way to the records room, to check on Michael and Laura's progress, he rang Emmet.

'Different county, same procedure – eh, Tom? I barely get to look at the evidence before you start harassing me.'

'Come on, Emmet, you've been in Limerick for hours. What have you got?'

'I spoke to the pathologist. They took samples from the body last night. The priest was indeed injected with Epinephrine, which in turn caused him to have a massive heart attack. Lucky guess on my part. You have a double murder.'

'Marvellous. Any forensic evidence?' Tom asked, hopefully.

'Yes. The priest had DNA under his fingernails. I got the sample myself from the mortuary, with the pathologist's assistance. It's minuscule but it's there. Just as well I came down.'

'That's good news.'

'This DNA will only be of use if you've got a suspect to match it to. Have you?'

'That's the plan. Will you be here soon?'

'As soon as you want me, Tom. Sure I'm just kicking my heels here, shooting the breeze with the rest of these useless, lazy scientists. We were turning the Bunsen burners on and off and talking about a round of golf . . .'

Tom hung up and smiled to himself.

The case was moving. In what direction, he wasn't sure, but he could smell a breakthrough.

'I have three names,' he said, handing his notepad to Laura.

'Who are they?' she asked. She had been fruitlessly rechecking boxes to ensure they hadn't missed a Liz Downes.

'The women who made accusations that Father Seamus got them pregnant.'

'So it's true!' Michael exclaimed, shaking his head.

Ray had joined the others and took the notepad from Laura to study the names.

'I just saw that woman's name, Noreen Boyle. Are we speculating that Margaret Downes is actually "Liz" Downes?'

'Yes, I think so,' Tom said. 'Her house name was Maggie. Maybe she gave herself a new first name in a bid to put this place behind her.'

Tom knew this was all conjecture, but there was so much similarity between Margaret and Liz's stories.

'I want the other two files, asap,' Tom said, 'but we can't get carried away with these three women. They got pregnant, so they couldn't hide what had happened to them. Others may have been raped and never spoke of it.

Remember, we found photos of more than three girls in the priest's attic.'

Ray pulled out a file from the box he had been going through. 'Noreen Boyle,' he said, handing it to Tom.

'Oh, hold on,' Laura said. She crossed to another box. 'Bríd O'Toole. I remember seeing it yesterday.'

Tom held the two files as though they were eggs that would break if dropped.

'Right,' he said, opening the first one.

He read aloud the pertinent facts.

Noreen had been admitted to the home in 1971, aged fourteen. She had been sent there from an industrial school. Her house name was Ivy. A note attached to her file stated bluntly that her mother had been a prostitute, father unknown.

It seemed the young girl had been accustomed to institutional life when she entered the laundry because there were scant entries recording disobedience in the years leading up to 1973, when she fell pregnant.

A handwritten page noted the pregnancy.

Ivy has made outrageous, sinful claims about how she conceived this baby. Due to her quiet nature, none of us have been watching her particularly closely and she has abused our trust. It is a reminder that we must never take our eyes off these girls, especially the ones that come from backgrounds like Ivy's. She has been punished for the sins of her fornication and pregnancy and we are now considering a suitable chastisement for the sin of lying.

Laura clicked her tongue with disgust as Tom read aloud.

The remainder of the file charted Noreen's admission to the infirmary in late December 1973. A short note revealed her baby had been adopted at eight weeks of age. It seemed there had been some difficulty getting Noreen to sign the adoption release, but her assent had eventually been secured.

A period of rebellion followed, before she was released from the laundry in 1977, aged twenty, to study as a nurse in Dublin.

Bríd's file was equally harrowing.

The youngest of six children, she had been placed in the laundry, aged twelve, following the death of her mother in 1969.

A handwritten note stated:

> Her father did the right thing in placing Bríd in our care. One can see that even at the tender age of twelve, this girl has all the markings of promiscuity. The figure of womanhood has already begun to bloom on her, something she considers a great delight, and she is entirely aware of her effect on men.

Bríd was pregnant in 1974, aged seventeen.

Tom thought back to the Downes file. She was around seventeen in 1974; he'd have to recheck it. Had Father Seamus not raped the younger girls? Maybe he was smart enough not to take the risk of impregnating them at that age for fear of a closer investigation. Or maybe he took pleasure in grooming them over a lengthy period.

Bríd's file was littered with punishments. She was obviously a serial rebel, which may have delayed her release from the laundry until 1981, aged twenty-four. The file didn't record what she went on to do.

'That reminds me,' Tom said. 'There was nothing at the end of Margaret Downes's file, either, to say where she'd gone or if she even left the laundry.'

'So, we're dealing with two crimes,' Ray said, when Tom shut the second file. 'The murders and the rapes.'

The inspector nodded. 'It may turn out that Sister Bernadette killed Mother Attracta and Father Seamus, but we've established that the probable reason for their murders lies in the past. These laundry women have been ignored for too long.'

'I think we're right to focus on the women who got pregnant as other potential suspects, though,' Laura suggested. 'Can you imagine the psychological damage that would do to someone – being raped and then having your child forcibly taken from you?'

'But if they'd been raped, surely they wouldn't have wanted the babies?' Michael said.

Laura shook her head. 'I did some training in rape counselling. Most women are usually treated early to ensure against pregnancy. But not all those who find out they're pregnant too late react as you'd expect. They don't necessarily associate the child with the assault, especially when they see the baby. It's hard to have those feelings about a newborn.'

Tom stared at Laura, an idea forming. It was a theory that had been scratching at the edge of his consciousness.

Just then, the door behind them opened and Ciaran came in. 'Tom, sorry to interrupt, can we have you for a minute?'

Behind Ciaran stood a tall, well-built man. He was in his forties and deeply tanned, his slicked-back hair lightened by sun streaks. This had to be the prodigal son from California. He smiled to reveal a set of gloriously white teeth, the likes of which had probably never been seen in Kilcross before.

'Ronan O'Neill,' he said, pleasantly, shaking Tom's hand vigorously.

'Detective Inspector Tom Reynolds,' Tom replied, hoping his fingers would still work when released. 'Thanks for your help with this, Ronan. Do you have something for me already?'

'I do. The sender of the emails wanted to remain anonymous but made an amateur error. They had to provide an existing email address when they set up the Yahoo! account – to verify passwords. The email address provided was Mother Attracta's.'

Tom's eyes widened. 'Go on,' he urged.

'Well, to access the nun's account from their personal computer, they'd have needed to find out her password. But if they used Attracta's own computer, they would have had easy access to her emails because she probably had her password saved, so the email account would have opened automatically. Just give me access to her computer and I can find out more.'

'By all means.' Tom turned to Michael. 'Could you find Sister Concepta?'

Over Michael's shoulder, Tom could see Ray was completely distracted. His deputy held a piece of paper and was frowning as he stared at it.

'If I'm right, I should be able to see when the Yahoo! account was set up,' Ronan said. 'After that, I'll try to find out as much as possible from cyber fingerprints.'

Tom said nothing. If Mother Attracta's account had been accessed on her own computer, then all the evidence was now pointing in one direction – towards one of the other nuns.

So why couldn't he shake the niggling suspicion that they were on the wrong track altogether?

Tom and Ciaran watched as Ronan's fingers flew over the keyboard, pulling up settings and history on the desktop.

The door opened, and Sister Concepta stepped in. Tom marvelled at how these nuns seemed to be invisible most of the time but so easily found when they were needed.

'Sister Concepta, I've asked this gentleman to look up something for me. You might know him from the village?'

The nun looked from Tom to Ronan and, after a moment, nodded uncertainly.

'Sister, did the other nuns ever have access to Mother Attracta's computer? Was it in communal use?'

Sister Concepta gave him a tight smile. 'No. Mother Attracta didn't like anyone else in here.'

'And it was just you and Sister Bernadette who had another computer?'

'Yes.'

Tom rubbed his chin. 'We believe someone was sending Father Seamus poison emails.' He studied her closely for her reaction.

She looked back at him blankly.

He turned back to Ronan. 'Will you be long, Mr O'Neill?'

The man didn't look up from the keyboard. 'Give me a half-hour, Inspector.'

Tom left the room with Sister Concepta.

'Sister Bernadette told me you'd spoken to her,' she said, when they were outside. 'Inspector, I've known Sister Bernadette a long time. I know what she's capable of and what she's not. Believe me, you are barking up the wrong tree.'

His phone rang.

'Nobody knows what anyone is capable of when they're pushed, Sister,' he responded, distractedly.

It was McGuinness again.

'Sir,' he said, indicating with a nod to Concepta that he had to take the call.

She glared at him, but left.

'What's happening, Tom?'

'We have some progress. Our focus at this point is on

another nun from the convent. She has no alibi for either murder. She appears to have motive and means.'

'Well, then, maybe my precautionary measure was taken too soon.'

Tom's mouth felt suddenly dry. 'What precautionary measure?'

McGuinness coughed. 'I've sent down Linda to help with the witnesses.'

Tom cursed silently and choked back his immediate response. He closed his eyes and tried to breathe steadily. Linda McCarn, Emmet's nemesis.

'You can call her back, sir. She's not needed.'

Silence met him on the other end of the line. Then, 'That's not going to be easy, Tom. She's booked into the B&B down there and left at eight this morning.'

This time the profanity escaped Tom's lips before he had time to stop it.

He took a deep breath.

'You do realize I've Emmet McDonagh here, too? What were you thinking?'

Linda and Emmet, it was rumoured, had once been engaged in a torrid extramarital affair. While part of Tom could see how two such driven, egotistical and stunningly clever people could have ended up together (and imploded), the thought of it made his stomach, unfairly, a little queasy. Nobody knew what had caused the rift between the two, but everyone knew of their now mutual animosity – and the hassle it caused when they were both thrust on to the same investigation.

One of these days, Tom intended to stop indulging them and call time on their childish carry-on. He'd also just realized who Ray had been referring to when he had mentioned another character staying in the village B&B.

McGuinness's response was as swift as it was defensive. 'Tom, what other action could I take? A murdered nun and a priest? That rings every psycho alarm bell there is. Of course I'm going to send down the state's leading criminal psychologist to assist you.'

'Well, there's not much I can do about it now,' Tom barked into the receiver.

'Let her help,' McGuinness said. 'She's good. And you know it.'

Tom was still grousing when the doorbell rang.

He knew that the person outside the door was Linda McCarn. She radiated crazy.

McGuinness had timed his call to perfection.

His heart sank.

CHAPTER 47

Tom opened the door and found himself eyeballing what he hoped was a fake fox.

Underneath the animal, which looked remarkably calm for a creature that had been transformed into a hat, stood the psychologist.

Just a head shorter than the inspector and skinny as a rake, Linda McCarn had decided early that the way to ensure her beanpole frame would never be overlooked was to adorn it with outrageous clothing and accessories.

Today, her dress sense was almost demure. Except for the orange fox hat, the tail of which was wrapped around her neck as a scarf, she was wearing a white puff parka jacket and an ankle-length green velvet skirt. She was a walking Irish flag.

Her wild frizzy brown hair was tucked into the hat, with just the odd delinquent curl escaping. The inspector often wondered whether Linda's clients, on first impression, were confused as to who was supposed to be analysing whom.

'Tom, darling,' she bellowed, in her privileged accent,

air kissing both sides of his face. 'I hear you need me!' She pushed past him, pausing only to whisper in his ear, 'I've dressed down. My Catholic upbringing.'

She laughed uproariously, and he backed away slightly.

'Come in, Linda,' he said, as she swept into the hall.

'Well, this is just adorable,' the psychologist said, looking around her.

Though they were standing in the large hallway of an even larger house, Linda spoke as though she'd just entered the tiny parlour room of a two-up, two-down.

'It's all very intriguing, isn't it, Tom? I've been hoping I'd get called in on this one.'

She moved through the hall, virtually stepping over Ellie, who looked up at the long legs moving through the area she was examining with a mixture of astonishment and annoyance.

'That's Ellie Byrne, from the Tech Bureau. Emmet is on his way, Linda,' Tom said.

'That odious man. Marvellous. Charmed, I'm sure.' Linda spoke first to Tom, then to Ellie. 'Can I get a drink? Only a soft one. I have to drive back to my lodgings later to write up this fascinating case.'

'You'll have solved it by then, I suppose,' Tom replied, tartly.

She put her large hazel eyes on full swivel and fixed them on him. They were searching, brilliant eyes. When they were focused directly on an individual, that person realized, often too late, that behind Linda's overbearing, eccentric manner lurked a genius, one who took in everything.

'All of the letters after my name lead me to believe you are being sarcastic, Tom.'

He sighed. 'My apologies. Let's get you some tea and we can talk.'

'Do they have a little sitting room we could retire to? I like to be comfortable when I'm analysing.'

Tom thought of the nun's main sitting room, into which he could fit half of his own downstairs rooms. It was a space Linda would find suitably charming.

He first checked the room was empty. He didn't want the psychologist discommoding the nuns just yet. The inspector wasn't sure any of them would be able to withstand a probing from Linda.

He deposited his guest, and left to fetch the tea.

No matter how hard he watched the kettle, the water still boiled. He returned to the sitting room within minutes.

She had made herself comfortable on the couch, legs tucked under her. The parka had been discarded, revealing a white blouse dotted with little black skulls. The hat rested on the chair beside her; she was stroking it like a pet. Her wild hair, now liberated, sprung in every direction, like a cartoon electrocution.

The overpowering scent of her pungent perfume had already permeated the room, and he coughed as it hit the back of his throat. Everything about the woman was overwhelming.

She was flicking through Sister Clare's copy of *Wuthering Heights*.

'Very disturbing, but so well observed. Phenomenal, considering how sheltered the author was.' She tossed the book to one side and held out her hand for the hot drink. 'Lovely, darling. You missed your vocation. Now, tell me what you have so far in your little mystery.'

Though he knew Linda described everything as little, perhaps because she herself was larger than life, it still managed to irrationally irritate Tom.

He filled her in on the twists and turns of the investigation.

She rolled her eyes upon learning the nuns had cleaned up the murder scene in the hall, and snorted when he described the priest's attic.

He finished by telling her how everything was pointing towards Sister Bernadette but that he was still looking into the backgrounds of former laundry girls.

'Hmm,' she responded, and stared into the distance.

He looked out at the darkening sky and ignored the low growling of hunger pangs from his stomach.

'Any thoughts, Linda?' he asked, after another minute of her nodding her head and saying 'hmm' had passed.

'Oh, lots of them, Tom. It's not as challenging as I'd hoped, I'm afraid. I envisaged it being much more sinister and twisted.'

He grimaced. 'Most people would find the facts of this beyond shocking.'

She sighed. 'The locals might be shocked to find out

about the priest's little indiscretions, Tom, but it's hardly earth-shattering. I suppose the people who enter religious life these days feel that they have some kind of vocation or other, serving the great sky-fairy.

'Back when half these people joined –' she waved her hand vaguely in the direction of the sitting-room door – 'it was rarely a choice. In families then, one son got the farm, one joined the gardaí and the last poor sod was sent to the seminary. Women who weren't married either found one of the few jobs for a spinster fast, or ended up in a convent.

'Unless you have a true vocation, being forced to join religious orders is like a form of torture. Expecting men and women to go against nature – it turns people insane. And by nature, Tom, I mean good, honest carnal knowledge.'

Tom wasn't entirely convinced that everyone who ended up living a life without sex turned insane, but he recognized a kernel of truth in what Linda was saying.

'You rolled your eyes when I said the nuns had cleaned the hall after they found the blood and smashed glass. You weren't shocked by it?'

'Good God, Tom. Of course I wasn't. You didn't attend a convent school but you can't be that unknowing of the world. Nuns are obsessed with cleanliness. I remember a girl in our class used to have the most amazing nosebleeds. I'm talking projectile. We had a sister who taught us. What was her name? Never mind. It's irrelevant. Anyway, all the while this little one . . . Eithne!'

'The girl was called Eithne?'

'No. The nun. I can't remember the girl's name. Just the nosebleeds. Anyway, she'd be standing there, scream-ing, blood spurting everywhere and the nun would be running around the classroom like a headless chicken, mopping it up and roaring at us to get the girl a towel. The point is, she was more concerned about the mess than the girl, Tom. Anyone taught by nuns knows the saying – cleanliness is next to godliness.'

'From what I've told you, do you think it's possible a laundry resident could have done this?'

She reclined on the couch, appraising him intently. 'I thought you were concentrating on this Sister Bernadette. She certainly meets the profile. There'd be no great sur-prise for someone in my profession if an individual like that, who had seen so much violence themselves over the years and been too insignificant to do anything about it, just snapped.' She clicked her fingers. 'And the theatrical presentation of the first victim – very religious, very . . . martyred. A converse insult, no doubt. But I find the Mag-dalene proposition far more interesting.'

'I'm sure you do. Could someone harbour vengeful thoughts for that length of time, though? The laundry was closed twenty-five years ago. Why snap now? Would anybody have picked up her behaviour changing, do you think? Is the perpetrator slowly unravelling?'

'So many questions, Tom.'

He could see her brain spinning with theories.

'About twenty years ago, as part of my training, my

professor sent me to London,' she said, eventually. 'I assisted in studying a man who had walked into an estate agent's and shot the owner, another man, in the head. He'd walked out, gone home and said nothing. He had tea with his family, bathed the kids and put them to bed and then sat down to watch the evening news with his wife.

'They're watching this news and next thing a CCTV still of him is flashed on screen. He'd taken no precautions, made no effort to hide his identity, and a security camera had captured him full face. So the wife's looking at the telly and then looking at him, going through all the motions of laughing at the coincidence, to realizing it's him – from shock to rage to numb – and then the police are battering down the door and he's arrested.'

Tom glanced covertly at the clock on the wall. As interesting as this was, he was concerned that Linda and Emmet were going to be having an involuntary reunion any minute now.

'Anyway, why would a seemingly normal chap, totally law-abiding, no obvious connection to the victim, walk in, shoot him and slope off home to have tea with his missus?'

'You tell me.' There had to be a point. Somewhere.

'Thirty years earlier, the estate agent had brokered a deal for the man's grandparents' house on behalf of the man's father. But he diddled the father out of the cash. He was never found guilty of it and went on to establish a successful business – probably financed by ripping off early clients.'

'Seems a bit of an overreaction to being swindled.'

'Well, after he'd been defrauded, the man's father's life spiralled. He lost his job, lost his home, turned to drink and generally got hit with all the crap life can throw at you. He really could have done with his inheritance to soften all his misfortunes. His son saw and suffered through all this.'

Linda sighed before continuing. 'The father died young enough; he was in his early fifties. A broken man, a broken life. The day my subject went in and shot the estate agent was the twentieth anniversary of his father's death. He'd been planning to shoot him since the nineteenth anniversary. He'd obtained the gun and monitored the office so he'd know what time of day the agent was there. He very particularly wanted to shoot him in the workplace. Poetic justice. He'd done all this without his wife ever realizing anything was amiss. Never missed a day's work, a family event or incurred so much as a speeding ticket.

'So, Tom, what I'm saying is this. If it was one of the women who had been incarcerated here, she could have been planning this for a very long time. Something could have triggered this decision in her, but it might just be that now is the time. She could be functioning completely normally. She could in fact be living in the village, unrecognized because she's aged. She might have managed to get close to her victims. You may have met her.'

'Revenge is a powerful motivator, and most people who enact the ultimate fantasy plan it clinically. Have you checked that one of the sisters in here isn't a former laundry inmate?'

'Yes,' he said. 'I have, actually. I can't get my head around this – that someone could continue acting normally after cutting out someone's tongue, carving words in their flesh and then crucifying their dead body.'

'Well, Tom, I can't stand the sight of blood. But my husband's a cardiac surgeon who spends half his day up to his elbows in people's chest cavities. Your killer may just have a strong stomach.'

This was something Tom had already considered. And Linda's choice of words had jogged a memory. Something someone else had said recently about having a strong stomach. Sister Bernadette, in fact.

Linda noisily slurped the dregs of her tea.

'The man in London,' Tom said. 'Why didn't he care about getting caught? It sounds like he had a good life, so why not try to get away with it?'

Linda cocked her head. 'There were a couple of factors. The first was that, aside from wanting to kill the man who'd destroyed his father's life – and, therefore, his family's – he was a good man. He wanted to do the time for the crime. There was no plan in his head beyond getting revenge. That was the end game.

'The second was that he wanted people to know what his victim had done to deserve execution. The agent was a seemingly respectable businessman. If he'd been murdered and the police couldn't catch the man's killer, motive may never have been established.'

Tom frowned in concentration. 'So, do you think our killer wants to be caught? Why go to such great lengths to conceal his or her identity?'

'Well, if it is a former inmate, she no longer needs to be apprehended so she can tell you what the nun and the priest did. You've done a good job of establishing that yourself. And presumably she had to keep her identity safe so she could carry out the second murder. Has it crossed your mind that there might yet be a third?'

That, of course, had worried him and every member of his team since the second victim had been found. He had been clinging to the blind hope that perhaps their killer, whether it was Sister Bernadette or someone else, had specifically targeted just these two victims.

It had also just dawned on him why Father Seamus had been stuffed in the closet. By hiding the body, the killer ensured the house was thoroughly searched, hence the expeditious discovery of the attic's secrets.

'Linda, could it have been someone other than one of the women in here? I mean another family member – a father, or brother?' he asked.

The psychologist tapped a finger on her chin and considered. 'Perhaps, Tom. My London case notwithstanding, the usual reaction of a father or a brother to that kind of situation, sexual violence in particular, would probably be immediate and public. You can imagine them marching up to the priest's door and beating him to a pulp in the middle of the village. And it's unlikely that the nun would be targeted. Her actions wouldn't incite as much rage in a father as the thought of the priest raping his daughter.'

Tom knew she was right.

'But there is another possibility . . .'

A car pulled slowly into the driveway.

Tom's face must have given away who the new arrival was, because Linda swung around on the couch and stared out the window.

'Is that who I think it is?' she asked.

He sighed. 'Yes. Linda, you were saying . . .'

'That man. My blood pressure is rising, and there's concrete and glass between us. I'll tell you what, Tom. I might just drive to the B&B and check in, then come back and talk to your nuns. Give *him* time to finish.'

She was muttering now, cheeks flushed, shoving her wild hair back under the ridiculous fox hat.

'Hold up! Your theory about another possibility?' he asked again, frustrated.

'What? Oh, yes. Another family member. A child. Like in the London case. Oh God, there he is at the door now. Is there a back exit?'

Tom felt like a light bulb had been switched on over his head. That had been the idea loitering on the edge of his consciousness for a while now.

Not a laundry girl – but the child of one.

CHAPTER 48

Tom brought his focus back to the psychologist, who was complaining volubly about Emmet McDonagh's imminent arrival.

'Tom, are you listening to me? I do not want to meet the oaf. Get it together.'

'For heaven's sake, Linda. There's no way out of here without bumping into him. You're adults; can't you just say hello and goodbye like normal people? What the hell happened between you two, anyway?'

She shook her head crossly. 'There is no such thing as a normal person, Tom. And what happened between us is for the grown-ups to know, and none of your business. Aha! Where there's a will, there's a way.'

She moved to the window and unlatched it, just as Tom heard the front door opening and closing.

'You can't be serious?' he exclaimed, as she straddled the sill. 'Linda, I might be busy later. I want to ask you more questions.'

He hadn't wanted her there in the first place, and now he didn't want her to leave.

Irony was a bitch.

She gave him a pitying look. 'Tom, stick with your Sister Bernadette theory. You know it's always the most obvious suspect. The revenge fantasy is pleasing to someone in my profession, but you have this case worked out. Are you looking for a reason not to arrest this nun?'

The look on his face must have confirmed her suspicion.

'Just because you like someone doesn't mean they aren't guilty. See you later, darling.'

Linda ducked her head under the window sash, though the unfortunate fox sustained a mild concussion on the way, and swung her other leg through.

Looking left and right, she crossed the garden like a spectacularly uncamouflaged member of a SWAT team.

Tom pulled the window down, shutting out the freezing cold air.

'Certifiable,' he murmured.

Emmet accosted Tom in the hall, just minutes after his erstwhile lover had made her escape.

'Ellie says Linda McCarn is here.' The forensic scientist scowled accusingly.

Tom rolled his eyes. 'You've just missed her.'

He was saved from further interrogation about Linda by Ciaran's arrival.

'Tom, we need you.'

Emmet waved Tom away. 'Go. You've your hands full.'

'Great. Get yourself some lunch; one of the sisters will take care of you.'

Tom followed the sergeant into Mother Attracta's office.

Ronan was still sitting at the desk. 'Well, Inspector, I've found what you need.'

Tom perched anxiously on the edge of the desk. 'Give me some good news, Ronan.'

'I was right. The emailer used Mother Attracta's computer. I've traced the original message that confirmed the Yahoo! account had been set up. It was in Mother Attracta's trash. It had been binned, but the trash hadn't been emptied. That gave me the date and the time the computer was used.'

'Which was?'

'On 8 October 2009.'

Tom whistled. Over a year ago.

'She set up the mail just after 2 a.m. on that day,' Ronan continued. 'But here's where it gets interesting. She didn't just create an email address that night—'

'You keep saying "she", as though you know who she is,' Tom interrupted.

'I do.'

Tom turned to Ciaran, astonished.

'I told you he was good,' Ciaran said, rocking on the balls of his feet.

Ronan continued. 'She spent a half-hour pulling up various articles on Magdalene Laundries. They weren't new articles. She'd visited the sites before. Then she also spent some time searching through online booksellers. She pulled up some books similar to the article searches but didn't buy any of them. Now, here's what gave her away.'

Tom could feel the air grow dense with the weight of his own expectation.

'She visited another website on the night of 8 October. She'd signed up to it years ago to receive regular news updates on a specific area. She had to register with her own name when she signed up.'

'She used her real name?' Tom asked.

'Yes. There was no reason not to.'

'Do you want to know what the website was?' Ciaran asked.

'I'd rather know her name.'

'Yes, but if we told you that it concentrated on religious life in Latin America . . .'

Tom felt his spine tingle. He closed his eyes for a moment, then opened them to see Ciaran and Ronan looking at him expectantly.

'Sister Bernadette,' he said.

In that moment he felt a surge of pity for the nun. The woman seemed so fundamentally good. Had she been driven to do something so utterly wrong?

And in addition to that, he felt an overwhelming sense of anticlimax.

Something in his gut had been leading him down a different road – one on which the crime had been committed by someone from the laundry's past, not the convent's present.

But there was no denying everything pointed to the

most unlikely suspect he'd ever encountered. A very pleasant nun.

'Ciaran, can I talk to you outside for a moment?'

'Sure. Ronan is just going to do some checking for us on Catherine Farrell. Even if it turns out not to be relevant, she's a mystery I'd like to solve.'

'You'll get a job with us if you're lucky, Ronan,' Tom said, standing up.

'It's interesting work, Inspector, but I can earn more in a week, doing what I do, than most guards would in a year.'

'We have a development.'

Tom had gathered his team in an empty office.

He struggled to keep his voice even. He didn't want them to get too excited. He filled them in on Linda's visit and her initial assessment. Then he landed the whammy punch.

'The emails that were sent to Father Seamus were sent by Sister Bernadette . . .' He paused.

'What more do we need?' Michael asked.

'Physical evidence would be nice, but if we could press her into a confession . . .' Ray answered.

'Ray's right,' Tom said. 'I want you two to take her in for more formal questioning.' He wanted somebody other than himself to interrogate her now. He'd deliver the final blow, when it was needed. 'Put the email evidence to her. This means she was in Mother Attracta's office at night – she was the one breaking in and messing with the woman's head. Another deception.

'Ciaran, Laura, try to find out where she could have brought Mother Attracta – where the nun was actually killed. Ciaran, maybe Ronan could help with that. Does she have family or friends we don't know about on the way to Dublin whose house she could have gone to . . . somewhere that's empty? If there's physical evidence to be found, that's where it is. What is it, Laura?'

'Are we dropping the laundry girls avenue, sir?'

'No, Laura. I want to know how many girls that priest raped. And let's not shut down any avenue until we have confirmation that the killer is, in fact, Sister Bernadette. If it is her, we can't even be certain she worked alone. But right now, she is the priority.

'Right, Ray, find Sister Bernadette and take her to the station – if that's okay, Ciaran? She needs to understand this is serious now. If she refuses, place her under arrest. I want her out of here so we can search her room and try to find out from the others where she could have brought the victim. I'm not entirely convinced yet she'd have had the physical strength to carry out these murders, but stranger things have happened.'

He didn't say it aloud, but if Sister Bernadette was their killer he wanted her in the station so she could cause no further harm – either to herself or to somebody else.

'I'll have one of the lads heat up the interview room and get ye some sandwiches and tea,' Ciaran called after them.

Tom walked to the hall and noticed the door to the corridor was ajar. He'd meant to go in earlier just to take a quick look, but it had slipped his mind.

Inside, Emmet was giving Ellie a lecture.

Ellie was glowering at her superior, her arms crossed defensively. Her boss sighed and gave her shoulder a conciliatory pat. She winced and turned away, spotting Tom.

'Never bloody good enough,' she snapped, storming off indignantly.

Tom raised his eyebrows.

'You only learn through criticism,' Emmet called, innocently, at her retreating back.

'Emmet . . . a word, please.'

Tom joined the other man in the corridor. He shivered in the frigid air. The smell of candle wax assailed his nostrils, for some reason evoking memories of funeral homes. The large glass windows gave the corridor a fishbowl effect. At night, with the lights on, people would be able to see in, but anyone inside wouldn't see out as well. It was an unpleasant thought.

'We have movement, Emmet. I have a suspect but I have no confession. And as of now, no physical evidence. You said there was something under the priest's fingernails?'

Emmet nodded. 'Yes, DNA, probably scraped when he tried to defend himself. Ellie should have caught that at the scene.' He looked over Tom's shoulder. 'Feisty, that one. I love that in a woman—'

'Maybe if you'd come down immediately, she wouldn't have been covering two sites on her own,' Tom interjected. 'That Jack seems bloody useless.'

'Jack?' Emmet said, puzzled. 'I didn't send him down.'

Tom squinted at Emmet, his brain processing. 'She said he asked to come down.'

They both heard a cry, and then the sound of the front door opening.

Ray and Michael were walking Sister Bernadette to the car.

The nun looked back at her home and, in doing so, caught sight of Tom and Emmet watching from the corridor.

She shook her head mournfully. Tom immediately felt guilty. It looked as though he was hiding.

Ray opened the car's back door and gently protected the nun's head as she got in.

No sooner had the vehicle pulled out of the drive than the door to the corridor burst open.

Sister Concepta stood before them, her fists balled by her side, her face a furious shade of red. She was shaking with anger.

'You stupid, stupid man,' she raged at Tom.

He was completely taken aback. He'd seen the woman angry. Not this irate, though.

'Sister—' he began.

'Don't! Don't you dare say anything. I've told you, Sister Bernadette could not have done this. You want to know the truth? Those two deserved to die horribly. But I'm more capable of killing them than Bernadette. She is a truly good woman. And you are putting her through this. I can't let you . . . I need to . . .'

Whatever else she wanted to say was lost in an

anguished sob, which broke from her lips and convulsed her body.

Sister Clare, who had also appeared, turned Sister Concepta round and tried to embrace her. The nun allowed herself to be held for a second, but then realized who was doing the embracing.

She pulled back, and Tom saw something like a sneer cross her face.

'Don't you dare comfort me,' Concepta snapped at the other woman. 'You were as bad as Mother Attracta. You don't care what happens to Bernadette.' She stormed off.

Sister Clare stood there, looking like she'd been slapped.

Tom was left reeling at the passion and fury Sister Concepta had displayed.

Emmet moved towards the door, the whole display a little too awkward for him. 'Excuse me, please; I think I'll do some work.'

A gloom had descended on the convent.

CHAPTER 49

Darren, Ciaran's deputy, had set out a platter of generously carved roast beef and horseradish sandwiches and a
large pot of piping hot coffee.

A recording device sat on the end of the rectangular
table. A foot above it, a plain clock adorned the otherwise
bare wall.

'Have you eaten, Sister?' Ray asked the nun, as they sat
down.

'Strangely, I have no appetite at the moment, Detective.'

The nun was pale, her forehead creased with worry.
She was trying to hold herself erect in the chair but was
failing. Her shoulders sagged from the weight of what
was being implied.

'Do you know why we asked you to accompany us to
the station?' Michael asked.

'You think I'm a murderer. I've already spoken at
length with your inspector.'

'Sister, when did you realize that Father Seamus had
raped girls in the convent?'

Ray spoke quickly, as though the premise of the question had already been established as fact.

Sister Bernadette balked. 'What do you mean?'

She was flustered. The right nerve had been struck.

'Well, that was the reason you sent the emails, wasn't it? When you realized that he'd raped those girls and got away with it.'

Sister Bernadette looked from one to the other of the detectives, her face betraying confusion, realization, then distress.

Her final expression was acceptance.

Just two questions in and Sister Bernadette had adopted the demeanour of a defeated person about to unload. Maybe she wanted it over.

'Ah,' she said at last. 'How did you know I'd sent the emails?'

She hadn't denied it. That was a good start.

'You didn't hide your tracks very well,' Ray answered. 'You used Attracta's computer, but our IT expert tracked the internet search history and found the Latin American website you'd subscribed to.'

She laughed, unnerving both of them.

'I'm no technological expert. I worried something like that could be done, though. That's why I didn't use the computer I shared with Concepta.'

Sister Bernadette spoke lightly, but her manner was still resigned – like someone who'd been caught out and could do nothing about it. She'd obviously decided to face her predicament with dignity.

'So you don't deny you sent the poison messages? The

ones that read . . .' Michael picked up a sheet of paper and started to read the lines printed on it.

Sister Bernadette held up her hand. 'There's no need. I know what they say. I don't deny it.'

Ray looked to the coffee pot. 'Do you mind, Sister?'

'My goodness, no. Drink, eat, do what you have to. Looks like we're here for the long haul.'

Michael poured the coffee, and a glass of water for Sister Bernadette.

'When did you figure it out?' Ray asked.

'When Sister Concepta and I were going through the files. It didn't take long. Girls who'd been in the convent since they were children? I do some nursing up in the old folks' home and eventually Barney Kelly started to talk to me. It took a while. He hates nuns. But he knew I'd been a missionary, and in his mind that was enough to differentiate me. So he told me about his suspicions.'

She took a sip of her water. 'I tried to raise it with Mother Attracta. Of course, she dismissed me out of hand. You know the quote? "The darkest places in hell are reserved for those who maintain their neutrality in times of moral crisis."'

Ray took a deep breath. Everything rested on this next question. In the absence of forensic evidence and witnesses, a confession was the key to this case.

'Is that why you killed her? Because she let those rapes happen?'

Sister Bernadette sighed and sipped from her water

again. She looked up at the clock, back to the tape recorder, and then at Ray.

'Yes,' she said. 'She didn't take those girls seriously, and more were raped because of it. So I killed her.'

Ray feared his heart might have stopped.

He looked at Michael – to make sure he'd heard it too. Now that she'd admitted it, he couldn't put the questions in his head in order.

'I'm going to do it again,' Sister Bernadette spoke again. Her face was dark, threatening. 'You'll want to know my next target. It's a former Taoiseach.'

The two detectives looked at each other, confused.

Sister Bernadette chortled. 'Yes, as the state's political leader, he could have intervened. Instead he just let the Catholic Church impose a moral code fit for the eighteenth century.'

Ray shook his head slowly. *She's lost it*, he thought. *Stark raving mad.*

She stared at him.

Then she snorted. 'For heaven's sake. You think I'm serious. I didn't kill Mother Attracta. I didn't kill Father Seamus. And this might come as a shock, but I've no intention of killing a former head of government either. My goodness. Yes, I sent those emails. But I didn't follow them up with murder. They are my greatest crime. I'm mortified and ashamed of them. Not of their content, but because I didn't have the courage to speak those words directly to Father Seamus. I feared you'd find them, and you have.'

Inwardly, Ray groaned.

Outwardly, he tried to look as though he was still in control of the interview.

'Sister, bearing in mind you admit to sending those emails, you can see why we have brought you in for further questioning. I searched the biblical reference you used for the email address. "Vengeance is mine"? It was your vengeance you were referring to, wasn't it?'

'No, Detective. The passage you take those words from, if you read it properly, refers to the Lord. Vengeance is his, not mine. This isn't some Hollywood movie. Do you think – what is it they say? – I'm "packing" under this habit? That I'm on some sort of holy crusade for justice?'

She laughed, and sat more erect. 'If you are honestly thinking of charging me with murder because I sent anonymous emails, I have little faith in your ability to ever find the person who committed these crimes.'

She glared at both of them. The humility and dread were gone. They had been replaced with righteous indignation.

Ray was unsure what to do. She could be an extremely clever woman who was playing them, but everything about her manner told him otherwise.

He looked down at his notepad and swallowed. 'You sent the emails, Sister. Did you make anonymous calls to Father Seamus accusing him of these things? Did you contact the police?'

She shook her head. 'No and no. I spoke to Mother Attracta and Sister Concepta. Concepta had come to the same conclusion herself, anyway.'

'What do you mean, Sister Concepta came to the same conclusion?'

Sister Bernadette narrowed her eyes. 'Everyone in the convent knows exactly what happened to those girls, even if they won't admit it.'

Ray sat back from the table. 'Everyone?'

'Yes.'

'But—'

'Why didn't someone do something about it?' The nun scoffed. 'Why do you think? Half are in denial, half are in fear. Where was my proof? I made the most innocent remark to the newspapers about the laundry, and all hell broke loose. Don't you understand? It's called speaking out of school. I went as far as I could.'

Michael placed his elbows on the desk.

'But is it as far as others in the convent would go?' he asked. 'Sister Concepta seems like a good woman. How did she react when she found out what Father Seamus had done?'

'Please don't do that.' Sister Bernadette's voice was scathing.

'Pardon?' Michael looked puzzled.

'Jump from me to her, to someone else, and someone after that. Isn't it enough to drag me in here without a shred of evidence to prove I killed anyone, without subjecting others to it as well?'

Ray cleared his throat. 'Sister, we'd like to take a DNA sample from you. You can either volunteer it or we can obtain an arrest warrant.'

The nun looked disturbed.

'Also,' Ray added, 'I need you to tell me if you have any family or friends who reside in or own houses between here and Dublin. Or if you yourself own or are renting any properties.'

He'd taken back control of the interview, but he didn't feel any better for it.

CHAPTER 50

Tom cursed. He and Laura had just eaten the creamy chicken and mushroom pie that the sisters had left for them. The atmosphere in the convent had changed. The nuns were cooler now that suspicion had fallen very obviously on one of their own.

The inspector hoped fervently they could get this wrapped up sooner rather than later, though that was looking less likely after the phone call he'd just taken.

'What is it?' Laura asked.

'Ray. He says Sister Bernadette admits to sending the emails but to nothing else. They're taking her DNA.'

The door flew open and Ciaran came in, his face flushed with excitement. Hot on his heels was Ronan.

'Is it related to Sister Bernadette?' Tom asked, standing up. 'Did you find a property?'

Ciaran shook his head. 'No. Nothing there, Tom, sorry. It's Catherine Farrell. Ronan went back to trace activity on the account she used to pay for the house next door to Father Seamus—'

Ronan interrupted. 'Inspector, I think you should know

that I was recruited in the States because of my hacking skills. I had to breach—'

Tom held his hand up. 'Don't say anything more, Ronan. What I don't know ...'

There was no correct way for a senior garda to finish that sentence, but the other man got the gist.

'Ciaran, make sure you get the warrants for that account sorted, asap. And retrospectively request that information. Right, tell me what you found.'

Ciaran deferred to the younger man. It was Ronan's discovery, and he should be the one to reveal it.

'She's been renting a lock-up for the last six weeks. Just outside Portlaoise. It appears to be a furniture storage facility in an industrial estate. You get a key; you can back your vehicle right up to the door of the unit and store whatever for the period of time you've rented. There's security on site, but not in each individual warehouse.

'There's an office that's staffed during the day to deal with administration, but it closes at 6 p.m. Unfortunately they don't have CCTV trained on the doors of the units, or on the entrance to the facility itself. But I found something that is going to blow your mind ...' Ronan paused.

He was starting to enjoy police work.

'Don't leave us hanging,' Tom blurted.

'Three weeks ago, the company went live with a computerized security system. It's very basic, it just logs times unit doors are opened and closed. Apparently, last summer the company had a problem with an employee using the master key to break into the lock-ups and steal small items. The owners didn't automatically miss their possessions because these are generally people moving house with lots of gear in storage. But a pattern was identified. The company sacked the employee and set up this system so owners can check online to make sure their unit hasn't been accessed.

'The company decided to use the system for a month to make sure it worked before advertising it as a security feature. I'm not sure if they were taking liberties on disclosure, but it certainly worked in our favour. Catherine Farrell wouldn't have known her key use was being recorded. The company thought we already knew about it when Ciaran rang, and they were pretty forthcoming with their records after that. Probably afraid you'd pull them for not informing their clients.

'Anyway, Catherine – or someone – opened her unit at 1 a.m. last Thursday morning. She exited it at 11.30 a.m. She returned to it at 4 p.m. Thursday evening, leaving twenty minutes later. Her final visit was at 10.30 p.m., and she exited at 2 a.m. on Friday morning.'

Tom felt his jaw drop.

The visits to the lock-up matched the timeline for Attracta's abduction, killing and removal to the Phoenix Park. The final visit could have been a clean-up operation.

He turned to Ciaran. 'What do you think of this?'

'I think we need to check out this facility sharpish. The company is planning to tell its customers about the new security this week. We tried to get them to hold off, but they've bought advertising slots that are set to go. Catherine hasn't been back since. But she's still paying rent, and could return at any time.'

'And we'll know if she does,' Ronan added.

Tom's mind raced in several directions. But there was one thread in particular that unnerved him. After crossing the Rubicon and marking Sister Bernadette as a suspect, now any of the nuns were potential candidates. When he spoke to Sister Clare yesterday, she'd referred to Sister Concepta as an actress. It was ridiculous to imagine that Sister Concepta and Catherine Farrell were one and the same, wasn't it? Or was Catherine Farrell actually Margaret Downes?

Then there were the dates the three women had been raped. Sister Concepta must have been born in the mid-seventies. And hadn't she said her parents were dead?

It couldn't be, could it?

Exactly what had been Sister Concepta's name before she became a nun? In fact, if it was a child of one of the women who'd been raped, that opened up the suspect list to several other men and women. Linda McCarn had said that Tom could have already met the killer. She'd also said it was always the most likely suspect. But what if it was the most unlikely . . .

His mind was racing with possibilities that he couldn't give voice to yet.

'How long does it take to drive to Portlaoise from here?' he asked.

'About an hour and fifteen minutes in normal weather

conditions,' Ciaran answered. 'Could take two hours in these conditions. But they've been clearing the main roads all day, and there hasn't been any snowfall since this morning.'

Tom wasn't about to lose another minute.

'Right, I'm heading to that lock-up right now. Ronan, can you monitor that storage unit and keep digging into this Catherine woman?'

'Absolutely. I am so rethinking my career choices right now.'

Tom pulled his ringing phone from his pocket.

It was Ian, hopefully reporting on the backgrounds of the three women whose names Sister Clare had given them. What had seemed less important just an hour ago was suddenly to the forefront of the investigation.

'Ian?'

'I have good and bad news,' the sergeant said.

'Start with the bad.'

'Right. Of the three names you gave me to check, two are deceased: Bríd O'Toole and Margaret Downes. Bríd died in the late eighties. She was the victim of a hit and run in Manchester.'

'What a tragic life,' Tom said.

'You think that was tragic? Margaret Downes died in the psychiatric unit she was transferred to by the nuns. She only passed away in 2008.'

The inspector ran his fingers through his hair and shook his head.

Could she have made the phone call to Kilcross and

posed as Liz, from a psychiatric hospital? Or, if Margaret was dead, then the Liz Downes who rang the station could have been a family member, ringing in grief. Did that make her a suspect? Or was the remaining woman on the list the key to the case?

'Did they have families?' he asked.

'Bríd was married but had no children outside of the baby that was adopted. There's no evidence they ever reconnected. The husband's dead as well. I don't know about Margaret. I spoke to someone briefly down there who said she might have had visitors. I'm looking into it.'

'What's the good news, Ian?'

'Noreen Boyle is alive and well. We have no number for her, but we have an address in Newbridge, County Kildare.'

'Excellent. Keep looking into possible family for Margaret, will you? Send that address for Noreen through.'

He hung up and tried to gather his thoughts. His gut told him the lock-up was where Mother Attracta had been murdered. But Noreen Boyle was the only remaining victim of Father Seamus who had been forced to give up her child.

Was she the person who had sought revenge?

The others stared at him, eagerly awaiting his orders.

'Right, we've more to do now. I've got an address in Newbridge for one of the women who accused Father Seamus of rape, Noreen Boyle. She's the only one on that list of three still alive.

'Ciaran, I want you to go with Laura to interview her. We can't rule out the possibility that she is the killer. And in that case, she could even be posing as Catherine Farrell. I know you barely saw her, but you are the only one of us who has any chance of recognizing her. Get local backup. And Laura, bring your firearm.'

It was 5 p.m. and already fully dark outside. If they left the convent now, Tom reckoned he could be in Portlaoise by 6.30 – as long as the roads weren't too bad.

Ciaran and Laura would be lucky to get to Newbridge for 7 p.m.

'Ciaran, I'm leaving Ray in charge here. I want a close eye kept on these nuns. I don't know if our murderer has finished what was started. On the other hand, it could still be one of the sisters doing this. Can some of the local guards come up here this evening?'

Ciaran nodded gravely. He had the same fears.

'Of course, I'll ask a couple of the lads to spend the night here and to patrol the grounds. One of them left earlier for Limerick city with Sister Bernadette's DNA sample, but there are still some guards here from the next village.'

Tom left him to rally the troops, and found Emmet in the hall. The forensic scientist was on his hunkers by the hall table where the glass vase had smashed, holding a pair of tweezers and staring intently through a magnifying glass at what they held.

'Deep breaths, old friend,' he said, when he noticed Tom. 'I found a tiny piece of glass. I can see how it would have been missed in the day. It was the ceiling light reflecting on it that caught my eye.'

'Could it be from someone's shoe?' Tom asked. 'People have been walking in and out of here for the last couple of days.'

'Not unless one of the nuns was table dancing. It was embedded in this curve.'

Tom dropped down and saw the groove at the edge of the table, a natural indent in the wood.

'What's the significance, though?' he asked. 'We know the vase was smashed here.'

'It's discoloured.'

'What do you mean?'

'It's discoloured with blood. It could be Mother Attracta's. Or it could be your killer's.'

'You truly are gifted, Emmet. Where's Ellie?'

'She said she had to check out of wherever she stayed last night. But to be honest, I think I was getting on her nerves.'

'I can't think why.'

'Did you just track me down to insult me, Tom, or can I get back to going over this area for you?'

'I've just got a tip about a lock-up in Portlaoise. I'm going to check it out. This could be Mother Attracta's murder site.'

'All right, let's go. But we need to take a quick detour

and leave this glass with the technicians in the city. They have the DNA from under the priest's fingernail. If this is the killer's blood, it could be a match.'

Tom hesitated. The seed of an idea germinating in his head had suddenly rooted itself.

He wanted to get to the lock-up as quickly as possible – they had better make this detour quick.

Before they left, Tom gave Ray an update and instructions about keeping a watchful eye on the convent.

'Ray, there are a number of people I want you to monitor in particular,' Tom said, his voice low and grave as he listed the names.

Ray gave him a puzzled look.

He opened his mouth to say something, then shut it. He knew better than to question how Tom's mind worked. The inspector was typically several steps ahead.

'And where's Sister Bernadette?' Tom asked.

'We brought her back with us. We didn't have enough to detain her. Anyway, she may as well be here if we're keeping an eye on all the nuns.'

Tom nodded.

'By the way,' he said, 'Linda McCarn is due back here to talk to the nuns. Tell her to act normal will you? Bloody woman.'

Ray nodded in sympathy.

The psychologist was the least of his worries.

Especially after the names Tom had just listed as suspects.

CHAPTER 51

Laura and Ciaran had passed Portlaoise by the time Tom and Emmet were leaving Limerick city. The back roads from the village had been thick with snow, and Tom was rueing their decision to detour. They had a local police car stationed at the storage facility, though, so if anyone turned up there, they'd be detained.

'Linda McCarn jumped out a window to avoid seeing you,' he said to Emmet, as they drove along the deserted motorway.

'She jumped out a window because she's mad as a bat,' came the reply. 'Just the ground floor, I take it. That was her coming up the road as we were leaving, wasn't it?'

Tom said nothing. He'd thought Emmet was too focused on driving to notice.

The inspector's phone buzzed.

'Ray?'

'Sir, Michael has found something in one of these old files.'

'What? How's it going there, anyway?'

'There are plenty of guards, and we're taking turns patrolling the house. I keep checking on the ones you told me to watch, but it's difficult when they won't stay in the same place. Anyway, remember Sister Concepta told us that Sister Bernadette was the only one who had proper medical experience?'

'Yes . . .'

'That's not true. Michael found a file of a woman who had a baby here. She came in pregnant; she's not one of the names we were given. Anyway, she nearly died in childbirth but two nuns saved her. They weren't fully trained midwives but had experience delivering babies. Seems Mother Attracta had been ill and couldn't attend to the woman.'

Tom was impatient to hear the names.

'Sister Gladys and Sister Clare were the nuns.'

'Ask Sister Concepta why she didn't mention them,' Tom said.

He felt cold. He knew Sister Gladys had been with some of the girls who'd had their babies taken.

But could she and Clare be potential targets for the killer? And why hadn't Concepta said anything?

Noreen Boyle's home was lit up like a Christmas tree. All the dwellings in the pleasant little cul-de-sac offered welcoming porches and living-room lights, but this cottage had entered into the Christmas spirit with particular vigour. Festive lights hung from the eaves of the roof, and a Christmas tree twinkled behind the living-room window. The illuminations cast a warm shimmering glow across the front garden, where a little family of snowmen sat.

Laura and Ciaran exchanged a look.

The background check on Noreen indicated she lived alone, but this was a house and garden that looked as though little people were very much a feature.

They lifted the wrought-iron gate off its latch and entered. Just behind the garden wall sat a printed sign urging 'Santa, please stop here'.

'This place is a winter wonderland,' Laura observed.

'I know. Any chance this is the wrong Noreen?'

'Our station sergeant is very thorough.'

'Well, if there are no children here, we're dealing with someone who's a few cakes short of a picnic,' Ciaran commented.

A garda car was parked up on the other side of the street. The uniforms inside waved over at the visitors to their local Lapland.

'It's now or never,' Ciaran said, and pressed the door-bell beside the giant Christmas wreath that adorned the front door.

A merry 'Jingle Bells' tinkled through the house.

Laura didn't know whether to laugh or run.

A moment later, the door opened and a little old lady stood in front of them.

'Yes?' the woman asked, smiling at them broadly.

Her hair was silvery white and framed her face in soft short waves. She wore thick-lensed glasses over sunken eyes. Her smile was kindly and welcoming. If a picture was to accompany the word 'grandmother' in the diction-ary, this could be her.

'I'm afraid we might have made a mistake,' Ciaran said, flashing his badge. 'We're looking for Noreen Boyle.'

The woman nodded.

'Yes, that's me.' She kept smiling.

Something jarred with Laura. Normally when the police called to the door, people reacted with worry.

'Eh, the Noreen Boyle we're looking for would have spent some time living in a place called Kilcross in the seventies . . .' Laura said, then stopped.

The woman was still nodding and smiling.

'Yes, that's me.'

'But you're . . .' Ciaran looked at her, uncomprehending. 'Could you give us your date of birth, Ms Boyle?'

She laughed, a clear tinkling sound.

'I was born in 1957. I know – I look like I'm bordering on octogenarian. It's amazing how hardship can speed up the ageing process. I can assure you, I'm the Noreen Boyle you're looking for. I've been expecting you since yesterday. I know why you're here. Now, would you like to come in? The heat is escaping and I've got biscuits in the oven I'd like to rescue.'

Laura and Ciaran cast a nervous backward glance at the car across the road, then stepped over the threshold and into the woman's house.

The industrial estate was just on the outskirts of Portlaoise town. At its entrance, Tom and Emmet passed a giant plastic snowman holding a sign pointing to Santa's Wholesale Grotto.

The drive down had been easy enough but both Tom and Emmet had been eyeing the temperature monitor on the dashboard nervously, as the number slowly fell. A freeze would make the roads lethal, and they didn't yet know where they'd be staying tonight.

Emmet drove slowly as they followed the numbered doors to the lock-up unit they were looking for. Unit 40b. He pulled the car into the designated loading bay and got out.

Tom looked around furtively as he slipped the key they'd been given by the factory owner into the lock of the door. Two local guards had met them with the search warrant they needed to enter the storage unit. They didn't have a huge evidential basis for obtaining the warrant, but Sean McGuinness was known as a man who rarely asked for something on a triviality, so it had been secured easily enough.

Right now, an open web page on the computer Ronan was sitting at would inform him that the door had just been unlocked. He wouldn't react; they'd called him when they arrived.

Tom felt along the inside wall until he found the light switch.

He swung the door open fully and looked into the unit. The large space could comfortably accommodate most of the furnishings of an average-sized house.

This unit, though, was empty – bar two items.

Two plastic chairs with steel legs, like those found in waiting rooms, sat in the corner.

The harsh artificial light bounced off the four grey walls, the white ceiling and concrete floor. Tom stepped in, closely followed by Emmet.

Their eyes travelled around the near empty unit, before coming to rest again on the chairs. Neither man said anything, but they were both thinking the same thing.

Was this a random coincidence and the chairs nothing more than unwanted pieces of furniture, left behind?

Or had Mother Attracta been tied to one of them when she met her fate, her tormentor facing her?

'This place has been cleaned,' Emmet said, lifting his head to smell the air.

'You look like a bloodhound,' Tom said.

'Bleach. The place reeks.'

Tom sniffed. He picked up the faint whiff of bleach. His crooked nose didn't seem to work as well as everyone else's.

'Would the factory owners have cleaned it after the last use?' he ventured, unconvinced.

'Why?' Emmet responded. 'Furniture is stored here, not foodstuffs or anything else that's likely to leave a mess or smell. I can imagine them giving it a run over with a sweeping brush but using industrial strength bleach after each rental seems an unnecessary expense. And the smell wouldn't be as strong if it had been cleaned some time ago.'

Emmet approached the chairs.

'This is what I'd use,' he said.

'What do you mean?' Tom asked.

'Wood would absorb the blood, no matter how much you cleaned it. This place is perfect, in fact. The floor and walls could easily be washed – or if you were a professional, draped with plastic sheeting. There's only one problem.'

Emmet walked out to the car and returned carrying a small stepladder.

'You've come prepared,' Tom remarked.

'Always.'

He beckoned the inspector over.

Tom crossed the room and supported the scientist as he mounted the ladder and reached up to the ceiling.

'Plaster,' Emmet said and licked his finger. He rubbed the ceiling with his finger and brought it down to show Tom. 'This was painted recently.'

Tom felt his spine tingle.

CHAPTER 52

In Noreen Boyle's cosy sitting room, the Christmas fir tree was adorned with an eclectic mix of ornaments that looked to have been collected from all over the world.

A fire was blazing in the grate, and the comforting smell of peat and the sound of crackling wood filled the room. Four stockings hung along the fireplace; the names of two girls and two boys had been stitched on their front. Little candy canes poked from their tops.

Along the mantelpiece, amongst the holly and ivy and assortment of globes, porcelain Santas and reindeer, stood framed photos of the four young children.

Laura hauled herself up from the deep couch and examined the photos. In the centre, Noreen was pictured between a red-bearded man and a ginger-haired woman. Neither of them particularly resembled Noreen. If anything, the man looked a little like Jack, their crime scene technician. Laura peered closer. No, the man in the photo had subtly different features.

'Does Noreen look anything like Catherine Farrell?' she asked Ciaran in hushed tones.

'She could have been wearing a wig for the red hair, but no, she's not tall enough. Catherine had about a foot on her.'

'The woman in this photo has red hair, and she's taller,' Laura said. 'Her daughter, maybe?'

Ciaran stood up to look, and nodded.

'Possibly,' he said.

The door opened and Noreen came in bearing a tray of tea and biscuits.

She was smiling gaily, but Laura couldn't shake the feeling that there was something off about the woman's cheeriness. Was it a little manic?

Ciaran stood up to help, taking the tray and placing it on the coffee table in front of the couch.

'Family?' Laura asked, indicating the photos.

Noreen beamed even wider.

'Yes. My son and daughter,' she said. 'Those are their children. They were here yesterday. That's when we decided to turn the place into the North Pole. Well, it was my idea. They helped; they like indulging me.'

She chuckled and sat down in the armchair nearest the window.

'Please, try some of my biscuits,' she said, as she poured the tea. 'I've been fine-tuning this recipe for a month and I think I have them just right now. They're chocolate-covered shortbread, but I've added a hint of nutmeg and cinnamon as it's Christmas.'

Laura sat back down next to Ciaran, propping herself

up with cushions as he had done. She tasted one of the delicious-smelling biscuits and let herself drift to heaven for a moment.

'I think you've nailed it,' Ciaran said.

'Oh, I'm glad. The children will love them.'

'Noreen, we know from your file in Kilcross that you were forced to give up a child for adoption,' Laura said. She glanced across at the photos on the mantelpiece. 'Did you have more children after you left the laundry?'

'No, but I did reconnect with my baby.'

'Was it a son or daughter you gave up for adoption?' Laura asked.

Noreen's smile vanished, replaced with a thin-lipped scowl. It completely transformed her face.

'It was my son. That's him in the picture, with his wife.' She pointed at the mantle. 'I didn't give him up. He was taken from me. There is a very significant difference.'

Her tone was bitter.

Laura took a deep breath. They'd decided in the car that it would be better if she handled the conversation. She knew now that she would have to play her ace card to get Noreen to relax and talk to them properly.

'Noreen, before I went down to Kilcross I found out something very distressing about the place. My mother's sister was sent to its laundry in the sixties. I've seen her file and know what happened to her. I know what those nuns were capable of. And if I ask you something silly it's because I don't know everything, not because I have any preconceived notions.'

Noreen observed Laura keenly.

'Who was your aunt?' she asked, suspiciously.

'Peggy Deasy.'

'Oh. I remember her.' The woman looked at Laura sympathetically. 'I'm not ashamed of telling you what happened to me there, though I cringe every time I think of the place. I want to tell people what happened. I've had a happy ending, but so many others haven't. The truth needs to come out. You must realize that yourself.'

Laura nodded. 'You said your son was taken from you, that you hadn't given him up. Your file says you signed the papers, if reluctantly.'

'I didn't sign the papers. I didn't sign anything. I refused. And I wasn't the only one. My signature was forged. And most of those who did sign were threatened into doing it. The only thing worse for your child than adoption was being taken into care and left in one of those orphanages. Everyone knew that.

'We were nothing, you see. We were treated like dirt. It was hard for any woman in those days who got pregnant out of wedlock. Most were forced to give up their babies. We girls, though, who got pregnant while in the laundry, were treated as the lowest of the low. I wasn't given any choice about keeping my baby. He was just taken.'

Laura and Ciaran listened in shocked silence.

'I didn't even understand what was happening to me when I got pregnant. I'd been sheltered. They said things about my mother, but they weren't true. I had that "prostitute" label rammed down my throat so many times. I remember my mother. She was a hard-working, loving woman who had the odd boyfriend. She just couldn't escape poverty, and then she upset some married man's family in the town and I was taken from her. I think he was my father and she asked him to help out. It didn't go down too well. Right until her death she tried to get me back.'

She shook her head sadly.

Until her death, Laura thought. Obviously the mother and daughter had never reunited.

Noreen sighed and drank her tea.

'It's been on my mind so much recently,' she continued. 'I got out as soon as I could. Came up here. Made a life for myself. Travelled, everywhere I could. Had boyfriends, but could never get married. I felt dirty. Soiled. Couldn't settle with anyone. I nearly went mad.

'Then I realized that I would never be happy until I found the baby they had stolen from me. You know, I didn't even know if it was a boy or a girl because they never let me see him. They just whipped him away as soon as he was born.

'I didn't care that he was the result of . . . of what had happened to me. I had felt him moving inside me. All I wanted to do when he came out was hold him.'

She shook her head. Her eyes glistened with tears.

'It took so long to find him. I got very depressed. Drank, lost my job. Then it happened. Ten years ago. He was looking for me, too. He doesn't know who his father was. I would never, ever tell him. I told him I was an innocent and a local boy got me pregnant and that I didn't even know his full name.'

Noreen sat quietly, staring into her teacup.

Laura was perched on the edge of her seat.

'You said you didn't know what happened to you when you got pregnant,' Laura said. 'What do you mean?'

Noreen blushed but held her head high.

'Like I said. I was an innocent. He told me to lie there and be quiet or he'd get angry. He'd give me sweets afterwards. Like that made it better. And I didn't know that was how you got pregnant. I told Sister Clare everything that had happened and she just slapped me in the face.'

Laura paled. 'So you were raped?'

Noreen looked her straight in the eye.

'Yes. Me and others. By that . . . man. Don't ask me to say his name.'

'If I say his name, will you nod if it's correct?'

Noreen pursed her lips. 'Go on.'

'Father Seamus.'

The woman's face flushed, and she nodded.

Laura exhaled. 'Did the nuns know what he was doing all along?'

'We told Mother Theresa, Clare, Attracta . . . all the ones in charge. That made it worse. They'd been letting him take us up to his house for years. No one believed us when we said what he was doing. They beat me while I was pregnant, for making up "lies". But after a couple of us got pregnant, one of them kicked up a fuss. Gladys. She was the only decent skin there.'

Laura could feel the tension in every part of her body.

'How did your son react when you found him?'

Noreen smiled. 'Very well. His adoptive parents were elderly when they got him and had died two years before I found him. He never would have looked for me if they'd still been alive. He had a good life, and I'm grateful for that. His name is Padraig. It took me ages to get used to that. I'd picked Matthew for a boy or Roisin for a girl. Even now, sometimes I think of him as Matthew.'

She smiled. 'But you'll be wanting to know about the woman who came to find me. So full of anger. So full of hurt.'

'The woman who came to find you?' Laura parroted.

'Yes. I thought that was why you were here. It's hardly to hear my story. After I heard about those two being murdered, I thought, she's done it. She's taken her revenge.'

Noreen crossed herself.

'You mean Mother Attracta and Father Seamus's murders?' Ciaran asked, feeling stupid even saying it.

The woman they'd come to see clicked her tongue.

'You can use their titles but there was nothing religious about them, I can tell you that. If ever two people deserved to die, they did.'

CHAPTER 53

The additional police presence from Kilcross had created an even tenser atmosphere at the convent – and word that a crazy woman was calling the nuns in for second interviews in the sitting room hadn't helped.

The sisters were nervous. Were they suspects or potential targets?

Michael had gone to talk to Sister Gladys while Ray went out to lock the front gates for the nuns. He needed a break from watching everyone and fetching things for Linda McCarn. There'd been a few phone calls to the convent from reporters who'd arrived in the village, and he didn't want to risk them getting to the front door.

The snow was starting to fall again and he half skated, half fell back to the convent.

Jack opened the front door for him.

'When did you get here?' Ray asked, suspiciously.

He hadn't seen the other man arrive. That didn't augur well, considering he was meant to be watching all the toing and froing at the convent.

Jack shrugged. 'About an hour ago. Figured I'd stay here and give Ellie a hand instead.'

'Ellie's back? Where is she?'

'Dunno.'

Michael had just come out of the kitchen.

'Find anything?' Ray asked, crossing the hall.

'I just talked to Sister Gladys. She confirmed that herself and Sister Clare helped deliver some of the babies, and said they had some medical training. She said Concepta would have known that.'

'Let's ask Concepta why she didn't tell us. I'm meant to be keeping an eye on her, anyway.'

Michael raised his eyebrows. 'She was in the chapel, last time I checked. Probably praying for all this to be over. Shall we?'

Ray opened the door to the corridor, and bumped into Ellie.

She smiled with genuine pleasure when she saw him.

'God, I'm glad to see you,' she said. 'I wish I could get out of this place. I'm sick of it. Where have Tom and Emmet gone, anyway?'

Ray was about to tell her when Michael interjected.

'There she is,' he said.

Sister Concepta had just rounded the corner at the end of the hall.

Ray turned apologetically to Ellie. 'Sorry, I've got to see a nun about a dog, but I'll come find you.'

Her disappointed look was like a dart to his heart.

He was about to say something comforting but didn't get the chance. Sister Concepta had clipped up the length of the hall and was eyeing him and Michael expectantly.

Ray had remembered something – something so important and so explosive he couldn't quite believe it. And what Tom had said before he departed now made sense.

Working fast, Emmet managed to carefully scrape a large section of the new paint from the ceiling.

'Plaster, you see, can be washed, but it tends to just spread the stain,' he said. 'Some stains are harder than others to shift. If I were the killer, I'd have cleaned the ceiling as much as possible then given it a couple of fresh coats of paint.'

Underneath the top layer of white paint was another, dirtier layer. But it wasn't the grimy grey colour that caught their attention. It was the light brown stains that someone had tried to scrub off.

'Is it . . .?' Tom asked.

'I'm pretty sure. I'll need more technicians here.'

'Headquarters are sending some of your team.'

Emmet took scrapings of the old paint, putting them into a bag.

'I imagine we'll confirm easily enough that this is Mother Attracta's blood,' he said. 'I'll go over this room and the chairs as best I can. Though I'll be shocked if there's anything else. Taking the time to paint the ceiling, after washing it . . . that's efficient. I suspect your killer probably covered the floor and walls, then bleached the place afterwards for good measure.'

The lock-up was chilly, but neither man was feeling the

cold at this point. Tom knew they were standing in the room where Mother Attracta must have awoken after being bludgeoned and kidnapped from the convent.

Freezing, in shock, tied to one of the chairs and placed in the centre of the room. What had been said to her before she was killed? Had her attacker told her she was going to die? Was murder the intention, or had the killer wanted to force the nun to confess to something? Or even just apologize? Was that why her tongue had been cut out – because she refused to comply?

It was imperative now that they move fast.

Something had started in this room. But was it finished?

'So who came to see you, Noreen?' Laura asked, her stomach awash with butterflies.

She had spent hours in the records rooms and had read every file from the mid-seventies period. Sister Clare had told them the names of the three women who'd been made pregnant by Father Seamus, but they knew he had also molested others. Was it one of those women who had sought out Noreen Boyle?

'I assumed you had come here because you already knew,' Noreen said. 'She said it was her mission. I thought that rather apt. A mission from God. If I hadn't found such happiness, I would have been tempted to do the same. That's why she opened up to me. She could see I'd suffered, too.'

Noreen looked down at her feet, ensconced in pink

fluffy cat contraptions. Now they'd spent some time with the woman, Laura was starting to suspect the monstrosities were her own choice rather than a well-meaning gift from her grandchildren, as the detective had first assumed.

'I knew they deserved it, but I hoped she wouldn't go through with it, for her sake. If only she'd found her happy ending. Like I had. The more I got to know her, the more I liked her–'

'Hold on,' Laura interrupted. 'Are you actually saying she told you she was going to murder people? Do you know what that means? You should have told the police.' The detective shook her head, exasperated. She had been correct. There was something not right about this woman. 'And you say you saw her more than once?'

Noreen's eyes widened. 'Well, I wasn't sure . . . I mean, I didn't really think she'd do it. I saw her dozens of times and she was always fine with me. She wanted to know so much. And I have such an excellent memory. She even rented the house next to that beast to find out more.

'I suppose I should have taken her more seriously, with all that planning. And she was in the perfect position to do what she needed to do. I presumed she'd see sense. But then she couldn't have her happy ending . . . because her mother wasn't like me. And then she died.'

'What?' Laura was struggling to keep up. 'Sorry, who died?'

'Her mother. She'd found her.'

'But why was she looking for her mother? What do you

mean? Do you mean she was a mother, looking for her child?'

Noreen blinked. 'Her child? Of course not. She was the child. It was her mother who was raped.'

'I just didn't think!'

Sister Concepta didn't even try to hide her frustration with Ray and Michael.

'Sister Gladys and Sister Clare weren't proper midwives. I doubt they could even dress a cut at this point. I'm not trying to mislead you, I just forgot. I wasn't here then, for goodness' sake; I'm only thirty-six.'

'Sister, when we met you first, you told us your parents had died,' Ray said. 'Who raised you?'

'Why is that relevant?'

'Answer the question, please.'

'My aunt took me in.'

Ray stood up.

'Please stay where I can find you,' he said.

Michael followed him out.

'What was that about?' he asked.

'I'm just wondering how much she's been keeping back from us. Keep an eye on her, will you?'

He found Ronan still in Mother Attracta's office at her computer.

'You need a drink or something?' Ray asked, postponing the question he really wanted to ask.

'I'm good, thanks. The nice nuns keep bringing me tea and snacks. They're not sure what I'm doing on the computer but they don't seem to realize I was complicit in having Sister Bernadette hauled up to the station. They keep giving out about you lot.' He laughed.

Ronan was enjoying being part of this fast-moving case. He'd no idea how slowly murder cases usually progressed, and what it was like to be involved in investigations that remained unsolved for years.

'Ronan, could I ask you to do something important for me?'

Ronan reacted to Ray's solemn tone. He sat up straight in his chair, all smiles gone.

'Sure. I'm just tracking this Farrell woman, but I keep arriving at dead ends. It's obviously a pseudonym. I'd welcome a distraction.'

'I want you to talk to my station sergeant, Ian Kelly. He's looking into this already, but I'm going to give you a name. I want you to find out everything you can about that woman's child for me. The difficulty is, the child was adopted, and I don't know the gender or what it was named.'

Ronan rubbed his chin, thoughtfully. 'This will be tough. I'm pretty sure adoption records are tight in this country, and older ones may not be digitized. Unless it was in the last few decades?'

'It would have been the mid-seventies.'

'Well, in that case we could get lucky. Look, I'll have to go into servers I really shouldn't be in.'

'That's why I'm asking you,' Ray said. 'If we need to use it as evidence later, we'll go through the proper channels, but right now I just need something confirmed. You can do this in one hundredth of the time it's going to take us to do it. I'll just ring Ian and see if he has anything.'

Ray leaned over to the phone on the desk and dialled the sergeant's number.

Ian picked up on the first ring. 'Hello?'

'Ian, Ray here. I have you on speakerphone.'

'No problem. What can I do for you?'

'I have a chap here who's giving me a hand with something. Did you get back on to the psychiatric unit about Margaret Downes's family? Tom said you thought she'd had visitors.'

'I spoke to them. It wasn't a whole lot of help, though. They didn't have a name. They have a visitors' book and it had been signed, but the nurse said it was completely illegible.'

'But they remembered seeing someone?'

Ray's stomach was sick with anticipation.

'Yes. A young woman. The nurse didn't know if she was a daughter, a niece or just a friend, but said she turned up a couple of years ago, shortly before Margaret died. Said she was absolutely devastated when the woman passed. They hadn't been able to ring or contact her when it happened because she hadn't left a number – and, of course, they couldn't read her name. She just turned up to see the old dear one day and they had to inform her she was dead.'

Ray sucked air into his cheeks. 'Okay, Ian. Thanks for that. We're trying to track down that woman. If you turn up anything else, let me know. In the meantime, could you get a warrant sorted so we can get access to adoption records in Limerick city?'

He turned to Ronan, whose California-tanned face was looking distinctly pale and worried.

'We're looking for Margaret Downes's daughter's adoption records?'

Ray nodded. 'Can you do it? Ian will sort a warrant for us. But like I said, that will take a while. And if you can, I really need to find out everything that happened to the daughter after that.'

'You're the boss.'

Sometimes, Ray reflected grimly, the rules had to be bent ever so slightly to hurry things along.

He crossed the hall to the records room. He found the box he'd been looking in earlier and pulled out the photograph. It was the same group photograph that, unknown to him, Laura had been looking at yesterday. He turned it over and read again the names on the back.

The year was 1976. He scanned through the names corresponding to each woman's row position. There it was – Maggie Downes. Second from the left, first row. Just a few faces along from Mother Attracta.

He looked at the picture again and this time focused on Margaret.

He had been right. He knew it.

He slumped on to the boxes behind him and put his head in his hands. Tried to rationalize what he'd just seen. He was still in denial.

His brain switched to automatic. He'd get Ronan to confirm it, then he'd act. There were police officers all over the convent, and all the nuns had been converging on the chapel for evening prayers when last he checked.

Everyone should be okay for now.

He pulled out his phone to ring Tom but stopped short. He couldn't, not yet. Not until he knew for sure.

He did need to talk to someone, though – someone who might be able to help.

CHAPTER 54

'Whoever did this had some energy.'

Emmet had traversed the entire floor of the unit, moving as fast as his knees would allow. Tom had been relegated to standing in the doorway and observing his colleague, to avoid further contaminating the scene.

The adrenalin rush he'd felt when they found the place had passed, and the plummeting temperature was getting to him.

'Isn't it unusual for a scene to be so clean?' he stuttered.

Any longer out here and he'd have hypothermia. Emmet, on the other hand, was sweating profusely in his full white suit; the tech unit assigned to assist him was still an hour away.

'Absolutely,' Emmet replied. 'Using plastic sheets – that's somebody who has done their research.'

Tom was so cold his brain was starting to freeze. He had to keep moving and keep talking.

'I was thinking of something when I was talking to Linda, Emmet.'

'Please, stop mentioning that woman's name. Every

time you do I get a stabbing pain in my shoulder like I'm going to have a heart attack.'

Tom looked up to the heavens. 'Give me strength.'

'Just tell me what you're thinking and leave loopy Linda's name out of it.'

Tom sighed. 'I'll find out what happened between you two eventually. Anyway, I began this case wondering if our victim had been killed at random – if we had some maniac on our hands. When I found out she was a nun, I was concerned that somebody was making a statement about the Church. There's been so much controversy in recent years.'

Emmet worked as Tom talked.

And as Tom laid out the bones of his theory, he temporarily forgot how cold he was.

'I went to the convent and met all these nuns who'd had fractious relationships with Mother Attracta. Most of them seemed too old and none of them came across as unstable, but I ruled nothing out. It's usually someone close, isn't it? Even in gangland murders, it often turns out to be a cousin or an accomplice who ends up firing the fatal bullet – someone who could get close enough to the victim and knew the routine.

'The evidence kept pointing to the sisters. And I've enough experience to know that there is no such thing as a cut and dry profile of a murderer. From the start, the laundry issue intrigued me. I was concerned it might lead the team off on a tangent. But it kept coming back up – especially when Father Seamus was killed. It just seemed obvious that revenge was the motive.'

'What's your point, old friend? You believe it was a woman from the laundry?' Emmet stood up and looked at Tom. 'You'd better stand in a bit, that snow is coming down again.'

Tom looked up at the sky and stepped over the threshold.

'The age issue, of the nuns and former laundry inmates, concerned me. The person who killed Father Seamus climbed over a ten-foot wall.'

Emmet nodded patiently and returned to the floor.

'Then we learned something else,' Tom continued. 'Father Seamus had raped girls in the laundry and made three of them pregnant. Laura and Ciaran are gone to interview one of those women tonight. She'd be well in her fifties now. Not exactly decrepit, but maybe too old to be scaling walls and carrying dead bodies into the Phoenix Park.'

Emmet nodded. He was half listening, trying to concentrate on what he was doing.

'When I was talking to our mutual friend, the psychologist, I asked her if a family member of a laundry inmate could have carried out the murders. I was thinking a father or brother. She entertained the theory and suggested another angle. That maybe I should be looking at a child.

'The more I thought about it, Emmet, the more it made

sense. Can you imagine what it would do to you if you found out not only that you were adopted but how and why you'd been adopted? And worse, that you'd been the result of rape?

'There are some people involved in this investigation who are just the right age to be a child of one of the rape victims. Sister Concepta is one. Hell, I've even given consideration to Jack.'

Emmet stopped what he was doing and looked at Tom.

'Jesus, Tom, I know he's useless, but it's not Jack. I know Jack's parents. I've known the chap since he was a kid. That's some bloody conclusion you've jumped to.'

Tom looked at Emmet, snapped back from his train of thought.

'What do you mean?'

'Well, first your killer has to find out they're adopted. Then they have to do this whole background search – which, believe me, is no easy feat. This state does not make it easy for people who've been adopted to find their birth parents. So, according to your theory, they defy all the odds and discover their adoptive mother's history and by the close of that story you have them committing a double homicide? It seems like too much of a perfect storm for me.'

Tom chewed his lip and absorbed what Emmet had said. What he wouldn't give for a cigar right now.

'I hear you, Emmet. But this crime *is* unusual. A nun and a priest killed within a couple of days of each other? The way that nun was left?'

Emmet shrugged. 'But if you're right and this is pre-meditated revenge, why did your murderer end up killing the priest when you were standing outside the bloody door? That doesn't seem planned. It looks pretty ad hoc, if you ask me.'

Tom considered for a moment before replying.

'We've already thought about that. The priest wasn't there on Wednesday when the killer struck first. He'd travelled to Dublin. Ray went over his bookings in the brothel. They were erratic. If someone had been watching him, they probably knew he disappeared the odd day, but there was no pattern.'

'Okay. You've an answer for that. To be honest, though, I don't think you've any idea how difficult it is for adopted people to find their real parents. The further back you go, it's especially hard. And where the nuns were involved, the state's records are appalling.'

Tom was getting irritated with Emmet. This was the problem with scientists. They were finicky about facts – you couldn't hypothesize without them ripping holes in your theories.

'You're very defensive of people who've been adopted, Emmet,' Tom said. 'I'm not claiming they're all running around murdering the people who decided they should be given up for adoption. I'm just wondering if there wasn't a strange confluence of events that ended up with this person deciding to take matters into their own hands when they discovered the truth. What's the matter? Are you adopted or something?'

'Yes. I am, actually. And you know others who are, too.'

Tom's eyes widened as he stared at his friend.

'I never knew you were adopted.'

'Why would you? I never told you. It's not something people generally talk about. Some people know I am, though – and I've tried to give them some help finding their parents, too. Adopted people tend to find one another.'

'You sound like an authority on the subject.'

'I am. I searched for my birth mother for years. Never found her. My records don't go beyond my adoptive parents. I suppose *I'm* a suspect now.'

'Wait a minute,' Tom said, warily.

He'd already formed a theory, but he needed to hear Emmet confirm it. That had been his missing link – knowing who was adopted.

'You said I know plenty of others. Who do I know?'

'Well, there's Bridget in your station, for a start.'

Ronan found Ray in the kitchen talking to Sister Gladys.

'Detective, can I see you?' he asked.

One of the other nuns bustled past him, and he gave her a broad smile. She'd brought him cake an hour ago, a delicious rich chocolate sponge with a hot raspberry filling.

Ray looked like he'd aged in the half-hour or so since Ronan had last talked to him. 'Sure,' he said, rising to his feet.

Sister Gladys grabbed Ray's hand as he stood. She was

sitting in her usual chair, her leg raised on a pouffe. The nun appeared to Ronan to have been crying.

Ray nodded to her, visibly dazed, before following Ronan out of the kitchen.

'What was that about?' Ronan asked, as they headed back to the computer.

Ray didn't speak for a moment, lost in his thoughts.

'Nothing. Just an old lady's memories. I was asking her about some of the pregnant girls she attended. She . . . she saw a lot of heartache. She was with Margaret Downes when her baby was taken from her.'

Ronan looked closely at the young man beside him. Ray was attractive. Tall, dark, a chiselled face, lean. But he had none of the swagger that good-looking men his age generally had. His eyes were intense but kind.

Ray caught the other man staring, and Ronan blushed. He did that a lot in Ireland. He wasn't openly gay here – it wasn't like California – people knew, but it was unspoken. He'd developed the habit of being self-conscious around other men, even when it was unnecessary. It was a sad fact that, among certain Irish people, homosexuality was still considered contagious.

'Well, wait until you see what I've found,' Ronan said. 'Talk about heartache.'

'You've found something already?' Ray said, amazed.

He opened the office door and stood back to let Ronan pass through. Ronan took up his seat at the computer screen.

'I've found everything. It was a piece of cake in the end.

In relative terms, this was a modern adoption. Further back and we'd have had trouble. Margaret Downes's daughter was born and adopted in 1975. Adoption became legal in Ireland in 1952, so the records are better from the late fifties on.'

Ray stood in front of the desk, fidgeting nervously.

'It was easy to find the birth and adoption certs because I knew where the daughter was born and from where she'd been adopted. The Health Service Executive in Limerick has all the files that were once held in this convent. After that, I tracked where she'd gone in the system. If she'd had an easy life it would have been harder, but this girl kept popping up. To a point, anyway.'

'What do you mean by "if she'd had an easy life"?' Ray asked. 'What happened to her?'

'What didn't happen to her would be a better question. This girl really got the shit stick. The couple that adopted her were not suitable. They were in their early fifties – too bloody old to adopt, but obviously well connected and moneyed. But they clearly couldn't cope with a small baby. She ended up in care when she was two. There was a series of foster homes, and it appears from her file . . .' Ronan stopped.

'What?' Ray asked, unable to keep the tremor from his voice.

'She was abused as a child. In one of her foster homes. It must have been pretty horrific because the adults were struck off the fostering register. I bet that doesn't happen too often in Ireland.'

'Go on,' Ray said, his voice strained.

'There's not a whole lot more,' Ronan continued. 'She was in care until she was fifteen and finally got some decent foster parents. They seemed to be involved in local religious groups and charities. Good people. When she turned eighteen she went off the health service's radar.'

'What age was she when she was abused?'

Ronan swallowed. 'Seven. To nine.'

Ray nodded but said nothing.

'Do you want to know her name?'

Ronan realized he'd gone from being thrilled at having unearthed so much in such a short time to feeling like he'd just told Ray that everyone he loved had been killed in a car crash.

'Yes. Tell me her real name,' Ray whispered.

'I don't understand.'

Laura stood up, agitated. In that moment, the beautiful Christmas tree, the sparkling ornaments and lights, the candles and the smell of shortbread faded into the background. All she could focus on was Noreen, tiny in her huge armchair, giving the detective a perplexed look.

'You said it was a child who came looking for you?'

'Not a child,' Noreen shook her head vigorously. 'She's an adult now. But she was Maggie's child. Maggie Downes.'

Laura brought her hand to her chest, where her heart was beating like that of a racehorse. She forced herself to sit down again and take a deep breath. She even managed a sip of tea.

'Maggie's child came to find you. How did she know to look for you?'

Noreen sat back, a little uncertain now, but willing to proceed.

'Maggie had brought only one thing to that hospital of any importance. A diary. That was the key to the whole thing, really. I suppose if she hadn't brought that, Liz would never have known—'

'Did you say Liz?' Ciaran spoke before Laura had a chance to react.

That name had been playing on his mind ever since he realized the mistake he'd made in not taking the phone call from Liz Downes seriously.

'Yes, Liz Downes. Maggie was her mother. When she found out her mother's surname, she liked to use it.'

'Why did she come to you?' Laura asked, impatiently.

'She'd done the research and found her mother. But when she finally came face to face with her, she met a woman so far gone she couldn't even speak. Liz said the hospital room had a bed and a little locker and that the diary was the only personal thing the woman possessed. God, it's depressing. It was exactly like that in the convent dormitories.'

Laura's mind was spinning. 'And the diary – what did it say? Did it say she'd been raped?'

Noreen shook her head. 'Good gracious, no, it didn't say that. The nuns wouldn't have let her keep it. It didn't even mention Liz. But Maggie did write about the other girls in the laundry. My name was one of them, and Liz found me. She knew nothing about her mother except that she'd been in Kilcross. Of course, I remembered Maggie. She was such a lovely girl. But after what happened to her, she was never the same.'

'How do you mean?'

'She lost her mind. God, the trauma I went through when they took my baby from me. But Maggie never recovered. She obsessed about it, couldn't think of anything else. Then she couldn't talk, couldn't eat. She was full of hate. She just kept repeating that they all deserved to die. She loved Liz so much, but then when her girl found her they couldn't even be properly reunited. Her body was there but her mind was gone.'

Noreen sniffed and extracted a white lace handkerchief from her sleeve, dabbing her eyes and nose.

'I told Liz everything I could,' the woman continued. 'I was so happy to meet her and be able to tell her how much she was loved, what Maggie had been like before it had happened. So beautiful, Maggie was. Just like her daughter . . .'

As Noreen talked, a theory was slowly forming in Laura's head. She realized why she had thought of it – a photo she had been looking at in the convent but to which she hadn't given enough attention. And names. At some point, she'd meant to ask one of the nuns about their names – obviously the saints' names they took weren't their actual names.

'Noreen,' she interrupted. 'What does Liz do for a living?'

CHAPTER 55

Ray was on the move. He needed to make sure everyone was safe.

The killer wasn't finished yet.

He flew through the most populated rooms in the convent – the kitchen, the dining room and the sitting room. He found most of the nuns gathered in the chapel. Sister Gladys had been moved to the sitting room, where she was trying to convince one of the guards to roll a cigarette for her. Only two people were unaccounted for, from what he could see.

He ran back to the kitchen. Sister Mary was distractedly chucking flour at a ball of dough and was startled when he banged open the door and stormed in.

'Where's Sister Clare?' he demanded.

'What's the matter, Detective?'

'Just tell me, where is she?'

Ray had no time to explain, but his agitated tone convinced the nun he was serious.

'I haven't seen her for hours. She went out earlier to mark out the foundations that have been buried under the snow, so no one would fall again. She knows where they are better than any of us. It was getting dark, she should have left it . . .'

Ray felt ice coursing through his veins.

'Shit!' he exclaimed.

He rushed to the back door, yanking it open. It was still unlocked.

'Get Detective Geoghegan! Get me Michael now!' he roared at the shocked and confused nun.

Sister Mary dropped the lump of dough and rushed to the kitchen door, panic spreading across her face.

'It's okay, she wasn't alone,' she squeaked.

'That's why I'm worried,' Ray shouted back.

He darted outside. The lights from the convent windows illuminated a very limited area of the grounds, and the fast swirling snow further impeded visibility. He looked left and right frantically, his breath coming in sharp, adrenalin-fuelled bursts.

He hastened forward before halting. He might as well have a bell around his neck, the noise he was making, panting as he sloshed heavily through snow and ice. He took a deep, calming breath and began moving more stealthily towards the old orphanage foundations.

The grey brick stones he first encountered were just that, small stones. They were probably larger under the snow, but he could only see their tips. No wonder Gladys had fallen over one earlier. In the distance, though, the remains of some walls still stood.

Instinctively, he knew this was where to go. Making careful progress, he reached the first of the higher standing brick mounds.

'Sister Clare,' he called out.

He paused, listening for a response or movement of any kind. Nothing.

He moved to the next wall. His whole body trembled with the cold, and the tips of his fingers were starting to go numb. The snow stung his eyes as he searched, unblinking, for signs of life.

'Sister Clare?'

He thought he heard a whimper this time, just to his right.

To hell with quiet.

He lifted his knees and started barrelling through the snow as fast as he could in that direction, casting nervous glances behind him every few yards. Ray had never seen anybody who had frozen to death, and he didn't want Sister Clare to be his first.

As he frantically fumbled around in the darkness, Ray spotted the nun's hands. Her arms had been tied behind her, looped around a narrow wall, the wrists knotted with rope. When he rounded the stone, he came face to face with a vision straight from a nightmare.

Sister Clare was in a seated position. More ropes had been placed over the tops and bottoms of her legs, held in place with iron pegs. The ropes and pegs had probably been brought outside by the nun herself to cordon off the foundations; they had been cruelly turned against her.

The elderly nun's coat was discarded to one side. Her scarf was tied around her mouth. Blood oozed from a nasty-looking wound to the side of her head.

Her eyes were, literally, frozen wide open. The nun's tears had turned to ice and her eyelashes were glued to her skin. Her face was white, and her hair and clothing were disappearing under the falling snow.

Amazingly, she was alive and found the strength to moan weakly when she saw him.

He fell to his knees and pulled the scarf out of her mouth. Alerted by the sound of ragged breathing and running feet approaching, he stood up.

Michael emerged from the snow. 'What the hell?'

'She's alive,' Ray shouted. 'Help me.'

He started pulling the pegs out of the ground. Michael joined him. When they had the ropes off Sister Clare's legs, Ray moved round the back of the wall.

'Shit, shit, shit, the knot's frozen. We need to stand her up and lift her until we can get her arms over the top. Do it gently.'

The two detectives carefully manoeuvred the near dead woman into a standing position, both men heaving and sweating from the exertion. Ray lifted her until Michael was able to raise her arms over the wall without hurting her. They were blessed it wasn't any higher.

Sister Clare fell forward.

'Take her,' Ray directed Michael.

The other detective scooped her up in his arms. Ray pulled off his fleece, draping it over her.

'Bring her back to the convent. I need to end this.'

Sister Clare mumbled something through chattering teeth.

Ray moved closer to her. 'You're safe now, Sister.'

The nun mumbled again.

Ray leaned his ear to her mouth and heard the one word.

A name.

He stood back.

'I know,' he said. 'I know.'

Emmet was putting his driving abilities to the test. Parts of the road were like glass. Anything over fifty kilometres per hour risked sliding off the road as the tyres struggled for grip. Adding insult to injury, the snow had started to fall again, obscuring their vision. The saving grace was that nobody else was mad enough to be tearing down the main road at this hour in these conditions.

They emerged unscathed from a particularly hairy stretch. Both men exhaled loudly in relief.

'Considering you've asked me to put my life and yours in danger, can you not just tell me what the mad panic is to get back?' Emmet asked, his eyes firmly focused on the road.

'I wondered,' Tom said, also staring out the windscreen intently, 'why the first victim had been left in the Phoenix Park. The killer didn't need a national team to discover what had gone on in that laundry. The body could have been left in Limerick for the local squad. I've been looking at this from the wrong angle . . . For God's sake, why can't I get a signal on this phone?'

'What was the right angle?' Emmet asked, exasperated.

He'd told Tom all the people they knew who'd been adopted. Tom had taken one deep breath, nodded his head, then roared at him to get in the car.

Now they were haring back to Kilcross as fast as conditions would allow, with Tom swearing every few minutes because he couldn't get through to anyone on his phone.

'Why would somebody kill a woman from Limerick and leave her in Dublin? Once we had the second victim, it should have been obvious. The person who'd killed Attracta had to gain access to Kilcross once more and be able to move through the village with impunity to finish the job. We gave the killer the free pass. We invited her down to the village.'

'What does she work at?' Noreen said. 'I thought you knew. She's a scientist of some sort. She kept it vague, but it's something to do with the police. Her mother would have been so proud. I told her that.'

Ciaran shook his head and turned to Laura, who was streets ahead of him.

'What does she mean?' he asked.

He, too, had cottoned on that Noreen was indeed, as he liked to put it, a few cakes short of a picnic.

Laura ignored him, her gaze never leaving the woman in the chair.

'Noreen, you said you wanted to call your son Matthew

but he was called something else when he was adopted. How did Liz get her name?'

'Ah. She was lucky. Her mother had a name for her. Sister Gladys felt so guilty that she put Maggie's chosen name for her daughter on the birth and adoption certificates. The nun claimed she'd made it up herself, but we all knew that Maggie had picked Elisa.'

'Elisa? I thought you said Liz?' Ciaran said.

'Yes, Maggie's daughter shortened it,' Noreen said. 'But it's actually "Lis" with an S, not "Liz" with a Z.'

Laura felt the room close in. She turned to Ciaran.

'What else is a shortened version of Elisa?'

Ciaran looked at her blankly for a few seconds.

Then he shot to his feet as realization dawned, sending his cup and saucer flying.

The convent was silent – bar the distant echo of voices raised in harmony.

The nuns were singing a mournful hymn in the chapel, blissfully ignorant of what had just occurred to one of their own. That unknowing state would shortly be shattered by the arrival of an ambulance and the expanding shockwaves of the frenzied activity now taking place in the kitchen, where Michael, Willie, Sister Mary and Sister Bernadette were trying to revive a now unconscious Sister Clare.

Ray climbed the stairs, his steps as heavy as his heart. The chorus of voices grew distant, replaced by the noise of his own shallow breathing.

The convent was haunted tonight. He could almost feel the presence of the women who had lived and died here. He sensed their souls around him in the air and shuddered, imagining whispered memories of suffering and desolation.

He knew what floor she'd be on, but he didn't know which room to try first.

He didn't have to think about it for long. It had to be the one with the open door. He walked slowly along the corridor. He had his pistol but he didn't want it. He wouldn't be capable of using it.

He arrived at the open door. It was the second dormitory the team had walked into on the first evening.

She was sitting on the floor, beside the unit between the windows, tracing with her finger the MM initials carved there. Her dark hair covered the side of her face. The windows were open and the snowflakes came through in flurries as the wind changed direction. Some landed in her hair, but she didn't move.

She reacted when she heard him cross the threshold, though, turning her head, a smile breaking when she saw who it was.

He didn't know if it was the eerie white light spilling in, or the angle from which he viewed her, but he could see now that her smile, as endearing as it was, didn't reach her eyes.

She stood up to face him.

'Ellie,' he choked, his heart breaking.

CHAPTER 56

'So are you saying . . .?' Emmet asked, turning to look at Tom.

The other man was still waving his phone around, trying desperately to get a signal.

As he spoke, the car hit an icy patch and the front wheels skidded to the left.

Tom dropped the phone and grabbed the door rest. Emmet was an experienced driver and let the car slide before he corrected the wheel.

'Jesus!' the Tech Bureau chief exclaimed, panting heavily.

Tom groaned. 'Emmet, let's arrive alive,' he said, before returning to his theory. 'Yes, that's what I'm saying.'

'But that can't be right. I mean . . . what the hell, Tom? No, I don't believe it. Not Ellie. She's happy in her life. I wouldn't have even known she was adopted, except an old university colleague told me she'd been asking how somebody would go about tracing birth parents. Ellie wanted it kept private but appreciated my intentions when I brought it up.

'She'd already decided she didn't want to pursue it.

Bridget is far more eager to meet her real mother. You're jumping to conclusions, Tom, dangerous conclusions.'

The inspector shook his head.

'It was all there, Emmet. I asked you to send Mark down with her. Was it you who decided she could select who she brought?'

Emmet hesitated before replying.

'No. I said they could both go down,' he remembered. 'But Mark was busy this weekend, and he'd done some late shifts last week.'

'Covering those shifts for Ellie, was he? I remember now, she looked bloody exhausted on Friday morning when we found the body. She must have just made it back from the lock-up.

'Ellie probably talked Mark out of travelling. She couldn't risk having him on site. I think she brought Jack as a decoy. It was a good strategy. I should have been watching her, but she kept directing me to look at Jack – pointing out when he abandoned her, as though he was off doing something suspicious.'

Tom continued his train of thought. 'Jack's incompetence shouldn't have been a problem, though. She's meant to be an excellent crime scene technician, yet she found no forensic evidence. You'd barely arrived when you picked up on the DNA under the priest's fingernails. And how come she didn't spot that glass fragment in the hall?'

'She could have easily missed what was under the priest's nails, Tom. You said yourself, she was trying to cover two sites. The pathologist would have found it, anyway. And the glass was minuscule.'

'She didn't miss the priest's nails for want of trying,' Tom said. 'She knew he'd scratched her, but she must have been in too much of a rush to clean up properly after she killed him. She was conscious of us outside and of her need to establish an alibi. In any case, she thought she'd have unfettered access to the body when she was called on site. She wasn't counting on there being guards in the priest's hall the whole time she was working with her victim.

'And she went over and over that convent hall, Emmet. She wasn't looking for evidence; she was making sure there was none, and missed the glass fragment. God knows how much she removed. That's why both scenes were so clean.'

Emmet shook his head, still unable to believe what he was hearing.

'There's so much that only started to make sense tonight. She's met Ray a few times but never showed any interest. Suddenly, on this case, she's making eyes at him. She was keeping him close, ingratiating herself with us so she could keep up with developments. I wasn't having team meetings that included her, and I didn't talk to her – not the way I'd talk to you – so that's why she helped us find out that the priest had been up to Dublin. It was evidence she was certain of, and it brought her closer to the team. But it would come to nothing for our investigation.

'I know you're struggling with this, Emmet, but think it through. Ray told me he met her outside the priest's house just before we found the body. She must have gone in, done the deed, then driven round the front. If anyone saw her and asked why she was up in the village, she had a reason and an alibi – lunch with Ray.

'I think she was posing as Catherine Farrell and renting the house next door. Does she work full time?'

Emmet shook his head.

'Not this year,' he said. 'She's studying. She puts the hours in when she's there . . . I can't believe this. If you thought it was her, why did you leave her down there?'

'I wasn't sure,' Tom said. 'I kept going through the people who fitted the age profile in my head, but I didn't know who was adopted – Concepta, Jack, Ellie. I took precautions, making sure neither Ellie nor Jack were in the convent when we were leaving. I told Ray to keep an eye on them once they showed up, and to monitor Concepta. When we saw how clean the storage unit was, the pieces clicked.

'If I'm honest, Emmet, I didn't want it to be her. She was on the shortlist, but I entertained doubts right up until you told me she was adopted. She knew you'd send her down, Emmet. You said she had a way with men . . . was she working her magic on you?'

Tom could see his friend blushing. 'Once you'd brought her in to work the Phoenix Park site, it all fell into place. She knew you'd be too busy to leave Dublin. She knew what she was doing.'

'Tom, listen to me, I've known this woman for years. I've had drinks with her. She is smart. She's kind. She's mature. And more importantly, she's stable. Do you hear me? She's not insane.'

Emmet's tone didn't match his words. The cogs in his brain were turning.

'You're wrong. I think she's probably the most traumatized person either of us has ever met. I just hope to God she's finished what she set out to do.'

Tom looked down at his phone.

The signal was back.

As fast as his fingers could move, he found Ray's number and dialled.

'Why, though, Noreen?' Laura asked again.

She had been trying to get through to Tom for the last five minutes. Then she tried Ray. They either had their phones turned off or had no reception. She cursed and banged the phone on the table.

She was afraid.

Ray had been spending time with Ellie. Was he with her now? She didn't know what was holding Ellie together. When would she snap?

'I'll try my lads,' Ciaran said, excusing himself from the sitting room, still dazed.

'Why what, dear?' Noreen responded.

'Why did you tell her everything? Why did you tell her what had happened to her mother?'

'Because she wanted to know,' Noreen replied, raising her hands, as if it was obvious.

'But did she have to know that her mother had gone mad because of it? Did she have to know she was the result of rape? That you'd all been raped? What was the point all those years later? You didn't need to tell her. You spared your own son that terrible truth. And why did you tell her Maggie was obsessed with getting revenge?'

Noreen looked at Laura oddly.

'Why wouldn't I tell her? Her mother wanted them to die. It drove her mad. That's the truth of it. They deserved it.'

Laura stood up.

Noreen Boyle was insane. Did she even realize what she was admitting to?

'You keep saying that they deserved to die. But you didn't kill them. You planted the seeds for her to do it. You don't seem to realize it, but you share the responsibility for this. The girl was obviously disturbed. She needed help, but you used her.'

Noreen tucked her handkerchief back into her sleeve, the same manic smile on her lips.

Had her son noticed the illness? Laura wondered. Or had he been blinded by pity and love?

'I would have killed both of them, if I hadn't found my family. It took me on a different path. I lost years of my son's life. I can't lose any more. Those nuns sat on the high moral ground, brides of Christ, and looked down at us as if we were prostitutes. Well, they were the whores. Satan's whores.'

Laura flinched.

How many times had Noreen repeated those words to a vulnerable Ellie? Was Ellie unstable before she met Noreen, or had the woman manipulated the young woman's emotions to the point of insanity?

Noreen sniffed. 'Anyway, I imagine you can charge me, but can you make it stick? I didn't kill anyone. I thought the girl was a fantasist. That's what I'll say in court.'

Laura felt rage surging through her.

'So you think you're going to get your revenge and the happy ending?' she challenged Noreen. 'Not if I have anything to do with it.'

The other woman looked as if she was about to reply, but didn't. Instead, she smiled enigmatically and twirled one of the Christmas tree ornaments.

Laura, disturbed, looked at the decoration.

It was a globe hanging on a piece of red ribbon. Inside was a little grey house, snow falling all around it.

CHAPTER 57

Ellie had moved to one of the window sills. She held her hand out and laughed when snowflakes landed in her palm.

She was so beautiful, Ray thought, and his heart lurched. A snow princess. But now he saw her in a new light. Instead of a confident, attractive woman, he saw what she had once been – a frightened little girl, dragged from pillar to post, abused, mistreated, abandoned.

His phone buzzed in his pocket, but he ignored it.

'Aren't you going to get that? It's good to talk.' She laughed again.

He shook his head.

'You look so sad, Ray.' Her smile changed to a pout. 'What's the matter? Isn't it beautiful here? The snow ...' She perched on the sill now and caught some more. Her laughter was as pure as the icy flakes. 'It's just perfect. How cold it must have been for the girls all those years ago, though. You know that's something the nuns used to do as a punishment? They'd leave the windows up all night so the girls would be freezing.' She shuddered and wrapped her arms around herself.

'Ellie,' Ray said softly. 'You're cold. Come away from the window.'

'No. I don't think I will, Ray. You want me to come over there so you can warm me up, do you? Tut tut.' She winked at him, coquettishly.

He recoiled at the tone of her voice. Instead of flirtation, now he heard a forced sexualization. He took a step towards her.

'Don't,' she said, her voice normal again. She tucked her hair behind her ear. 'I know you know.'

He stopped, inhaled deeply.

'I don't know how, but I saw something register on your face downstairs. I knew you'd figure it out eventually. Maybe not you, but Tom. He's renowned, isn't he? So handsome, too. I like the older men. Like Emmet. So easy to manipulate. Tom, not so much. I researched everything I could about him but I hoped that I could do what I had to before he found me out.

'And then at some point, I started to think, maybe they won't figure it out. You were so intent on it being one of those nuns. I really thought my luck was in. And I wasn't finished.'

Ray took another step.

'Tom was on to something,' he said. 'He told me to keep an eye on you and a couple of others. I realized he was right when I saw you downstairs. I'd seen a photo of your mother in one of the boxes earlier.'

Ellie shook her head. 'No.'

'Yes.'

She looked shocked, upset. 'I didn't see any photos. I went through lots of those boxes. I had to stop when the two nuns started going into those rooms at night. I had no idea what they were up to. Fair play to them, I guess. A bit too late, though. Laura said more or less the same when Concepta helped find her aunt's file. How considerate the nuns are . . . now.

'So, you know something I don't know. You know what my mother looked like when she was young. I don't. I only ever saw her in the hospital, and she wasn't herself then.'

'The first time I saw the picture, I knew there was something in it speaking to me,' Ray said. 'I didn't know what it was until I passed you in the hall earlier. Your face . . . your mother looked like she'd lost something. Sad, but still so beautiful. You're always smiling, so I didn't see it straight away, but downstairs you had that same look. When she smiled, she must have looked like your twin.'

'When she smiled,' Ellie said. 'I can't imagine that was too often. You know she died in a psychiatric hospital? I didn't go in to see her much. It was too hard. She didn't know who I was. I tried so hard to make her understand. When I read her diary, I knew she'd been in one of these places and then I found out she'd had to give me up.

'It's funny, because before that, I hated her. I wasn't even sure I wanted to find her. I fought so hard to make a good life for myself, and she had given me nothing. I didn't know single women were forced to give up their babies, back then . . .' Ellie paused. 'They say a tiny percentage of people are adopted, but a huge percentage of adopted people end up in institutions. We have addictive personalities, apparently. Always trying to find something to fill the hole inside us. Believe me, the void in me is huge, Ray.

'The nuns claim they were doing us a favour. It's the only trauma you're supposed to be grateful for. You're supposed to be *thankful* for your adoptive parents. You've no idea what I had to go through in my life. Oh!'

Compassion filled Ray's face. Ellie looked at him with a dawning realization.

'You do know. You seem to have figured out a lot about me, Ray. Do you always do this much research on potential girlfriends?'

'Don't,' he said, sadly.

'Don't what?'

'Don't make jokes. You don't have to. I understand.'

'Understand? Are you kidding? You understand what it's like to be ripped from your own mother? A pain so bad that it drives her insane and eventually kills her? To find out that you're the result of rape – and not just any kind of rape, but the rape by a priest of a young girl in his care? And to spend your childhood being pulled from one house to the next and being labelled trouble because you can't settle and won't stay quiet when the bad man hurts you?

'My my, I underestimated you. It seems you have no end of talents if you can understand all that. I was only seven when my foster father started raping me. I didn't even know what he was doing. Like mother like daughter, he used to say.'

Ellie's tears flowed freely now.

Ray's chest ached looking at her. He wanted to put his arms around her. He didn't see a killer. He saw a little girl, wounded beyond repair. He saw a daughter and her mother, destroyed.

'You told me you had parents,' he said, trying to stay focused. 'I asked you if they minded what you did.'

She smiled. 'I'm an excellent liar, Ray. Honestly, you'd think you would have figured that out by now. Always use a smidgeon of truth, though. I had good foster parents later on. They were lovely people, and I was with them until I went to college. They're very proud of me. I've no real family, though. When I found Margaret, I researched her background to see if I had any relatives. There's no one. I didn't bother with that pervert. There's no one left, Ray. I come from nothing.'

Unconsciously, he was walking towards her.

'No,' she shouted.

'I'm sorry,' he said, halting abruptly.

She shook her head. 'You don't have anything to be sorry for, Ray. You've shown me a lot of kindness. I know you're a good man. I don't want you to come closer because I'm trying to protect you.'

She reached down to the floor beside the cupboard and the object that lay there.

He saw the glint before he realized what it was. A knife.

His head snapped back.

She looked up at him calmly, the tears no longer flowing. 'You think I wouldn't use this, Ray? I already have.'

He stared at her, then at the knife. 'That was the—?'

'Yes. Attracta. She was the one who took me from my mother. I have no memory of it. Obviously.' She snorted. 'I was only a few minutes old. My mother swore revenge on her. A woman who was here at the time told me everything. How my mother would literally repeat that over and over, that she would kill the people who had hurt her and taken me. So I had to do it for her, you understand? I had no choice. You want to know how I did it?'

Ellie was holding the knife up in front of her, its tip resting precariously against the index finger on her other hand.

Ray shook his head. 'There's time enough for that, Ellie. Please, come downstairs with me. We'll get you a drink and you can warm up.'

In his head, the words 'you have the right to remain silent' repeated themselves.

'No, Ray, I need to tell you now.' Her voice was desperate.

He didn't know what to do. A confession up here was useless. They were on their own. But she'd started talking already.

'It was Emmet McDonagh who showed me how to find her, actually. Do you know he's adopted, too? He had no luck finding his mother, though. Too long ago, the poor man. I told him I'd no interest, just to get him off my case, but I was already searching. I did what he wouldn't do – I hacked into adoption records and found my original birth certificate. Do you know my mother gave me the name Elisa? It was the only thing she was allowed to give me.

'I wrote to this convent then. To Attracta. I asked her about my mother. She said there were no records left and she didn't remember Margaret Downes. Lies, Ray. I knew she was lying, so I broke in here to prove it. I found the records.

'When I met Noreen Boyle and realized what had happened to my mother, I tried to do things right. I rang Kilcross garda station. I used my real surname. I'm Lis Downes, you see. Lis was my name growing up, but I've been calling myself Ellie since I started college. I wanted to leave Lis behind.'

She sighed. 'The guards paid no attention to me. Then I rang the priest and told him I knew. He just roared at me and hung up. So I started watching the convent and his house. I even rented the house next door. I'm Catherine Farrell. A woman of many names.'

She giggled, then composed herself. 'I had to break into the convent a few times to familiarize myself with Attracta's routine, but all I had to do with the priest was befriend him. I was always careful to make sure no one else saw me, but Father Seamus and I became quite the best of pals. I wore a red wig as part of my get-up. It was a lucky pick. He loved the redheads.'

Her face showed the distaste Ray felt.

'He was vile. I'd rap on his back door when he was there alone on the pretext of going in for a cuppa. I told him I was a famous writer hiding out incognito. Said I couldn't handle dealing with the plebs in the village but his intellect stimulated me. Played up to his arrogance. He'd be all flirtatious . . . disgusting. No idea who I was. His own daughter.'

She covered her mouth, looked like she was going to vomit.

Ray put his hands behind his head and groaned. He felt so angry he wanted to smash something.

'I was furious on Wednesday when he wasn't in the bloody house. There was no pattern to those squalid little visits to Dublin. In the end, it didn't matter because Emmet sent me down, like I knew he would. I appealed to Mark's ego, told him this was just a kidnap scene and his many skills were needed in Dublin. I'd never have been able to prevent him spotting things. Jack leapt at the chance to come down, and he's so bloody useless I knew he wouldn't cause me any problems.

'Anyway, I went to the priest's house yesterday. I climbed over the back wall and banged on the back door for ages, but I had to ring him in the end. I was so nervous with you standing out front. I told him it was urgent. He arrived down after a couple of minutes, all flustered. He'd been up in his dirty little hovel, but he still found time for little old me next door.'

She smiled. 'You can't imagine how exhilarating it was. I told him I had something I'd been meaning to tell him, as I twirled my lovely red hair. By the way, those foot-prints Tom found. I borrowed Jack's boots. They're in the back of the van.

'So, priesty-beasty was a bit on edge, but being up in that attic must have got him excited. God, he was thrilled when I leaned into his ear. And I whispered, "You know how you were saying I remind you of someone? Well, actually, I'm your daughter." He was so shocked, he just stared at me as I rammed the needle into his neck.

'He could barely react, standing there, clawing at me. He scratched me a little.' She pointed at the bottom of her neck, under her sweater. 'I tried to get everything out from under his fingernails, but you lot were standing there looking at me. I watched you out the window for a minute, you know. I thought you were looking right at me at one point.'

'Does the glass fragment Emmet found in the hall table have your DNA on it, too?' Ray asked.

She frowned. 'I didn't know about that. I don't know how I missed it. Stupid, stupid girl.' She shook her head vigorously, before rolling up the sleeve of her sweater.

Ray saw cuts dotted all over her right arm.

'Hazard of the job,' she said, her voice light. 'Emmet grabbed my shoulder earlier, I thought I'd scream with the bloody pain.'

'Why did you cut out Attracta's tongue?' Even as Ray asked the question, he couldn't believe he was directing it to Ellie. 'Why the carving and the crucifixion?'

Ellie sighed. 'I just wanted her to say sorry. I was going

to kill her anyway, so it wouldn't have mattered, but I wanted her to apologize. But she got quite fatalistic when she realized she was going to die. She went from being frightened to laughing at me. To laughing at my mother. When I told her I'd been abused as a child, do you know what she said? "Oh, really?" Like I was making it up. You can't imagine what I felt when I heard that.'

'No, I can,' Ray said. 'I imagine you felt just like your mother did when she told Attracta that Father Seamus had raped her, and wasn't believed.'

Ellie nodded emphatically. 'Yes. I was furious. So I told her what I was going to do to her. I told her she wasn't a bride of Christ, that she was a whore – worse than a whore, because she'd been like a pimp for that man, giving him access to all those young girls. Her and that Theresa bitch who was in charge at the time. God knows how many he raped. And when the girls reported him, Attracta and the others told them they were liars.

'The priest did her favours. Got her elected as head of this snake pit. It was meant to be the other one, Clare. I found Clare's diary, too, when I went through their bedrooms. Egotistical maniac, that one. She was another one responsible for taking the babies away.'

Ray was terrified. Ellie's voice wavered between maniacal and light, happy and sad. It was as if there were different people speaking out of her mouth.

'I told Attracta I'd kill her and crucify her like the martyr she thought she was. I said I'd carve those words into her. I slapped her to make her listen to me, but she just laughed. So I said I'd nail her to a tree where perverts went and I hoped they'd vomit on her when they found her. I guess you kind of did.'

'Ellie!' Ray exclaimed.

'Sorry. Bad taste. The point is, nothing scared her. You know what she did? She spat at me. So I pulled out her tongue and cut it off. It was so easy, you wouldn't believe. Just a quick slice. Then she was scared. Jesus, was she scared. She must have seen that look so often on the faces of the girls in her care. And then she realized I was going to make good on my promises.'

Ellie was composed now. Her voice was sad, but calm. 'I held the knife to her heart and just plunged it in. I stabbed her again and again. It wasn't necessary, but I was so angry.' Ellie's eyes glazed over as she relived the moment, her face horrifically intent and satisfied.

Ray shivered.

'I wanted people to know what she'd done,' she continued. 'That's why I left her in the park – that, and I wanted to make sure I could be down here to deal with the priest and the other nun. I couldn't rely on being "Catherine" again, not with you lot here.

'That's all there is to it. I mean, there's lots more, but I think you're big enough to figure it all out after. You know, I am a little sad that we won't get to go on our date. You're very handsome. We'd have made beautiful children.' She grimaced. 'But I'm too damaged for you, Ray. I was damaged before I did what I did. Now . . . I've killed three people. There was a sort of symmetry to all their deaths, even though only the nun's went to plan. Attracta was left exposed. Seamus was hidden away like his disgusting obsession. And Clare – you've yet to find her, but she's as frozen now as her heart was towards all those girls who asked for her help.'

Ray edged towards her.

She had placed one leg out the window.

He shook his head. He knew now what she planned to do, and why she'd felt the urge to confess.

'Stop, Ellie,' he said. 'I can't let you do it. You've done terrible things but I understand why you did them. And if I understand, others will, I promise you. You need help. But I will be there for you.'

He didn't want to say he'd found Sister Clare in time. He'd no idea how she'd react to that. He'd gone from wondering what was keeping the ambulance for the nun to praying that it wouldn't have its sirens blaring when it arrived.

'Oh, Ray. I have to do this. It's over. I know, when people find out what happened to me, I won't go to jail. I'll go to an institution. Do you think I can go somewhere like that after what happened to my mother? You see how beautiful I am? My mother looked like me once. Noreen told me, and you said it yourself. But she didn't look like me when I met her. She didn't even have her hair . . .'

The last sentence was a whisper.

They both cocked their ears at the sound of an approaching car. Everything outside was so silent that its struggling progress on the snowy road could probably be heard for miles around. It stopped just outside the convent. Then they heard its doors open.

Ellie looked out the window and Ray stood paralysed, wondering what this development would bring.

She turned back to him. 'You know, I think that's our bosses. I should go down to meet them.'

Though it seemed like everything was happening in slow motion, Ray still couldn't reach the window in time.

He yelled and reached out for her, just as she slipped her other leg over the sill and jumped, leaving his desperate hands grasping at air.

CHAPTER 58

Tom and Emmet had just pulled up at the gate of the convent. Sister Concepta had taken the inspector's advice about being prepared for the media, and the gate was locked.

Tom cursed. How were they going to open it? He pulled his phone out and started dialling. Why the hell wasn't Ray answering?

'What's the plan here?' Emmet said. 'Which one of us is going to give the other a leg-up?'

As they stood holding the bars of the gate, something caught Tom's eye and he looked up.

The words he intended to say caught in his throat. It was Emmet who swore and yelled, 'What in God's name?' as he noticed the woman half in and half out of the second-floor window. 'Is that Ellie?' he said.

Then they were both panicking and shaking the gate, realizing they couldn't get in to stop what was about to unfold.

It didn't seem like it happened in real time.

Ellie's other leg emerged from the window, and then she was falling. Hands reached out after her and, for a second, Tom wondered if she'd been pushed, until he realized the hands were trying to grab her.

Ray's pained face appeared in the window, accompanied by a stricken cry.

Ellie fell on to the roof of the outside corridor with a sickening thud. She didn't fall through it, as Laura's aunt had all those years ago. The snow-covered tiles broke her fall – and probably her neck.

Then Tom heard another thud and realized that Emmet, the man who routinely looked at dead bodies for a living, had just fainted beside him.

Tom rubbed his tired eyes and shifted wearily in the uncomfortable chair beside Emmet's bed. 'How are you, my old friend?'

The other man looked around him, confused.

The inspector watched his face as the memory of what he'd witnessed came back.

'It used to be, Tom, that waking up like this in a strange bed with no idea of how I got here meant I'd been on the beer the night before. What happened – did I have a heart attack?'

Tom snorted. 'Do you think you'd still be in the convent if you'd had a heart attack? You don't think we'd get you to a hospital for an ECG or something?'

Emmet sat up, grunting as he tried to raise himself into a comfortable position. 'Well, I know you didn't keep me here because it's a five-star establishment. Would it kill you to get me another pillow?'

Tom stood up and fetched a pillow from the wardrobe behind him. Emmet sat forward as he placed it behind his back.

'Thank you. Is my body clock wrong? I feel like it should be morning, but it's pitch black outside.'

'It's two in the morning. You had what they refer to colloquially as a "turn". You fainted.'

Emmet shook his head mournfully. 'How embarrassing.'

'It was a nasty shock. Unsurprising, really.'

Emmet's expression turned grave. 'I was no use to you. When she fell. I should have been able to help. I presume they've taken her.'

'She's gone to Limerick University Hospital,' Tom said. 'They brought Sister Clare up, too. She's in a bad way. Almost froze to death. Ellie tied her up outside and left her to die. She never left the convent after she rowed with you. She just carried out the rest of her plan.'

Emmet raised his eyebrows. 'They should have taken Ellie to the Dublin mortuary. Headquarters could have taken care of her.'

'It's not a mortuary she needs,' Tom said.

'What do you mean?'

'She didn't die, Emmet. She has a broken leg, fractured ribs, a broken wrist and concussion, but she's not dead. If it hadn't been snowing, she might be. But as it turned out, the drop was too short and the snow too thick for her to kill herself. She misjudged it. I'd say she wasn't in her right mind, but that's a given.'

'My God!'

'Yes. She was saved. Though it might take her a long time to appreciate it. Ray travelled with her in the ambulance. Broke Laura's heart for a second time.'

'Laura has a thing for Ray, does she?' Emmet asked, struggling to keep up. 'Well, I suppose she has a chance now. Nothing like your love rival being a multiple murderer to give you an edge.'

'Ray's completely oblivious to Laura – and anyway, I think it will take him a while to recover from this. Laura has more self-esteem than to allow herself to be a shoulder to cry on. She has enough on her own plate; her aunt was in this place, and now she knows what happened to her. She has to go home and tell her mother the story ...' Tom paused.

His mind flashed back to earlier. Willie had opened the convent door and let them through the gate. He hadn't even realized what Ellie had done, just heard the two men yelling outside. Willie saw to Emmet while Tom roared at him to ring an ambulance, before racing into the house and up the stairs. His heart was pounding so hard he thought it would explode.

He found Ray collapsed at the window, his whole body shaking. Tom sank to his knees beside him.

'I couldn't stop her, Tom, I couldn't reach her. She did it. She did it.'

Tom sat with him until the others arrived – in the dormitory and outside – pointing at the prone figure on the roof of the corridor.

They hadn't realized she was alive until Michael

managed to hoist himself, with Jack and Willie's help, up on to the roof. He checked the young woman's pulse, then started yelling that she was alive.

This shook Ray from his despair. The first ambulance took Sister Clare. A second arrived shortly afterwards for Ellie, after Ciaran convinced emergency services that, yes, they did need another vehicle.

Emmet listened now, as Tom relayed the night's events.

'I don't know whether to feel anger at her for what she did, or relief that she's not dead,' he said, when the inspector had finished. 'Is it right that I should feel this conflicted about a murderer, Tom? I thought I knew her.'

Tom shook his head. 'Of course you feel conflicted. You liked her. I liked her. But she was very disturbed. She had an awful life. Ray told me something of her background before the ambulances arrived. And it seems she was manipulated into doing what she did. Laura got back here not long after us. She and Ciaran met Noreen Boyle. Turns out she dropped as much poison as she could into Ellie's head.

'That woman wanted Ellie to kill Mother Attracta and Father Seamus. Ellie was a puppet to her. She's an accomplice, and I'll see her charged for something. I'd have had more respect for the woman if she'd committed the murders herself.'

'Sad, sad, sad,' Emmet said, shaking his head.

Tom said nothing for a minute, then 'Will I fetch you something to drink?'

'Please. My mouth feels like sandpaper.'

'Have a sip of the water there, and I'll get you something stronger from downstairs.' Tom stood up but paused at the door. 'You know who'd be good to talk to, to get your head around what's happened?'

'If you say that quack's name, I'll have another heart attack.'

'You didn't have a heart attack the first time, you old fool. All right, then. Wait there.'

'Like I'm going anywhere. I probably have low blood sugar or something. It's unlikely I just fainted.'

'I'm sure that's it,' Tom smiled.

Most of the nuns were in bed at this stage, though the guards were still up, trying to come to terms with the shock of discovering one of their own had committed such heinous acts.

The inspector found Linda McCarn loitering in the hall.

'Is he all right?' she asked, nodding her head up towards the rooms on the balcony from which Tom had emerged. 'Silly old man. He's not actually sick, is he?'

Her tone was dismissive, but Tom could detect a hint of concern. He hesitated for a few seconds before replying.

'I won't lie, Linda, he's not in a good place. In his head, I mean. It's more your kind of doctoring he needs at this stage.'

'Do you think I should go up? I should go up, shouldn't I? We are adults, after all. I mean, I'm qualified . . .'

She looked uncertain, clearly torn between not wanting

to see Emmet, genuine worry and an overriding mischievous desire to see him incapacitated.

Tom shrugged.

Linda's eyes widened with determination.

'Right, then,' she said. 'Into the breach. A sacrifice for my profession.'

He stood at the kitchen door and counted. He'd got to twenty when he heard it.

'What the hell? Jesus Christ! No, you don't. Get out! Help!'

The yelling must have woken half the convent.

Tom smiled a self-satisfied grin.

They didn't mind pulling him into their little drama, but they wouldn't tell him the backstory. If they were going to act like children, why should he be a grown-up?

In the kitchen, Sister Concepta and Sister Bernadette sat in a huddle with Sister Gladys. They all had glasses of whiskey, their hands wrapped around the spirit like it was the only thing propping them up.

Sister Concepta stood up, shakily, when Tom came in. 'Inspector, you look exhausted.'

Tom yawned. 'I didn't want to leave my colleague before he came to. I wanted to tell him that Ellie had survived the fall.'

Tom was unsure what Sister Concepta and Sister Bernadette were going to say to him. He'd had a long day and really wasn't up to an argument. But they were looking at him with compassion.

'I just want to get Emmet a glass of whatever you're having yourselves,' he said. 'If that's okay.'

'More than okay. Let me get it for him, and one for you as well.' Sister Bernadette stood up and fetched the bottle. Tom imagined the nuns' stores of alcohol had diminished somewhat over the last few days.

'How is he?' Sister Gladys asked.

'Cranky. Relieved. Confused. Looking for drink, which is a good sign.'

'I meant your deputy.'

'Oh.' Tom dropped his head. Ray had told him he'd gone to Sister Gladys and asked her about Maggie Downes. 'He's very shaken at the moment.'

'Not surprising, after what he witnessed,' Sister Bernadette said.

'It wasn't just that,' Sister Gladys spoke again. 'He was very taken with that young woman. I didn't see her when she was here. There were so many of you running in and out. But I heard him talking about her with the other lad you have. If I'd seen her, I think I would have recognized her. Her mother's face is imprinted on my brain.'

Sister Gladys clasped her hands together and brought them to her breast. 'I was there when Attracta took her baby from her. I can still hear her screams.'

She was transported back thirty-five years to the hospital ward, where Mother Attracta stood wrapping the newborn while Maggie begged to hold her baby, just once. She'd agreed to give her up for adoption. But once the young women had delivered and laid eyes on their children, it was always the same. And she, Gladys, had held Maggie firmly in the bed when Attracta called her a whore and strode from the room with the infant.

'I should have stopped Attracta. I was afraid and weak. I'm a stupid woman. I wish her daughter had killed me.' Tears streamed down the elderly nun's face.

Sister Concepta reached out and placed a sympathetic hand on the elderly nun's arm. There was little that could be said to make the old woman forget, or forgive, herself.

'We were just talking about it,' Sister Bernadette said, handing Tom his glass, placing Emmet's on the countertop.

Tom lifted the tumbler to his lips and took a good swig.

'It's a tragedy,' he said. He owed Sister Bernadette an apology, even if he had just been doing his job. 'I want to—'

'Don't.' She held up her hand and shook her head dismissively. 'There's no need to say it. I understand. And if I'm honest, there's part of me that feels we are all guilty. We are part of a system that set in motion a chain of events, the consequences of which unfolded here in the last few days. Mother Attracta and Father Seamus were the authors of their own misfortune.'

'That's not really how the law works,' Tom said.

'You worry about the law,' Sister Concepta said. 'We'll worry about the morals of what happened. I don't blame that young woman. She is quite obviously ill. The real sin is that she was made that way.'

Tom raised his glass to the three women, humbled by their insight and grace.

'I'd better bring Emmet up his prescription,' he said. 'By my reckoning, he'll really need it now.'

He left the sisters bent over their drinks, whispering and remembering an appalling past that had led to a calamitous present.

Everything else in the convent was quiet.

The ghosts that haunted it were silent, for now.

EPILOGUE

Five months later

'Can't you drive any faster? They're not going to wait for us.'

'Boss, do you want me to break the law?'

Tom glared at Ray. He would buy a new car next week, and this time he'd let Pat Donnelly, his mechanic, choose it.

'To hell with this.' He reached into the glove compartment and pulled out the portable siren. Rolling down the window, he leaned out and placed it on the roof.

Ray looked at him, amused.

'All right, then, just this once,' he grinned. 'Hold on to your hat.'

They managed to get to the hospital without killing themselves – or anybody else – though Tom was pretty sure that owed more to luck than Ray's driving.

'Fast doesn't have to mean dangerous,' he yelled, jumping out of the car, relieved to be in one piece.

Ray shouted after him. 'Make up your mind. I'll park and get the cigars.'

Tom ran in through the front door. He looked around, uncertain. The main reception area of the maternity hospital was to the right. He spun on his heel and almost crashed into a heavily pregnant woman.

'I'm so sorry,' he said, grabbing her arms to make sure she was okay.

Something about her was familiar. Then he clocked it. It was Anne, Michael's wife.

'Anne!' he exclaimed. 'What are you doing here?'

He hadn't seen her in months but knew that she was doing well with her pregnancy. It showed in her radiant face.

She smiled broadly at him. 'I'm fantastic, Tom. I was just in for an antenatal appointment and I saw Louise bringing Maria in. Things seemed to be moving so fast for her, I thought I'd hang on and see how they went.'

Tom nodded politely. Happy as he was to see Anne, he really wanted to find his family.

Anne laughed at his frantic look. 'Go. Tell them she's in the labour ward.'

He kissed her on the cheek and raced over to the reception desk.

The man standing behind it was on the phone and smiled at Tom politely, indicating he'd be finished in a moment. Tom was about to flash his badge to speed things along when the receptionist hung up.

'How can I help you?' he said.

'My daughter, Maria, she came in here an hour ago. She's in the labour ward.'

The man smiled at him. 'We usually only allow the father of the baby up there, sir. Would you like to sit in the waiting room? I'm sure the new dad will come down and tell you when the baby's arrived.'

'There's no dad up there,' Tom said. 'Her mother's with her.'

The man sighed, the smile never leaving his lips. 'Her name?'

'Maria Reynolds.'

The receptionist typed something into his computer. 'Oh. She's been moved to St Mary's ward already. You must be Tom Reynolds, are you? You're a designated visitor.'

'What? Yes. What do you mean, she's been moved?'

'It means she's had her baby. I'll just get you to fill out this card and you can go up.'

Tom felt the world spin. 'She's had the baby?'

His heart felt like it was about to stop. In the last few minutes he'd been made a grandfather, and he hadn't felt anything change.

He filled out the card impatiently and then took the man's instructions, flashing the visitor's pass at security and racing up four flights of stairs when the lift didn't come fast enough.

Eventually, he found the ward.

Some of the mothers looked up at him with interest; others were too busy with their new arrivals to notice.

He saw them immediately. Maria was in the second bed. Louise was sitting beside her, alternately stroking their daughter's hair and the head that poked out of a small bundle in Maria's arms.

'Dad!' she exclaimed.

He stood at the end of the bed, speechless.

'You just missed it,' Louise said. 'She nearly had the baby in the car. We only got into the labour ward and out she popped.'

Tom found his voice.

'She?' he asked.

Maria nodded. 'She. Born thirty minutes ago. Seven pounds, eight ounces. Two weeks early. Well, come on, Grandad, come round here and have a hold.'

'Oh, see who's the lucky one,' Louise said. 'I only got to hold her when they were moving us up to the ward. Maria hasn't let go of her since.'

Tom edged round the bed.

A little hand flew out of the yellow bundle, accompanied by a cry.

He reached out and took her, cradling the infant's tiny head in the crook of his elbow. It had been so long since he'd held a baby. He felt like a novice. After a few seconds, though, that comfortable feeling came flooding back.

The little face gurning up at him was love itself. Her scrunched-up nose and perfectly pink pout were glorious. Her hair was dark, like Maria's. She could have been Maria. Her eyes were closed, but when he ran his thumb gently along the side of her cheek, they opened and looked up into his.

'Hello, beautiful,' he said. 'Welcome to our family.'

'Her name is Cáit,' Maria said.

Tom laughed. For the last few weeks Maria had been tormenting him with reality TV stars' names. Cáit was Louise's mother's name.

He brought his head down to the baby's forehead and inhaled her newborn smell, overwhelmed with happiness. A lump formed in his throat, he was so overcome. And then there was that little pang of sadness in his stomach.

The case was a few months old now, but the memory remained as fresh as ever. So many women had been denied this feeling, their babies ripped from their arms or stolen from their cots as their mothers slept. He closed his eyes and allowed himself to imagine their pain for a moment.

He and Laura had volunteered for the last few months with the campaign to win justice for the women who'd been in the Magdalene Laundries and the mother and baby homes.

Sister Bernadette and Sister Concepta were helping as well. They had got into trouble with their order for joining the campaign – but not too much. Publicly, the Church was trying to convey an image of doing whatever it could to help the women. Privately, the powers that be were still hoping it would all just go away.

The two nuns continued to visit Ellie. She was being held in a secure ward in a psychiatric hospital in Dublin, awaiting trial. Tom and Ray had been to see her twice but she had made it apparent she didn't want to see them, so they hadn't gone back.

She had yet to come to terms with the fact that she was still on this earth, and reminders of her former life were too painful. Tom had tried to explain to Ray that the only reason she wanted to see the nuns was because she wanted to ask more about her mother. After Ellie's initial recorded confession, in the hospital ward in Limerick, she'd said nothing to the police, except one word. When they told her Sister Clare had passed away, following a protracted bout of pneumonia brought on by her ordeal, Ellie had said, 'Good.'

Ray was heartbroken for the young woman, but he was getting over the shock.

As Tom suspected, Laura had stood back and offered friendship and support to Ray but nothing more. She was a good girl. Intelligent. He hoped Ray would notice her eventually. The detective had helped Laura and her mother when the Brennans set about finding Peggy's unmarked grave. No doubt he was compensating for the things he couldn't do for Ellie – but it was a kind gesture, nonetheless.

Tom now squeezed his new granddaughter one more time, counted his blessings and gave her back to her mother. Then he sat on the other side of the bed and picked up Louise's hand, their daughter and granddaughter between them.

There was nowhere any of them would rather be.

I am frightened.

They try to keep it quiet in here, but there are always doors banging, the sharp footsteps of sensible nurse's shoes in the corridor, the occasional screams from some poor tortured soul.

It's getting dark now.

I don't like the dark.

The room is locked, but I still feel vulnerable. The lock is on the outside, not the inside. It's like I'm that small child again, waiting for the door handle to turn, quivering in my bed, clutching my teddy bear and praying my foster father won't come tonight.

There are footsteps approaching. They're coming to my room. They're coming for me.

They realized I wasn't taking my pills, so now they inject me. Every night, every morning. I spit, I wrestle, I bite, but there's very little you can do when you're being pinned to the bed by two strong nurses. I have to resist, though. I need my wits about me.

They think I'm insane.

Maybe I am.

I don't feel crazy. Everything I did felt very sane to me.

But I don't live in a society where you're allowed to take justice into your own hands. And yet, I don't live in a society where real justice is delivered unless you dish it out yourself.

Now . . . I no longer live in society at all.

I have my memories. Real and imagined. The imagined are where my mother keeps me. Where she cuddles me as a baby and promises to protect me from harm. My mother, telling me how much she loves me. My mother, walking me to school, helping me choose my first pretty dress, wiping my runny nose. Normal, happy, loving – what my childhood should have been.

The real memories are of driving the knife into the heart of the woman who stole all that from me and watching her eyes widen in terror when she realizes nobody is going to save her and I'm going to make good on all my promises of desecration.

Or whispering in the ear of the man who began this pain, before I force a syringe into his neck and watch as his heart shrivels up and dies. Daddy dearest.

The door handle is turning. They're coming to try to continue my living nightmare.

They don't realize they're too late this time.

All the pills they gave me when they thought I was a good girl just swallowing them . . . I stashed them. Now they're dissolving in my stomach. Tonight's injection will be the icing on the cake. I won't fight tonight.

Mother, it's me, your little Elisa. Are you waiting for me? I'm scared, but I feel so sleepy. I just want to be with you. It's all I've ever wanted.

And now, I can feel her arms around me. Holding me tightly, telling me not to worry.

I'm being lifted from the bed, raised from its clinical white sheets. I'm floating through the air, long tubes of light filling my vision, like I'm speeding down a fast tunnel. There are panicked shouts and movements in the background. They're telling me I'll be fine and they're running. The noise is jarring, hateful, but it's growing more distant. It can't reach me any more.

I no longer exist.

Revenge tasted sweet. But this is sweeter.

I'm coming, Mam. I'm coming back to you.

ACKNOWLEDGEMENTS

My dad, who passed away in 1995, never knew the tragic circumstances of his adoption from an Irish mother and baby home. I do, now. *With Our Blessing* is a work of fiction but it visits the sad history of such institutions and is written in his memory. I miss you every day, dad.

Thanks to Fern, Pearse and Roisin, for reading my very rough manuscript from start to finish, for all the constructive critique, but mainly, for loving it. And thank you to all those who read the first few chapters and offered suggestions and comments. You know who you are. Your support helped me write the rest.

To Stefanie Bierwerth and the team at Quercus, for spotting my work and pushing for it, I can never thank you enough. You've helped to make my dreams come true.

Thanks to my family and friends for your unending encouragement and love.

My four lucky charms, Isobel, Liam, Sophia and Dominic. You make everything achievable, little ones.

And finally, to my husband Martin. I couldn't have done this without your amazing editing skills, your insights and, most of all, your terrific cups of tea. Here's to many more joint enterprises.

Keep reading for the first page of Jo Spain's next book, *Beneath the Surface*, the second novel in the Inspector Tom Reynolds series . . .

Ryan Finnegan, a high-ranking government official, is brutally slain in Leinster House, the seat of the Irish parliament. Detective Inspector Tom Reynolds and his team are called in to uncover the truth behind the murder. As the suspects start to rack up, Tom must untangle a web of corruption, sordid secrets and sinister lies.

At first, all the evidence hints at a politically motivated crime, until a surprise discovery takes the investigation in a dramatically different direction. Suddenly the motive for murder has got a lot more personal . . . but who benefits the most from Ryan's death?

BENEATH THE SURFACE BY JO SPAIN

The Death

I am going to die.

I know this as surely as I know I don't want to.

I can't bear it. I cannot stand the thought of leaving my girls, of not seeing them again.

Kathryn will never recover. We have defied the odds of so many married couples and are as much in love as the day we met. Sweet, beautiful, funny Kathryn.

And Beth. Oh, my little baby girl. The newness and perfection of her skin. The smell of her soft hair. Her little pudgy hand clasping my finger like she'll never let go. She's part of me, but she'll never know me. People will tell her I loved her but she will never understand how much. She won't know the almost physical pain I felt when she was born, so overwhelming was my love for her. I couldn't speak when I held Beth for the first time, the lump in my throat was so large. Kathryn laughed. She'd never seen me cry before and it was because I was so happy.

I'm crying now.

Did I know it would come to this? Why didn't I realise that I *was playing Russian Roulette not just with my own future, but with my family's too?*

I fall forward into the cold arms of the angel. The images fall from my hands, scattering across the floor.

My leverage and my downfall.

How little they mean now.

I would give anything to turn back time and be with my girls, to take them in my arms and squeeze them tight, my heart exploding with love.

Because too late, I know that's all that matters.

My body writhes in agony as I try to turn my head.

I want to look my executioner in the eye. Who is this person who will steal everything from me?

My punishment is cruel. My threat was to a career, not a life. This is not fair.

I will beg. I will wail and I will plead and maybe God will intervene. He will forgive my naivety, my arrogance. This angel will carry me not to Heaven but to help, and I will fight to live. I will fight for them, Kathryn and Beth.

But all hope of salvation evaporates as I behold my attacker.

My mouth struggles to form the word.

It's not 'Please.' It's not 'Stop.'

It's . . . 'Why?'

And then I see it, but I don't see it. The end.

There's no shot at redemption.

I am going to die.

The gun is in my eyeline as the second bullet is fired.

That's the one that kills me.

www.quercusbooks.co.uk

Quercus
Join us!

Visit us at our website, or join us on
Twitter and Facebook for:

- Exclusive interviews and films from
  your favourite Quercus authors

- Exclusive extra content

- Pre-publication sneak previews

- Free chapter samplers and
  reading group materials

- Giveaways and competitions

- Subscribe to our free newsletter

www.quercusbooks.co.uk
twitter.com/quercusbooks
facebook.com/quercusbooks